Adventures
of
Regen the Bremen

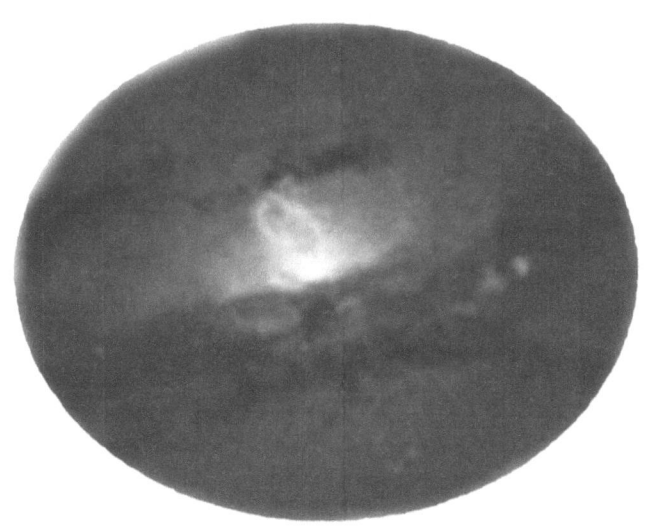

M. L. Hollinger

TotalRecall Publications, Inc.
www.totalrecallpress.com

TotalRecall Publications, Inc.
1103 Middlecreek
Friendswood, Texas 77546
281-992-3131   281-482-5390 Fax
www.totalrecallpress.com

ISBN: 978-1-59095-111-8
UPC: 6-43977-41115-0

Printed in the United States of America with simultaneous
printings in Australia, Canada, and United Kingdom.

FIRST EDITION
1   2   3   4   5   6   7   8   9   10

*To my family, but particularly to my wife, Jan,
who never stopped believing in me.*

Preface

This book is the result of a lifetime enchantment with space travel. When my grandmother gave me Wiley Ley's book, *By Rocket to the Moon*, in 1947 she had no idea it would launch me on a career in aerospace engineering. I was fortunate enough to be part of several major projects in the military space program and played a minor role in the Space Shuttle Program. Now that I am fully retired, I've devoted my time to writing science fiction novels and short stories. If this were 3012 instead of 2012, and I were forty years younger, I'd be Regen.

Introduction

Regen is a Bremen. By nature he loves only his pet skeen, sensual women, money, and adventure in that order. Bremens are known for their sexual prowess, their tough exterior, covering a sensitive interior, and their tendency to leap before they look. I hope you enjoy following this arrogant, self-confident, egotistical and narcissistic bastard through a series of adventures in disparate sectors of the galaxy.

CHAPTER 1

There was nothing that remarkable about the tall Bremen, but the Space Witch Saloon grew suddenly quiet as he walked in the door. Bremens have a reputation for being tough guys, but the thing that silenced the crowd and attracted all eyes in the room was the animal skulking along behind this one, trying to conceal itself in his shadow.

It was a skeen, and few there had ever seen a live one except in a very heavy steel cage. It ambled along on large, fur-covered hind legs with its rat-like tail tucked safely between them. The usually fearless patrons parted respectfully as the Bremen walked up to the bar.

"You can have anything you want in here, but that thing has to stay outside." The bartender nodded toward the skeen.

"He goes where I go. Gimme a double Gordian bourbon and a menu."

"You don't get nothin' 'til that piece of shit's out o' here."

The Bremen turned to the skeen and spoke almost lovingly.

"Hear that Hitler? This guy don't want to serve us."

As if in response to the insult, the skeen jumped up on the bar and glared at the bartender with beady red eyes. It opened its mouth to reveal an array of stiletto-like teeth and sat back on its hind legs, front claws extended. A low, hissing sound came from somewhere deep inside its leathery chest.

"Get that bastard away from me, or I'll call security."

"Now you know Hitler, here, would be eating your liver for dessert before they could gun him down. He does exactly what I tell him to do, and he won't hurt a fly 'less I give him the word. Right now we're both hungry, and I've got a mighty mean thirst. We were planning on spending some dough here, but if you ain't interested, there's plenty of other bars in Loba City."

"Okay, just get him off the bar."

"Git down, Hitler." In response to the Bremen's command, the creature hopped back to its place near the big man's feet and curled up into a ball.

The bartender placed a dog-eared menu in front of the man and poured the whiskey out of a tall bottle. He was about to put the bottle back in the rack when the Bremen spoke.

"Leave the bottle. Hitler might want a drink too."

The Bremen perused the menu while he gulped down the bourbon then shoved the greasy paper across the bar.

"I'll have three smurgers, well done, and Hitler'll have the gartog special, very rare."

"Whatever you say, mister." The bartender scribbled the order on a computer pad and left to serve other customers.

Now that the confrontation was over, the bar returned to its previous condition of joyous chaos. The short, fat Aandie on his left was the first to comment on the skeen.

"I've seen a pack of those things eat a whole cow in a matter of minutes. We had them on the Belarius. How did you ever get one to follow you around like that, especially one that big?"

"I raised him from a egg I found in the hold of the Honida Maru. I always wondered if you could tame 'em, but I knew it was no use startin' with a baby. I seen guys try it and get torn up for their trouble. I thought you might have a chance if you hatched one and he thought you was his mama. You gotta feed 'em good, though. If they get hungry, they'll eat anything, 'cludin' you."

"Where have I heard that name 'Hitler' before?"

"I found it in an old book I read while doing some time in the penal colony on Gaba 3. From what that book said, this guy Hitler was a real bad ass. I figured it was a good name for a skeen."

"I remember now. Hitler was a man of 20th century Earth. He killed a lot of people in ovens or something. Yes, he was a bad actor. Can the skeen do any tricks?"

"Sure, but he has to have a treat after each one, and our food ain't here yet."

"No problem." The Aandie reached over to a nearby table and lifted a chunk of meat from the platter in front of a small Tumeg. The victim protested loudly in his shrill, whiney language, but made no move to stop the theft.

"Here, Hitler, roll over!" the Aandie commanded as he held the morsel out in front of the skeen. The patrons near the animal watched enthralled as the hideous creature rolled over several times and sat up with its mouth open in anticipation of its treat.

"That is remarkable!" The Aandie lowered his hand to the skeen.

"Look out fer yer..." Regen didn't get to finish his sentence. Hitler jumped to grab the meat and took two of the Andie's fingers as a bonus.

"AAAAghhh!"

"...fingers," Regen finished.

"Ahhhhgh! The damned thing bit me! Help somebody!" The Aandie screamed in pain as blood poured from the severed joints, and the victimized Tumeg giggled with glee.

A security man rushed to the scene and applied a dressing to the wound.

"We'd better get you to a hospital," the security man said. "Those things carry all kinds of germs."

The Aandie turned to the Bremen with a shocked expression. "What did he do that for? I thought you said he was tame."

"Ever'body knows skeens like fingers better'n anything. You should'a been more careful." Regen poured himself another glass of bourbon as the security guard rushed the Aandie to the door.

Another guard approached Hitler with a drawn laser pistol. "That skeen's had his last meal."

Regen drew his pistol and stepped between the guard and Hitler. Luckily, the confrontation was interrupted by a woman in the uniform of the royal palace guard.

"Okay, boys, turn down the testosterone a notch." She turned to the security guard. "I'll take care of this."

The guard holstered his weapon and walked away grumbling.

Regen studied the woman. She was almost as tall as he was, and her build, though slender, showed the lines of a powerful frame under the black jump suit. Her hair, nearly the color of the red piping on her uniform, was tied back in a bun, and she wore very little make-up. Emerald green eyes fixed the Bremen in a gaze combining admiration with official authority. She was every bit as beautiful as the last time he'd seen her.

"I've got five men looking for you, Regen, but I thought I might find you in here," she said.

"How'd you figur' that out?"

"It was easy. You're a Bremen, Bremens like low places, and this is the lowest dive in Loba City. Besides, I don't see anyone else in here with a pet skeen. I'm surprised someone hasn't shot it by now." She scowled at the skeen, and it scuttled behind Regen's legs to lick up the Aandie's blood.

"It's good t' see you too, Varda. You must've really enjoyed our last meetin' to come down t' this level o' the city."

"Don't flatter yourself. I just wanted to see if what they said about you Bremens was true."

"Well, was it?" He smiled at her with an oily confidence in his sexual prowess.

"I wouldn't want to shatter that gigantic Bremen ego with an answer. I came to see if you were interested in making some good money."

At that point, the bartender placed a platter in front of Regen and held another over the bar. "This is for the skeen, but you give it to him. I want to keep all my fingers."

Regen placed the platter on the floor in front of Hitler who dove into it with gusto. Evidently, the Aandi's fingers only served as an appetizer. "Want a smurger?" Regen asked Varda.

She looked at the greasy mess on the bar and screwed up her face in disgust. "No thanks, but you go ahead and eat. I've got a business proposition for you."

Regen picked up a smurger and took a large bite. "Go ahead," Regan said around his mouthful.

"I came looking for you because you're the only guy I know who's familiar with the Banguilla region."

"I been there, and I ain't interested in goin' back." Another bite of smurger replaced the first.

"I got an assignment there, and I need a guide. The pay's good, and it should only take a few days."

"What's 'good'?" Regen asked. He knew the royal pay scale was not nearly as generous as that of the many smugglers and drug dealers in the bar. That motley group was keeping a watchful eye on the royal guardswoman. They thoroughly distrusted anyone wearing that uniform.

"How does two hundred fifty thousand sound?"

Varda definitely had his attention now. He wiped his mouth on his sleeve and turned to face her. "What's the job?" Regen asked.

"Bringing back the Prince's lost dog," Varda answered.

"That must be one helluva dog."

"The Prince loves that mutt, and the Banguers took it because they knew it would get the King's attention. He spoils that kid rotten. They've offered to trade it for two terrorists scheduled for execution next month. They say that if their people die, the dog dies. The kid's been giving his parents a fit since the dog vanished, and I drew the job of getting it back."

"Why don't the king just give 'em the terrorists? That region's full of tough guys who don't like the monarchy. What's two more?"

"These guys blew up the shuttle craft taking the Rillian Ambassador back to his ship. If they don't get executed, the Rillians will cut off our supply of nuclear fuel. He can't let them go."

"This planet'd be a pretty dead place without nuclear fuel, and I like some of the whore houses. Do you know where they've got the dog?"

"Yes, but I can't talk about it here. Come on back to the palace with me, and I'll tell you all we know."

"Hitler ain't finished his dinner yet, and I could use some more bourbon." Regen signaled the bartender to bring another glass. "Have a drink and relax for a while." He poured Varda a double shot and another for himself, then continued with his smurgers.

The pair walked through the crowded streets of the royal city. This particular sector was a vivid contrast to the skyscrapers rising like a mountain range to the West. Here were only dives, brothels and warehouses sitting unlighted in dark contrast to the glowing windows downtown. Only the occasional streetlight or security lamp broke up the sinister shadows harboring some of the vilest predators in the city, but none dared confront a Royal Guardsman and a mean looking Bremen, particularly a Bremen followed by an extremely large skeen. The guards balked at allowing a skeen inside, but Varda asserted her authority to get them past the gate. Once in the courtyard, however, Varda led Regen and Hitler to a sturdy cage.

"Hitler'll have to stay here. I can't take him inside the palace."

"He don't like cages much, but I can talk him into it if we're not gone too long."

"An hour or two is all we need. You can come back to him here after that." Varda beckoned to a reluctant looking guard who saluted smartly as he joined the group.

"Misha, here, will look after Hitler. He's even got some treats for him." Varda patted a leather bag hanging from the man's belt.

"Make sure you throw 'em to him," Regen advised. "He likes fingers real good." Regen bent down and whispered to the skeen as he opened the cage door. "He's okay. Just throw one of them treats in there, and he'll go in after it."

The guard pulled a human thumb from his bag and dropped it through the bars at the rear of the cage. Hitler salivated as he entered the steel cell and was soon gnawing on the grisly prize.

"We had some punishments to deal out this morning, and I

thought Hitler might as well benefit from them," Varda explained to a smiling Regen.

They left Hitler in Misha's care and found their way to a briefing room deep inside the palace. The guard at the door looked skeptically at Regen, but accepted Varda's word the Bremen could be admitted.

Inside, Varda called up a map on the large screen.

"The camp where they have the dog is here." She used a laser pointer to indicate a spot. "Do you know the area?"

"Yeah, that's all jungle with only a few good trails. The double canopy is a good thirty meters off the ground. Ya could hide half o' Loba City in there."

"We've got some photos." Varda called up a satellite photo of the camp.

"You know you only see what they want you t' see in them photos, don't ya?"

"I know, but they definitely want us to see this." Varda used the pointer to show a large pen containing a huge, furry animal.

"Is that a dog? Looks more like a bear."

"It's a Malma, and we've positively identified it as the prince's dog, Cuddles."

"Cuddles? Malmas are almost as bad as skeens. You didn't tell me I'd have t' bring out a Malma."

"You didn't ask. Besides, he's pretty well behaved. He only tore up two of the Banguers who were in on the snatch. The prince seems to be able to make him obey pretty well."

"Yeah, but I ain't the prince, and I don't think his old man'd think too highly o' me taking his kid along t' keep the dog quiet."

"No, the prince can't go for obvious reasons, but we can tranquilize the dog and bring him out quietly."

"We? How many're going in with me?"

"That's what I want you to tell me. Is there a good way to get a battalion sized force in there?"

"Battalion? No way! They'd have ambushes set up every hundred meters along the trails. You'd loose most o' yer men 'fore you got t' the camp. You need surprise, and there's no way a force that size could move quietly through that jungle."

"What about a vertical attack?"

"The double canopy makes any kind o' vertical attack impossible. This'll have to be a covert operation, two men at the most."

"Two people," Varda corrected. "I'll be going in with you even if nobody else does."

"You? Did you see that dog? That monster must weigh 120 kilos! I said two men 'cause that's what it'll take t' carry out a tranquilized Malma."

"I bench press 120 kilos sixteen times every day, how about you?"

"Don't worry 'bout my end. How far do we have t' carry this mutt?"

"All we have to do is get it outside Banguilla territory. I'll have a detachment of rangers waiting for us with transporters so we can make a quick getaway."

"That's still about four klicks for us to carry that beast. Are you sure you're up to that?"

"I wouldn't ask any of my men to go into Banquilla with a crazy Bremen who keeps a pet skeen. I'll hold up my end of the deal."

"I'm still not convinced we're looking at the real thing here. Have you sent in any crawlers?" Regen was referring to the tiny surveillance devices built to resemble insects or small rodents.

"Seven, but the Banguers detected every one. One flyer got to the camp and took these pictures." The screen shifted to show the same camp but in more detail. "It also dropped a listening device which they haven't found yet. We'll be able to listen in on them before we penetrate the area."

"That's good, providin' they don't find it 'til we're outta there. How many men do th' Banguers have in that camp?"

"We count twenty nine, but there may be more. There's a known terrorist camp three klicks in this direction, though. Maybe a whole battalion there."

"Wonderful! You and me 'gainst twenty nine Banguers. Sounds fair."

Regen's sarcasm was not lost on Varda. "I'm open to suggestions."

"Well, I kin git in pretty easy. The Banguers know me, and they trust me, but you have t' be in every computer they got."

"I'll dye my hair and the make-up boys'll help a lot. I don't think they'll recognize me in time. They'd have to do a DNA match, and that'll take a while."

"You know the only way they'll believe ya is if yer my whore?"

"That wouldn't be such a bad assignment." Varda smiled warmly at Regen. Having sex with him would not be a new experience. They met once before on Waldara while she was on vacation and he was negotiating a drug deal at the same hotel. He looked a lot different then. Instead of the rough dress of a Bremen, he wore the swanky clothes of a Molon Federation representative. He looked like a real gentleman, and she was fooled completely.

"I just hope they make me prove you're what you say you are." Regen smiled back at her.

"That's the only way we'll have time for any sex on this trip.

What do you think?."

Regen studied the pictures of the camp and looked at several maps before replying.

"The only way I see this workin' is if we go into th' camp as drug dealers. We spend a day or two there trading drugs and casing the camp's operation. Once we know the layout, we can put together some plan fer gettin' th' prince's mongrel back to him."

"If we need any help, I can call in the rangers."

"We can't risk any kind of transmission, and you can't carry anything that might tie you to the palace. You know what the Banguers'll do if they catch on?"

"I've seen their work before. That's why we'll take these." Varda handed him a small pill.

"Wadda we do, ask the goons t' wait a minute whilst we takes a poison pill?"

"No, we'll have these implanted inside our cheek. If we need them, all we have to do is bite through the skin. They act in a matter of seconds, and the medics tell me they're painless."

"Which one of 'em tried it and survived t' give that evaluation?"

"Don't be a smart-alec, Regen. They work, and no matter if there is some pain, it's better than what you'll get from the Banguers."

"We'll have to get hold o' some drugs t' trade."

"We've got two tons of drugs in the royal police warehouse—any kind you like. We can have all we want."

"We'll only take in ten kilos apiece, but we need a stash of a couple hundred somewhere outside their territory. They'll just take what we have on us, but we can use the stash as our insurance. It's how I al'ays done business with them weasels."

"Anything you want in the way of equipment?"

"We can't take in any GI stuff. What you got in th' way o' contraband?"

Varda led Regen to a storage room containing weapons and gear the police confiscated from various felons and terrorists. Regen looked the stuff over with a practiced eye.

"This 's good," Regen pronounced as he hefted a laser pistol. "It's Parsan, and I was on Parsa just a month back." He found the holster and strapped it around his waist. "Got any energy packs fer it?"

"Over here." Varda led him to a cabinet holding ammunition for any weapon he'd ever seen.

"What'll you carry?" Regen asked.

"If I'm your whore, one of these." Varda lifted a small lead firing automatic pistol in a holster that strapped around one leg. "And, one of these." The second item was a knife with a poison groove that fit into a woman's boot.

"Good, we'll need a lot o' water too. Better take these two backpacks with tanks. We can put the drugs in 'em. We'll take these, too." Regen lifted two pack harnesses out of a pile and held them up in front of Varda.

"What are those for?"

"Fer carryin' th' dog out. We can rig 'em like this." He showed Varda how the harnesses could be reconfigured to provide a means of lifting the dog on a pole between them.

"Good idea, but how do we hide these from the Banquers? They'll be sure to search us and our packs."

"We don't take 'em in with us. They'll want t' sample the goods 'fore they make a big buy. I'll send you out with one o' their guys to git th' buy. You bring it in usin' these. Speakin' o' hidin' things, how do ya plan t' get the tranquilizer stuff in?"

Varda led Regen to another table where a walking staff lay. She handed it to the Bremen.

"It's all hidden in here."

Regen hefted the staff and inspected it thoroughly. "Looks pretty good. How do you get to th' stuff?"

"I can't show you without breaking the camouflage, but they'll never find it, believe me."

"I'll take your word fer it. Let's go'n pick out the good stuff."

In the drug storage area, Varda signed out several hundred kilos of a particularly nasty item. Most of it was consigned to the rangers to hide in the location designated by Regen, but some went into the back packs.

"When you want t' start this operation?" Regen asked.

"The sooner the better—your call."

Regen consulted his watch before answering. "It's close to nine now. Kin ya git everythin' arranged 'fore midnight?"

"Sure, we just have to get our poison pills implanted before the medics close up for the night. Everyone else is on standby waiting for my orders."

"Midnight it is, then. I'd better get back t' Hitler 'fore your man runs out o' fingers," Regen said.

Varda led Regen to the medical section of the castle where their poison pills were implanted. She told him it was a painless process, but Regen still insisted on anesthetic.

"Regen, you're a real wimp! Anybody with a pet skeen should be able to do this without Novocain."

"I don't like nobody pokin' 'round inside m' mouth 'less I'm sure I can't feel it."

The procedure went well, and Varda left to undergo her cosmetic changes while Regen returned to the courtyard to relieve a very nervous guard.

"How's he been?" Regen asked.

"I'm glad you showed up. I'm about to run out of things to

feed him, and he looks like he's getting hungry."

"That's just th' cage. I'll let him out now."

"I think I'll move over there while you do that." The guard beat a hasty retreat to a safer location.

Regen opened the cage door, and Hitler scurried out then turned and lifted a leg to relieve himself on the cage.

"Well, at least ya got some good food." Regen addressed the thing as if it could comprehend his every word, and it looked at him with a fondness seeming to convey complete understanding. "Come on! We'll walk 'round th' yard and git some exercise."

Varda appeared just before midnight, but Regen almost didn't recognize her. Her hair was now pitch-black, and instead of the smart guard uniform, she wore a loose fitting, low-necked blouse and full skirt. Long earrings dangled from her lobes and a necklace of gold coins hung heavily around her neck. The crimson sash at her waist identified her as one of the girls from the bordellos of Loba City. Even with garish and overdone makeup, she still radiated exotic charm. Regen whistled softly.

"I don't care what you cost. Let's go to your place."

"Don't get any ideas, Regen. This is strictly business. Did you get your water tank filled?"

"All set'n ready to go."

"Fine, I'll call for the transporter." Varda pulled out a communicator and spoke into it. Within minutes, a transporter appeared overhead and lowered itself into the courtyard. The big vehicle almost filled the space, but a door in the side slid open to let in Varda and Regen, who had to coax a cowering Hitler into the cargo compartment.

A company of rangers sat in the troop seats on either side of the cargo compartment, and boxes of stores tied down on pallets filled the center of the cavernous compartment. Varda and Regen took their seats near the rear door while Hitler found cover between Regen's legs and the skin of the transporter.

"The Banguer will see this thing coming for miles," Regan shouted to Varda over the whir of the engines.

"Don't worry. The cover story we leaked is that this is a re-supply mission to the outpost where we're landing. You and I are listed as traders. It'll all look routine to them."

The transporter landed at a ranger base just outside the Banguillan border. It was a favorite jumping off point for smugglers and drug traders who bribed the government for the opportunity to make millions or die horribly through dealings with the Banguers. Regen and Varda checked their equipment and left the compound through a hole in the fence with Hitler close behind. Moonlight provided enough illumination to let them make their way past the border guards, then they stopped to rest and wait for sunrise. Varda checked for any traffic from the listening device before burying her receiver and communicator at the base of a tree.

CHAPTER 2

The next morning, the pair began their approach to the Banguer camp. The dense jungle canopy let in very little light, but Regen knew the trails well. A dank mist rose all around them as the splotchy sunlight warmed the ground and drove off its moisture only to have it condense again a few inches off the sodden mass of the jungle floor. They moved without regard for noise. The object was to be noticed, and it was not long before they were challenged.

A small Banguer appeared in the pathway as if by magic. His rifle was pointed at Regen's belly, but once he saw the skeen, it moved to cover the animal. Hitler responded by bounding off into the bush.

"Stop where you are!" the Banguer shouted.

Regen and Varda complied as three more men materialized out of the jungle behind them.

"We're here t' trade with yer chief. We got some good kourma for'im t' try." Regen used the Banguer word for the hallucinogenic drug favored by those people.

One of the men behind them approached Varda and tore open her backpack. He reached inside and pulled out a plastic bag of yellowish powder.

"Ah! The Bremen speaks the truth. Let's take them to camp and try this stuff. If it's not what he claims, we can always enjoy his screams as he dies."

"And his woman after that," another of the men shouted

and was met with a chorus of laughter.

"Take us to yer commander. We got a lot more'n we carry, but its location'll die with us if you get rough."

"Take their weapons, Vishna," the man in front ordered. One of the Banguers relieved Regen of his gun and knife while another pulled the knife from Varda's boot.

"Under her skirt too," the leader reminded his man.

With great glee Vishna lifted Varda's skirt and exposed the small pistol.

"The Bremen's whore has her own stinger. I will pluck it out," he yelled as he reached for the weapon.

Varda's walking staff came down sharply on the man's neck sending him sprawling on the jungle floor. As the others moved to subdue her, she carefully pulled out the pistol using only two fingers and handed it to the leader.

"I will not be pawed. All you had to do was ask for my weapon."

The men laughed heartily as they herded the strangers past their fallen comrade who was just now shaking the cobwebs from his skull.

"Come along when you can walk, Vishna," the leader called as he led the party down another path to the main camp.

Varda was right. The Banguer had made no effort to camouflage the camp. It was just as they had seen it in the photos. They were met by about a dozen other men shouting insults at them accompanied by the hoarse, thunderous barks of Cuddles from his pen.

"What's that monster ya have there?" Regen asked even though he knew full well it was Cuddles. The sight of a full grown Malma in a Banguer camp should provoke a great deal of interest from any outsider, and he would have been foolish not to comment on it. As they passed the enclosure, he carefully noted every detail of the pen's construction.

"It's trade goods," was all the patrol's leader would say.

They were ushered into a metal tent, and both were relieved to find it was climate controlled. A refrigerated atmosphere replaced the heat and humidity of the jungle morning and shocked their sweat covered skin, turning their damp clothes into ice cubes. The leader spoke to a fat Banguer in a turban and brown robe who Regen guessed to be the camp commander. They conversed in Banguilli, but Regen understood enough to determine the commander was interested in dealing. The patrol leader stepped back, and the commander addressed Regen.

"Who are you, and what do you have to trade?"

"I am Regen the Bremen, and I got some fine quality kourma fer th' right price."

"How much is your right hand worth?" the commander answered with no sign of emotion at all.

"Yer welcome t' all we carry as a gift to yer most noble highness, but we can 'range for th' delivery o' much more'n that, long as we're dealin' with such honorable persons as yourself."

The commander rose from his chair and walked toward Regen. He studied the man carefully then moved to Varda. A smile crossed his face as he felt her body from top to bottom and opened her mouth for inspection.

"You have a fine whore here. Is she for sale?"

"I promised her pimp I would have her back in a week. He's the one who supplies the kourma to me, and I wouldn't want to make him angry."

"I understand, but you could still loan her out for a night or two, couldn't you?"

"I don't know. She's pretty expensive, and I have t' pay fer ev'ry one o' her tricks."

"How much?"

Regen thought for a moment while he studied Varda's face. She was playing the role well by keeping silent and pretending to appreciate the fat man's attention, but he knew she was cursing him mentally and hoping she could find some way out of this situation. Regen knew the price of whores very well. A woman of Varda's caliber would command over 2,000 credits, but that sum was probably within the commander's budget, even after buying the kourma at street prices. He decided to double that figure and add some to boot.

"I'd have t' have at least five thousand a night."

Regen noticed Varda's right hand flashing all five fingers twice, but ignored the signal.

"Ahhh! I can't afford that and the kourma too, and the drug is much more valuable than even a night with this beauty." He turned to inspect the things from their backpacks and the weapons they carried.

"This pistol is Parsan. When were you there?"

"Last month. I sold some durdu to the lord of Franga."

"How is old Nerda these days?"

"I don't know no Nerda. The guy I dealt with was named Oolla."

The commander smiled and handed the pistol to Regen.

"Welcome to my camp, Regen. You may stay until you have sold your goods or until we move on. You will not be allowed to leave the camp until then, but you have my promise of safety while you're here. You are fortunate your reputation precedes you. I've heard of your fair dealings with others of my countrymen, but I've also heard you possessed a pet skeen. I was suspicious when you showed up without it, and I had to make sure of you."

"My skeen was scared off by yer men, but he'll find me pretty soon. I'd 'preciate it if you'd tell yer men not t' fire on 'im if they see 'im, yer excellency."

"My name is Gudra, please let us drop the formalities. You must be hungry and tired. My man will show you to some quarters and provide you with rations. We have no kitchen here, as this is a temporary camp, I hope you don't mind."

"Not at all. I've eaten Banguer rations before and found them quite tasty."

"Good, good. We'll talk more this evening. Relax until then."

Gudra issued instructions in his language, and the patrol leader led Regen and Varda to another metal tent.

"You may have this tent. The two men who lived here were casualties in a recent action. I will send a servant with your things."

Varda collapsed on one of the beds and was about to speak when Regen silenced her with a gesture and whispered in her ear.

"Make some noises that'll sound like we're makin' love whilst I search the place."

Varda nodded and began to moan sensually. "Yes, Regen, yes, yes, yes," she pleaded while fighting to maintain a straight face.

Regen nodded in approval, then moved around the tent inspecting every place where a camera or microphone could be hidden. He even lifted the ornate carpet on the floor of the tent before joining Varda in the ruse.

"Oh, oh, oh, oh, yeah!" he shouted and fell silent as he whispered to her once more.

"I don't think we're bugged, but we'd better be careful for a while. Why don't you muss up your clothes a bit and take a walk around the camp. I'll stay here and talk with the servant they send."

Varda nodded agreement and assumed an appropriate state of disarray. Before leaving the tent, she said, "Thanks for setting my price high enough to discourage that fat-assed Gudra."

When the servant arrived, Regen found she spoke only the Banguer dialect, but he understood enough to find out the camp was set up a week back and one third of the men were always out in the jungle on sentry duty. Each shift was four hours long, and the men slept most of the time during the eight hours they were back in camp. She had no idea where the sentry posts were, but she did know there was never a guard on the dog. She hated the animal and would not go near the pen. Several people had been bitten by the monster as a reward for their attempts at affection.

Her name was Villina, and she was one of six servants in the camp who also doubled as whores. The woman was not bad looking for a Banguer, and she proudly informed Regen her price was ten thousand Gritta, about one hundred credits in good money, but a princely sum in Banguilla's currency. Regen declined her services.

The servant cleared out the effects of the men who died kidnapping the dog and left the tent to Regen. He laid down on one of the bunks and fell asleep easily.

CHAPTER 3

An hour later, Varda shook Regen awake.

"Rise and shine. Lunch is served." She handed him a box full of olive drab cans.

Regen rose on one elbow and surveyed the labels.

"This stuff's good," Varda said as she showed him the label on the can. She stabbed another morsel with her plastic fork and popped it into her mouth.

"Yeah, I like the boiled lizard testicles too," Regen said.

Varda choked for a moment then spit the portion in her mouth back into the can.

"I guess I should have waited for you to tell me what this stuff was." Varda washed out her mouth with a large swig from the bottle of whiskey that came in with the rations.

"You said it was good. Give it t' me, I like th' stuff." He took the can from Varda and finished it off with gusto.

"What's in this one?" Varda asked holding up another can for Regen's translation of the label.

"That's all vegetables. Nothin' you wouldn't eat somewhere else."

Varda popped the lid off the can and waited as the automatic heating element warmed the contents to serving temperature.

Regen lifted another can from the box and popped the lid. This time, a layer of frost appeared on the outside as the contents were cooled near the freezing point.

"Try one o' these," Regen said as he offered the can to Varda.

"What are they?"

"They're like shrimp, only I think they taste better."

Varda pulled out a long, meaty tail and took a tentative bite.

"Hmmm! They are good." She shared the rest of the can with Regen.

"What'd you find out on yer walk?" Regen asked.

"There isn't any guard on the dog pound, and nobody wants to go near it. One guy lost a hand when he tried to pet the thing, and that lesson wasn't wasted on the rest."

"The servant confirmed that, an' she told me a third o' the men are out in th' jungle on sentry duty at any one time. Did ya see any communications gear?"

"There's a commo tent and command post attached to the tent we were in earlier, and one of the servants told me it's always manned. I'd guess they have a hot line to that larger bunch down the trail to the East. They're ready for any kind of attack by conventional means, just as you guessed."

"I'm sure they don't trust us as much as Gudra implies. We'll have t' be very careful about askin' questions. Everythin' we say'll be reported."

"We've got a while until we have to meet with Gudra this evening. Have you thought of anything?"

"I'd like t' get some idea o' where their observation posts are 'fore I make any plans. We won't be able t' use any o' th' trails, that's fer sure, but I'm also sure they have th' jungle staked out too. Is there a lock on th' gate to th' dog's pen?"

"It's a four button keypad."

"We'll have t' see if'n we can just happen t' be around next time they feed th' dog. Maybe you can express some interest in th' thing or lay some charm on whoever has the duty."

"They only feed him once a day, in the evening. I'll hang around the pen door after supper and see if I can pick up the code."

"Good. Do ya need a nap?"

"I think I will sack out for a while. Speaking of feeding vicious creatures, where's Hitler?"

"He does this sometimes when we're out in th' wild. He musta found somethin' t' eat by now or he'd 've sniffed me out t' feed 'im."

"I'd be just as happy if he'd stay around here and harass the Banguers."

"When we leave, I'll give 'im a call." Regen showed Varda a small whistle on a silver chain around his neck.

"I hope that's silent, like a dog whistle,"

"Same thing. Only he'n th' dog kin hear it. I'm goin' t' take a look around whilst you nap. Sleep tight."

Varda lay down on a bunk, and Regen left the tent. He walked around the camp and noted that his steps were being dogged by one of the Banguer women. Restricting his movements to those areas he thought appropriate for a drug trader, he still managed to get a good look at the command post. It would surely contain a map showing the location of the outposts, but there was no easy way in except through the other tent.

Some men appeared to be stirring from a row of tents he guessed were the barracks. He walked toward a group opening rations around a mess table shaded by a canvas canopy. They fell silent as he approached, but smiled as he greeted them in their native language.

"Hello, stranger," one of them spoke. "What brings you to our camp?"

"I'm a trader in kourma, and I come t' do business with yer

commander. How's th' duty here?"

"Some kourma will make it livable," the man replied. "The whores here are too expensive for me. Kourma's cheaper and accomplishes the same thing."

The men relaxed now and began to talk among themselves. Regen continued his conversation with the original man while listening carefully to the others.

"I hope I don't get that swamp post today," one of them said.

"That place is the home of every mosquito in the province. Jumita and I had it yesterday evening when they were all hungry," another one said.

"It's better than the northern post. Too many snakes for my taste, and all of them deadly," a third chimed in.

Regen finished his tour of the camp and returned to the tent. Varda was just returning from the latrine area as he walked up.

"Any news?" she asked.

"Yeah, come on inside."

They entered the tent and Regen filled her in.

"There must be five observation posts. They send out ten men ever' four hours, and from what I kin make out, they got two men at each post. Now, four men met us on th' main trail, so there's gotta be two posts near that. Let's see that map."

Varda produced a map from her backpack, and Regen spread it out on one of the beds.

"That's here," he pointed to the main trail. "One of the guys I heard talkin' was complainin' 'bout th' mosquitoes in th' swamp. That must be somewhere in here." Regen moved his finger in a small circle defining the area on the map. "Another man was talkin' 'bout a lot o' poisonous snakes. That might be this-here place near the trail to the south. There's one more som'eres."

Varda pointed to another part of the map. "This looks like the place one of the gals in the latrine was talking about. She said her favorite lover brought her some mangoes the other day after his tour of duty. The only place they could grow around here is this area."

"That makes sense. They could see half way t' Loba City from them heights. They got ever' possible way in or out covered pretty good."

"What about this ravine, here?"

"No good, the walls're too steep. We'd never be able t' get us and a Malma down t' th' riverbed. 'Sides, this time o' year the river'll be up. We'd either have t' swim or have a boat."

"But the river flows toward home. If we had some way to get Cuddles down there and some floatation, we could use the river to make our escape."

"I don't think it'll work, but keep your eyes open fer something we could use as a life jacket fer Cuddles. We could al'ays swim."

The two relaxed until a man called for them near dusk. They entered Gudra's tent to find a meal, of sorts, spread out on a low table surrounded by pillows.

"Come in and sit, Regen. It's not much, but it's the best I can do with canned rations. You over there, and your lovely woman between us."

Two women served what appeared to be wine. It had a sweet, dusky taste Regen recognized as vodka mixed with the blood of a small deer found in the area's swamps. He didn't tell Varda what she was drinking, but he knew this was a symbol of Gudra's trust and his promise of fair dealing. After the drink, they dove into the meal, and when they finished, the women returned with a hot, dark beverage resembling coffee but made from ground up tree bark.

The dinner hour was consumed with Gudra's questions on happenings in the galaxy since his assignment to this post a week ago. Regen made sure he brought up the kidnapping of the prince's dog.

"That Malma ya got in yer pen sure looks a lot like th' dog in all th' TV news stories," Regen said.

"You've discovered my reason for being here, Regen. It is the prince's dog, and we hold it as the ransom for our comrades falsely condemned to die by the king's courts. As soon as our men are released, we will be breaking camp. I expect the king's answer soon, so let us get down to cases on your kourma. How much do you have, and what is your price?"

"I assume you've tried th' stuff b'now," Regen asked.

"Yes, and the quality is not what I would choose, but it's good enough to give to my men. They have been asking me to provide it since we came here, and I want to keep them happy."

Regen knew he was lying. The stuff he'd taken from the police warehouse was top grade. Gudra was only trying to drive down the price. He must counter some way.

"Then yer are used t' mighty fine kourma indeed. Only th' royals kin afford that degree o' refinement."

"I did not mean to degrade your product. I just meant that I had tasted finer kourma, but not in quite a while, mind you."

"Thank ya. Let's see, yer duty here's pretty hard, and I'll make allowance fer that. Let's say 100,000 Gritta a kilo?"

Gudra blinked but maintained his composure. The price was high, but the drug was first quality stuff. He could cut it ten to one and still have something his men would prize. Back in his base city, the stuff would go for half again that much uncut or he could cut it again there and still make a tidy sum.

"How many kilos are we talking about?"

"I have 100 ready to deliver now, and another 100 within

one day's journey."

"Ten million is a lot of money. I don't have that much here in the camp. Would you accept my note?"

"I know yer a man o' honor, but in my business I gotta deal in cash. You understand, I hope?"

"Certainly, but you may have to stay longer to allow me to secure the funds I need to buy 100 kilos."

"Perhaps you could buy a smaller amount right away then more later?"

Gudra smiled. He knew what Regen was doing. The man was deeply in debt to buy the original 100 kilos. He needed some fast cash to settle that debt and purchase the rest, hence the one day delay on the second 100.

"At your price, I could afford only 60 kilos, but that would probably satisfy my men for the time we plan to spend here. Would that be satisfactory?"

"More'n satisfactory, commander Gudra." Regen offered his hand, and Gudra took it to seal the bargain.

Varda noticed the sun was about to set and spoke to Regen.

"They feed the large dog now. May I go watch them?"

"Let her see it, Regen. The monster is quite interesting. We feed it a small deer every night, and the thing reduces it to bones in a matter of an hour or so."

"You kin go, but be in our tent right after." Regen could almost feel Varda's anger at being ordered around, but she put up a good act.

"Thank you, master. You are most generous." Varda bowed low as she backed out of the tent.

"If I could prevail on yer good will fer some o' the kourma we brought in today. We'll need a little for our evenin'. I'll repay ya when th' shipment arrives."

"Certainly, how do you plan to get it here?"

"My whore will take the money out in the morning and return with the goods. Could you send a man with her to carry some of the load?"

"Certainly, but we dare not leave our own territory."

"If I may be allowed to use my communicator, I will have my people deliver the amount agreed upon to the border by morning."

"Go ahead."

Regan called for the delivery of the kourma using the code words Varda gave him to indicate that Cuddles was well.

Varda fell in with a crowd following a man carrying a deer carcass toward the dog pen. As Gudra said, this was one of the highlights of the day at the remote camp.

Cuddles knew it was mealtime and set up a steady howl as he watched his dinner approach. She moved into position to watch the man punch the keypad and noted the sequence. In response to his command, the outer door opened to a small, fenced in area at one corner of the pen. The man dumped in the deer and punched the keypad again in the same order. This time, the outer door closed and the inner door opened allowing Cuddles to grab the deer by the neck and drag it to the center of the pen.

She watched in horror as the beast tore the deer into pieces and began to consume it in large gulps. An image of the men who had been mauled in the kidnapping came into her mind, and she shuddered to think how horribly they died. The crowd of Banguers cheered each time the big dog tore a limb from the deer, and whistled encouragement as it consumed the animal's entrails. She wondered if there were enough drugs in the tranquilizer gun to make the behemoth manageable.

The next morning, Varda left the camp with the money and one of Gudra's men. She'd filled in Regen on the feeding ritual at the pen, and he was confident they could handle the task of doping the dog and getting it out of the area. The camp closed down after sunset except for the changing of the guards. Regan timed that process and found it took only thirty minutes or so for the old guard to be sound asleep once they returned to camp. That left plenty of time to get the dog out of the camp and to the edge of the ravine. The only rub was finding some kind of life jacket for the tranquilized dog.

He walked back to his tent and noticed the servant woman carrying out their trash in a large, black plastic bag. It suddenly dawned on him that he could use his laser pistol set on a low energy range to seal the bags. It should only take three or four of them to float the dog, and they could be tied on to the same harness they would use to carry the beast out. He approached the woman.

"Villina, would you leave us some extra bags? My whore wants to pick some of the mullana berries we saw walking in from the kingdom."

Villina looked at the small roll in her hand and offered it to Regen. "Take the rest of the roll. There's only four or five left anyway."

"Thank you, she'll appreciate that."

Varda returned that night with the goods. She and Regen sat in Gudra's tent while he tested several bags of kourma.

"It is as you said, Regen. This is fine kourma and well worth your price. I'll make arrangements to ship in the money for 100 more kilos. When can you bring it in?"

"I can have it at the border one day after you get the cash. We can use the same arrangement as today," Regen said.

Gudra nodded his approval as his men removed the drugs. "Done! It is truly a pleasure doing business with you, Regen.

Varda and Regen left the commander's tent making sure they had the pack harnesses. They sat in their tent waiting for the midnight shift change of the guards.

The camp was silent in short order, and Varda put on an outfit more suitable for moving through the jungle, though it still looked like something out of a Loba City whorehouse. At least it was black to blend in with the night.

They crept to the pen where Cuddles was sleeping soundly. Varda pulled a small perfume bottle from her backpack and poured its contents over the end of the walking staff. A fine line appeared, and she unscrewed the cover with a left-handed motion. From the inside she shook out four tranquilizer darts and a blowpipe. Inserting one of the darts in the pipe, she took aim at Cuddles rear end and blew sharply into the long tube.

Cuddles yelped as the dart struck home and immediately turned to pull the offending item from his hide. Regen and Varda waited to see if the yelp aroused any interest, but nothing stirred.

"He's not getting very sleepy," Regen whispered.

"It'll probably take two darts," Varda replied as she loaded another shot.

The second dart elicited another yelp, and this time, a head appeared from a tent near the enclosure. The man surveyed the area, but the dart in Cuddles' behind was hidden from him by the big dog's bulk. Satisfied the dog was not harmed, he ducked back inside the tent.

This time Cuddles felt the effects of the drug. He tried to rise but flopped back down immediately. His tongue lolled out of his mouth and his eyes rolled back in their sockets.

"I think he's out," Varda whispered. "You got the stuff?"

"I've got the harnesses, and I'll get one of the poles holding up that canvas over there." Regen indicated the canopy over the dinner tables.

"Okay, go get it while I open the pen."

Varda punched in the code and the gate swung open. Regen joined her with the equipment and they opened the inner gate. It only took a moment to truss up Cuddles in the slings and run the pole through rings in the harnesses.

"On three we lift him up," Regen said, and Varda nodded. He counted softly, and the pair shouldered the pole and Cuddles. The dog's toes dragged the ground as they carried him out of the pen.

"I'll have to tie up his legs," Regen whispered.

"Wait until we're out of the camp," Varda replied.

They carried the dog into the jungle and stopped when they were well out of sight of the camp. Regen had managed to find a climbing rope in the Banguer's stores, and he cut a piece from it to secure Cuddles dangling feet against his body. Now that the dog was secured, they made good time through the jungle toward the ravine. Regen was in the lead using his night vision goggles to make sure they did not run on to any unexpected problems like an outpost they had not counted on or some jungle creature that might impede their progress. All was going well until just before reaching the ravine. Regen suddenly signaled Varda to stop and indicated they should drop the dog. Varda moved to his side.

"What is it?"

"It's an observation post, but there's only one man there. I don't know where the other one is. We're going to have to take this guy out before we can get to the ravine, but I need to make sure his buddy isn't around anywhere first. Put on your night vision stuff and check to the left. I'll check out the right side. We'll meet back here."

Varda nodded and moved out. Regen checked her progress for a while then began his search of the right flank. He found no other Banguer and returned to the dog. Varda joined him in a moment.

"His friend is about twenty meters to the left manning a communicator. I can't take him out the way he's situated. Go take a look and see if you have any ideas."

Regen nodded his understanding and moved off to see what Varda was talking about. He found the man easily, but saw the problem. He was in a foxhole with only his head above ground. A camouflaged metal cover with four vision slots prevented any surprise attack. Regen moved back to Varda.

"He's in there pretty solid, but I think I may have a plan." Regen pulled the tent pole from Cuddles' harness arrangement. "If you can take this one out, I'll take care of the other one with this." Regen hefted the pole, and Varda smiled in understanding. She gave him a thumbs-up sign. "Three minutes from now." Once more Varda nodded, and Regen moved back to the dug-in Banguer.

He situated himself behind the foxhole and carefully moved the pole into position where it was aimed directly at the back of the Banguer's head through one of the vision slots. He checked his watch, and as the numbers fell to zeroes, he used the pole like a pool cue to knock the man senseless. He waited for any sound from the right and was rewarded by the appearance of Varda cleaning off a bloody knife with a large leaf. He moved to the foxhole and opened the cover. A quick knife slash cut the man's throat.

"I don't know how often he had to check in, but we'd better

hit that ravine quick," Regen said, and Varda nodded her agreement. They moved back to where they left Cuddles, but the dog was gone.

"Where'd he go?" Regen asked.

"I don't know. He was here when I moved out to kill that Banguer. The drug must have worn off."

"If he's walking around, we'll have to hit him again with the tranquilizer. You got any more shots?"

"Two more, but I figured we'd need those to get him down the river. He can't be wide awake yet. He probably just came-to enough to stagger off a short distance. You check that way, and I'll go this way."

The pair searched for Cuddles for several minutes but found no trace of him. They met back at the original spot.

"Any luck?" Regen asked.

"None, how about you?"

"Likewise. He must be more wide awake than you figured."

At that moment they heard the noise of panic from the camp behind them.

"Oh, oh. They either found Cuddles or found he was gone," Regen said.

"Either way, they know we're not there and the pen's open. They'll check the OP's, and when this one doesn't answer, they'll be all over us," Varda said.

"Time to save our own behinds. The ravine's that way." Regen pointed ahead and took off at a trot with Varda close behind. As they passed the communications foxhole, they heard the radio come alive with frantic commands. Regen broke into a dead run.

By the time they reached the ravine, they could hear the sound of men crashing through the brush and see the beams of their lights probing the darkness for their quarry. Regen secured the rope to a tree and threw it over the side of the cliff.

"How deep is this thing?" Varda asked. "Do you have enough rope?"

"Whatever rope there is, it's all we got. I'll go first and let you know."

Regen slid over the side, and Varda saw the rope grow taut. It seemed like hours before he called up to her.

"It's about a two meter drop to a ledge just above the river. No sweat."

Varda dropped over the edge and lowered herself hand over hand to the end of the rope. The ravine was too dark for even her night vision device to spot anything.

"Two meters, you say?"

"Yeah, two meters. Let go of the rope."

Varda released her grip and fell into Regen's arms knocking him to the ground. They tumbled into the river and were quickly pulled along by its wild torrent. The pair bounced against rocks on each side and slammed against boulders in the center of the stream. Attempts at swimming were useless. It took all of their efforts to stay afloat and to divest themselves of the now useless equipment they carried.

"Varda! You okay?" Regen shouted above the roar of the water.

"I'm fine. How long until we're out of this?" At that point, she took in a mouthful of muddy water, and swallowed half of it before she could splutter out the rest.

"Don't know. We must be moving at close to forty klicks. At that rate, it should only be a few minutes. Hang on."

Varda tried to find the bottom a few times, but never succeeded. Her body ached from hitting the rocks, but she fought to go on. As she was about to relax and let the river take her, she sensed the current easing somewhat, and heard Regen's call.

"Swim to your right. You can stand up over here."

She obeyed and soon found she could crawl against the current using the sandy bottom for leverage. A huge hand took her arm and pulled her from the water.

"You okay?" Regen asked.

"I'll live, but I'll be black and blue for weeks. I don't think any bones are broken. Where are we?"

"We're out of the ravine." Regen pointed upward at the bright starry sky above them. "I figure we're maybe one or two kilometers from the rendezvous point. We can wait on sunrise to move on."

"What about the Banguers?"

"It'll take them hours to get to this point moving through the jungle. We'll be long gone by then." Regen pulled the chain from around his neck and fumbled until he found the whistle. He blew into it several times.

"Are you trying to call Cuddles?"

"No, Hitler. I figure Cuddles went back to the pen. He knows there's food there."

"If he did, there's no way we'll get him out now. Those Banguers will never let anyone else into their camp."

"Well, baby, we did our best, and that's all anyone can ask." Regen blew the whistle again several times.

"You don't know the king. I'll probably lose my commission over this."

"There's always a partnership with me."

"Somehow, I don't think I'd fit in very well with the smuggler and dope dealer crowd. I can always get a job with the bomb disposal squad, it's a lot safer."

Varda sank back on the rocky bank and tried to sleep, but each place her body contacted anything radiated waves of pain. She stared at the stars overhead and tried to name each one to focus her mind elsewhere. Regen said nothing more but continued to blow his whistle from time to time.

Dawn turned the sky to gray and faded out the stars. Varda saw they had drifted down to the edge of the jungle and agreed with Regen's estimate of their distance from the rendezvous point. Regen was fast asleep on a large, flat boulder a meter or two to her left. She rose with great difficulty and moved to his side.

"Wake up! We need to get out of here before the Banguers get here." She shook him violently.

Regen awakened with a low groan, wincing in pain as he lifted himself to one elbow.

"What didn't hurt last night is screaming at me this morning," he said between clenched teeth.

The pair moved off down the riverbank, but Regen continued to blow his whistle.

"I say good riddance to that skeen."

"I know he'll find me if he's not dead. One of those greasy Banguers probably shot him once they found we were gone."

"Good for them."

Regen gave her a sharp glare but moved on toward the rendezvous.

"Is that you, Captain Varda?" a husky male voice called from the cover of some brush on their right.

"Tomich, is that you?" Varda replied.

"He asked first," Regen quipped.

A group of heavily armed rangers appeared from their hiding places and surrounded the bloody pair in torn clothes still damp from their swim.

"There may be some Banguers behind us," Regen reminded them.

"Jarva, take Sten and check back down the river," Tomich

commanded, and two men moved off smartly. "Mikkan, get a transporter in here fast." Another man pulled out a communicator and began to give coordinates. "Where's the dog?"

"We lost him back in the jungle. The tranquilizer wore off too quickly, and he got away while we were taking care of an unexpected outpost," Varda explained.

"There's going to be hell to pay with the king," Tomich said.

Regen blew his whistle again, and was surprised by the sound of husky barking in reply. All eyes turned in the direction of the sound as it turned from a bark to an eerie bay.

"Owoooo! Owoooo!"

"What the blazes is that?" Regen asked.

"It's Cuddles," Varda shouted. "He's chasing something. Blow your whistle again, maybe he'll come to it."

Regen complied and the sound seemed to be coming closer.

"Keep it up," Varda commanded.

As she spoke, the huge dog came bounding toward them across the river with Hitler in hot pursuit.

The rangers raised their rifles to shoot, but Varda acted quickly.

"Don't shoot! It's okay."

Regen was laughing uncontrollably.

"Call him off, Regen," Varda shouted, but there was no need. Hitler ran to Regen's feet as soon as he saw the big Bremen.

Regen leaned down and patted the top of Hitler's head while surveying his pet skeen for any damage.

"I guess you did okay," Regen said as he moved to pat the thing's stomach. "Doesn't look like you missed too many meals, either."

Cuddles did not stop to find out what happened to his

pursuer. He ran on into the open plain while the rangers stood looking perplexed. Tomich recovered first.

"Mikkan, tell that transporter to keep track of the dog. There's a tranquilizer gun on board, and Rusor knows how to use it. Tell him to bring down the dog so we can load him into his cage."

The two rangers who had gone to check for pursuing Banquers returned to report no sightings of any, and the group waited while the transporter ran down Cuddles. Regen and Varda took advantage of the pause to get the worst of their cuts looked at and drain two canteens of water apiece.

Hitler was the talk of the group, but Regen warned them to stay well back and keep their hands away from the skeen's mouth.

"Why do you suppose Hitler was chasing Cuddles?" Varda asked.

"To Hitler, Cuddles was just breakfast. He must have found him this morning and was chasing him down when I blew the whistle. Cuddles probably heard the whistle and figured there was human help where the whistle was, so he headed for it. Hitler gave up on him when he saw me because he knew I'd feed him, and he wouldn't have to waste energy running after that dog."

"Skeens are pretty smart animals," Varda said just as the transporter landed near them with a doped and caged Cuddles aboard.

CHAPTER 4

The royal family turned out to welcome Cuddles back home. As the transporter landed, a band struck up a martial air and the entire court cheered the new heroes. The cage containing the giant dog was the first item out the door, and the prince ran to it. Varda hung back embarrassed by the state of her clothing, and Regen stayed with her. The rangers filed off to their barracks except for Captain Tomich. He approached the pair with a big smile on his face.

"Aren't you two going to bask in your hard-won glory? The King will want to thank you personally."

"I can't go out like this," Varda complained. "I look like a hooker who's been beaten-up by her pimp."

"The only thanks I want is money in my account," Regen added. What brought all this on?"

"I had to make a report," Tomich said. "The reception must be the King's idea."

"All of this'll scare Hitler to death," Regen said as the skeen cowered behind his legs. "I can't take him out there." Regen indicated the assembled nobles with a wave of his arm.

"Just a minute." Varda spoke to one of the transporter crewmembers, and the man left the craft. He returned a few minutes later with the cage the skeen occupied a few nights before.

"Well, this will take care of Hitler, but I'm still a mess," Varda said.

Tomich took off his field jacket and handed it to Varda. "Take this. It'll cover up the worst of it. As for you, Regen, the Queen'll love you the way you are. She's into the rugged, unfinished types. Now get out there." He shoved them out the door to the cheers of the crowd.

The Prince was busy having his face washed by Cuddles, but the King stood and walked toward Regen and Varda. The pair knelt on the carpet laid over the rough cobblestones of the courtyard and waited for the King to speak. The crowd fell silent as the King raised his arms and turned from side to side.

"My fellow citizens," the King began. "Thanks to the gallant efforts of Captain Varda and Regen of Brem, my son's pet is restored to him, and we have avoided a diplomatic confrontation with a valued ally. I hereby promote Captain Varda to the rank of Major and grant Regen of Brem full and complete pardon for any past crimes committed in my realm. Let tomorrow be a day of feasting and rejoicing in honor of these brave subjects."

The assembled nobles applauded respectfully, but the mob outside the gate cheered wildly at the news of the feast day. The King's larders would be opened to the public, and many would receive their first decent meal in weeks.

The King lifted Varda to her feet and embraced her as he said, "I'm sure you'll want to rest and change into something more suitable for the party tonight. You are excused, Major." He turned to Regen.

"You don't know how my chief prosecutor begged me not to issue your pardon, but here it is." He handed Regen a plastic card bearing the royal arms.

"Thanks, your majesty, but I'm more interested in the money Varda promised me," Regen said.

"Without that, you'd have no need for the money." The

King pointed to the card. "You'd be enjoying the hospitality of our penal colony. Varda has all the authority she needs to pay you what she promised. Is this the skeen that saved the day?" The King pointed at Hitler's cage.

"Yes, it is. His name's Hitler," Regen responded.

A wry smile turned up the corners of the King's mouth. "A very appropriate name for such an evil animal." The King moved his hand toward the cage, and before Regen could shout any kind of warning, the monarch pushed two fingers through the steel mesh to pet the skeen. Hitler responded in his usual fashion by snapping at the offered treats.

To Regen's astonishment the King's hand moved back so fast he barely saw it happen. He was relieved to see all five of the royal digits in their usual places.

"Hmmm, they are as fast as everyone says they are. I thought a Middian Viper was the fastest thing alive, but Hitler has them beat by a good tenth of a second."

"Your Majesty's not so slow yourself. I've never seen anybody do that and come back with all his fingers."

"We play a game here on Loba you're probably not familiar with. It's called Ujibba, which means 'the death game' in the language of one of our more primitive races. It involves snatching a prize of gold from the cage of some deadly snake without being bitten. I was quite good at it as a young man, and I'm still faster than most. I'd like to borrow your skeen for a game tonight. I don't think any of the other players know how fast they are. I should make a lot of money, and your pet should have some tasty treats."

"Hitler's bite ain't poison, yer Majesty."

"No matter, the penalty is less severe but the permanent disfigurement will compensate for the absence of mortality. I'll return him to you in the morning. You will stay for our party tonight, won't you? Let me introduce my Queen." He beckoned for a stately looking woman sitting on a companion throne.

An attractive middle-aged woman in a very expensive outfit stepped forward and offered her hand for Regen to kiss. The perfume was almost overwhelming, but the Bremen maintained his composure as he kissed the soft skin.

With her free hand, the Queen lifted Regen's chin and fixed his eyes in hers. A slight upward pressure told him he should rise, and he dropped her hand as he stood. She was only a few centimeters shorter than Regen and a bit taller than the King, but it was her eyes that fascinated the Bremen. They were gray flecked with bright blue, and they seemed to transmit pure passion. He felt his hormones begin to respond and suppressed the urge to take her in his arms. A quick glance at the King revealed an aura of total indifference to the subliminal seduction transpiring an arm's length away. He was much too preoccupied with Hitler to notice.

"Yes, do join us Regen," the Queen echoed her husband. "You won't be sorry."

"I'm a Bremen, yer majesty, and Bremens don't turn down parties, long as there's lovely ladies present. I'll be there, and you can use Hitler if you like, yer Majesty. Just see he gits fed first."

"Good! We'll see you tonight, then. I'll take care of Hitler until then," the King said.

With that, the audience was ended. The royals turned and marched back to the assembled nobles as a guard motioned for Regen to follow him.

He led the Bremen to a spacious room and indicated a closet full of expensive clothes.

"You should be able to find something here to fit you. Use that communicator over there if you want anything to eat or drink. The party starts at 2100 local time." He pointed to a digital clock set into the far wall. It read 1100. "You're free until then."

"I need to talk to Captain Varda. How do I find her?"

"Just punch her name into the communicator. It'll find her. Anything else?"

"No, I'll take over from here. Oh, one thing. Could somebody see that my ship's fueled up and ready to go by 0900 tomorrow?"

"I'll take care of that. See you at the party." The guard left and Regen surveyed his quarters.

It was large, with all the amenities anyone could expect, including a marble hot tub in the center of the thickly-carpeted floor. A hint of steam rising from the roiling surface told him it was ready for use. He slipped out of his ragged clothes and let the hydraulic massage work the pain out of his muscles and joints. He was about to go to sleep when Varda appeared.

Her hair was now back to her original red, and she wore a slinky black gown with sheer panels in all the right places.

"May I join you in the hot tub?" Varda asked.

"How the hell did you get in here? I locked the door myself."

"This is a royal palace, Regen. You've got to expect a few secret passages here and there. You didn't answer my question."

"Sure, sure, get in. The water's fine."

Varda shed her gown in one deft motion and stood naked a moment before gliding into the tub. Her bruises were turning several shades of blue and purple now, but they couldn't detract from her athletic figure.

"God! That feels so good," she cooed as she closed her eyes and leaned back against the side of the bath.

"I see you got beat up pretty bad in the gorge," Regen said pointing to a black and purple bruise on her shoulder.

"The medics say I'll live. What about you? I heard you moan a few times on the way out."

"Nothin' an hour or so in here won't cure, particularly since you're in here with me." He reached across the tub and took her hand, pulling her toward him. She didn't resist and re-settled next to the big Bremen.

"I was hoping I could take care of your needs for tonight so that you didn't have to service the Queen."

"Why couldn't I just do both of you?" Regen asked.

"You don't understand. The King is insanely jealous. If he caught you with the Queen, you'd die a very messy and slow death. It's not worth it, Regen."

"I thought the old boy'd be tied up in his game of chicken with Hitler all night."

"He probably will be, but he'll want to know she isn't playing a different game somewhere else in the palace. He has cameras planted in all the good hiding places, including her boudoir. I wouldn't doubt they're all over your ship by now. The minute you two would get hot and sweaty, he'd be there to nab you."

"They ain't watchin' you, are they?" Regen said as he pulled Varda into his arms.

"I don't have a jealous husband, and I couldn't pass up this opportunity to catch you all cleaned up," Varda answered as she pressed her lips to his. They soon left the hot tub for the silken-sheeted bed.

Varda awoke first and roused Regen with a rude slap on his bare buttocks.

"Get up, Regen! We've got to find you something suitable to wear for the party this evening."

Regen growled as he turned over and watched Varda dress.

"What's wrong with my regular clothes?"

Varda held up the ragged remains of his usual uniform. "I rest my case," she said.

"I got another outfit in my spaceship. Just send one of your stooges out to get it."

"No, you need something more suitable to the occasion than body armor and a weapons belt." She walked to a large closet and opened the door revealing a large array of princely attire. "We should be able to find something in here."

As she worked her way along the rack, she changed the subject. "What bank do we send the credits to for your services in rescuing Cuddles?"

Regen joined her at the closet as Varda handed him an expensive suit in light mauve. Regen sneered at the outfit and tossed it aside.

"I been thinkin', I don't want your money."

Varda turned to him with a shocked expression. "You don't want money? Who are you, and what have you done with Regen?"

"When we got the dope to deal to the Banguers, I noticed a lot of Petro in the warehouse. I'll take my payment in that."

Varda pulled out a sharp looking uniform in dark burgundy and held it up for Regen's appraisal. "We just got that stuff recently when we busted a big drug dealer in Loba City. We'll need some of it for evidence, but you can have the rest. I think that would amount to some 1,000 kilos."

Regen raised his eyebrows in reaction to the uniform and took it from Varda's hand for closer inspection. "That'd be enough. I know where I can peddle that stuff for a good profit." He felt the sleeve of the uniform and nodded his approval.

"This'll do."

"I'll have the stuff loaded on your ship tonight." She nodded toward the uniform. "Try it on."

As Regen put on the suit, Varda used her communicator to issue the order for the narcotic to be loaded on Regen's spaceship.

"A bit large, ain't it?" Regen modeled the oversize uniform.

Varda laughed and sent Regen's heart racing again, but he knew it was too close to the time for the party to enjoy another roll in bed with her.

"They're all extra large size, but we can size it real fast. Just step in here." Varda opened another closet door revealing a fitting cabinet. Regen stepped inside, and Varda set the controls for the unit. In less than two minutes, Regen emerged wearing a perfect fit.

"Pretty snazzy contraption," Regen said.

"You look like a million credits," Varda complimented as she turned Regen around for inspection.

"More like 1,000 kilos of Petro," Regen corrected.

"Whatever. You need to do something with your hair, and shave." She rubbed her hand across his dark stubble. "I'm going back to my quarters to clean up a bit. I'll see you at the party." She turned to leave.

"Wait a minute! Where is this party? I don't know anything about the palace."

"A guard will knock on your door when it's time. He'll show you the way. See you later." Varda blew him a kiss and left.

Regen was just splashing aftershave lotion on his face when the guard knocked.

"Come on in. It's unlocked," Regen called from the bathroom.

The guard entered and sniffed the air. He stifled a smile as he spoke.

"I've been sent to escort you to the party Mister Regen. Follow me please."

"Do I smell that bad? The only stuff they had here was a bit on the fluffy side for my tastes."

"Not at all, sir. The Queen herself selects the toiletries for the guest rooms. This way please."

The guard led Regen through the corridors of the palace toward the sound of revelry and a rather loud dance band. They entered the ballroom where expensively dressed men and women were gyrating sensually on a large, marble-mosaic dance floor. Incense burned in a dozen braziers around the room leaving a blue haze hanging just above the dancer's heads. In alcoves cut into the walls around the room, couples were indulging in whatever sex acts fit their mood. Filmy curtains of gauze-like material did little to hide the action. Some were already feasting on dishes brought in by liveried servants, and wine flowed freely.

A servant showed Regen to a seat at the head table between two empty chairs. He calculated the one on his left belonged to the Queen since the King sat on the other side of that vacant spot. The King welcomed Regen profusely.

"Welcome Regen. I've been getting acquainted with Hitler while Varda was entertaining you. He doesn't seem to like me very much."

Regen took his seat, and an attentive servant promptly filled a huge wine glass with a rich, red liquid. Regen wasn't much on wine, but this stuff had an aroma like molten gold. He took a sip before answering the King and smacked his lips in appreciation.

"Hitler don't take much to strangers. This wine's pretty decent. Where's it from?"

"It's a local concoction made with a merlot from the Southern provinces spiced with a bit of majira. It's supposed to be an aphrodisiac."

Regen was familiar with majira. He'd sold several tons of the junk over the last year on planets where it was legal. About half the galaxy considered it no more harmful than alcohol and taxed it accordingly while the rest banned it as a narcotic. There was very little profit in the stuff.

"Maybe it'll work for one of those ladies tonight?" Regen nodded toward the dance floor where three women clad only in thongs and pasties were gyrating to the music.

The King laughed. "Not on them, Regen. They much prefer each other's company to any man's, but that one might be on the menu." The King pointed to a stately brunette just walking into the room. She wore a filmy sheath of light blue material, and as she walked, it showed her bare skin color where it clung closely to her body. She wore undergarments of a slightly darker color hiding strategic locations. She was a beauty, but right behind her Varda appeared wearing the dress uniform of the palace guard.

The contrast couldn't have been more stark. The brunette radiated sensuality while Varda projected a no-nonsense military demeanor. The uniform hid most of her feminine assets, and the beautiful red hair and classic face were hard-pressed to overcome the image. He decided Varda was a better choice in spite of the almost irresistible attraction of the other woman.

"Oh, there's Varda," Regen announced in an effort to change the subject.

"Regen, you disappoint me. Didn't you get enough of her this afternoon?"

Varda told him the King had cameras in every room in the

palace, and the monarch probably knew every detail of his session with her.

"She's a fine lady, yer highness," was all Regen could muster. He wondered if the King was as familiar with Varda as he was.

"Alas, I've only been able to enjoy her vicariously. The Queen keeps a close eye on all the palace staff. She'd cut off my balls if she caught me with Varda."

The King rose as Varda approached the table and raised her quickly to her feet after her bow to the royal personage. The King seated her on Regen's right after the usual pleasantries.

Before Varda could engage Regen in conversation they were joined by a perspiring Queen.

"My God! Dancing makes me thirsty," the Queen announced as she plopped into the chair.

A servant hastened to fill her glass with white wine, and she drank half of it in one gulp. As she returned the glass to the table, she noticed Regen.

"It's Regen, isn't it? I didn't recognize you at first. You clean up pretty good, and you weren't that bad dirty."

Regen smiled at this lady who, obviously, thought any man with a pulse rate should go mad with desire at the very sight of her. He remembered Varda's warning, but it was currently doing battle in his head with a strong impulse to lick the sweat from her nearly exposed bosoms. Her gown, if you could call it that, barely covered the sensitive parts of her upper body on top and didn't extend much past her hip joints on the bottom. She had good legs, and her figure was that of a woman fifteen years her junior. Platinum blonde hair shone almost as bright as the jewels and pearls holding it on top of her head. Her face had classic lines with the exception of cheek bones protruding a bit too much. Her eyes were her main attraction. Regen remembered them from that morning, a curious combination of gray and blue compelling a man to tear his gaze from her body and submit his soul to her will. He finally recovered from her spell enough to answer.

"Thank you, yer Majesty. I must say you certainly look lovely tonight yourself."

Varda saw the ship sinking and nudged Regen with her knee under the table. The big Bremen only patted her leg with his right hand to acknowledge the reminder.

"They tell me you're a drug smuggler, Regen. Is that true?" the Queen asked.

"I like to think of myself as someone who supplies a need the government neglects," Regen replied.

"I've tried kourma and majira, but neither one of them produced any memorable effects on me. I understand our police just confiscated a great deal of a new drug called petro. I'll have to try some of that. They say it's a powerful aphrodisiac. But my ladies in waiting tell me I don't need any aphrodisiac with a Bremen."

Varda broke in. "Your Majesty, Regen has requested payment in petro instead of credits. I'm afraid all but the evidence quantity has already been loaded aboard his spaceship."

The Queen's eyes lit up a bit at the news. "Well, perhaps you could spare a bit for some experimentation, Regen?"

"I never use any of the stuff I sell. I've seen what it does to people who get hooked."

At that point, dinner arrived, and the conversation turned to other subjects. The food was exquisite, though a bit on the fancy side for Regen's tastes. The wine was fantastic and produced a slight buzz inside his head. The more he drank, the more irresistible the Queen became.

After dinner, the entertainment began. A troop of jugglers was first on the bill, and the King excused himself.

"I leave the acrobats and jugglers to you and Major Varda, Regen. I'm off to test my reactions against Hitler. What time do you want to leave tomorrow?"

"As early as possible, yer Majesty, but make it easy on yourself."

"Fine, I'll have Hitler at your ship by 0900 tomorrow. I hope you and Major Varda enjoy the evening." The King gave Regen a surreptitious wink as he left his chair.

The Queen seemed to be enthralled by the jugglers, and Varda leaned close to Regen.

"This would be a good time for you to make your exit. The Queen will make her move as soon as the entertainment's over," she whispered.

Regen turned toward her with an evil grin on his face. "What about us making an exit together?"

"Not tonight. I've got an early day tomorrow, and I'm going straight to bed," she said in a slightly louder tone, then added, "Alone!" for Regen's benefit.

"In that case, I might as well enjoy the entertainment. I can handle Her Majesty okay. Don't worry about it." He nudged Varda with his shoulder in a playful manner.

A magician followed the jugglers, and Varda made her excuses to the Queen, leaving Regen to face his fate alone.

The Queen didn't say much through the magician's act, but when some female dancers in minimal costumes appeared, she turned to Regen.

"I'd like to try some petro, but you have all we can spare on your ship. Take me there, and show me how to use it."

"How could I leave the floor show now? This looks like the best part," Regen answered.

"I think I can give you a better show on your ship.   Besides, it's the only place my husband doesn't have spies or cameras. He hates for me to use narcotics. I'll make it worth your while, Regen." She let her right hand brush over his private parts as she smiled invitingly.

"Just so you can try the petro, darlin'. I can't afford to git on His Majesty's bad side."

"Lead the way," the Queen said, and rose to her feet indicating Regen's path with a sweep of her arm.

When they reached the ship, Regen checked out his load. The petro was stored properly, and the ship was fully fueled for his departure in the morning. He took a small bag of the white powder from one of the metal chests and led the Queen to his cabin.

"You got to have pure water for this stuff," he said. "I'll git some from my recycler unit, it's s'posed ta be as pure as it gits."

He filled a small glass with water and broke open the bag of petro. Taking a small spoon from one of the storage drawers, he measured out two spoonfuls into the water and stirred it vigorously. He handed the glass to the queen.

"Here, Your Majesty... Say, what is your name, anyway? If I'm goin' ta be yer pusher, I need to know something 'sides yer title."

The Queen laughed as she took the glass from Regen. "It's Yolanda, and what am I supposed to do with this, drink it?"

"Nope, just hold it so's it gits up ta yer body temperature. We'll inject it when it's warm enough. I gotta find an **in**-jecter, though. Be right back."

The Queen placed the glass between her legs and smiled at Regen. "I'll be right here waiting," she cooed.

Varda decided to make a visit to the security center before turning in for the night. Her crew had the duty, and she needed to make sure all was well with her Lieutenant in charge. She walked into the control room to find the officer watching the panel of monitor screens but concentrating on the one showing the King fleecing his aristocracy in the Ujibba game. He noticed his boss enter the room and stood to attention.

"At ease, Sumann. Anything happening?"

"Not much, Major. By the way, congratulations on the promotion." He extended his hand, and Varda took it in a firm grip.

"Thanks. How's the King doing?"

"The royal surgeon's been busy treating some nasty bites, and Count Tulla lost a finger, but the King hasn't lost a bet yet."

Varda perused the monitor in the King's gaming room and zoomed in on Hitler. The ugly little half-rat seemed to be enjoying every minute of the game.

"Where's the Queen?" Varda asked.

"She was in the banquet hall on the last cycle, but I'll check her again."

Lieutenant Sumann called up the banquet hall camera system and was surprised to see empty chairs at the head table. "She's gone, and your smuggler's gone too. I'd better find her."

A flurry of keyboard entries produced a new display on the main monitor, and Varda sighed heavily in disgust. The Queen was, obviously, high on something and busy undressing Regen.

"That idiot just can't resist a sexy woman. He's all Bremen," she said through gritted teeth. "Can we talk to him through that camera?"

"Sure thing. Here's a mike."

"Regen! Can you hear me?" Varda almost shouted.

Regen turned his head trying to find the camera, but the Queen continued undressing him oblivious to any distractions.

"Who the hell is that?" Regen said.

"It's me, Varda. What are you doing?"

"Queenie here, or I should say Yolanda is about to make me a very happy guy. You wanna come down and help or just watch from there?"

The Queen stopped undressing Regen and slipped out of her gown to stand naked in front of the spy camera. "Who's talking, Regen?" she slurred. "I don't mind another woman involved if you don't. I think it's fun sometimes."

Varda interrupted. "I told you about her, you dummy. Don't do anything more. I'll be right down to get her, and you'd better head for space on the double. The King'll be checking up on her any time now, and when he finds out where she is there'll be hell to pay."

"I can't leave without Hitler, and the King's busy with him right now. Relax and don't get so excited. I'll take care of Yolanda, here, and bring her back to the palace in, say, an hour or so."

"The Queen's got nice tits," Sumann said, he thought low enough to keep Varda from hearing him.

"Sumann! Get this straight. You haven't seen any of this. We're going to have a system breakdown about thirty minutes ago. I don't care how you get it done, but I want all of this and any more until I get the Queen out of there, erased completely. Let's just hope the King stays occupied that long."

As she spoke, another screen came alive with the King's image. "Where's the Queen!" he demanded.

Sumann reached for the switch that would let the King see the control room, but Varda stopped his hand.

"Tell him she went to try some of Regen's petro. That's

probably the truth as far as it goes. He doesn't need to know any more right now. I'm not here. Give me time to get out of the camera field before you turn him on."

She moved to a position behind one of the consoles and nodded to Sumann.

"Yes, Your Majesty," Sumann answered.

"Didn't you hear me the first time? I said, where's the Queen?"

"Yes, sire. She's with Regen. She wanted to try some of the petro he has aboard his ship."

"Connect me with that camera. I need to see what she's doing," the King commanded.

Sumann glanced at Varda who shook her head vigorously.

"Well, sire, we have a bit of a problem there. That circuit went out a few minutes ago, and we haven't been able to bring it up yet. We're working on it now."

"Ah hah!" the King shouted. "I smell a rat here. I'll go myself to find out what she's doing. Keep working on that circuit." The monitor went dark.

Varda emerged from hiding and called up the link to Regen's ship. The Queen was busy performing oral sex on Regen, and Varda nearly gagged at the sight.

"Regen! The King's on his way right now. You'd better get her dressed and off your ship in a hurry. Then, I suggest you head for deep space as fast as that thing will go."

"I can't leave without Hitler," Regen protested. "I'll git her off, but you gotta bring Hitler to me."

"I can't manage him and the cage too, it's too heavy. You'll just have to come back for him when this has all died down a bit."

"The King will probably kill Hitler for spite. Tranquilize him and put him in a bag. If you take a small transporter, you can beat him here easy."

Varda did some mental calculations. The King would take several guards with him. It would take him a few minutes to round them up, and they'd take the royal underground to the spaceport. She could nab Hitler and be there a few minutes ahead of him if she hurried.

"Okay, I'll try to make it, but get the Queen out of there now!"

None of this fazed the Queen. She continued to work on Regen through all the shouting and panic, but now, he pushed her away and began explaining the situation. A look of sheer horror spread across the royal face, but the words didn't match the expression.

"You mean we aren't going to bed?" she pleaded.

Varda looked around the room for something to carry Hitler in. The only thing at hand was a canvas cover over a console being sent to the shops for repair. It would have to do. She ripped it off the unit and turned to Sumann.

"Give me your stun gun," she demanded.

The Lieutenant pulled the weapon from a small pouch on his belt and handed it to Varda.

"Thanks, now get busy destroying the record of that camera on Regen's ship. I'll check with you in a half hour, if I'm not in the dungeon keeping Regen company." With that, she sped out the door.

The King's gameroom was empty of nobility now. Only the cage containing Hitler remained among the servants cleaning up the blood on the floor. She moved to the skeen and pulled out the stun gun.

"Sorry about this, boy, but I don't have time to check out any tranquilizers," she said to the skeen. Hitler cocked his head to one side and gurgled his lack of understanding. Varda set the gun to its lowest range, hoping it wouldn't kill the thing. A quick blast surprised the servants, but they only stood watching as she opened the cage and stuffed the mini-dinosaur into the canvas cover. They were used to strange goings-on in this particular room. Varda was relieved to feel a heartbeat as she pulled the animal from the cage.

Tucking the skeen under her arm, she bounded up the two flights of stairs to the palace roof and the transporter station. Only one sleepy Sergeant was on duty, but he jumped to attention as Varda rushed through the doorway.

"No time for paperwork now, Sarge. Official royal business." She rushed past him and onto the landing zone before he could say anything.

As she jumped into a waiting transporter, the Sergeant muttered, "Yes, Ma'am."

Back at Regen's ship, he was having a hard time getting the Queen's clothes back on her.

"But Regen, daaaahhhling, we've only just begun to enjoy the evening. Don't be such a party pooper," she protested.

"It's okay, Your Majesty, er, Yolanda. We're gonna git it on back at your place soon as the transporter gits here. Now, help me git yer big boobs inta this dress."

"Not until you kiss each one of them as sexy as you can." She assumed a pouting attitude with her hands on her hips.

"Okay, but this is all ya git 'til we get back to yer place." He gave each one the "royal" treatment and was just finishing as Varda stormed in.

"Regen, for God's sake, the King's right behind me. Get her dressed," Varda shouted.

"Did ya get Hitler?" he asked.

"Here he is, now let me help you with her." Varda dropped her package to the floor and took over dressing the Queen.

"Captain Varda! I would never have expected you to be the third party in our little ménage-a-trois." She kissed the Major on the cheek as Varda lifted the Queen's dress back up to her shoulders.

"Please, Your Majesty, the King is on his way here now. Try to understand the seriousness of the situation." She turned to Regen. "What's she high on?"

Regen extracted Hitler from the makeshift bag and looked up from inspecting his unusual pet to answer Varda. "Just some petro, but it should be wearin' off by now. I only gave her a small dose."

"You were too stingy, Regen," the Queen slurred. "I added some more while you were looking for the injection thingey."

Regen stood up and grasped the Queen by the shoulders. "How much?" he asked, his voice growing angry.

"Only a pinch or two. What's the harm in that? Kiss me, you big hunk." She threw her arms around Regen, but the Bremen pushed her away.

"Is that an overdose?" Varda asked.

"Probably not, but she'll be like this for another hour, or so, if she added that much. You got her dressed?"

"She's presentable. I'll take her into the terminal. Give me that bag." She pointed to the cover she'd used to carry Hitler.

"What do ya need that fer?"

"I have to account for Hitler some way. I haven't figured that out yet, but I'll find something. You'd better get out of here as quickly as you can. The King can't be much behind me."

Regen leaned past the tipsy Queen and kissed Varda on the lips. "Bye, darlin'. I'll always remember that hot tub."

"Regen, you're a misogynistic Bremen asshole, and you'll forget me five minutes after you leave this planet, but it was great sex. She kissed him back then hustled the Queen down the ship's ramp and into the terminal. She waved as the smuggler's ship lifted into the night sky, and it blinked its running lights in response.

The King and his party bounded up the stairs from the underground station to find a drunken Queen being supported by a disheveled Major.

"What's been going on here?" the King asked.

"Her Majesty's been sampling some petro, Sire. I'm afraid Regen let her have a bit too much."

The Queen recognized her husband and flew into his arms.

"Reggie, baby. That nasty old Regen wouldn't fuck my brains out, but I know you'll take good care of me once we get back to the palace. Won't you, pleeeeease?"

The King looked at Varda with a confused expression.

"I think you'd better take advantage of this opportunity, Your Majesty. Regen says the petro could last another hour, or so." She winked at the sovereign who smiled in response and ordered the party back to the palace at all possible speed.

CHAPTER 5

Once Regen cleared Loban space, his first concern was for Hitler. The skeen lay motionless on the cabin floor ever since Varda dropped him there. He felt for a heartbeat and was relieved to find a strong, steady pulse. Hitler appeared to be breathing normally, but Regen had no idea how Varda tranquilized him, thus he had no idea how to revive him. He picked up his animal companion and laid him softly on his own bed hoping for the best. He returned to the navigation console and sat thinking about a destination.

The best place to peddle the petro was Gobra, but he'd need a visa to get through immigration. As a convicted felon wanted on several planets allied with Gobra, there wasn't much chance of obtaining one through normal channels. He'd have to visit old Trodius, the best forger in the galaxy, and he dreaded that encounter.

As he laid in the course to Villia, Trodius' planet, he was distracted by the clatter of claws on the metal floor. Before he could turn around, a somewhat groggy Hitler jumped into his lap.

"Well, it's good to see you back in the land of the livin'," Regen said as he stroked the leathery head.

Hitler cooed contentedly and looked up at his master through heavy-lidded red eyes.

"I know, you're hungry. Let me set the course, and I'll feed ya."

Usually the mention of food was enough to send Hitler scurrying for the compartment where the small rodents he relished were caged, but this time, the skeen only dropped its head into Regen's lap. Once the course was in, Regen dumped Hitler and headed for the animal cages.

"I hope those guys on Loba replenished yer supply o' varmints. If they didn't, it's dry kibbles for you, old boy."

As Regen opened the door to the skeen's food compartment, the chattering of several dozen rodents changed Hitler's expression from one of dismay to one of eager anticipation. Regen took one of the cages and dumped a small, furry creature on the ship's deck. It scampered off with Hitler in hot pursuit, and Regen returned to the control room.

He sat at the console thinking about Trodius. The old forger always subjected his clients to tall tales about a mythical city of gold on a planet that couldn't be found in the data banks of any navigation computer. Everyone knew the place didn't exist, but old Trodius made it his life's work to prove it did He would have to be patient while the old man prattled on about the mysterious place he called Agam Valeem. There was only one good thing about the trip—Hitler was particularly fond of the small rodents called koosa infesting the old fortress Trodius used for a hideout. As he thought of this aspect of the visit, his pet skeen jumped into his lap.

Regen stroked the leathery head while Hitler gurgled his appreciation. "Not long now, boy. We'll be at Trodius's soon and you can eat all the little critters you want."

Regen turned on his communicator and called the eccentric old forger.

Trodius was expecting Regen, but none of his sensors were picking up the smuggler's spacecraft. He was beginning to worry about the big Bremen when he heard the noise of the ship's drive system as it descended to a landing near the ancient stone fortress he called home. He ran outside to greet his old friend and noticed the ship was a kind he had recently been investigating himself. As Regen stepped from the hatchway, Trodius ran to embrace him.

"Regen! I've been looking forward to your visit, but this ship is a big bonus."

Regen pushed the old forger back a bit and gave him a quizzical look. "What are you talkin' about, you old fraud?"

"Your ship! It's just what I need to make a fortune on Agam Valeem."

"Aw not that old garbage again?" Regen turned to go back inside his ship.

"No, wait Regen! I've done a lot of research on this subject, and a stealth craft like this one is just what we need. I got some new information last month that's bound to interest you."

"Trodius, I've heard yer stories 'bout that imaginary planet ever since my first phoney pilot's license. What makes you think I'd believe 'em any more now than I did then?"

"The place is real, Regen. This is reliable info, and you're going to flip when you see it. Come on inside."

"I came here for a visa to Gobra. Can't we just do some business and leave it at that?"

"One of my flunkies can take care of that while I show you this stuff. I promise, if you aren't convinced by the time your visa's done, you can have it for nothing."

Regen considered that listening to Trodius's latest fairy tale was well worth the price of a visa, and he was sure he'd be no more convinced than he had been by the last "absolutely genuine, verifiable, proof-positive" evidence of the mythical land of gold to be had for a song.

"Okay, Trodius, I'll give you the time it takes to make the visa, but no more."

"Did you bring Hitler? He may be the most important part of the whole deal."

At that point, Hitler bounded from the spacecraft and headed straight for the darkest parts of the ancient castle, brushing rudely past Trodius on his way.

"Good to see he's still around," the older man was almost gleeful at seeing the skeen.

"I wouldn't part with him for the world. He's a lot of company on long trips, and he's good entertainment in the dives I have to frequent to line up deals."

"Still ripping fingers off unwary suckers?"

"Oh, he gits a few ever' now and then, but he loves your rats better 'n fingers."

"They're not rats, they're koosa, and they don't do any harm. Shame he has to kill so many of them. Takes the time between your visits to repopulate the place. Oh well, he's welcome to them. Come on in. I got some really marvelous stuff to show you."

Trodius led Regen into a large room filled with bookshelves and computer equipment. Several display screens showed what appeared to be old documents, and Trodius led his guest to a rather large unit in one corner.

"Sit down, Regen, and look at this." Trodius indicated a chair in front of the screen.

A few commands produced an ancient looking document in a script Regen recognized from past visits. It was, supposedly, the language of Agam Valeem.

"What now? You know I can't read this stuff."

"I've translated the text. Just look at this picture." The screen changed to a series of simplified drawings showing what

Regen guessed to be various gods or kings. Most of them were half animal, half human, but one in particular caught his eye. It couldn't have been a better representation of Hitler if it had been a photograph.

"So they got skeens, so what?"

"The text says this is their god Duru. He's a mythical combination of some kind of kangaroo-like thing and a miniature dinosaur-type creature. According to this document, Duru rules the underworld and judges the souls of the dead. If your soul doesn't pass muster, he eats it."

"Sounds like a skeen, alright, but what does that have to do with Hitler and me?"

"It says the only way to appease the god is to offer it gold while you're alive. Don't you see? The priests must have used this as a way to raise money. You could buy your way into their version of heaven before you died. It was sort of an insurance policy."

"Okay, why should that interest me?"

"We could go there and pass Hitler off as the god. People'd shower us with gold, and we could be in and out of there with a fortune before they got wise."

"That's assuming this document's authentic. How much did you pay Harbon for this one?"

Regen was wise to Harbon. The man made a living peddling fake artifacts and documents around the known planets. He'd sold Trodius several pieces of junk about Agam Valeem.

"This didn't come from Harbon. I got this one from a guy whose great grandfather'd been there, except the guy didn't know that. He found this scroll, and some other stuff, in his father's place after the old man died. Somebody told him I bought old stuff, and he wanted to see what it was worth. One of the items was great grandpa's navigation log. Check this out." Trodius placed a data disc in the computer and called up the log. He paged through it to one section in particular and magnified the text for Regen's benefit.

"Look, this shows the great grandfather went to Kimos about 120 years back. From there, he went to Loomisa and stayed for ten years."

"Lots o' people 've been to those planets. They're pretty far off the beaten path, but they're on the charts," Regen countered.

"I know, I know, I'm coming to the good part. Look at this next entry. He had to leave Loomisa in a big rush because the law was after him. Seems he'd deflowered one of their temple virgins, or something. He headed out into unknown space, for that era, and found a place he calls Aga Valam. He spent several years there pretending to be a holy man. He says they would have killed him immediately, but he was wearing a robe they mistook for some kind of monk's habit, and they thought his ship was some kind of flying temple. The scroll is their holy book. Don't you see, Regen? His ship was just like yours, and Hitler is just like Duru. All we have to do is pretend to be holy men attached to your skeen, and we've got it made."

"Wait a minute. They didn't have stealth ships 120 years back. How can my ship look like his?"

"Well, it's not exactly like his, but it's close enough. It was a Ramand ZGA 998, and they revived the basic design for the ZHS 1160 because they found out it was a good stealth profile. Look at this." Trodius called up an image of the older ship next to one of Regen's ship."

Regen surveyed the photos. "Yeah, they look a lot alike, but so what?"

"The people there don't know about spaceships. They thought his ship was a temple, and they'll think yours is one too. They might even be looking for the old guy's return. We could be the fulfillment of some kind of prophecy, for all we know."

"Or the return of a wanted con man and put our necks right into a rope. Besides, that was 120 years back. They probably know all about spaceships by now, and there's a good chance they've seen skeens, too. Maybe there's been a few more great grandpas since your guy, even if we can believe his log."

"I doubt it. They've been isolated all that time. Nobody goes there because they don't think the place is real. Regen, I tell you it's a cinch. With Hitler as part of the deal, we can con those guys like crazy. What do you say? Are you game to give it a try?"

Regen weighed his life on the scales of greed, and was not too sure which way they tipped. He'd risked it before at pretty short odds, but he was more certain of the dangers he'd have to face. Cops and rival drug smugglers were one thing, but enraged worshipers who'd been swindled out of their life savings were something else. If Agam Valeem was still a primitive planet, they could have some very painful and drawn out ways of making a swindler pay for his crimes.

"Too risky, Trodius. Count me out," Regen said.

"Don't you want to know how much great grandpa made?"

"You can't believe anything in that log, Trodius."

"I don't have to. The guy who sold me this stuff was so rich he didn't even get a good price for it. He let me have the whole package for less than a fourth of what I'd have given him for it if he'd bargained a little bit. I looked him up after he first contacted me, and the guy has billions. He told me neither he nor his father had worked a day in their lives. The whole family fortune came from great grandpa's trip to Agam Valeem."

Suddenly the scales fell heavily on the side of greed.

"Okay, tell me your plan."

Trodius briefed Regen on his plan for fleecing the poor suckers on Agam Valeem, and Regen considered the plan might have some merit, but only if the place was still as backward as it was then.

"I still think these guys might have wised-up over the last century?" Regen said.

"That's where your stealth ship comes in. They can't be very sophisticated in only 120 years, and a ship like yours could get past any sensors they could develop in that short time. It's a cinch."

Regen rubbed his chin trying to coax all of the pitfalls in the plan out of his brain. He remembered the petro.

"I only got room for another 1,000 kilos. I got a load o' petro takin' up half my cargo space. That enough?'

"You can stash the petro here while we're gone," Trodius said. "Why settle for half a load of gold?"

"Look, 1,000 kilos o' gold is enough to make both of us richer than old King Gog. How do I know the petro'll be here when I git back?"

"Regen! You insult me. My people will make sure it's safely locked up, and they don't do narcotics. Wouldn't you rather have 1,000 kilos for yourself?"

"Well, if you're sure you can trust 'em." Regen snapped his fingers suddenly remembering he'd need a lot of fuel to get to Agam Valeem. "I just thought, where can we refuel? If I have to make it all the way from here to that part of the universe in one hop, we won't even be able to take on 500 kilos o' gold." The pair called up a navigation display, and Regen found several places to refuel where he was not a wanted man.

The next morning, they left for the long trip to an isolated planet on the fringe of the galaxy. During the voyage, Regen spent a great deal of his time acclimating Hitler to the wardrobe Trodius insisted he wear, and training the skeen to strike and hold a god-like pose. After hearing what the old man's plan was for his pet, Regen stocked several cages full of koosa to use as bribes.

He had not underestimated the difficulty of the task, and by the time they reached the planet, the koosa population had been decimated in spite of the fact they were even more prolific than Trodius imagined.

While Regen was training Hitler, the automatic sensors of the ship scanned for any electronic emissions from the planet, but they found none. One light year from their destination Regen made a detailed scan of all possible frequencies with Trodius looking over his shoulder. The old man practically danced with delight at the negative results.

"They haven't discovered electronics yet. We're in luck, Regen," Trodius shouted.

"That doesn't mean they haven't progressed beyond worshiping skeens. We still could have made this trip for nothing, you know."

"Don't be such a pessimist, Regen. 120 years isn't that long in human development, particularly where religion is concerned."

"I'll feel much better when we can git some good pictures of the surface that don't show any modern weapons."

Regen eased the ship into an orbit suitable for photographic work and began to map the planet. It was a typical life-supporting world with large oceans and sizeable polar ice caps. There were four large landmasses, two in the northern hemisphere and two in the south. Trodius steered him toward one semi-arid area on the smallest northern continent. After several orbits, Regen had a complete picture of the target area in daylight. They waited for that part of the planet to enter darkness before finishing their scan using infrared frequencies. The men sat down in front of the display to have lunch and study the results.

"Not much showin' up on the infrared," Regen said.

"They don't have electricity, then," Trodius said. "All the better for our purposes."

"This city seems to have the largest signature. Let's look at it in daylight." Regen called up the same area and the pair surveyed the image.

"Zoom in on this area." Trodius used a laser pointer to indicate the spot, and Regen enlarged the picture to reveal a complex of large buildings around a plaza. Trodius moved closer to the screen and studied the complex.

"Yes, this is the temple complex our man described in his log. Could you put your ship down in that plaza?"

Regen called up an image of his craft scaled to fit the photo and overlaid it on the plaza. It fit easily.

"Phew, that's a huge area. There's plenty of room, but it's a poor place to get stuck if things turn sour," Regen protested.

"Don't worry, we won't stay very long on any visit. Let's get into our priestly garb so we can make a grand entrance," Trodius said.

Regen hovered over the temple complex plaza long enough to scare the people away from his landing site and dropped the ship into the center of the paved area.

"Show time!" Trodius beamed as he pushed the button opening the main door at ground level.

"Let's do it," Regen replied as he slipped his hood up on his head and fastened a leash to Hitler's collar.

The spacecraft's door opened to an audience of

thunderstruck men and women who backed away fearfully at the sight of a hooded Trodius walking out to meet them. Regen held back inside the craft holding Hitler's leash firmly. He need not have been so concerned. Hitler was cowering behind his master's loose-fitting robe trying to be invisible.

Trodius spoke. "People of Agam Valeem! We have come from the heavens at the bidding of Duru to warn you of the end of the world."

The crowd began to mumble, "Duru, Duru."

Trodius motioned behind his back for Regen to come forward, and the Bremen walked into the sunlight dragging a reluctant Hitler.

The crowd now began to shout, "Duru, Duru," and the front ranks fell prostrate before the embodiment of their god.

Regen whispered, "I guess Duru still swings some weight on this planet."

"Can't you get Hitler to take on a more god-like pose?" Trodius said under his breath.

Regen looked down to see Hitler cowering between his legs. He knelt and spoke the command he used in the training sessions. Hitler immediately moved to the front and struck a very regal pose while the crowd continued to make obeisance and murmur, "Duru, Duru."

Trodius spoke again, "People of Agam Valeem, prepare yourselves. Bring your offerings of gold here when the sun is directly overhead tomorrow, and Duru will bless you. Farewell until then."

Trodius backed away from the crowd, and Regen followed suit. Once inside the spacecraft, they shed the robes, and Trodius piloted the ship in a hasty exit while Regen removed Hitler's disguise and rewarded him by releasing two of the koosa. The skeen took off at high speed after the closest prey.

Trodius approached the hold just as Hitler sped past him in pursuit of his lunch. "Can't you just give him those things?" Trodius asked.

"He likes it better if he can run 'em down," Regen said. "Do you think we did any good out there?"

"Well, we'll see how effective we were tomorrow," Trodius said.

"Those rubes'll have time to sober up by then," Regen said. "I suspect we'll have some sort of official delegation to contend with when we land tomorrow."

The next day, a big crowd assembled in the plaza, but they took shelter once they saw the ship descending. When the dust settled around the spaceship, they moved back to the door where their god appeared the day before. Trodius opened the door, and a chorus of "Duru, Duru" greeted his appearance. Regen led Hitler out behind Trodius.

This time, the skeen seemed to know what was expected of him. Regen only had to give the command for his pet to assume the regal pose he'd been taught during the voyage. At Hitler's appearance, the crowd surged forward. People began to place golden objects before the skeen and mumble to Trodius. The older man nodded his understanding and made what Regen guessed was some kind of blessing sign as each one passed by him and spoke his piece. The mound of precious metal had grown to a good size by the time they heard the trumpets. The crowd fell silent, and as the sound of the horns drew closer, the mob parted to make a pathway for the ornate procession.

A squad of musicians blowing long, brass trumpets led the parade. Behind them, several men dressed in ornate black robes walked in a solemn group. Their heads were shaved, and golden loop earrings hung from each ear. Their robes were decorated with gold and silver thread stitched into intricate patterns, and heavy gold chains hung around their shoulders holding what Trodius guessed were badges of office. Behind that group, a chorus of women followed singing some kind of hymn and banging tambourines in rhythm to their song. The parade stopped in front of Trodius, and one of the men in the ornate robes approached him. When he was within a few feet of the fake priest, he stopped and bowed low from the waist. Trodius greeted him, and they began a conversation.

Regen couldn't tell what they were talking about, but Trodius's body language told him the subject was not a comfortable one for his partner in crime. After a few moments, Trodius turned toward him.

"This guy says he's the high priest of Duru here at Agam Valeem. He also says he wants us to take him into heaven to meet with the god and a few other deities of interest. He says he's already told his buddies that if we're real, we'll take him, and if we don't, they'll know we're nothing but frauds," Trodius whispered.

"Sound like he's a wise guy. What should we do?" Regen said.

"We'll take him up with us and rub him out. When we come back, we'll claim he was so holy the gods wanted to keep him. Everybody'll be happy, and nobody's the wiser."

"Good plan. Tell him we'll take him up as soon as the gold's loaded."

Trodius turned back to the priest and conversed with him again. He turned back toward Regen with a look of utter disgust on his face.

"This guy's pretty smart. He says he's instructed his people to keep the gold here until he returns. Looks like we'll have to bring him back."

"Well, next stop, heaven," Regen said.

Trodius returned to the priest and they spoke again. This time the priest turned to the crowd and made a long speech before turning back to Trodius. Trodius led him back toward the ship, and Regen and Hitler followed.

Once inside, the priest sat down in one of the cabin chairs as if he were quite accustomed to space travel. He then spoke in the common language shared by Trodius and Regen.

"Well, gentlemen, I have to congratulate you on your approach to fleecing these people. No one has ever produced such a fine reproduction of Duru." He reached forward to pet Hitler, but Regen stopped him.

"You lose fingers that way. He don't pet."

Hitler hissed menacingly at the priest who leaned back in his chair and surveyed the animal.

"What is it?" the priest asked.

"It's a skeen, and his name's Hitler," Trodius replied.

"What does it eat? It looks like a carnivore."

"Whatever little rat-like critter you got around here," Regen replied.

"Interesting, we have a creature here we call a grut. They're quite a delicacy, and I'm sure Hitler, here, would like them. I'll have several dozen sent to your craft," the priest said.

"That'd be right neighborly o' you, Mr. ..." Regen said, fishing for the man's name.

"Let me introduce myself. My name is Morgh, and I'm high priest of Duru, as I told you. We make a very fine living doing just what you two are doing, and we don't like outworlders coming in to spoil our show."

"So you've seen other ships before?" Trodius said.

"Only a few, and most of them rank amanteurs compared to you two. I was about to expose you for frauds when I saw your animal. He convinced me we needed to talk privately, hence this excursion into the heavens." Morgh waved a hand above his head in a lazy manner.

"How do you know this language, anyway?" Regen asked.

"As I said, we've had other visitors. One group was an archeological expedition with no interest in gold. They stayed for several years, and I worked closely with them during that time. They spoke this language, and I only hoped it was one you'd understand."

"Don't expect to talk to no gods here," Regen said.

"Oh, I don't. I don't quite understand all of this," Morgh swept his hand around the cabin, "but that's not important. The important thing is that you and I cooperate in your venture."

"What cut do you want?" Regen said.

"First of all, half of your take in gold," Morgh said.

"Half!" Regen interrupted. "Half!? We travel all the way across the galaxy, and you expect half? We'll give you a third, and that's generous."

"Gentlemen, you're in no position to bargain. Without my approval, the people will give you nothing."

"You saw what they laid at our feet without your help," Trodius said. "I imagine we could do that well at any city. It's you who are in no position to bargain. We could kill you now and claim the gods wanted to keep you in heaven."

"True, but I've left orders with my subordinates to give you the test of the hearts if I do not vouch for you on my return. I have a rival for my position as high priest who will gladly administer that test once he gains the priesthood as a result of my miraculous assumption."

"What's a heart test?" Regen asked.

"I read about it in great grandpa's log," Trodius said. "They use it to find out if a prophet is legit. Since Duru is the judge of the dead, they use the hearts of two recently dead men to test him. He has to pick the heart of the good man to be considered genuine."

"Correct, but if you don't know the trick, you won't pick the right heart," Morgh said.

"What's the trick?" Regen asked.

"Oh no, if I told you that, you'd have no further need of me. But, let me tell you the other half of my proposition before you do anything rash."

"Go ahead," Trodius said.

"As I said, my rival covets the high priesthood. He's always looking for some chance to depose me. If you two will back me up with your fake Duru, I'll see that you get away with as much gold as your ship can carry, though it would only be half of the total haul."

Trodius looked at Regen, and the Bremen shrugged his shoulders.

"What choice do we have? There's no way we could pass the heart test without him," Regen said.

Trodius nodded his agreement. "Okay, Morgh, you've got a deal. What do you want us to do?"

"Just keep doing what you were doing a while ago. I'll back up your claims and keep the suckers coming in. Gold isn't that hard to come by on this planet, and you'll have a load in less than two of our weeks."

"How do we make the split?" Regen asked.

"You take everything and leave, but you drop my cut at a place in the mountains I'll show you. Can you take this craft back to the city?"

"Yeah, but I got a better idea. I'll show you the map, and you can point the spot out to me from that," Regen said.

"Very well," Morgh said, and the trio moved to the map wall.

Regen called up the area around the city, and Morgh indicated the target. A closer image of the area pinpointed a cave where Morgh said his share was to be stashed.

"Don't try to short me," Morgh said. "I'll have a man checking out the cave every day. Double cross me, and you'll have to leave with what you have at that point. You won't be able to come back for more. Got it?"

"We got it. When I make a deal, it's a deal," Regen said.

"Good, the man at the cave will also be my means of contacting you. If he has a message, he'll wave a white flag at the cave entrance. Now, you'd better get me back," Morgh said.

The spaceship landed in the plaza once more. The temple delegation approached the craft, and Morgh emerged from the door. He made a long speech, and the crowd pressed forward once again to bring gold to the imposters while Morgh fell into place in the procession back to the temple.

When the crowd thinned out, the men loaded the gold on the ship with the help of a tractor beam. Regen rewarded Hitler with a generous helping of koosa while Trodius set a course for the agreed-upon cave.

There was no sign of life at the cave, but they deposited half of their load safely inside with the tractor beam and left for a low orbit and a good night's sleep.

The operation went smoothly for several days, but the take was beginning to die off. They were nearing the weight limit for the ship at this point and figured that one or two more days would do it when the man with the white flag appeared at the cave entrance. Regen landed the ship nearby, and Trodius walked the short distance to the messenger. He returned carrying a parchment scroll sealed with wax.

"That from Morgh?" Regen asked.

"Yeah, it's got his seal on it. Let's see what it says."

Trodius broke the seal and unrolled the parchment.

"It's in their language, and it'll take me a while to translate," Trodius said. He spread the document on a chart table and studied it for several minutes.

Regen was hard pressed to keep Hitler from munching at the edges of the parchment. They had run out of koosa, and a local rodent Morgh supplied them with didn't seem to strike the skeen's palate. The Bremen's pet often used paper as a dietary supplement when he was off his feed.

"It looks like Morgh's rival for high priest is planning a move on our next visit. He plans to make us pass the heart test," Trodius said.

"Does he tell us what the secret is?" Regen asked.

"Yes, he says the bad heart is from a recently executed prisoner, and it'll be on the tray with a missing handle on one side. He says we'll have to look closely because the flunkie holding the tray will try to hide the missing handle. Otherwise, the trays'll be identical. Looks like they plan to do it tomorrow."

"Well, we've about milked this city dry anyway. We could just cut out with what we have," Regen said.

"I'd like to have a full load before we give up," Trodius said. "We need at least another three days to do that. With Morgh's tip-off, we can pass the guy's heart test easy. That should give us the time we need."

"Okay, but I'd feel a lot safer if we left now."

"Don't worry so much, Regen. We've got this one made."

The next day, the temple delegation was there to meet them when they landed. A different priest led the group, and Morgh was nowhere to be seen when Trodius, Regen and Hitler emerged from the spacecraft. The priest approached Trodius and bowed low before speaking loudly enough for the crowd, as well as Trodius, to hear. Regen didn't understand a word, but the smile on Trodius's face gave him confidence they were still on firm ground.

He began to worry when two of the other priests stepped forward. Each one held a silver platter covered with a domed lid. They removed the lids to reveal two human hearts. The crowd's reaction was stunned silence. Regen saw Trodius bend low over the platters and was a bit unnerved when his partner turned to him with a bewildered look. Regen moved closer, bringing Hitler with him.

"What is it?" Regen asked.

"Both the platters are the same. Morgh's information's no good. The old boy here must have switched platters on him."

"We're toast, then. Let's get out of here while we can," Regen advised.

As Regen spoke, Trodius noticed a cordon of armed men moving to block their entry to the spacecraft.

"Too late. They've got us hemmed in," Trodius said.

Regen was about to reach for his pistol when Hitler suddenly tore the leash from his hand and leaped for the trays. Surprisingly, the priests holding them held firmly while Hitler rested his foreleg claws on the left platter and sniffed at the heart. To Regen's surprise, the skeen dropped to the ground and moved to the other tray. Hitler repeated his performance, but this time he gobbled down the heart in short order.

"I hope he got the right platter," Trodius moaned.

Regen retrieved Hitler and held the pistol under his robe in case the skeen picked incorrectly.

The look on the priest's face told them Hitler guessed correctly. The holy man turned to the crowd and made a long speech. He ended by turning back to Trodius and prostrating himself on the ground before him. Trodius lifted him to his feet and addressed the mob himself. The trumpets sounded, and the temple procession made its way back to the sanctuary.

"That was close," Regen whispered as the people moved forward to present their gold and receive Trodius's blessing.

Trodius only smiled. "You wouldn't expect the great Duru to make a mistake, would you?"

The day's haul nearly filled the hold without Morgh's share. The trip to the cave was routine, and they moved the ship to a low orbit for the night.

"Well, one more day should do it," Regen said. "We can only take on about another 50 kilos if we want to make Loomisa for refueling."

"I agree, let's have one more go at it before they get wise. I think the old boy was amazed today, but he'll think of something else pretty soon. I didn't see Morgh there. I wonder what happened to him," Trodius said.

"I'll bet he's room temperature right now," Regen offered.

A green light began to blink on one of the consoles, and Regen looked to it immediately.

"What's that?" Trodius asked.

The look of surprise on Regen's face made Trodius nervous. The Bremen was paying far too much attention to his instruments, and punching far too many buttons.

"There's another ship in orbit around the planet," Regen said. "It just took off from an area near Morgh's cave. It's hailing us."

Regen pushed more buttons, and an image of Morgh appeared on the screen. They recognized the bald head and earrings, but the priest was wearing modern clothes.

"Hi guys, thanks for the help," Morgh said.

"Morgh! What are you doing in a spaceship?" Trodius said.

"It's my ship, and the name's Sugra. I just used Morgh for the sucker's benefit."

"What happened?" Regen asked.

"The guy I told you about made his move on me. I was in jail and about to be executed when your skeen passed the heart test. He had to let me go, but I figured this well was about dry and made my exit."

"I guess Hitler was lucky picking the right heart," Regen said.

"I think there was more than luck in it," Morgh said. "He was supposed to eat the bad heart, which represented the bad guy's soul. That guy had been in prison, and didn't have access to the delicacies of their cuisine, including roast grut."

"What does that have to do with it?" Trodius asked.

"The things you've been feeding your skeen are grut, and I guess he doesn't like them very well," Morgh said.

"No, he doesn't. Lately, he chases them around an kills 'em, but he doesn't eat 'em," Regen said.

"Well, the good guy's heart would have smelled of grut. That's why your skeen went for the other one. Take care! See you guys on the next trip."

Morgh signed off and they watched as the track of his ship vanished from their screens.

Both men sat stunned for a moment. Before Regen could recover, Hitler appeared at his feet with a dead grut in his mouth. He dropped the animal in front of Regen and looked up at him with a pleading look.

"Sorry boy," Regen said as he patted his pet tenderly. "It's dry food for you until we get to the next stop, but I'll see that you get the best stuff they have when we get there."

CHAPTER 6

Once away from Agam Valeem, Trodius busied himself with inventorying the gold artifacts while Regen scanned data sources for gold prices. He was quite surprised to find gold at 37 credits per gram on Algaren III while it was trading at only 32 on most other planets. Algaren III would not be too far out of their way, and the extra profit would be worth the detour. He could hardly wait to tell the old forger about their good luck, but Hitler interrupted his session by jumping on the console. He looked up at Regen with what could only be described as a sheepish grin, something totally out of context for a skeen.

"What you bin up to now?" Regen asked, but his question was answered as an irate Trodius strode into the room holding a badly mauled grut at arm's length.

"Regen! You have to do something about that animal of yours. I found a dead grut in my boot for the third time in so many days."

"Sorry 'bout that. He don't like 'em much, and he hides 'em once he kills 'em. I'll chuck the rest of 'em out the airlock."

"Good riddance. I hate for him to have to survive on dry food, but my boots are beginning to smell like a slaughterhouse."

"I was just comin' ta get ya anyway. I found a good price for gold on Algaren III, 37 credits a gram. We got over 2,000 kilos aboard which means 37 million apiece."

"More than that, Regen," Trodius corrected him as a smile spread across his face. "Some of the objects in our cargo will fetch much more than bullion price to artifact dealers. They've never seen stuff from Agam Valeem, and they'll go wild over it."

"Holy shit! How much more?"

"We could be talking about over twice bullion price. We'll just have to sample the market once we get to my place. We've got at least two stops to refuel before we get there, and we don't want anyone along the way to know what we got. There may be pirates in this part of the galaxy."

"I know a few fences who deal in this kind o' stuff, but I'm sure you got a better knowledge o' artifacts and what they're worth than I do. They'd probably skin me alive."

"Let me do some investigating before we split up the loot. We need to find out which things the collectors will go for. That way we can be sure we each get a fair half. We're rich, Regen! Rich as Phoban politicians." The two men danced around the control room to Hitler's astonishment. He found a safe haven under the navigation table and watched the antics with his head tilted to one side in astonishment. All he knew was that he was hungry, and dry food was not his idea of a proper meal.

At the first refueling stop, Regen managed to purchase a good supply of live meals for Hitler, and they made it back to Villia with no further dead animals in the old man's boots. Once the gold was unloaded at Trodius' fortress hideout, one of his flunkies made an electronic catalog of the stuff and began to circulate it to all the fences they were aware of. It wasn't long before the offers came pouring in.

They divided the gold between them based upon the bids they'd received, but Regen was sure he could get a better price from one man Trodius' people didn't know about. He loaded his share on his ship along with the petro, bid the old forger a fond farewell, and headed into a part of the galaxy honest people avoided, but it was a place where most Bremens felt right at home.

"Oooofff!" The impact of Hitler on Regen's lap distracted him from the task of entering new course coordinates for the planet Volla. The skeen, looked up into his master's face with a pleading expression the big Bremen knew only too well.

"I know you're hungry, but I gotta set in this-here new course for Volla. Gimme a few minutes, will ya?"

The ugly animal gave a gurgling moan and jumped back to the deck of the spaceship. He sat down near Regen's feet but kept his beady red eyes glued on his only source of food.

"Yer gettin' too fat anyway. You nearly knocked the wind out o' me that time. I should put you on a diet."

Hitler cocked his head to one side and hissed softly at the suggestion of any cutback in his daily rations.

The course lights finally blinked green all around, and Regen led Hitler to the room housing the food animals. As soon as the rodents saw the skeen, they began a nervous chatter and raced in circles inside their wire cages. Regen dumped the unlucky victim on the deck, and it scampered off in stark terror with Hitler in hot pursuit. He watched amused until they vanished down one of the stealth ship's many cable tubes.

Regen returned to his consoles and found the communicator light blinking with a call waiting. He punched the receive button, and the screen came alive showing a middle-aged Andran smiling broadly.

"Hi, Rollum, what's up?" Regen asked.

"I've looked over your inventory of gold artifacts, and I think I can use some of them, if the price is right."

"Give me your best offer, and we'll see if we can do business."

"Well, this one's worth four times its bullion value." The screen changed to show an eight-centimeter tall golden antelope mounted on a marble base.

"Okay."

"I can give you six times bullion value for this one." A curious looking statue of some goddess with the head of a lion filled the screen.

"Okay."

"I'll take all of these things you got?" The screen showed a smaller object about two centimeters long shaped like an insect of some kind.

"I got about a hundred and fifty, or so. They dumped those things on us by the handful back on Agam Valeem. The natives said they're some kind of magic charm."

"They're chakmas. You find them in a lot of primitive cultures. The priests at the temples sell 'em to the superstitious suckers. This one's supposed to cure whatever ails you. All you have to do is say the right prayer, bake it in some bread and feed the stuff to whoever's sick."

"What if they swallow the thing?"

"No chance of that. You'd notice something this big in your mouth no matter how sick you were. They spit it out and sell it for its gold value, usually about ten percent of what they paid for it. It's a real racket."

"What makes people fall for that garbage?"

"I've heard it works, sometimes. The most popular ones are the kind that make a member of the opposite sex fall for you. They come in all shapes depending on where you get 'em. This one's from Binta. Kind of obvious what it's for."

The screen showed a small phallic symbol.

"What do you do with that one?"

"You drop it into a glass of wine, and it's supposed to drive the gal nuts for you. There's all kinds. I'll give you ten times bullion value for any of 'em, but more for this one."

The screen showed a stylized fish of some kind. It was tiny, not more than a centimeter in length. "I've never seen one like this. What's it for?" Rollum asked.

"The suckers we got this from think it grants your fondest desire. Sort o' like a genie in a lamp kind o' thing. All ya do is swallow it, and all your dreams come true."

"I've heard about these things, but I've never seen one before. I know a collector who'll pay through the nose for it," Rollum said.

"Maybe I should find this thing and try it out myself," Regen said.

"They're only good for one wish, and it's almost certainly been used up, or the sucker wouldn't have parted with it. You have to get it re-blessed, or something, for it to work again."

"Too bad, that 'un had possibilities. What about the rest o' the load?"

"Bullion price minus 30% for my cut."

"You payin' alimony, or somethin'? That's a pretty healthy cut."

"Shop around. Times are tough right now. We got a deal on the non-bullion stuff?"

Regen didn't need a lot of time to think about the deal on the artifacts. It was as good as any he was likely to find, but he made a note to shop the bullion stuff around a little more.

"Deal on the non-bullion items. You sure that's all the good stuff? I'd hate t' melt down the rest and find out I just destroyed the Mona Lisa, or somethin'."

"You know I'm the best art fence in the business. Would I

let you melt down something I could make a buck on?"

Regen knew the little Andran wouldn't pass up anything of artistic value. Andrans were avid collectors of all kinds of artwork, and they often paid well above market price for anything striking their fancy. He was lucky to have Rollum on his side.

"Okay, I'll sort out your stuff and see you in about two o' your days, if all goes as planned. Mark the things you want on the video and transmit it back."

"Nice doin' business with you, Regen. See you in two days."

The screen went dark, and Regen waited for the data transmission to end before moving to the compartment housing his share of the loot from Agam Valeem. Opening the bulkhead door, he was surprised to see Hitler sitting on a pile of golden objects, wolfing down the creature Regen released earlier.

"How'd you get in here?" Regen asked as he looked around the cargo bay for any possible access point suitable for a skeen. He figured the small rodent could probably go anywhere he liked, but Hitler was much too big to follow by the same route. The skeen didn't look up from his meal.

"Oh well," Regen selected a medium sized container and called up Rollum's marked listing on the computer screen. He sorted through the loot, placing Rollum's items in the container. After two hours of sorting gold, his back and arms needed a rest. He was about to find his bunk for a nap when Hitler jumped at a small pile of booty in one corner of the bay. He barely caught sight of the furry head before Hitler scooped up the hapless animal in his powerful jaws, along with some smaller gold objects. Before Regen could intervene, the gold and the animal were sliding down Hitler's gullet.

"Stop that, Hitler! You're eatin' up my profits. Get out of here!"

Regen shooed the skeen into the companionway and closed the door behind him, then yawned, stretched his arms and back, and turned toward the control center. He checked the ship's sensors and the communications log before laying down for a well-deserved nap.

He hadn't slept long when he was awakened by a heavy object pouncing on his chest. A pair of red, beady eyes stared intently into his face, and the foul breath of the skeen assaulted his nose. It hissed like a fiend from hell, and Regen swept it to the floor with a quick motion of his arm.

"What're you doin'?" Regen roared as he swung his feet over the side of the bunk and reached for his pistol. The skeen crouched just out of his reach in the dark room and continued to hiss like a cornered snake.

"I guess you've finally gone wild like ever'body said you would. God, I'd hate to shoot ya, but if you don't calm down, I'll do it." He raised the pistol and waited for the skeen to make its move. The hissing continued, but Regen thought he heard a harmonic in its tone. The animal's eyes seemed to soften, and it bolted for a ventilation shaft.

Regen re-holstered his pistol and scratched his head. "I'm gonna have t' test those rats for rabies. Hitler must've eaten a bad one, for sure."

He went to the hold and passed each cage through the medical unit. None of them tested positive.

"Oh well, maybe he was just in a bad mood."

At that moment, Hitler walked through the doorway and settled calmly at his master's feet staring up at him with pleading eyes and cooing softly.

"Oh, you wanna make up now, eh?"

Hitler cocked his head to one side and gave the Bremen a quizzical stare.

"Don't give me that innocent act. You're gonna hafta be on your best behavior the rest o' the afternoon if you want another snack. Now get outta here!"

The skeen recognized the tone, though he understood none of the words, and ran through the door just ahead of his master's kick. Regen returned to the cargo hold and resumed sorting out Rollum's part of the treasure. He moved a crate full of odd bits and found the cable run both Hitler and his victim must have used to enter the compartment earlier. It was a bit small, but skeens seemed to be able to shrink as needed in order to get where they wanted to go. The sort was finally complete except for one object – the chakma Rollum identified as being worth so much more than its bullion price. He went through the smaller pieces again, with no better luck.

"That must'a been one o' those Hitler swallowed. Well, I'll have to check out his skeen box every day now."

Regen had trained Hitler to use a litter box, but cleaning it out was no pleasant task. The skeen's diet of small, furry creatures was not conducive to sweet smelling stools. Now, he would have to tear apart each of the little balls to find the chakma, and he was not looking forward to the job. As he turned to leave the cargo hold, a leathery head appeared in the cable run opening and began to hiss at him.

"I told you, no snacks 'til you can behave. Now git!" Regen threw one of the larger gold objects at the skeen, and it ducked back inside the small metal cave.

Regen sat down at the ship's control console and checked the progress of his flight. The craft had received a good boost from the outer planets of the Volla system, and would easily make the target planet in twenty-four hours. He needed to check bullion prices quickly, and sent out an electronic message to a dozen potential partners for illegal gold. As he worked he noticed Hitler skulking about near the bulkhead on his left. Evidently, the skeen got his message about leaving him alone for a while. He turned his seat to recheck the navigation console and saw a brown streak vanish down the passageway to the cargo holds. He turned back to where he'd seen Hitler, but the skeen was gone.

"I knew you was fast, but that's a new track record," Regen said to the empty cabin.

Dinner was the next item on the agenda, and Regen moved to the food console to select his meal. The long journey from Loomisa had consumed the best parts of his food supply, but the remaining choices weren't that bad. He punched in his selection just as Hitler scampered through the door. The skeen sat obediently at his master's feet and looked up at him with as much affection as a skeen could muster.

"Well, that's more like it," Regen said as he reached down to pet the repulsive creature. "How 'bout some dinner for you too?"

Regen led his pet back to the cage room and selected a victim. The creature ran for its life as soon as its feet hit the deck, but Hitler only continued to look up at Regen with his usual mealtime expression.

"Oh, that one didn't suit your fancy, eh? Well, I guess now that you've turned over a new leaf, you can be picky."

A second release saw Hitler off in hot pursuit of his meal. Regen returned to his own dinner, enjoying his favorite movie while he ate.

After dinner, Regen prepared for his last night in space before landing on Volla. As he changed into his pajamas, he noticed Hitler's head protruding from one of the ventilation tubes.

"Hi big fella, do you need a snack?"

A hissing noise behind him made Regen turn around. There, sticking out of another ventilation tube, was another skeen's head. His gaze rebounded to the original head. Was he seeing double? How could Hitler be in two places at once? Then he noticed the hissing head was a little smaller and had no collar. Spinning around toward the other skeen, he saw the familiar studded collar Hitler always wore. Like a man at a tennis match, his head swiveled back to the first sighting, but the strange head was gone. Hitler jumped into the room and ran to his master's side.

"What's goin' on, boy?" Regen knelt to pat the leathery head as Hitler responded with a frantic gurgling noise he always made when he was frightened.

"We got a ghost, boy?" Hitler only hissed and jumped up on the bed.

"Well, I don't believe in ghosts, at least not yet, but if you're scared, you can sleep with me tonight."

Regen joined his pet and was soon sound asleep.

The next morning, Regen fed Hitler. As before, he rejected the first rodent only going after the second one his master released.

After eating breakfast, Regen hailed Rollum.

"You ready to do business?" Rollum said in response to Regen's greeting.

"Yeah, you got all the artifacts, but Grutchik beat ya out on the bullion. I'll be at your place in an hour and a half."

"See you soon," Rollum said as the screen went blank.

Regen landed his ship close to the Andran fence's seaside villa. It was a lovely area with high, snow-capped mountains in the background. The sand dunes surrounding the huge villa faded into a white beach running for miles in either direction. Lush forest started at the base of the mountains and marched up to the snow line.

Rollum stood at the low stone wall surrounding a large patio and waved to Regen as the ship came to rest only a few meters away. Regen shut down the drive system and opened the ground level hatch. It was only a few steps down the spiral ladder to reach the fresh sea air and the hot scorching smell of the sand. Rollum moved toward him.

"Welcome to my house, Regen. Where's Hitler?"

As the Andran spoke, a greenish brown blur streaked past Regen and vanished into the dunes.

"I guess he can't wait to get some real food," Regen said. "I think he's tired of the rats I got him on Loomisa. You got anything around here he'd eat?"

"We've got vulla by the hundreds. I'll have my people trap some for you, and you can see what he thinks of them."

"Sounds great. How 'bout some of your boys unloadin' my stuff?"

Rollum called to some men observing the pair from the patio. They moved down to join the group, and Rollum gave them orders.

"Regen'll show you the stuff. Bring it inside to the sorting room." He turned to Regen. "After you show them what to bring in, we'll have a drink or two before we settle up. You had breakfast?"

"Only spacefood junk. I'd appreciate a home cooked meal for a change."

"You got it." Rollum turned to another man. "Wait here and show Regen to my library. We'll have breakfast in there. See you in a few minutes, Regen." Rollum strode off towards the villa while Regen led the men into his ship.

"The stuff's in there in a container marked for Rollum," Regen said as he opened the door to the cargo compartment.

One of the men jumped back in surprise as a green streak sped past his legs.

"Holy shit! It's a skeen!" the man shouted.

"How'd he get back in here?" Regen said as he scratched his chin. He turned to the men. "Don't worry. Hitler won't hurt ya, and there's no more skeens aboard. Go on in."

With the cargo moved to the villa, one of Rollum's men led Regen into an ornately decorated room with bookshelves along two walls. Large, open windows made up most of the other two walls, and the pleasantly cool sea air blew lazily through the ceiling to floor curtains. Rollum rose to greet the Bremen extending a glass of light golden liquid.

"Welcome Regen. Have some of this stuff. It's the best Mourlin wine I've ever tasted." He raised his own glass toward Regen. "Here's to a profitable deal for both of us."

Regen raised his glass in response and they both took a long sip of the wine.

"That is good stuff," Regen said as he smacked his lips loudly. He knew that Andrans required such indications of appreciation for fine food or drink.

A woman appeared in the doorway carrying a large tray.

"Breakfast is ready, sir."

"Just set the tray on the table, Azirah," Rollum said. "By the way, this is Regen, a friend of mine."

"Pleased to meet you, Azirah," Regen said. Azirah responded by dipping to one knee and extending her right hand, palm up.

"Touch her palm with your right hand, Regen. She's a Vollun, and that's how they say hello."

Regen did as requested, and Azirah rose and backed out of the room.

"Hard to get good help like that anymore," Regen offered.

"Here on Volla, there's a lot of people out of work right now. If things pick up, she'll probably leave me for a good job the first chance she gets. Sit down and eat."

The pair sat down, and dove into the delicious meal. Regen suddenly stopped eating.

"You did tell your men not to shoot Hitler, didn't you?" Regen asked.

"Oh sure. Don't worry about him."

As Rollum spoke, Hitler came bounding in through an open window and curled up next to Regen's feet.

"I guess he got his fill of whatever kind o' rat you got 'round here," Regen laughed.

Rollum joined in the laughter just as one of his men appeared carrying the carcass of a dead skeen.

"Sorry, boss. Rikka saw this thing and shot it out of habit. He was in the city when you put out the word on skeens, and nobody filled him in."

Rollum and Regen looked from the dead skeen in the man's arms to Hitler sleeping soundly at his master's feet.

Regen got up and moved to inspect the animal's corpse. He carefully opened the mouth and then lifted one of the hind legs.

"This one's a female. I didn't think you had any skeens here," Regen said.

"We don't. She must've come in on your ship," Rollum said.

"No way. Hitler'd never tolerate another skeen aboard," Regen countered.

"But, you said this one's a female. Wouldn't that make a difference?" Rollum asked.

"It might, but where would I get a female skeen? I've been in space since I left Villia, and they got no skeens."

"Well however it got here, it's dead now. Let's go check out the loot," Rollum said. "Just go bury that one, and tell Rikka he shot a stray – and not to worry."

"Sure, boss." Rollum's man left the room with the skeen as Rollum and Regen moved to the sorting room. The treasure was laid out in order, and Rollum inspected the artifacts.

"Where's the one shaped like a fish?" Rollum asked.

"Hitler ate that one, and he ain't passed it yet. I'll go back to the ship and check his box."

Regen found several new stools in Hitler's litter box and carefully tore apart each one with a plastic knife. The putrid smell even penetrated his filter mask, but he found the tiny golden fish on the second try. He cleaned it up and returned to Rollum.

"Yeah, he passed it. I think I got all o' the stink off it." Regen handed the chakma to Rollum who sniffed it and pronounced it sufficiently cleansed.

As Rollum was transferring the funds into Regen's accounts, a thought suddenly hit the big Bremen. Yes, it had to be the only plausible explanation.

"Remember what I told you about that thing-a-ma-jig?" Regen asked.

"The fish chakma? Sure, it's supposed to grant your fondest wish if you swallow it," Rollum replied. The realization of the situation suddenly hit the Andran.

"You don't suppose Hitler made a wish, do you?" Rollum said.

The two men stared at each other for a moment before their eyes came to rest on a contented-looking Hitler curled up in one corner of the room.

CHAPTER 7

Regen departed Volla the next day and set a course for Gobra. His old friend Homerk would pay well for the petro in his hold, but now that his account boasted over 52 million credits, he wasn't too worried about the price. Trodius' passport and visa, along with some of his usual disguises, fooled the immigration people completely. Customs went over his ship with a fine-toothed comb, but the petro was very well hidden.

Regen set his stealth ship down in a grassy swamp area less than 100 meters from Homerk's island compound and waited for a helicopter to pick him up. The "Camp", as Homerk called it, was the envy of every drug dealer on Gobra, being in the middle of an almost impenetrable swamp. The marshlands stretched over 200 Kilometers in any direction, and served as home to the most vicious predator on the planet, a large alligator the locals called "Coya". The swamp was not deep, which meant only shallow draft boats or skimmers could navigate it, and these light craft were no match for the huge reptiles.

The average coya measured more than four meters in length and weighed in at a good 700 Kilograms. They were known to turn over boats, and they could lunge out of the water far enough to tip a skimmer off balance. Like all gators, they drowned their prey first and ate it later after the flesh assumed a sufficiently aged condition. Not even Hitler dared venture into those swamps, and that said a lot, since skeens were generally regarded as fearless.

The "Camp" was safe from the usual police attack. Big military swamp buggies could manage the trip, and airborne assault was possible, but Homerk had an excellent missile based defense system. This and his timely payoffs to government officials, insured serenity at this swampland oasis.

Camp was hardly the word for the place. There were no tents or open fires here. Several large villas dotted a green campus created by dikes holding back the swamp water. Storage buildings and quarters for the lesser members of Homer's army surrounded the more opulent housing for Homerk, his officers and his guests. Regen was looking forward to his stay.

The helicopter hovered just above the spaceship, and Regen and Hitler jumped aboard. Homerk was in the passenger compartment to greet them. He was on the heavy side bordering on fat, but Regen knew that was a deception. The big man was as quick and powerful as he was when he weighed twenty kilos less. His mop of red hair was the same color as the curly growth peeping from the top of his shirt and covering the large, muscular arms. Greenish gray eyes twinkled with a love of life seldom seen in his dour profession.

"Regen! It's good to see you. How's Hitler doing these days?" Homerk asked. He knew better than to try petting the creature even though Hitler seemed to be smiling at him.

"He's fine. I hope you've told your boys not to shoot any skeens while I'm here."

"Sure, sure, they all know about you and Hitler. What'd you bring me this trip?"

"I got some first class Petro, but I had to pay through the nose for it. I won't be in much of a mood to bargain."

Homerk laughed merrily. "Negotiating with a Bremen is like pleading with a coya to spare your life."

The helicopter rose into the air and made the short journey to the camp.

A delegation of women met them as they landed, and Homerk led Regen to the group.

"Regen, these are my harem girls. Aren't they lovely?" Homerk boasted as he swept his arm across the panorama of beauty.

Regen gave a soft whistle and turned to Homerk. "You've added a few since my last visit. How do you keep them all happy?"

"I don't. I share these beauties with my captains, and that seems to give them all they want. Every one of 'em is a first class whore, and they don't care about anything but money. I won't have a woman around who gets romantic notions about anybody. If I catch 'em, they're outta here on the next chopper, but as long as they don't get attached to any one man, they can stay here and bank money like crazy. Which one would you like?"

"That's very generous of you, Homerk. I wasn't expecting treatment like this."

"When you're in my camp, you go first class. Besides, a few good rolls in the hay might bring down the price of that petro."

Regen surveyed the group and picked out a black haired Mangin woman. He knew they were experts at driving a man wild with pleasure.

"Ah, Mila! A great choice, Regen."

The woman came forward and knelt before Regen. The Bremen lifted her to her feet and kissed her hand. "I know my stay here will be pleasant now that your beauty is part of it," he said.

"Hold on, Regen. This is just for tonight. We switch girls every night here. Like I said, no attachments," Homerk bellowed. "Mila will take you to your rooms and see that you're settled in. Do you need a cage for Hitler?"

"No, I'll just let him roam around once he knows where home is, lead on Mila"

Mila showed Regen to a spacious apartment on the ground floor of a villa near Homerk's palace. Hitler sniffed around the rooms for a few minutes before leaping out an open window.

"Aren't you afraid your pet will get lost?" Mila asked.

"Nah, he's got the scent of the place now. He won't have no trouble."

"What will he do?"

"He'll hunt somethin' to eat and soak up some rays. He'll be gone 'til sundown."

"I'm glad, I don't feel comfortable around him, and I want to be comfortable with you." Mila moved to Regen and pressed her body against his while her face tilted upward in an open invitation for a kiss. Regen didn't need any more hints, and fell into the mood of the moment.

That evening, the intercom woke Regen from his sleep and caused Mila to stir beside him.

"Get up, Regen. Dinner at my place in an hour." It was Homerk's voice, and Regen looked at the clock to find he had been making love and sleeping all afternoon.

"Is this formal, or what?" Regen asked.

"God no, wear whatever you like. Mila'll find you some clothes around there. I think we got some stuff big enough for your frame. Remember, one hour!"

The intercom went dead, and Regen turned to Mila. "That don't leave you much time to get beautiful."

"I don't need much, and I'm insulted you think I need *any* time for that."

Regen laughed. "You can wear what you got on now and be the most beautiful woman there."

Mila smiled warmly as she pulled a sheet around her naked body and marched off to find Regen some clothes.

Dinner resembled the pictures of old Roman orgies Regen saw in Earth books. There was music and women and entertainment besides some very exotic food. Homerk introduced him to his captains.

"Regen, I want you to meet Mikka. He's from here on Gobra, and one of the toughest guys you'll ever run across. He handles all of my distribution on this planet."

Regen shook the big man's hand and made a mental note not to offend him.

"Pleased to meet you," Regen said, but Mikka only nodded and went back to his meal.

Regen and Homerk walked on a few paces and stopped in front of an Andran.

"This is Rollous. He's my bookkeeper and business manager. If it wasn't for him, I wouldn't have a nickel."

The Andran rose and bowed to Regen. "I've heard much about you, Regen. It is a pleasure to know you."

"Same here," Regen said. Before he could extend the conversation, Homerk rushed him off to a man in a motorized chair.

"This is Turris, he used to handle my deliveries until a coya overturned his skimmer one day. Now he does my security."

Turris smiled up at Regen. "That coya got my legs, but he left the parts I need the most." Turris pulled a sexy redhead into his lap to emphasize his meaning.

Regen met three other members of Homerk's team before

they returned to their place at the head table and began the feast. The food was excellent, and the wine flowed freely while they enjoyed various forms of entertainment. It was a noisy operation, but the house grew silent after a fanfare from the orchestra.

"You'll love this one, Regen," Homerk said as he elbowed the Bremen in the ribs.

The band began a sensual melody, and silk curtains parted to reveal a living goddess. She was barely clothed, but she would have looked stunning with none at all. Regen estimated her height at a few centimeters under two meters, but she couldn't have weighed more than 60 kilograms. Her sun-bronzed skin and golden hair gave the impression of a gilded statue. Deep, blue eyes shown like sapphires under her long lashes, and full, red lips promised a myriad of sexual delights. She moved like a shark stalking its prey, smooth and calculating. The room erupted with cheers.

"Who is she?" Regen barely gasped.

Homerk laughed loudly. "I thought you'd like this one. That's Varuda, and there's no woman like her in the galaxy. She's also the most expensive item on the menu here."

Regen was transfixed by her performance, but managed to ask, "How much?"

Homerk laughed even louder. "To you, old friend, 150,000."

Homerk was unaware of Regen's windfall from Agam Valeem, and the smuggler wanted it to stay that way. He must not appear to be too cavalier about the price.

"I don't care. I have to have that woman," Regen said.

"Take a number. She's with Mikka tonight, Turris tomorrow night and me after that. But I'll tell you what, gimme the petro for 4,000 a kilo, and you can have my turn."

Regen felt relieved. It was a generous price, and he should react accordingly.

"Done!" Regen almost shouted.

"Done, that is, if your stuff tests out to my standards. We'll have a go at that in the morning. Just enjoy Mila tonight and dream of Varuda.

The two moons of Gobra were nearly set by the time the party wound down. Regen was busy enjoying Mila's expertise when a siren interrupted their passion.

"What's that?" Regen rose from the bed and threw a boot at the speaker in disgust.

"It's our alarm. It may be an attack," Mila said as she hurried to dress. "I must go to my shelter, and you should report to Homerk. He'll need every fighter he can get if it's the drug police."

"I guess you're right," Regen said grudgingly as he found suitable clothes and strapped on his weapons.

Mila bolted through the door just as Homerk arrived.

"Come on Regen, there's some kind of trouble, and you can be a big help," Homerk said.

The men made their way through the confusion to a command center near the outer wall of the camp. Turris was busy studying a computer display, but turned to acknowledge Homerk.

"It's not a raid, boss, it's Mikka," Turris spoke with a somber voice whose tone conveyed more than the words.

"What's wrong?" Homerk asked.

"The boys at the dock said he showed up there an hour, or so, after the party broke up and demanded a skimmer and a rifle. He said he was going coya hunting. He was really plastered, and the guys didn't want to let him have the stuff, but he insisted, so they let him go. They sent a chopper to keep tabs on him, though. Unfortunately, it wasn't enough."

"What do you mean?" Homerk asked.

"Here's the film from the chopper." Turris ran the chopper's camera tape.

The chopper's spotlight showed a skimmer running through the swamps at high speed while Mikka swung a spotlight back and forth in front of it. When the light revealed two red eyes just above the surface, Mikka slowed to a crawl and leveled his rifle at the spot. Before he could fire, the water beneath the skimmer exploded upward as a huge coya surfaced beneath it. Mikka was thrown from the skimmer, and before the chopper could act, the coya plunged beneath the surface with Mikka in its jaws. Several shots from the chopper produced no results, and no trace of Mikka was found. Several choppers joined the search, but it was useless.

"Poor Mikka," Regen said.

"That was a stupid thing to do!" Homerk raged. "What was that bastard thinking about? You don't hunt coya at night! He knows better."

"He was drunk," Regen tried to put a good face on the matter.

"I've seen him knee-walkin' drunk a lot of times, and he'd never pull somethin' like this." Homerk thought for a moment. "He was with Varuda tonight, wasn't he?"

"That's what you told me," Regen said.

"Turris, get her up here, now!" Homerk commanded.

In a few moments Varuda stood before them. Even dressed in normal clothes with no makeup, she was still as beautiful as ever.

"Yes, Homerk, you called for me?" Varuda said. Her voice was calm, and she seemed to be unaware of Mikka's foolish exploits.

"When did you leave Mikka tonight?" Homerk asked.

"I didn't. He left me. He was so drunk he couldn't perform, and he said he was going hunting."

"Why didn't you stop him, or at least, call someone?" Homerk raged.

"How was I supposed to stop him? He was angry because he couldn't get it up, and he'd have killed me if I got in his way. Besides, I knew the boys at the dock wouldn't let him out in his condition."

"Well, they did, and now he's a midnight snack for some coya," Homerk said.

"Oh no!" Varuda's face went pale, and she slumped to the floor crying uncontrollably.

Regen moved to her at once. "Get up, Varuda. It's not your fault. Get hold of yourself."

"Oh God, Homerk! I didn't think anything like this would happen," Varuda sobbed.

Homerk's face changed from rage to compassion at the sight of the woman's tears. "It's okay, darlin'. Go back and get some sleep or you won't be any good to Turris, here, tonight."

"I'm so sorry, Homerk. I know you and Mikka were great friends." Varuda spoke more calmly now, and she seemed to be regaining her composure quickly.

Homerk dismissed her with a backhand wave. "Go on, get back to bed."

Varuda left, and Homerk turned to Turris. "Keep looking for a body. I don't expect to find much, but we'll bury whatever there is."

"Sure, boss," Turris said as he turned back to his console.

Homerk and Regen returned to their own beds, but the thought of Mikka being eaten alive by a coya haunted Regen's dreams.

The next day, they closed their drug deal. Homerk was

pleased with the quality of the petro and announced he could cut this stuff another 50%. Regen kicked himself for not doing just that when he had the chance.

Another party followed dinner that night, but it was subdued compared to the night before. Everyone was sobered by Mikka's death. Only a boot with the remains of one foot was ever found, but it was given solemn burial by Homerk and an Andran who claimed to once have been a priest for some relatively minor god.

Regen decided to do without female companionship, but he watched with barely hidden jealousy as Turris left the banquet room with Varuda.

The next morning, Regen rose and toured Homerk's camp. Several changes were apparent since his last visit. The defense system was more complete and included several new weapons. More places were off limits now, and it seemed the drug dealer had expanded his operations to include some unusual vices. One fenced-in yard contained bales of what Regen guessed were Brogah roots. Primitive people on Miggo used the roots as an aphrodisiac, but the natives had decimated the plant to the point where imported root was worth more than gold. Regen thought he heard female voices from one walled off compound. This was, most probably, the source of Homerk's female companions.

He hadn't gone far when he heard a commotion near Homerk's villa. He ran back to the area to see two of Homerk's captains consoling a middle-aged woman. She was on her knees sobbing uncontrollably and wailing in a language he didn't understand.

"What's wrong?" Regen asked one of the captains.

"It's Turris, his wife just found him dead from an overdose of petro," the man said.

"Oh my god! Didn't he know to cut the stuff?" Regen asked.

"He never used any kind of drug before," another man inserted, glaring at Regen with undisguised hatred.

"Wait a minute! I didn't give him any petro. All my stuff went into Homerk's warehouse. He had to get it from there unless you guys have another stash somewhere."

"All I know is, he's dead, and Homerk's going to want to know why. How do we know you didn't have more junk on your ship?"

"I didn't even see him after dinner last night. He went out with Varuda right after we ate."

Turris' wife switched to a familiar language. "That whore!" she shouted. "I told him to stay away from her, but he wouldn't listen. She's the one who killed him. Get her!" She fell into the arms of a captain who led her away.

"What about Varuda?" Regen asked.

"She's in the clear. She was with Homerk nearly all night."

"I saw her leave with Turris," Regen said.

"Yeah, she screwed him, alright, but Turris throws out the whores after he uses 'em. She knew Homerk wanted her, so she spent the rest of the night with him."

"I just want you guys to know I never gave him no petro," Regen said.

"We'll let Homerk figure that out. He'll probably want to talk to you later. Don't try to leave the compound, okay?"

"I'll be here," Regen assured him.

Regen walked to the dike wall and sat down on a grassy spot. He stared into the vast sea of swampgrass contemplating the deaths. A coya cruised a hundred meters away in an open water area, and Regen wondered if it was the one that ate Mikka. He was startled by a hand on his shoulder and turned to see Varuda.

"Thinking of Mikka?" she asked.

"I was, him and Turris also. What a horrible way to die."

"Mikka or Turris?" Varda asked.

"Mikka, Turris was in la-la land before he bit the big one. He didn't feel a thing."

"How do we know what dreams he was having before he died?" Varda said.

"I guess we don't."

"I understand I'm with you tonight."

"Yeah, I don't know what kind of company I'll be. Homerk's people think I gave Turris the petro that killed him."

"I can clear that up for you. Turris had his own stash. He showed it to me before we made love. I didn't think he ever used any drugs, but he said he did petro from time to time. I told Homerk about it last night, and he was surprised too. You don't have anything to worry about."

"I'm glad of that. These guys can get pretty nasty if they think you've knocked off one of their own."

"I've seen it, and it's not pretty," Varuda shuddered. "Where's your skeen?"

"He's out hunting somewhere. He likes fresh food after a long space voyage."

"What does he eat when you're in space?" Varuda seemed genuinely curious.

"I keep some rodents for him, but he gets tired of the same thing every day. I'll have to see if you guys have anything I can use for his food when I leave here."

"I'm sure Homerk'll find you something. He likes you, you know."

"We've been friends for a long time, ever since we did some time together on a penal colony planet. I helped him make it through that ordeal, and he's treated me right ever since."

Varuda jumped as Hitler ran up to Regen and leapt into his lap.

"Jesus, Hitler, you scared me," Varuda panted.

"How'd you know his name?" Regen asked.

"It's all over the camp. Not too many people have pet skeens."

She stared at Hitler for a moment, and relaxed visibly. The skeen seemed to be entranced with the woman, and looked at her with a blank expression. Regen was shocked when the woman's hand crept slowly toward the animal.

"Careful, he likes lady fingers real good," Regen cautioned.

"He'll let me pet him, won't you Hitler."

Her hand rested on the leathery head for a moment then stroked his neck. Hitler stretched his head to make the skin smoother and cooed contentedly. "Good boy," Varuda cooed.

"I only seen that once before," Regen said. "There was this guy who could pet him because his body odor acted like a sedative for skeens. Most people lose a finger of two for their effort."

"Maybe it's my perfume?" Varuda said.

"I don't think so, women normally ain't interested in getting too close to a skeen. He usually don't like perfume anyway. Could be, though."

"Regen, Homerk wants to see you!" The call came from behind them, and Regen turned to see Rollus.

"I'll be right there," Regen replied.

"I'd better go with you to remind Homerk of our conversation last night," Varuda said.

The pair joined Rollus and walked to Homerk's villa. Inside, Homerk had set up a conference table with several chairs. Two of his captains were there with him.

"Regen, Varuda! Come in. We were just going over Turris'

overdose. What can you two tell me about it?" Homerk asked.

"All I know is I didn't give him any petro," Regen said.

"I can vouch for that," Varuda said. "I was with Turris last night, and he showed me a stash he said he only used on special occasions. He asked me if I wanted any, and I told him I didn't use the stuff. He said he'd wait 'til later to get high. He said he wanted to be sober to enjoy me."

"I can believe that," Rollus said.

"I know it wasn't your petro that killed him, Regen," Homerk said. "Danner, here, says the stuff that killed Turris was super pure. He's seen the symptoms before. My problem with all of this is Turris never used any kind of drug. Even his wife never saw him high, and she didn't know of any he might have had hidden away somewhere. Where was this stash of his, Varuda?"

"He kept it in the false base of a statue in his room. It was a black goddess of some kind with the head of a coya," Varuda replied.

"That's Wan," Rollus inserted. "She's these people's goddess of the underworld. I remember Turris telling me someone sent him the statue as a gift. He loved the thing, and it was worth some money too because it was made out of a rare kind of rock."

"Well, it all fits together. The statue's where we found the stuff. The base was open when his wife found him this morning," Homerk said. "Still, it's really weird. I never saw Turris high, even on alcohol. I still can't believe he'd try petro when he didn't even know how much to cut it."

"That's funny," Varuda said. "He asked me about that just before I left his place. I told him I didn't know for sure, but I'd seen some of the other girls mix it with silica powder. I told him he'd better get some good advice before using the stuff, but I guess he didn't."

"Okay, you guys can go. I know you didn't have anything to do with this, but I will find out who sent him that statue, and why. See you at dinner," Homerk said.

Varuda came to Regen's room that night dressed in her most sensual clothes. Regen whistled softly as she entered. Even Hitler stirred from his pillows in a corner of the big room and cooed with a sound Regen never heard him utter before.

"You're the most beautiful woman I've ever seen, and Hitler must be agreein' with me," he said.

"Do you like the outfit? I wore it especially for you."

"It's fantastic, but I think I'd like you better without it." Regen enfolded her in his arms and kissed her passionately. As he did so, his hand fumbled for the fasteners of her top.

"Let me do that for you," Varuda purred as she pushed the big Bremen away. With one deft motion the entire costume fell to the floor revealing every detail of her beauty.

"Now, let me do you," Varuda said as she moved to Regen and undressed him.

The two fell into ecstasy on the silk sheets, and Regen thought he never had a better sexual encounter in his life. At last, they lay together looking up at the stars through the skylight. Varuda leaned over and stared into his face.

"I hope that was as good as you expected," she said.

"It was marvelous. Where did you learn all that?" Regen said.

Varuda didn't answer him. She only stared at him intently. Regen began to feel his body go limp, and he wondered if this was some new form of sexual activity from her vast repertoire. Thoughts began to crowd into his head, but they were not sensual. He saw a young girl making love to a red haired lad. It was Homerk, but why should a young Homerk be in his head? He only met Homerk after he was a grown man. It was like a video playing inside his mind. The girl fell off of her lover and gasped in agony. Homerk tried to help her, but she was soon dead. Then Regen heard Varuda's voice. Hearing was the wrong term. Her voice was not coming in through his ears but like a radio broadcast with his brain as the receiver.

That's my little sister, Regen. Homerk introduced her to drugs and turned her into a whore addict. He gave her some petro one day not knowing she was allergic to it. I vowed to revenge her death, and it's taken me all these years to work my way into his confidence. Now I've eliminated his two top captains, and tonight was supposed to be his turn, but you brought in more of the evil stuff, and I decided one more murder wouldn't hurt anything. Before I'm finished, all of you dirty bastards will be gone, and the feds'll come in here and clean out this snake's nest. That is, they'll do it as soon as I sabotage the defense system. You see, Turris gave me a lot of useful information before he overdosed.

Regen tried to move, but his muscles wouldn't answer his brain's commands. He couldn't speak, but he knew Varuda could read his thoughts. *Why me, Varuda? If Homerk didn't buy my petro, he'd just get it from somebody else. I didn't have anything to do with your sister's death.*

It's no use, Regen. I made up my mind to do you as soon as your ship landed and I found out what you were bringing. Don't beg, I hate men that beg.

I'm not begging, I just want to know why me.

Because you're here, darling, and your pet skeen is such a convenient way of doing away with you.

Hitler? Hitler wouldn't harm me, or are you going to feed us both to the coyas like Mikka?

Smart! You guessed that I compelled Mikka to go hunting. I really enjoyed seeing that croc pull him under, but you won't be a snack for some coya. Come here, Hitler.

Hitler moved from his pillows with a jerky gait. He was resisting as best he could, but Varuda's will was too powerful for him.

You see, Regen, I've done some research on skeens. It seems everyone who's ever tried to tame one wound up being killed by it. They always revert to their wild state. Some take more time than others, but they all do it. I think it's Hitler's turn now.

Varuda concentrated on Hitler, and Regen could detect her thoughts. She was telling the skeen to kill, and Hitler was resisting with all his might. *Kill! Kill!* Her grip on Regen was slipping a bit, but still not enough to allow him to reach his pistol. He could move his hand a little and inched it toward the holster on the nightstand. He was using all of his own concentration now, and was shocked when Hitler jumped on his chest.

Regen looked at his skeen and saw a very familiar expression. The red eyes almost glowed, and the powerful jaws hung open revealing the razor sharp white teeth. Saliva dripped onto his chest, and the rancid breath almost overcame Varuda's spell. Regen knew the skeen would soon strike at his throat with deadly results. He forgot about the pistol. Now he concentrated on Hitler. He conjured up images of their early years together while Varuda's command of *Kill!* tried to overpower them. He thought he saw some softening in Hitler's expression and tried even harder to transmit friendly thoughts to the animal. He was slipping into unconsciousness, but he thought he heard a woman scream before all went black.

Regen awoke to Homerk and Rollus standing over him.

"Are you okay, Regen?" Homerk asked.

Regen shook the fog from his head and rolled on one elbow

to survey a bloody scene. Varuda lay on the floor in a pool of her own blood while Hitler skulked in a corner. The animal's mouth was smeared with red, and it seemed to be totally confused.

"Good old Hitler!" Regen shouted, and his voice seemed to bring the skeen back to his old self. It flew past the two men and landed near Regen's chest cooing contentedly.

"What happened here?" Homerk asked.

"It was Varuda," Regen said as he stroked Hitler. "She's a compeller. She made Mikka go hunting Coya, and she probably made Turris overdose on the petro. She just tried to get Hitler to kill me, but I guess it backfired by the looks of things."

"We'd figured out it was Varuda too," Rollus said. "We traced the statue with the dope to a dealer who recognized her picture and gave us her real name. Homerk remembered about her sister and made a connection. We were coming here to get her when we heard the screams. We busted in the door and Hitler was busy gnawing on her insides. I was going to shoot him when Homerk called me off. The monster hissed at us a few times then ran into a corner and hid."

Regen looked down at the skeen and wiped the blood from his mouth with the sheet. "Whoever said man's best friend is a dog never met a skeen, I guess," he said.

CHAPTER 8

The guard saluted smartly as the tall Bremen walked through the door. The clicking sound from his bionic knee echoed in the hallway of the ornate headquarters building, and Regen smiled as he remembered it was the center of what Homerk called a "camp." It would have been a very relaxing and profitable visit had it not been for the bizarre killings of the last few days. He had almost been a victim himself but for the loyalty of Hitler. The skeen obeyed his every command, and that obedience was the primary reason Regen could take his leave of the planet instead of finding himself a permanent resident of the "camp's" graveyard.

"Good afternoon, Regen. Is your ship loaded and ready to go?" Homerk bellowed as Regen entered the great hall.

"Yeah, all set. Just wanted to say goodbye and thanks for the deal."

"Sit down, have some lunch first." Homerk waved an arm across a table groaning with platters of food.

"Well, I could use a good meal before I take off. I got two weeks of space food starin' me in the face." The big Bremen sat down and dove into the tasty dishes with gusto.

"I wonder if I could ask a favor of you?" Homerk asked.

"If I can do it, I will."

"Could you make a delivery for me?"

"Where to?"

"I need to get some merchandise to Millin 4, and I need a

stealth ship, like yours, to do the job. It'd be worth 200,000 to me."

Regen liked the price, even though Millin 4 was a bit out of his way. "What kind of cargo you got?"

Homerk clapped his hands, and some guards led in five women. The plainest of them was beautiful, but they were all cuffed and hobbled. Regen understood immediately, prostitution was illegal on Millin 4, and these were high priced whores, indeed. Homerk had a lot of money riding on their delivery. The problem was, Regen's ship was not designed to transport passengers. It was a pure freighter.

"Shit, Homerk! You know I ain't got no way to carry passengers. I'd love to help you out, and I like the price, but these gals won't be in very good shape by the time I get to Millin 4 if they have'ta sleep on the floor of a cargo hold and eat space food."

"I got that covered. We'll load on some cots and some canned rations for 'em. Your ship's nearly empty, and it won't be anywhere near maximum weight."

"I ain't worried about weight or cg. I just can't take no women aboard. I don't even have a woman's toilet." The thought of five women aboard hit Regen full force. It was bad enough having to put up with another man aboard, but women were much too demanding for his tastes. They wouldn't take the hardships of freighter travel with equanimity. The constant griping would drive him nuts even if it were for only two weeks.

"We'll put a portable toilet aboard too. Look, they'll be locked in your hold until you get to Millin 4. They won't be any trouble at all. I'll make it 250,000."

Regen rubbed his chin as he surveyed the cargo. They were whores, maybe they'd make the trip a bit more pleasant if he asked nicely. Homerk and the pimp waiting for them on Millin 4 need not know they'd been used a little on the way.

"Okay, I'll take 'em, but I need to get goin' right away. How soon can you get it all aboard?"

"My men are ready to load you up right now. Just one more thing – no sampling the wares on the way. Got that?"

Regen smiled. Who would know? Homerk knew full well it was a meaningless condition.

"Yeah, I got it."

"I know you, Regen. That's why they've all got plugs. Only the customer on the other end has the code for releasing them. He's got some high class Johns waiting, and he's assured them they're getting fresh stuff. Understand?"

It was a blow. Trying to have sex with a plugged woman was almost lethal to both parties. He'd just have to grin and bear it for two weeks.

"Thanks for telling me. They'll get there intact."

The meal went on while Regen's ship was loaded with its human cargo. As the food was running out, and Regen calculated he'd had enough wine, one of Homerk's men announced the ship was ready.

Homerk rose and met the Bremen with a bear hug.

"Goodbye, Regen. It was a pleasure doing business with you, and I won't forget this favor."

"Same here, and you're payin' for this favor, remember?"

"As soon as I get the word from the customer that the cargo's delivered in one piece, I'll credit your account. Oh, you'll need this."

Homerk handed Regen a data disc. "The contact's information's on here. Don't use it until you're well out in space. It has its own encryption software, so you don't have to worry about anybody listening in. Thanks again, buddy."

Regen walked aboard his ship and met one of Homerk's lieutenants coming out.

"Here's the key card for the hold, sir. They got plenty to eat, sleeping kits and a potty. No need to let 'em out 'til you get there."

"Thanks." Regen pocketed the key card, and the man bounced down the entry stairway to the ground.

Regen inspected the cargo hold containing the women. It was locked securely, and no sounds came from inside. Maybe Homerk had trained his whores well. Just to be sure, he set the intercom for the hold on listen mode. He noticed that the TV camera inside had been covered effectively, but the audio still worked. All was quiet inside, at least for the moment.

The ship hadn't been in deep space more than an hour when it happened. Regen was almost asleep in his command chair when the intercom erupted with a chorus of screams from the women's compartment. He flicked the switch.

"What's goin' on in there?"

"There's a monster in here. Help!" a female voice in pure panic mode shouted.

Regen knew the cause of the alarm. Hitler had, undoubtedly, found his way into the hold. It was, after all, one of his usual haunts.

"It's only Hitler. He won't hurt nobody. Stay calm, and I'll be right there to get him."

He unlocked the door to find the five women in one corner of the hold hiding behind their bed kits and Hitler staring at them with wide, unbelieving eyes.

"Hitler, git outta there," Regen shouted.

The skeen looked at his master with a pleading expression, but a snap of the Bremen's fingers told the animal it was time to comply. He scuttled slowly out the door and peeked back at the females from behind Regen's legs.

"Thank you," a tall, blonde woman spoke. "He scared the shit out of us. Please keep him out of here."

"I'll try, but those cable runs go all over the ship. He hunts his food in there, and I got no way of keeping him out if he wants to come in. He won't hurt you long as you don't try to pet him or anything. Whatever you do, don't hit at him. I guarantee he'll attack you then, and it won't be pretty."

"I've seen skeen's work before," a shorter brunette said as she shivered at the thought.

"Can't you lock him up or put him in a cage?" this was the stunning redhead he'd seen before at Homerk's dinners.

"I can't lock him up for two weeks goin', but I will put him in his cage at night."

"Thank God," a silver haired, dark skinned woman sighed. "There's no way I could sleep knowing that 'thing' was around."

"He ain't no 'thing'," Regen protested. "He's a skeen, and he's my pet. Look, you gals are perfectly safe in here. I got the intercom on, so just call if you need anything."

With that, Regen closed the hold door and resumed his seat at the ship's controls.

It took two days for the girls to get tired of their confinement. Hitler behaved himself, but five women can only play so many card games, and the gossip was exhausted the first day. The sexy redhead was the first to complain.

"Oh Captain Regen," the sultry voice slinked out of the speakers on the flight deck.

"What is it Darlin'?"

"We girls have decided we should take turns keeping you company on the flight deck. Could I come up?"

"Ain't nothin' here worth seein', love."

"Well, what we really want is some real food. We're tired of these canned rations."

"Nothin' here but synthesized stuff. I think you got the best deal with the cans, if you ask me."

"Please? We need the male companionship as much as the food."

"You're all plugged, and I ain't interested."

"We just want to talk to a man for a change, please?"

Regen thought about it. It might be nice to have someone to talk to besides Hitler.

"Okay, I'll let you out, but only one at a time."

Regen's response was met with squeals of glee.

Regen unlocked the hold door to find the redhead dressed in her best gown. It was transparent in the right spots and covered what needed to be covered while providing subtle hints of the treats in store for her clients.

"Come on out," Regen said.

The woman glanced back at her companions with a wry smile as she stepped through the portal. Regen closed the door quickly behind her, though none of the other women tried to follow.

"Thanks for letting me join you. What's for dinner?"

"Anything the machine'll make. Your choice."

The pair moved to the flight deck, and the redhead stopped at the food synthesizer to select her meal.

"What do you want," she asked.

"I ain't hungry right now," Regen answered.

The woman took her tray from the machine and sat it on the console next to Regen as she plopped into the co-pilot's seat.

"What's to drink?" she said.

"There's some good whiskey in that flask there." Regen pointed to a magnetic bottle on the console.

"Any glasses?" she asked.

Regen retrieved two plastic tumblers from a storage bin and placed them in front of the redhead.

"Pour me one too," he said.

"I think all of this technology is simply wonderful," she said as she swept her gaze across the panels in the room.

"All I do is fly 'em. Don't know much about how they're made. What's your name? We might as well be on speakin' terms if you're gonna be up here."

"Mellina, I cost 100,000 a night."

"Well, even if I had the 100 grand to spare, you're plugged."

Mellina dove into her meal, and the cabin was quiet while she ate.

"Napkins?" Mellina asked.

Regen produced some paper napkins and handed several to Mellina.

"Thanks. We really appreciate this. There must be some way I could show you how we all feel."

At that moment, Hitler jumped into Regen's lap. Mellina let out a scream and leaped to her feet knocking over the food tray. Hitler returned to the floor and began lapping up the mess.

"It's okay, he won't hurt you. He just smelled the food. I always let him clean up my scraps."

Mellina inched back into her seat keeping the skeen in view and giving it a wide berth. She studied the animal as it ate.

"You know, they aren't too bad once you get a good look at them," she said. "Could I pet him?"

"You gotta be real careful. I'll tell you what to do after he eats."

The pair watched as Hitler licked the tray clean before jumping back into Regen's lap. The skeen kept an eye on Mellina as he curled up into a ball.

"Okay, move your hand slowly towards his head and keep the palm up. I'll guide you."

Regen took her wrist in his hand and moved it toward Hitler's head. The skeen suddenly came alert and growled deep inside its chest.

"Easy, boy. She's okay. I got her hand," Regen soothed as he placed Mellina's hand near the skeen's nose.

Hitler sniffed the hand and sneezed sharply.   Mellina recoiled.

"It's okay. Perfume does that to him. Try again."

Once more Regen guided Mellina's hand toward Hitler. This time the skeen sniffed the hand more tentatively before lowering its head back to rest on its forelegs.

"You can pet him now. He knows you're okay."

Mellina stroked the leathery head softly. Hitler responded with a soft cooing sound.

"It's soft. I expected him to be scaly and hard."

"That's just the way he looks. Fools everybody," Regen said.

"He's warm too. Aren't lizards cold blooded?"

"He ain't no lizard, he's a skeen. People don't spend too much time investigatin' 'em. They usually shoot 'em on sight."

"What a shame. He's kinda cute once you get to know him. What does he eat?"

"Mostly any kind of rat I keep for him. If I run out of those, he eats dry pet food and table scraps."

"Well, as I was saying before Hitler came in, there must be some way we girls can show our gratitude for letting us have a break from our makeshift cell."

"I think you could think of something, if you used your *head*."

Mellina took the hint.

The next girl out was the dark woman.

"What do you want?" Regen asked.

"I just want a real bed. Do you have one?"

Regen showed her to his cabin. She eyed the two bunks and plopped into the bottom one.

"Wake me up when you want me to go back in." She waved Regen out of the room. "Goodnight."

He let her sleep a full ten hours before rousing her.

Next out was the blonde. She was wearing a sweater and short shorts.

"You want food or sleep?" Regen asked.

"Neither, I just want to walk around the ship and stretch my legs."

Regen glanced at her bare legs and decided he should keep her under close observation while she roamed the ship.

"I'll show you around. There ain't much to see, though."

She said her name was Armenna, and her family was responsible for her situation, having sold her into prostitution at an early age. It was an honorable profession on her home planet, and she was surprised to find it was considered a crime on other worlds.

Next out was the shorter of the two brunettes. She wore sweats and athletic shoes.

"Have you got any exercise equipment aboard?" she asked.

Regen showed her to the weight machine and treadmill he kept in one of the other holds, and she spent over four hours working out before signaling her willingness to return to captivity.

Last was the tall brunette. Regen thought she was the prettiest of the lot in spite of the dark blue jump suit hiding the true shape of her figure.

"What's your pleasure?" he asked her.

"I need to talk to you, privately. Where can we go and not be overheard?"

"Well, we could go to my cabin. This way." Regen led her to the small room and closed the door. "What did you want ta talk about?"

"My name is Orianne, and I'm a princess of Bardour."

Regen laughed. "Sure, and I'm the king of Tennera. Welcome aboard, yer majesty."

"You don't understand. I'm not kidding, and it's your highness, not your majesty."

"Pardon me, *yer highness*." Regen made a low bow.

"I didn't think you'd believe me. Look, can you contact Bardour?"

"You don't talk to Bardour, they talk to you. That planet's off limits. Nobody goes there without a special visa, and they ain't granted none in over 100 years. You'll pardon me if I think you're givin' me a line of crap about being from there. You don't look no 100 years old."

Orianne sighed heavily. "I'm only thirty, but that's beside the point. I was on a diplomatic mission when Homerk's men kidnapped me. They sent my father a ransom note, but he wouldn't pay up."

"Some old man you've got," Regen said.

"He's hated me since I was born because my mother died giving me life. He was glad to see me gone. Besides, his counsel doesn't want a woman on the throne when he dies. They'd just as soon my cousin took over. Look, help me out, and I'll see that you get twice whatever Homerk's paying you for this trip."

Regen paused to think. She seemed to be sincere, but there was no way he could check her story easily. A message to

Bardour would take two days to get there, and then, they might not respond to it. Besides, if her story were true, they wouldn't want her back anyway.

"What good's it gonna do to call home? They don't want you back."

"I have friends who want me on the throne. The party was very strong before Homerk captured me six months back, and I'm sure they'd rally around me if they knew I were alive and on my way home. Please, Regen, you have to try for me. You're the only hope I've got."

She seemed so vulnerable. Her expression was soft and pleading, and the first hint of tears showed in her deep blue eyes. Regen quickly pushed the sympathetic feeling back down to the lower levels of his consciousness. He was no sucker for a forlorn woman.

"No dice. Even if I thought you was tellin' the truth, we're close enough to the Bardour system they'd send out destroyers to get me if they heard the message. Our lives wouldn't be worth spit."

"Wait, Regen, I have a special code that only my people can decipher, and I heard Homerk say this was a stealth ship. You could slip me in without being detected. Once I'm queen, I could make you a very rich man."

"A lot of if's in that story. If you're a princess – if you have a code they can't break – if your buddies are still alive – if you become queen – if, if ,if."

"All I ask is that you send one message. If they come after you, I'll give myself up to them. I'm all they want anyway." Orianne lowered her head, and the tears became a reality.

"Balls! I can't stand to see a woman cry. What's yer special code?"

Orianne smiled for the first time, and Regen led her to the

communications console.

"Space channel 349," she prompted.

Regen punched in the number and received a clear channel signal.

"What now?" he said.

"I'll take over from here," Orianne said as she nudged Regen away from the keyboard.

She pulled a comb from her hair and broke it in half. A small chip fell out, and she placed it in the receptor panel. After a moment, the screen came alive with symbols Regen was not familiar with. Orianne seemed to understand it all. Her fingers flew over the keys as a smile spread more broadly across her face. She hit the final key with a flourish.

"There, all we have to do now is wait for an answer," she beamed.

"That's four days from now. Meanwhile, I gotta keep a sharp lookout for any Bardon destroyers. I won't get much sleep that way."

"I'll help you. I'll take over when it's my turn out and you can sleep then."

Regen gave her a suspicious look, and Orianne responded quickly.

"You can lock all the other controls while I'm on duty."

"Okay, we'll start in two days."

Orianne was as good as her word when it came to giving Regen a rest, but the message was five days old and still no indication that either her partisans or the Bardon defense system heard it. Regen was feeling more comfortable about possible attacks, but Orianne was growing more morose by the day.

On the sixth day, she was watching the consoles while

Regen slept when the green indicator light blinked indicating an incoming message. She watched as the message filled the screen. It was her special code. She leaped to her feet and ran to wake Regen.

"Regen, Regen! They've answered. Come quickly." She shook the big Bremen awake oblivious to Hitler's snarls and snaps.

"What the..." Regen shook the sleep from his head and placed a comforting hand on Hitler to stop any possible attack on Orianne.

"They've answered, they've answered. They're still alive. It's wonderful, Regen."

"Calm down. Let me see what they said." He threw back the blanket and sat up, much to Orianne's consternation, as he slept in the nude.

"Regen!!" she shouted as she turned away.

"Don't tell me you ain't seen nothin' like this before. How long you been a whore?"

"It's just embarrassing when you don't expect it, and I'm not a whore, I'm a princess."

"Let's see what your subjects have to say, yer maj..., oh excuse me, yer highness."

Regen dressed and joined Orianne at the communications console. She called up the message.

"This is in your lousy code. I can't make heads or tails of this gobbledygook," Regen said.

"It says my father's dead, and my cousin's on the throne. They thought I was dead because that was what my father told the press. Now that they know I'm alive, they're ready to revolt once I reach Bardour. All you have to do is get me there. Isn't it great, Regen?"

"Sure, no problem. All I gotta do is penetrate three rings of defense systems goin' in, land you someplace where we hope there ain't a couple o' regiments o' bad guys waitin' for us, get me back out safely to space through a full blown revolution, explain to Homerk's customer why there's only four girls 'stead o' five, and convince Homerk I aint' got the fifth one hid away somewhere for myself. Simple."

Orianne's face fell, and they sat in silent thought for a long time. Orianne finally spoke.

"I've got it. Hitler kills me," she said.

"What! Do you know what you're talkin' about?"

"I don't mean he really kills me. We fake it so the other girls are convinced I'm dead. The customer can't complain, and Homerk's satisfied. He isn't out any money because you don't take any payment."

"Whoa, there. I need that money."

"Don't worry about it. I'll make you rich once I'm queen. I told you that already."

"Yeah, but a bird in the hand, and all that. Homerk's credit's good, but you're a long odds bet. Besides, we may never make it to Bardour alive."

"They said they might be able to disable a sector of the defense system for a short time. All we have to do is give them two day's notice. I know they can do it, Regen. All we have to do is fake my death."

Hitler jumping on his lap interrupted Regen's thought process.

"It's his feedin' time. Let me take care of him before you say any more."

Regen opened the door to the hold where Hitler's animals lived. They set up a raucous din and scurried around their cages when they saw the skeen. Regen picked a victim and released it on the floor of the cargo hold. Hitler was upon it in an instant and gleefully tore it to pieces before his master's eyes.

"God, what a mess you make," Regen said as the poor creature's blood spread across the floor. He knew Hitler would lap up all the blood before it could dry out, but he suddenly realized how he could fake Orianne's death. He returned to the flight deck.

"Your highness, are you sure your people could fix the defense system?"

"Yes, one of the leaders of my faction is in charge of the northern hemisphere. He's watched pretty closely, so he couldn't let it go off for very long. How long would it take you to get to the planet?" Orianne's eyes glowed with hope. Maybe this soldier of fortune could help her after all.

"I'd need an hour in stealth mode, but if the system was off, I could go in like normal. That'd only take a half hour."

"I think they could do that easily. If a system goes down, it takes about 45 minutes to bring the backup system fully on line. Now all we need to do is fake my death."

"I got that figured out. Hitler'll attack ya just like you suggested. It'll mean you getting' a little bloody, but I think it'll work."

"Count me in. When do we start?"

"I gotta check somethin' out first." Regen put Homerk's disc in his communications computer and waited. The screen soon came alive with a picture of the ugliest Andran he'd ever seen. The olive skinned little man smiled out at him with obvious expectations of delight.

"You must be 'omerk's courier. Is my merchandising in wonderful condition?" His round face was smooth and girlish. He was bald except for a fringe of shiny black hair above his ears. The dark eyes were deadly serious and belied his wide grin. He spoke with the peculiar accent of his race

"They're all here. I just need delivery instructions," Regen smiled back at the man.

"Is that one of the items I have been expecting?" the Andran asked.

Regen turned to Orianne and back to the screen. "Yeah, she's the ugly one."

"Oh delightful, delightful," the Andran's smile became even bigger, something Regen didn't think possible. "Here are the coordinates. It should be a journey of only two days to get here from where you are voyaging now, but you'll have to assume stealthy configuration to seduce the customs police. Will you have any problems?"

"I've slipped past a lot of customs people, and I don't expect your boys are any smarter. See you in 48 of your hours."

"I can hardly wait to see my beauties," the Andran said as the screen went blank.

"Well?" Orianne asked.

"Come along with me. We have to work fast. I'll get you dead then get the rest of the girls to the Andran before we head for Bardour." Regen picked up Hitler's cage and led Orianne to the hold containing the food animals. Without the skeen present, they remained fairly calm, but Hitler knew the sound of food when he heard it and came running in. Regen led him to his cage and placated the skeen with one of the furry creatures.

"That's disgusting," Orianne wrinkled up her nose at Hitler's eating habits.

"Don't get too grossed out yet," Regen said. He selected two more of the animals and cut them open letting the blood cover the floor of the hold.

"Sorry I gotta do this." Regen moved to Orianne and smeared the animal's blood over her face and arms. She recoiled, at first, but she quickly understood what he was doing.

"Now lay down in the blood and try not to breathe too much. I'm gonna let the other girls know you're dead, and they may want to see you."

Orianne complied, and Regen tossed the dead animals to an eager Hitler before washing up and moving to the intercom button.

"God almighty, Hitler's killed Orianne," Regen shouted in what he hoped was a convincingly agitated tone.

"What are you talking about, Regen?" It was the sexy blonde, Armenna.

"He got her. She wanted to feed him, and he got her. Poor kid."

"Regen, come in here now!" Armenna demanded.

Regen moved to the hold door and opened it to find a panic stricken group of women huddling in a corner of the hold with Armenna standing at the door, hands on hips.

"I knew that skeen'd cause trouble. If you don't kill it, I will." Armenna produced a wicked looking knife from under her gown and started toward the exit.

"Hold on, I got him in his cage now. He'll stay there until you girls are safe at your destination. I'm really sorry about Orianne. She'd been getting' along real good with Hitler, and she wanted to feed him. I didn't want to let her, but she insisted. Poor kid."

"Take me to her, Regen," Armenna insisted.

"This way, but it ain't pretty."

Regen led her to the hold and opened the door just enough for Armenna to see Orianne lying in a pool of blood. The blonde recoiled in horror just as he'd expected.

"Oh, there's so much blood."

"Good thing she's layin' on her stomach. That way you

can't see the worst part," Regen added leaving the rest to Armenna's imagination.

"That's enough, Regen." Armenna turned from the sight, and Regen closed the door.

"I'll take care of the funeral arrangements—prob'ly take her back to Homerk's camp for burial."

"She told me once she'd like to be buried in space," Armenna said as tears ran down her cheeks.

"We can do that, if you like. I got a body bag an' all."

"Set it all up, Regen. Mellina can say some words, she was once some kind of priestess. Call us when you're ready."

"Sure, sure, you just help those other gals pull themselves together. I'll keep Hitler penned up for the rest of the trip, so they're safe."

Regen deposited her back in the prison hold and returned to Orianne.

"You can get up now. They fell for it."

"Thank God. Those rat's blood smells awful." Orianne held her arms out from her body and shook her hands to get rid of what blood she could.

"You can take a shower in my cabin, and there's some extra clothes in there. All male stuff, but it's clean."

"What do I do with these?" Orianne pulled her top away from her chest.

"Better drop 'em here. I'll clean up this mess. Can't let Hitler out of his cage to lap it up as much as he'd like that. He might get away. Poor thing, he hates to be caged up."

"Turn your back, Regen. I don't intend to put on a strip show for you." Orianne began to undo her top.

Reluctantly, Regen did as she requested.

He heard the door close and set about the clean up. The clothes could go out in the body bag, but he needed a convincing body. He remembered a spare mattress in another hold and cut it up to make a suitable stuffing for the bag. A few ballast weights taped up in the mattress provided the needed weight. He threw the bag over his shoulder and headed for the dump port.

Regen opened the women's hold door and led them to the dump area. The women stood on either side of the bag while Mellina said something in a language Regen didn't understand, then signaled he could dump the bag. Regen loaded the phony body into the airlock and pushed the ejection button. With a swoosh of escaping air, the deed was done.

"I get her cosmetics," the small brunette yelled.

"Her shoes are mine," Mellina said as she ran back to the prison hold.

"Just remember I get her jewelry," Armenna reminded them.

Evidently the dark woman had no interest in any of Orianne personal effects as she silently fell in behind Armenna.

After locking up the women Regen returned to his cabin where Orianne was fuming.

"Oh, those harpies! No respect for the dead at all." She was turning red in the face, and Regen moved to calm her.

"Take it easy. What did you expect from a bunch of whores?"

"It's really true, there is no honor among thieves," Orianne shook her head in disbelief.

The next afternoon, Regen navigated his way through the customs check points in full stealth mode and landed at the Andran's complex. The beaming smile was there to meet him as he led the girls off his ship.

"This is insufficient. There are only four of them. What happened to the very exceptional looking brunette?"

"That's a sad tale. The girls can tell you all about it. I messaged Homerk about it, and he's only expecting payment for the four. Sorry to have to run off, but I got places to be. See you next time."

Regen quickly launched the ship back through the maze of sensors to deep space, set the autopilot and entered his cabin to find a fully armed Orianne. He couldn't resist a laugh.

"What's funny?" she asked.

"You, it's two days yet to Bardour, and you're loaded fer bear already."

"I found this stuff in your armory. I'll pay you for it when we get there."

"No need, it's all stolen anyway. Did you leave anything for me?"

"There's plenty left. You can buy more later."

"I just hope your boys know what they're talkin' about concernin' that surveillance system. This ship has no armor and no guns."

"You just get us there. I've already told them when to shut down the system. I can't tell you how much help you've been, Regen."

"If you didn't have that plug, you could show me your gratitude."

"Oh that." Orianne produced a small device from one of the pockets in her jump suit and tossed it to Regen. "Have a souvenier."

"How'd you get this out?" Regen hefted the object and resisted the temptation to sniff it.

"I felt it go inert a few minutes ago. The Andran must have disabled the rest of them, and this one followed suit. Now what were you saying about gratitude?"

Two days later the defense system was down, just as predicted. Regen sailed through to the planet's surface where her followers received Orianne like the princess she was. Regen watched as an adoring crowd surrounded his ship.

"I guess you are a *highness* after all," he said.

"You can stick around and fight with us if you like," Orianne said.

"No thanks. Me and Hitler got some explainin' to do with Homerk, and I got places to be after that. Take care, your highness."

"Wait a while, and it'll be your majesty." She smiled up at Regen and kissed him on the cheek. "Come back and see me then. You'll always be welcome on Bardour."

The crowd swept her away as Regen watched from the foot of the ramp. Hitler sat down at his master's feet to survey the spectacle.

"You know, boy, I'm gonna miss that princess," he said.

Hitler looked up at him with a forlorn expression and cooed softly.

CHAPTER 9

Regen sat staring at the idyllic scene on his navigation display. He knew every palm tree and grain of sand on that beach, at least as far as a picture could transmit that knowledge. Hitler jumped up on the map table and joined his master in studying the picture. It had no particular attraction for a skeen since they weren't much on water in any case and doubly so when the water crashed on the shore in huge waves and contained creatures capable of swallowing a skeen in one bite.

The big Bremen stroked the creature's leathery head and smiled at his only companion on these long space voyages.

"You know, fella, I've been lookin' at this here picture for two years, and now we can go there and live like kings."

Hitler cooed, appreciative of the tone even though he didn't understand the words.

"Look at this." Regen changed the image to one of a villa with luxurious gardens and a large swimming pool. "And this," the scene changed to a row of casinos and nightclubs. "With fifty million we buy a place like that and use the interest on what's left to live high for the rest of our lives." He checked the navigation display and said, "Only four more days to go. I'm sure they got some kind o' rat there you can feast on. If not, we'll import any kind you like."

Four days passed in the usual boredom of space travel, but Regen took advantage of the time by reviewing villas for sale and making arrangements for tours. The ship would have to dock at an orbital terminal, since the atmosphere of Terma was a bit too corrosive for long-term storage on the surface. He'd take a shuttle to Daq Vinas, the livliest city on the planet and a favorite watering hole and gambling den in this sector of the galaxy. All the beautiful people came there to relax and drop large sums of money in the hundreds of casinos populating the neon quarter of the city. Daq Vinas was the capitol of Ausland, the largest country on the planet and de-facto ruler of the rest of the largely arid sphere. The other nations were composed of nomadic tribes bound together in constantly changing federations. Only Ausland boasted a stable population and enough arable land to support it. It traded with the nomads for what could be had from the mountains and desert sands, and with the rest of the galaxy for the finer things in life.

Most of the hotels were a bit too upscale to accept skeens, so Regen opted for a dude ranch on the outskirts of the city where Hitler could hunt in the scrub desert areas surrounding the main complex. The name of the place was what really convinced him to stay there while he selected a proper villa. "The Velvet Saddle Ranch" conjured up such pleasant prospects he could hardly turn it down. Besides, the price was right and they accepted "pets."

Customs gave Hitler a jaundiced eye, but several minutes of pouring over the regulations and consultations with two higher levels of superior officers finally concluded there were no laws prohibiting the importation of ugly, mean-tempered animals. Hitler snarled at each approaching officer with enough vigor to discourage any close inspection of his cage. Immigration noted he was wanted on several planets, but none had extradition treaties with Terma, and he used his real passport.

The courtesy bus to the Velvet Saddle arrived on time, and Regen noted only men boarding the conveyance. He also was surprised to see that very few of them loaded luggage of any kind into the cargo bays. Hitler was forced to ride in one of the bays by himself creating grunts and hisses of protest as the door closed. The ride to the ranch took over 40 minutes, but the skimmer was well out of the city and into the bleak countryside of Terma before it pulled into the lane leading to the ranch.

The Velvet Saddle was much more than Regen expected. The skimmer bus dropped he and six other passengers off at a wood frame hotel modeled after old planet Earth Western movie sets. A bellboy in western garb, complete with string tie and pointed toe boots, corralled his luggage, but balked at handling Hitler's cage. Regen assumed personal control of his pet.

Inside, the lobby was decorated in red velvet everywhere you looked. Red velvet upholstered chairs and sofas. Red, flocked wallpaper covered each wall. In one corner, a robotic piano player clad in a red pinstripe shirt with red sleeve garters produced songs he'd never heard of about men who mistreated women and paid the price. Good-looking women in revealing lingerie lounged about the lobby in provocative poses, and Regen smiled knowing the name of the place was as accurate as he'd suspected. The other men began making the acquaintanceship of the whores, and Regen was about to follow suit but decided he'd best register first. The clerk behind the counter sported huge sideburns and a red suit straight out of a movie lot wardrobe.

"Welcome to the Velvet Saddle, Sir. Would you please register?" the clerk intoned officiously as he swung a computer input device to face Regen. The Bremen swiped his ID card through the slot, and the clerk's face blossomed into a broad smile.

"Ah yes, Mr. Regen. We've been expecting you. Our owner would like to speak with you privately. Please follow me. This way, Sir." The clerk motioned to his right and Regen followed him expecting the usual hassle over Hitler. He led the Bremen to an ornate wooden door and pushed an intercom button. "Mr. Regen is here, Madam," he said into the speaker. The latch buzzed and clicked, and the clerk opened the door. "Go right on in, Sir."

Regen walked into the perfumed atmosphere and studied the ornate furnishings. Red was still the dominant color, but gold leaf trim accented every piece of furniture. A huge, intricately carved golden desk sat with it's back to what was obviously a one-way mirror giving an excellent view of the small casino attached to the hotel. The office appeared to be empty, but a familiar voice from behind broke the silence.

"Regen! You bastard! Where have you been for the last three years?"

He turned to see a vision in red velvet standing before him. It was Mariva, and he felt a twinge of nostalgia as he studied her beauty. She was dressed in a low-cut gown fitted at the waist and flowing from there to the floor. The black lace trim accented her bronze skin and revealed the edge of an overlapping panel running diagonally from her right hip to her left ankle. Gold jewelry adorned her wrists throat and ears while each finger sported a ring with a large stone. She was every bit as gorgeous as he remembered her from Liban II three years back. The jet-black hair and the dark obsidian eyes were as enticing as ever, and she still had that slight hint of a mustache.

"Well, if it ain't Mariva. You sure come up in the world

from Liban II." Regen stood still not sure if he was welcome or not, but Mariva settled that issue quickly. She moved to the Bremen, threw her arms around his neck and kissed him passionately.

"Well," Regen said as he recovered from the shock. "I guess you are glad t' see me, at that."

"I thought I'd never see you again, and when your name showed up on the reservation list, I was hoping it was you. Sit down and tell me all about where you've been since the last time. Do you still drink that stuff from Gordia? What's it called?"

"Bourbon. I like it with a little water and lots of ice."

Mariva moved to a communicator panel and gave instructions. She turned to Regen before she finished. "You hungry?"

"No thanks. I grabbed lunch on the satellite port before the shuttle brought me down."

"That's all, Roddon," Mariva said then sat down in an easy chair opposite Regen.

"You wanna know 'bout me, but it looks like you've had all the good luck since we last met. How'd you ever find a place like this?"

"This place represents a lot of time on my back, Regen, but hitting the lottery for 500,000 helped a lot. One of my customers owned the place, and he was tired of screwing around with it. I got it for a song. He was trying to make money on it as a dude ranch and losing his shirt. You probably understood what I'm doing with it as soon as you walked into the lobby. I see you still have Hitler."

"Yeah, he's even saved my life a few times since I see'd you last. He's also responsible for my new-found wealth."

Mariva's eyes lit up with new interest. "Wealth? Did you

say wealth? You haven't had two credits to rub together ever since I've known you."

Regen told her the story of Agam Valeem, and Hitler seemed to take that as his cue to begin sounding his "I'm hungry" call.

"What a funny noise," Mariva said.

"He wants some food. Is it okay if I let him out to hunt?"

"Wait a minute. You'd better let me instruct the boys not to shoot him. They're not used to seeing skeens around here, and they'll probably think one of our larger lizards has been sampling the steroids." Mariva returned to the communicator and gave the necessary instructions. "You can let him out the back door—down the hall to your left. He'll find all kinds of lizard buddies to hang out with or have for lunch–whatever suits him. Come right back, though, I'm not finished with you yet."

Regen took Hitler to an open area near the fence before releasing him from his cage. The skeen sniffed the air and immediately took off at full speed after a medium-sized, green gecko. Regen went back to Mariva's office and buzzed the door. The familiar buzz-click told him it was open, and he walked in on a total surprise.

Mariva had converted the sofa into a large bed with red satin sheets and lay on it in a provocative pose wearing only a very sheer pink robe.

"Come on in, and we'll take up where we left off three years ago," she said.

Regen needed no more encouragement. He stripped off his clothes and joined her.

The buzzing tone of the door signal roused Mariva, and she shook Regen awake.

"Get up, Regen. There must be some sort of emergency.'

The Bremen pushed her hand away and rolled over. "Leave me alone. I need a nap."

"Get up, you skeen lover. My people wouldn't disturb me for anything less than inter-galactic war. It must be important, and I don't need you lounging in my sofa-bed."

Regen continued to resist rejoining the living while the buzzer kept up a steady pace of nagging. Mariva dressed quickly and advised whoever was outside the door to be patient. She pushed a button on a control console, and the sofa bed resumed its duty as a sofa, enfolding Regen in its bowels.

"Hey! What's goin' on? Let me outta here!" Regen's muffled protests were barely audible.

"Just lay there and keep quiet, Regen. I have to take care of this." Mariva tucked some stray sheet ends into the gaps between the cushions and opened the door lock. A breathless security man dressed in an old west sheriff's costume entered the room.

"Miss Mariva, we've got trouble with Senator Malinski, and I need your okay to throw him out."

Mariva had standing orders that no one was to be evicted from the premises without her personal approval, and the security staff followed her instructions to the letter.

"Lead the way, Burkin," Mariva said as she motioned toward the door.

A muffled shout from the sofa caused the fake sheriff to hesitate for a moment.

"Never mind about that. One problem at a time, and first things first," Mariva assured him.

Regen felt he was wrapped up in the sofabed for hours before Mariva returned and freed him.

"Damn, Mariva! You didn't have t' do that. I could'a hid in

the bathroom, or somethin'."

"You weren't hurt, and I had to take care of Senator Malinski. He's a good customer, and he keeps the law off our backs."

"I thought prostitution was legal here on Terma."

"It is, but there's always a faction in the senate trying to wipe out gambling and all the other 'sins' that go along with it. Malinski makes sure they never have enough votes to pass their bills."

Regen began to dress, and Mariva continued.

"Why do you want to buy a villa?"

"I need someplace to call home, and someplace where Hitler can run as he pleases."

"You can call this place home, and Hitler would have half the planet to wander around in."

"At your rates? I can barely afford the time it'll take to find a place and close the deal."

"Look, for what a villa will cost I'll put you up in style here for as long as you want to stay."

"Yeah, but I got nothin' when I leave. At least I could sell the villa and git somethin' out o' it."

Mariva went pensive for moment. Regen had a point, but she really wanted him to stay with her. The business side of her fought with the basic female desires inside her head. Finally, the female won.

"Okay, I'll make you a partner in the Velvet Saddle for the price of the average villa. How's that?"

Now it was Regen's turn to ponder. Mariva was a fine woman, no doubt about that, but he had no desire to make love to only one woman in his retirement years. With that arrangement, he might as well be married to her. Some ground rules were definitely in order.

"I'd haf t' have separate quarters?"

"No problem, you can have one of the line shacks."

"Line shack!"

"Oh, don't get upset until you see it.   They're special bungalows we rent to customers who want more privacy than the hotel affords. They're plush."

"Okay, and I don't want no responsibility for managin' this place?"

"Understood."

"Finally, my time's my own." This was not a question but a firm statement.

Mariva's face fell a bit, but she recovered quickly.

"I'd expect my partner to be available for 'consultation' on a regular basis."

"Now, you know I could never turn down an offer from you, Mariva."

A smile spread across her face, but she remembered one of her own conditions.

"And, you pay for all the whores you screw besides me."

"Aw, Mariva, I was hopin' you'd throw in the girls for a partner."

"No dice, Regen. I know you too well. Is it a deal?"

Regen bit his lip and considered the prospects for further negotiaion. It was as good a deal as he could get. He knew that.

"Deal!"

CHAPTER 10

The "Line Shack" was no disappointment. A spacious living room with a stone fireplace featured a hot tub under the floor accessible at the push of a button. A sensual bedroom with a king-sized bed sported a mirror on the ceiling. The adjoining bathroom's walk-in shower contained six different jets in the walls and floor besides the normal massaging shower head. A second bedroom provided a means of escaping the erotic and conducting business in a normal manner.

Regen had a special door installed for Hitler. It responded to a magnetic tag on his collar and opened whenever the skeen approached it. Water was the only thing lacking outside, and Regen placed a good-sized bowl next to the door. A float arrangement kept the bowl full at all times.

In no time at all he'd settled into a routine of riding, gambling and entertaining Mariva's ladies. The evenings belonged to Mariva, and she continued to surprise Regen with her knowledge of business, head for figures and undemanding sex schedule.

Mariva took an active hand in setting up a portfolio of investments for Regen since the big Bremen was totally ignorant of such matters. He trusted her implicitly, and his trust was not misplaced. Soon, he was making more money from his investments than even he could gamble away.

His favorite game was Jerillian poker. A curious blend of

poker, Tarot cards and Mah-Jongg played with a double deck of fifty picture cards in five suits. There was no normal rank of hands since the winning hand was a purely subjective judgment rendered by an android dealer. One needed a particularly attractive spread or one describing a propitious fortune in order to convince the computerized mind to select it as winner. The house took a cut of every pot.

On this particular day, the players were all new faces at Regen's favorite table. He liked the android dealer here because he usually favored the type of hand Regen tended to stay with. Where other dealers were suckers for love stories, this one tended toward the blood and guts hands with lots of adventure implied. Regen introduced himself to the players and promptly forgot their names. Unlike other forms of poker, tells were not important in Jerillian poker. The only person you had to watch was the dealer. Even though he was an android, he often exhibited a small tic or unusual eye movement when he was particularly impressed with a hand.

The first game began with the two hole cards to each player. Regen smiled inwardly as he looked at a Warrior of Swords and a Wizard of Swords. They were a good beginning, and he bet 1,000 credits. There were no raises, and the dealer dealt the first up-card to each player. A Warrior of Crowns added to his macho spread, and he bet another 1,000. To his surprise, a tall man in a brown business suit at the other end of the table raised him 1,000. Regen studied his exposed card, it was a Sage of Coins. What could he be going for with this dealer? Regen called.

The next card was a Priest of Hexes for Regen. It wasn't what he would have wanted, but he could weave a nice tale with those four cards. He checked, and the businessman bet 2,000. His card was a Sailor of Swords, which only added to

Regen's puzzlement. He called.

The third card up for Regen was a King of Hearts. Now he was ready to raise the ante a bit. How macho could a hand get? He bet 5,000. The businessman had drawn a Slave of Coins, and he raised Regen 5,000.

The players between he and Regen folded, and Regen called. The other players also dropped out leaving only the two men. Regen studied the dealer and found no clues in that impassive face.

The last card came down, and Regen lifted one corner cautiously to find a Queen of Hearts. His story was complete. This dealer would not be able to resist the appeal of his hand. He summarized it in his mind. A Warrior of Swords battles a Warrior of Crowns for the love of the Queen of Hearts, but he must overcome a spell cast by the Priest of Hexes by order of the King of Hearts. The Wizard of Swords helps him out. It was a sure thing, and he bet 10,000.

The man in the brown suit smiled as he upped the bet to 20,000. He seemed so sure of himself, and the dealer showed no signs of favoring either hand. There was just enough confidence in the man's demeanor to cause Regen to doubt his own hand, and he only called.

"Turn over your cards and arrange them as you desire," the dealer intoned in a steady voice.

Regen's opponent revealed the Thief of Coins, Queen of Crowns and Wizard of Swords. He arranged them in a row with the Wizard of Swords followed by the Queen of Crowns, the Sage of Coins, Sailor of Swords and the Slave of Coins. He explained his hand.

"I am the Wizard of Swords. I had a good business selling weapons to the military, but my wife, the Queen of Crowns, suggested I invest our money with a broker friend of hers, the

Sage of Coins. She and the broker conspired to swindle me out of most of my money while she ran away with the Sailor of Swords. I am now a Slave of Coins, working for others in an attempt to regain my lost prestige."

The other players murmured their appreciation of the story, but Regen's face took on a confident smirk. These sad tales might work with other dealers, but this one was too enamored with warriors and battles to fall for that kind of tripe. He arranged his cards and began his explanation.

"I am the Warrior of Swords. I stole the affections of the Queen of Hearts, and the King of Hears sent his champion, the Warrior of Crowns, to kill me. To be doubly sure, he had his Priest of Hexes make a special sacrifice to insure his champion's success. However, the Wizard of Swords interceded on my behalf, and I defeated the King's champion winning the Queen of Hearts."

The other players sat in silence. Here were two wonderful hands, both worthy of winning. What would the dealer decide?

The dealer studied both hands and leaned back in his chair.

"The tale of stolen love is most intriguing. It has all of the elements of a good adventure story befitting the personality of Mister Regen." He nodded toward the drug runner and smiled.

"However Mister Mulinor's story appeals to our sense of fair play and contains the classic betrayal plot. I detected a note of personal sorrow in his voice, and I think his story may apply directly to himself. It invokes our sympathy and our good wishes for his future success. I award the game to Mr. Mulinor." The dealer pushed the pile of chips to the man in the brown suit while Regen sat in stunned silence.

He'd never seen this before. An android wasn't supposed to have emotions. This dealer never evidenced any indication of feelings before, why now? There was no use thinking about it.

The decision was final, and there was no appeal.

"Antes please," the dealer intoned.

Regen picked up the few chips remaining in front of him and rose to leave. The loss of 33,000 credits was as much as he was willing to stand on any given day. There would be other days and other tables. The man in brown rose with him.

"Mr. Regen, may I buy you a drink?" he asked.

Regen looked at the man trying not to show his disappointment at the loss. Why not let him buy the drinks? He'd won enough.

"Sure, the bar's this way."

They took seats at the long bar. Regen ordered Gordian Bourbon and water while the other man ordered local brandy and soda.

Regen's opponent raised his glass in a toast. "Here's to lady luck."

"I'll drink to that since you seem to be her escort today." He touched his glass to the offered tumbler and took a sip.

"I'm sorry, I don't remember your name," Regen said as he set his glass on the bar.

"It's Mulinor, Favik Mulinor. Do you go by anything but Regen?"

"It's the only name I got. Back on Brem, people only have one name."

Favik smiled as he laughed lightly. "Must get a bit confusing at times."

"Our alphabet has 26 letters, seven of which are vowels, that gives a little over six million possible names. Brem is a sparsely populated place, but there's still over four billion people there. When I have to, I use my name number with my name."

"Interesting, what is your name number?"

"Mine's 5481, but most of the time I can just use Regen.

Where you from, Favik, or do you go by Mulinor?"

"I'm from Durma, and my friends call me Favik. I'd like to count you among those friends, if you don't mind."

"No problem, I just ain't interested in palyin' poker with you no more. I don't know what you did to that dealer, but he ain't called a hand like yours a winner since I been commin' here."

"No telepathy, magic or secret devices, I assure you. He must have sensed my recent loss."

Regen took another drink while he studied the man. Favik had light brown hair worn in a business cut. He was clean-shaven and had soft brown eyes. He was a bit shorter than Regen, but there was an athletic build under the conservative suit. He saw nothing about the man to evoke sympathy. The suit was an expensive cut, and the gold and diamonds on his fingers and hanging around his neck boasted some degree of wealth. Maybe it was the eyes? They had that lost puppy look women often went for.

"What loss is that?"

"My business partner just walked off with all the money in our account and left me holding a big sack of debt. I had to sell off the business to settle with the creditors. I got thoroughly screwed in the process, and he's on some planet without an extradition treaty for Terma."

"How much did he git?"

"About 10 million. Doesn't sound like a lot, but it was a year's profit we'd been keeping in reserve for any downturn in the market. I was okay until last spring when demand for our black boxes nose-dived. It was only temporary, but the creditors wanted their money and wouldn't negotiate. They knew they had me over a barrel, and they held my feet to the fire until I sold out."

"Too bad, what're you gonna do now?"

"A guy approached me with a deal just the other day, but it's a bit on the shady side. I'm not sure if I want to go through with it, and besides, it will take some up-front money I don't have."

"You're talkin' to a guy who's been on the wrong side of the law all his life, and I got a little money t' invest. Why don't ya tell me 'bout it?"

"You have to promise to keep what I tell you an absolute secret."

"Don't worry 'bout me. I got no reason to tell nobody nothin'."

Favik leaned across the table and spoke in a whisper. "This character claims to have a black box that makes spaceships invisible. He says he'll let me have it if I can find him a spaceship and cut him in for half the profits."

"What's he wanna do with this 'black box' and a spaceship?"

"There's a revolution on Bardour, and the rebels need weapons badly. They'll pay through the nose for almost anything. All you have to do is get through the space defense system and there's billions to be made."

The name of the planet struck a familiar note in Regen's head. He'd dropped Orianne off there only a few months back.

"I been there already, and the Bardour defense system is nothin' t' mess with, even with my ship."

Favik's eyes lit up. "You've got a spaceship?"

"Yup, a stealth model that's invisible to almost all sensors 'cept the ones around Bardour. They got some kind of radar there that can spot any kind of stealth technology."

"This guy claims they can't see his stuff. He stole the gear from an experimental Spaceforce ship that crashed out in the desert last year. He and his boys were on the scene first and looted the whole crash site. While his buddies were going for money and gold, he pulled the stealth gear. He figured some dope smuggler would pay pretty well for the item. They were able to bug out before the rescue people got there."

"Garbage! The army'd be all over that part of the country looking for those goons. Are you tryin' t' tell me they got away clean?"

"This guy says the army's afraid to go into their territory, but they're watching the borders pretty closely. Evidently, they want that stuff back real bad. He wanted to find out what all the interest was about and sneaked out a few weeks back. He found out the ship was testing some new kind of cloaking device. Somebody told him I'd help him peddle the gear, but I couldn't see how we could get it out of the hills and past the army. You've got a stealth ship. You could get in and out easily."

"You don't know much 'bout stealth stuff. It works good in space, but it ain't worth a damn once y' git inside th' atmosphere. My ship's big enough to register on the army sensors with all the cloakin' stuff goin' full blast. Nope, the only way is to git the stuff out the same way your man got out. How many boxes has he got?"

"I don't know. Probably it would be best if you spoke with him directly. I'll arrange a meeting, but how do I contact you?"

Regen gave Favik his contact information and went back to his cabin. Mariva was waiting for him.

"I had the restaurant make us a nice lunch, Regen. I figured you'd be back around noon. Sit down, and I'll heat it up a bit." She indicated a chair at the finely set table. A bottle of red wine was already open, and two glasses sat ready. She moved to the kitchen and placed two containers in the food heater unit. "Have any luck at poker today?"

"Nope, lost my limit, but I ran into a guy who might have a pretty profitable deal for me."

"Oh, who's that?"

"Some guy named Favik Mulinor. He beat me at the poker game and then offered to buy me a drink. While we were conversin' he told me about runnin' weapons to Bardour."

"Nobody runs guns to Bardour, Regen. It's a suicide mission," Mariva called from the kitchen.

"I told him that, but he said he had a guy with a new stealth unit the Bardourians couldn't see. Claims he got it off an experimental ship that crashed in the desert a while back."

"I heard about that crash. The army's still looking for a bunch of Zunids they think looted the crash site. From what I hear, they're about ready to attack the Zunid stronghold."

A chime sounded, and Mariva removed the containers from the heating unit. She dished the contents on to two plates and set one in front of Regen and the other at her place.

"Why don't you pour me some wine?" she asked.

Regen poured two glasses and raised his to Mariva. "Here's to good sex."

"I'll drink to that, but tell me more about this Mulinor character."

"Don't know much more. He's settin' up a meetin' with his guy, and I'll know more after that. If the device is as good as he seems t' think it is, we could run guns to Bardour and make millions. I didn't tell Mulinor this, but I got a special contact on that planet."

"Oh, in which whorehouse?"

"Ah, ah, ah, you got it all wrong. This gal's a real princess. Her name's Orianne, and she's real grateful t' me for rescuin' her from life as a slave whore. I reckon she'd be real glad to see me."

"I read about her. She's in charge of the whole rebel movement on Bardour. That's some contact. You might have a good deal there, Regen.   How do you like the curried rattlesnake?"

Regen looked down at his plate with an expression of pure disgust. "Is that what this stuff is?"

"Yup, fresh killed this morning."

Regen took a bite and savored it for a moment before washing it down with wine.   "Everbody allus told me rattlesnake tasted like chicken.   Tastes more like Cirrilian alligator t' me."

"That bad?"

"Nope, great! I love Cirrilian alligator."   Regen dove into the meal with gusto.

After dinner they made love and relaxed in the hot tub.   As they soaked up the bubbles, Mariva spoke.   "Let me check out this Mulinor guy before you agree to any meeting.   I think I've heard that name before somewhere."

"Whatever that little heart o' yers desires, darlin'."   Regen pulled her close to him and kissed her gently.

CHAPTER II

The next day, Mariva called Regen to her office and handed him a folder.

"This should give you some idea about Mr. Mulinor's credibility," she said.

Regen opened the folder to a picture of Mulinor in a prison outfit with a number under his chin. He read the four-page report from a private detective named Durban and smiled at the contents.

"This here Mulinor's a man after my own heart. Don't look like he's ever been involved in a legitimate business. I feel a lot better now that I know I'm doin' business with a thief and a con man. I'd figured him for a reg'lar guy up t' now."

"Regen! You can't be serious about giving this guy any money?" Mariva's face took on an incredulous expression.

"Look, another crook I can understand. I know how they think, and I can deal with that. I think I'll hold off any judgment until after I see what kind o' stuff his Bedouin buddy's got. Don't worry, I'll keep my money in my pocket 'til I'm convinced."

"Well, it's your funeral," Mariva sighed as she took back the folder. She knew there was no talking Regen out of at least investigating the deal.

That evening, Regen's communicator chimed, and Mulinor

appeared on the screen.

"Regen, can you meet me at the Black Hole Club bar at ten tonight?"

Regen knew the place. It was one of the least desirable clip joints in an area of Daq Vinas famous for undesirable dives.

"Sure, I can make it. See you then."

The screen went blank, and Regen punched the stop button on his end also. He checked his watch. There would just be enough time for the hotel skimmer to drop him off, but first, he checked the load in his laser pistol and donned its shoulder holster before putting on a coat.

The Black Hole was everything Regen expected. As he walked in the door he smelled every kind of dope he'd ever sold, and the smoke from the bongs hung in a psychedelic fog just below the ceiling. A recording of a native band playing at the threshold of pain assaulted his ears while a Bagalla woman gyrated sensually across the bar that doubled as a stage. She was completely naked except for a small gold thong barely covering her pubic area. The assortment of thieves, Bedouins and petty criminals surrounding the stage pushed money into the thong and called out bawdy suggestions, which she ignored completely. He spotted Mulinor at a booth to his left and joined him.

"Sit down, Regen," Mulinor greeted the Bremen.

"Where's the guy with the cloakin' device?" Regen asked as he took a seat opposite Mulinor.

"I wanted to go over the whole deal with you before he got here. He'll show up in an hour or so. Want a drink?"

A waitress clad in a skimpy outfit appeared out of nowhere. Regen gave her a thorough inspection then said, "I'll have a double Godian bourbon and soda."

The waitress left, and Mulinor continued, "I got a contact on

Bardour who handles the rebel's weapons buys. He's ready to take anything we can bring him if we can get through the planet's defense system."

Regen thought about his last trip to Bardour when only the deactivation of one quadrant allowed him to make a penetration. He wondered why the rebels couldn't do it again, but figured the boys in charge of the defenses had closed that door very quickly.

"I been there. I know 'bout the defense systems."

"Did your ship penetrate them before?" Mulinor's face took on a hopeful expression.

"Nope, they spotted me afore I got inside 10,000 kilometers. Took all the skill I got just to get away in one piece." Regen lied, but he figured there was no point letting Mulinor know of Orianne yet.

"Well, you understand why we need the latest gear to make it through."

"Yep, but even if we got one o' those doo-dads, where do we get the weapons?"

"The guy who has the stuff is a Zunid chieftain. His tribe's area borders Rugistan, and he claims he can get all the weapons we want from the Rugistani government as long as we ship them off the planet."

"I don't s'pose this guy had any idea o' the prices they want did he?"

"He thinks we can get a good shipload for ten million."

Regen knew the capacity of his ship, and doubted he could carry that much weight. "I don't know if'n my ship could carry ten million worth o' weapons. Cargo capacity from here to Bardour'd only be 'bout four metric tons."

"No problem, if this guys stuff is as good as he says it is, we can make all the runs we want. Mulinor scribbled on a napkin for a moment. "I figure at your ship's capacity, we'd have to pay around eight million at a crack. Of course, after the first load, we'd be operating on the profits."

"Who puts up the money for the first load?"

"That's where you come in. We'll need money for that and to grease the palms of the guy with the cloaking gear and a few people in Rugistan. He's supposed to tell me who and how much today."

"And how much o' this are you goin' t' cover?"

"I'm broke, Regen. All I got is the money I won from you the other day."

Regen pulled a folded paper from inside his coat and opened it up. "Let's see, accordin' t' this here bank statement you got over six million stashed away on Riga IV in the First Galactic Savings Bank."

Mulinor's face went white, and he edged toward the end of the booth. "How did you find that account?"

"Relax, I just wanted ya t' know you ain't dealin' with some rube. Don't ever try to con a conman, Favik. I got sources for this kind o' stuff."

"Well, that's my retirement fund, Regen. I'm sure you've made similar arrangements for yourself."

"My money's scattered all over the galaxy by now, but I can git to it if'n I need it."

The waitress sat Regen's drink on the table, and Mulinor downed the last of his and handed the empty glass to the woman. "I'll have another one of these," he said.

"Look, I'll use some of that money if you like, but no more than half of it."

"Sounds fair t' me, but you gotta expect t' git a smaller cut o' th' profits."

"I don't care. As soon as I get nine million out of this deal,

I'm gone, and you can have the rest all to yourself. I got an island on this planet that's begging me to come spend the rest of my life there, but it'll take 12 million to do it the way I want." Mulinor was distracted by the approach of a turbaned and bearded Bedouin. The crowd in the bar fell silent as the tall man strode through the tables with two brawny bodyguards behind him. His brown robe was loose-fitting in the Bedouin style and made of an obviously expensive material from the way it flowed around his body. A red sash around his waist held a jeweled dagger, and a large emerald hung from a heavy chain around his neck. His face was craggy and wrinkled by many days in the harsh desert sun, but his beard was black as ebony and curly. Dark brown eyes scanned the room until they spotted Mulinor. He moved to the table and indicated positions for his guards on either side of the booth.

"Good afternoon, Mulinor. I assume this is the man you spoke to me about." The bedouin indicated Regen with a nod of his head.

"Yes it is. Regen, I want you to meet Jahallah."

"Pleased t' meet ya," Regen nodded toward the Zunid.

Jahallah took a seat next to Mulinor. "A pleasure to meet you also. Mulinor, here, tells me you have a spaceship."

"Yep, I got a ZHS-1160 with full stealth capability."

"A bit smaller than we hoped for. It will mean more trips to deliver the same amount of weapons, and that will increase the danger as well as the expenses."

The waitress arrived with Mulinor's drink, and he asked Jahallah, "Anything for you?"

"My people never touch alcohol, thank you."

Mulinor dismissed the waitress, and Regen continued the conversation.

"Favik tells me you got a system that should make these

trips past Bardour's sensors a walk in the park."

"I do, I have the latest experimental unit from the Terman Space Force. They were testing it last month when the ship crashed near my tribe's stronghold."

"I'm curious, Jahallah. What made you go for the cloakin' unit? I understood you Zunids were only interested in gold and hearin' yer victims scream in pain."

Jahallah stifled a laugh at Regen's black humor.

"Ah, but Bremens are so boring to torture. They only grunt a lot and die too quickly," Jahallah said as a smile spread across his dark brown face.

"It's one o' our failings," Regen responded.

"You asked me why I took the cloaking unit, so I'll tell you. I am a rich man, Regen. I have over 300 horses and more gold than ten of them can carry. My oldest boy spent eight years in the Terman Space Force, and he was with me when we looted the wreckage. He spotted the new unit immediately and advised me to take it. I failed to see the value in a piece of electronic equipment, but he insisted it would bring a very good price from some drug dealer or smuggler. I humored him. I told him he could take that unit while I collected the fuel crystals. Are you interested?"

"How much o' th' system you got?" Regen asked. "The black box is no good by itself. You gotta have the control panel and all the antennae to make it work right."

"My son assures me he has all the components needed for full operation of the system."

"I understand the army wants their stuff back real bad. How do you plan to git it outa your place and somewhere we could put it in my ship?" Regen asked.

"The same way I came here. Our lands border on Rugistan, and the army dare not place a large force near that border.

Relations between Ausland and Rugistan are very touchy at the moment. There are only border guards at the usual crossing points. We Zuinids know many places to cross into Rugistan where there are no border police, and once we reach Rugistan, the authorities there don't care what we do as long as we stay out of the cities."

"So, you and a few o' yer boys would carry the stuff out on your backs, eh?"

"As you say, on our backs."

"Where could I land my ship?"

"My clan is allied with one of the Rugistani border tribes. Chief Yussah of the Hallami is married to one of my daughters. They would be agreeable to protecting your ship while the modifications are made. We could also use his territory as a base for our weapons smuggling operations."

"Seems like you got it all tied up with pretty ribbons. How much is this gonna cost?"

"My son put a price of 20 million credits on the unit, but he's had no buyers yet. I've suggested an arrangement where he would receive 10 million up front and ten percent of the profits from the arms deals. Chief Yussah requires 5 million but is not interested in any of the profits as long as we make some appropriate gift from our weapons shipments from time to time."

"How about you?" Regen asked Jahallah.

"As I said, I am already a rich man, but since no man ever has enough wealth, a simple five percent of the profits would satisfy me."

Regen thought for a moment. After the cut for the kid and his father, that would still leave 85 percent for him and Mulinor. "Who do we hafta bribe to git the weapons?"

"One or two minor customs officials and the defense

minister will need to be complimented for each shipment, but that should amount to no more than five percent, at most."

Regen smiled and leaned across the table toward Mulinor. "You know, I like the way he puts it, 'compliment' them. Sounds a lot better'n bribe, don't it?"

The Rugistan cut dropped the final net to 80 percent, but that would be enough if the cloaking unit were as good as advertised.

"Mr. Mulinor and me'll hafta talk this over among ourselves for a bit, if you'll excuse us, please," Regen said to Jahallah.

"I understand completely. I will avail myself of the local female menu here while you two decide. Shall we say in one hour?"

"Fine, come back in an hour," Regen said.

Jahallah left the booth followed by his bodyguards. Regen summarized the situation.

"Okay, 8 million for the first batch, ten million for this guy's kid and five million for Yussah. That's 23 million up front with only 80% left on the profit side. How much o' th' up front money you willing to pony up?"

"I told you, three million is all I can do."

"Well, that leaves 20 million for me plus I bear all the shipping expenses and assume all the risk. Th' way I figur' it, that don't leave much o' that 80% for you, Favik. Let's see, I figur' that's only 'bout 15% for you and 65% for me."

"Wait a minute, Regen. I deserve some credit for putting this whole deal together, don't I?"

"I guess there's somethin' in that. Tell you what, I'll go 25/55 with ya."

"I was thinking more like splitting down the middle."

"You ain't got eleven million t' put in, Favik, but tell you what, 30/50, and that's my final offer."

Mulinor sighed and leaned back in the booth. "Okay, let's drink on it." He raised his glass to Regen who responded accordingly.

After an hour, Jahallah returned to the booth. "Have you two come to an agreement?"

"Yup! It's all set, 5% for you, 10 million and 10% for your boy, and whatever it takes t' grease the Rugistan politicos." Regen offered his hand to Jahallah, but the Zunid made no move toward it.

"In my tribe it is traditional to seal such bargains with blood." Jahallah pulled the ornately decorated dagger from his belt and pushed an empty glass to the middle of the table. "Are we ready?"

"Whatever you got in mind's okay by me," Regen said. He was used to this sort of thing from long experience sealing drug deals with primitive people.

"I hate knives," Mulinor said as he gave the dagger a distasteful look.

"Only a small cut is required," Jahallah said as he cut his forearm and let some blood drip into the glass. "Regen?"

The Bremen held his arm over the glass and Jahallah took some of his blood also.

"Mulinor?"

Favik reluctantly bared his forearm and suffered visibly as the cut was made. He wrapped a handkerchief around the wound.

"A toast to our success." Jahallah raised the glass and took a sip before passing it to Regen. The Bremen followed suit and handed the gory cocktail to Mulinor.

"I have to drink some of this?" he asked.

"Only a taste is required," Jahallah answered.

Mulinor moved the glass as if a force field existed between

the glass and his mouth. He gagged a bit at the smell of the blood but took a deep breath and tilted the glass to his lips.

"Ugh!" Mulinor set the glass on the table heavily.

"Good! When do we meet again in Rugistan?" Jahallah asked.

"Well, I gotta git some money and bring my ship down. Let's say a week from today."

"Done! I will get the coordinates of the site to Mulinor before then. I look forward to a profitable association, gentlemen." Jahallah rose, and the bodyguards joined him. "Peace be with you until then."

That night, Mariva listened to Regen's description of the deal and grunted her disgust. "Regen, I'm surprised at you. Don't you know you can't trust any of these people? Mulinor is a first class con man, Zunids are known for screwing the people they do business with, and any border tribesman in Rugistan is bound to be a crook. You'll be lucky to get out of this with your skin."

"I know all that, but if the Zunid kid's got a super-duper stealth device, I could sure use it."

"I thought you were retired now."

"Well, y' never know when you'll hafta go back to work. There's nothin' sure in life, y' know. Besides, I ain't gonna let loose o' any cash 'til I'm sure the doohickey works. I set it up with Mulinor that you'd be the one to release the money on my say so. I'll give you a code word to let you know the deal's Kosher."

"Regen, the Zunids have tortures that could make Hitler talk. I have to have some way of knowing you're not having your balls pulled off when you give me the code word."

"I thought about that already. I'll give you another word to let y' know th' deal's off. If y' git that word, you'll know I ain't comin' back and you can just forget about me."

"I still don't like it. Who'll screw my brains out if you're not around?"

Regen took her in his arms and kissed her tenderly. "I know you'll miss me, but I'm sure someone'll come along better 'n me. Besides, you'll have all my money to console ya."

"Money doesn't make a very good bed partner," Mariva said as she led Regen to her bedroom.

CHAPTER 12

Regen's ship landed at the agreed upon spot in a narrow valley just across the Ausland/Rugistan border. Mulinor, Jahallah, a young man Regen guessed was Jahallah's son and a band of mean-looking horsemen were there to meet him. Jahallah took the lead as Regen descended from the ship.

"Welcome to Rugistan, Regen. This is my son, Amalek." The young man bowed to Regen and touched his chest with his hand. Regen figured this was the proper greeting and returned it in kind.

"Pleasure t' meet ya, Amalek," Regen said. A rumble of curses and the click of rifle actions welcomed the appearance of Hitler behind his master, and Regen acted quickly to save his pet.

"Tell these guys t' take it easy, Jahallah. Hitler here's my pet."

Jahallah held up a hand and gave some commands in his language. The horsemen returned to a waiting posture as the Chief explained the relationship of the skeen and pointed out the animal's spiked collar and gold tag. He turned to Regen with a broad smile on his face.

"I've never seen one of those things this close and alive. How did you manage to make him a pet?"

"That's a long story. If'n we ever git any time t' relax, I'll tell ya all about it. Who are the goons?" Regen pointed to the horsemen.

"They are men from my tribe who will serve as your security while you modify your ship. Yussah is camped two kilometers to the West between here and the capital city to protect us from the Rugistan authorities, but these fellows will protect us from Yussah."

"Well, I guess we'd better git started. Where's the cloakin' stuff?"

Amalek responded. "We've set up a camouflaged area over there." He pointed to an area Regen could barely find without a hint from Amalek. "If you will move your ship under the netting, we can begin at once."

"Okay, just be sure your men don't mistake Hitler fer lunch and shoot first."

Jahallah answered. "They have been instructed to refrain from shooting anything that even resembles a skeen. Besides, our religion prohibits the consumption of his flesh. I think he will be safe."

Regen moved his ship under the artificial cover, and Amalik showed him the new equipment.

"This is the main control unit." He held up a small box with a few switches. "We'll have to rig it into your display system, but I don't think that'll be a problem. The main black box we can put anywhere you like. I'd suggest where your current cloaker is now. We can probably use some of its wiring for this unit also."

"Sounds good t' me. How many sensors and antennae you got?"

"I looked up your ship's device, and we have one of these units to replace each one of yours. I think that should be enough."

"Don't think, know," Regen admonished. "Th' defenses 'round Bardour can vaporize this ship in a microsecond if they see anything that looks suspicious."

Amalek smiled and pointed to a large black box. "This thing is the difference, and what it takes to get you safely through any defense system. It's the main computer."

"Kinda big fer a 'puter ain't it?"

"You wouldn't believe what this baby will do if I told you. It's this big because it has one million times the computational ability of your ship's computer and over a billion times the memory. That's what the Space Force was testing when the ship crashed."

"Phew!" Regen whistled. "No wonder it's so big. Why so much c'mputer power?"

"This baby reads the radiation beamed at your ship and sends back the correct response to negate your reflection and give a picture of the space behind you at the same time. There's only a one picosecond delay, and I don't know of any defense system that can respond to that brief a signal."

"I'm impressed. Let's git busy. I'll help ya any way I can."

"Let's start by tearing out your old system. That way we can get an idea of where some of this stuff will fit and how much re-wiring we have to do."

Mulinor approached the two men and spoke to Regen. "I'm going into Rugibad to make our first buy, but I'll need you to transfer some funds to my account, Regen."

"Okay, I'll make the call." Regen moved into his ship and established contact with Mariva.

"How's it going, Regen?" she asked.

"Looks legit so far. Mulinor's gonna make our buy now. I approve codeword gamma."

"Got it. I'll transfer the money immediately. You got good security there? The buzz around here is the Ausland government is curious as to why you moved your ship to

Rugistan. You may get some heat soon."

"I think we got enough muscle to take care o' anything but an armored attack. Keep me posted if ya hear any more rumors."

"You just take care of yourself among those Zunids. I don't trust them. Combine them with Mulinor, and I'm really scared."

"We'll just hafta wait n see. Don't worry 'bout me darlin'. Talk to ya later."

Regen broke off the call and returned to advise Mulinor the money was now in his account.

"Good, I should be back in two days with the goods. Will you be ready to go by then?"

Amalek replied. "No problem, we'll be waiting on you."

Mulinor left in the company of several Zunids, and Amalek and Regen began work on the ship.

As they worked, Regen gained an appreciation for Amalek's knowledge of cloaking systems. It began when they started to remove his old system.

"This Sajo 440D is a great system, and you've got the military version too. Who do you know on Gobra?"

"I got contacts there, and there's a General in their Space Force who likes petro real good."

"Will you sell me your old system?" Amalek turned to Regen and noticed the wry smile on his face.

"I know this'un works. If'n yers works as good as you say it does, I'll sell mine to ya fer half the price you're chargin' me for the new stuff. If it don't work, you can have it, 'cause I won't be needin' any kind o' cloakin' system after I'm space temperature."

Amalek laughed as he realized the first test against the Bardour defense system may well be Regen's last.

"It's a deal." He offered Regen a dirty hand, and the Bremen responded in kind.

By that evening, the job was well over half done, and the men decided to stop for the night. They joined Jahallah and his men around their campfires.

Jahallah's fire was in front of an ornate tent, and a peek into the interior revealed a plush setting befitting the chief of the tribe. Jahallah welcomed them.

"Come sit at my fire, my son, and bring Regen along." Two men moved to make space for the newcomers.

"What's fer dinner?" Regen asked.

"Roast lamb and a special delicacy of our people made from the fruit of the large palm trees that grow near the mountains. You'll like it."

Their meal was interrupted by two of Jahallah's men dragging another man into the firelight.

"Who is this?" Jahallah asked. The air of impatience in his voice over the disturbance of his meal was unmistakable.

"Sir, we caught this man just outside the camp. He claims to be a Rugistani, but I suspect he is a spy from Ausland."

The man was dressed like a Rugistani in turban and loose-fitting tunic and trousers. His feet were shod in soft leather boots tooled in the fashion of the Wamani, Yussah's tribe.

"What are you doing here?" Jahallah asked him.

"I was only curious about the spacecraft. I've never seen one before, sir."

"How did you know it was here?"

"I saw it land earlier today as I was hunting bird's eggs in the hills to the North."

"And, what kind of eggs were you after?" Jahallah asked.

The man squirmed a bit and sweat popped out on his head. "Why, granna eggs of course."

Jahallah's face grew grim. "Tie him to that tree and bring the instruments," he directed the men.

"No, no, I was wrong. It wasn't granna eggs, they were scenie eggs."

"Another bad guess, my friend. Neither of those birds nest at this time of year. I think you are some kind of spy, and we will find out what kind very shortly."

The man's face grew ashen white. He'd undoubtedly heard stories about Bedouin tortures, and he knew he would never hold up to them. He might have had a suicide pill somewhere handy, but he opted for confession instead. Perhaps he thought his death might be more merciful if he admitted his mission.

"No, don't do that. I'll tell you what you want to know. I'm an agent with the Ausland Border Patrol. I was sent here to find out what you're doing to the spacecraft and if the new cloaking system is involved." He slumped against the ropes holding him to the tree expecting the worst.

One of Jahallah's men appeared carrying a small black case and what looked like an ornate crash helmet. He set them down next to his chief.

"You have saved yourself a lot of pain with that admission, but we can't let you go back now. Give him the injection, Karmou."

Another Zunid stepped forward and opened the black case. He removed an injection device from the center section and held it against the man's chest. After a soft swishing sound, the man's head dropped to his chest.

"Is he dead?" Regen asked.

Jahallah laughed. "I suppose he thinks so at this minute, but he's very much alive."

The chief picked up the helmet and placed it on the man's head.

"No, Regen, this man is worth much more to us alive than dead. All we need to do is modify his memory somewhat, and he will serve us instead of his masters back in Ausland."

Jahallah pushed a button on the front of the helmet, and a mechanical voice began to speak. "Watch out for that snake. It may be poisonous. Oh, oh, those guys have spotted me. I'll try to duck into this ditch. Oh shit! They had men there too. Got to play dumb. I'm just a poor bastard gathering wild eggs."

"Back two minutes," Jahallah commanded.

"Don't know what they're doing to that ship yet, but it looks like some of those components are from our test ship. I need to get a bit closer to read the markings. I think there's enough cover this way. What's that? Look out for that snake . . ."

"Stop there! Erase after 'but' and up to 'I think' and insert 'it looks like those are bales of hashinah. The guy's buying drugs from the Zunids.'"

"Are you tryin' t' tell me you just modified that guy's memory?" Regen said. Even in the dim light from the fires, his face showed his disbelief clearly.

"Wonderful gadget, isn't it? Yes, that's exactly what I did. This man will go back to his superiors and report what I just planted in his mind. They will check your records and find you have several arrests for drug smuggling. Our work here will then proceed without further interruption since buying hashinah is perfectly legal in Rugistan." He turned to his men. "He will revive in thirty minutes. Make sure the camp is dark, but post men to keep him away from the spacecraft. Leave his bonds loose enough to allow him to reach the knots and escape. You might cut him up a little for effect. He'll think he passed out from the torture. Follow him to the border to make sure he doesn't turn back. Tomorrow, bring several bales of hashinah here in case they send another spy."

"It will be as you say, my Chief." The Zunid bowed low and removed the helmet from the victim's head as other men retied the ropes.

"I'll be damned! I never heard of anything like that there helmet. Where'd ya git it?"

"Space Force ships aren't the only ones that crash in the desert. This was on a Trillian warship unfortunate enough to tangle with our defense system. As usual, we reached it before anyone else and helped ourselves to the weapons and what little booty was aboard. One of the survivors was a psychiatrist who traded this device for his life. We hid him out until he could arrange for false papers and escape, and he showed us how to use it."

"Never been to Trilla, but I think I'll stay away from the place after seein' that thing." Regen gave an involuntary shudder as he watched one of Jahallah's men remove the helmet and loosen the prisoner's bonds.

The next morning, the spy was gone, and one of the Zunids reported he'd run for the border as soon as he was free.

Regen and Amalek returned to work on the ship and there was no further interruption that day with the exception of a small drone photographing the area. Jahallah's men fired upon it but managed to miss each time so it would report the presence of the hashina bales.

Work progressed smoothly, and the job was finished by evening meal time. As they walked toward the camp, Regen commented, "I ain't seen Hitler fer nearly two days. I sure hope some guy hasn't popped him."

"My father's men were given strict orders about him, and the Wamani are staying well clear of our camp. He's probably just found some food he likes."

Shouting from the other side of the camp caused the men to

investigate the source of the commotion, and they found a group of Jahallah's men forming a circle around Hitler and a large, green snake. Money was changing hands at a rapid rate as the men watched the skeen deftly dodge the snake's strikes. Regen reached for one of the men's laser pistols, but his hand was pushed away quickly as the man jabbered in the Zunid language. Amalek interpreted.

"They have too many wagers going on this fight for you to kill the snake. I wouldn't try to interfere."

Regen studied the situation a bit and asked, "What's th' odds right now?"

"Your skeen is the underdog at 3:1."

"Tell 'em I got a thousand to put on Hitler." Regen smiled as he pulled a credit voucher from his pocket and handed it to Amalek. The Zunid handed it back to Regen.

"This is strictly a cash deal."

Regen found 500 in cash and offered that. It was quickly faded by the Zunids.

"I think you can kiss that 500 goodbye, Regen. That's a green maroba, one of the fastest and deadliest snakes on the planet. I've never seen anything survive an encounter with one. At least your pet will die quickly. The venom only takes a few seconds to act."

"You ain't never seen a skeen in action either. Just watch."

The snake appeared to be in more of a defensive posture. Regen assumed that was the case since Hitler was much too big for the thing to swallow. Hitler, on the other hand, saw the snake as food, and he stalked it carefully looking for a weakness in the reptile's strategy. The chess game seemed to go on for hours, though only a few minutes passed. The Zunids were encouraging the snake more than Hitler, and Amalek informed Regen the odds were now more like five to one and no more bets were being laid down.

Hitler knew what he was doing. The snake began to tire visibly after a large number of strikes, and the setting sun was robbing it of precious body heat by the moment. On one strike, it was a bit slow to recoil, and the skeen struck like lightening. He grabbed the snake just behind its head and bit down hard. The thing writhed and coiled around Hitler's body, but the skeen held on doggedly shaking the thing back and forth until the head separated from the rest. The body of the reptile relaxed, and the coils fell to the ground wriggling much less actively than before. Hitler dropped the head and jumped back in case there was still some life left in it. He need not have worried.

The Zunids groaned in astonishment and began to melt away to return to their chores. Two of them approached Regen and passed him a bag full of money.

"These men were keeping the bets, Regen. This part of the money is yours." Amalek pointed to three other men counting out their winnings. "You see, there weren't many people taking your side.

"I'm happy t' make 'em some money," Regen said as he watched Hitler tear apart the snake's carcass.

CHAPTER 13

Mulinor arrived early in the morning with fewer trucks than expected. Regen, Amalek and Jahallah were waiting for him with anxious expressions. He stepped out of the first truck and strode toward them in a black mood.

"Jahallah, you'll have to have a talk with your relative. That bastard Yussah took about a fourth of the weapons as his *gift*."

"Do we have enough left to make the trip worth while?" Jahallah asked Mulinor.

"It'll be a light load for Regen's ship, but we should make a tidy profit," he responded.

Regen moved off to inspect the trucks. He rejoined the group.

"Ya don't git much fer eight million these days, but I guess we kin git 'bout 25 million fer the stuff ya got here. As long as we got room, you might as well put on a few bales o' that hashina stuff. Might be a market for that among the rebels too. Have the boys load it up, and I'll be gone as soon as ever'thing's aboard."

"Since you have a light load, I'll go along with you, Regen." Amalek voiced it as a statement and not a question.

Regen looked at him with a puzzled expression. "I don't know why y'd want to. There's a good chance I may not even git ta the surface let alone git back out and safe here."

"Let's just say I'm looking after my 10% and my father's hashina."

"Yer funeral." Regen turned to Mulinor. "You got th' contact information?"

"It's all here on this chip. My man on Bardour says the government hasn't broken this code yet."

Regen took the chip and placed it in his pocket. "Let's git busy."

The load took most of the morning, but there was time for a lunch made from real food before departure. Regen and Amalek would have to make do with what the synthesizer produced for the next two weeks. Amalek was looking forward to the adventure since he had never been into deep space before, but Regen knew it would not live up to the boy's expectations.

They boarded the ship with Amalek taking the co-pilot seat in the command center.

"I worked on dozens of these things while I was in the Space Force, but I never got to fly in one. I'm really looking forward to this trip." Amalek's enthusiasm was interrupted by a harsh hissing noise, and he turned to see Hitler glaring up at him from the deck.

"You're in his seat, but don't pay no 'tention to him. Get outta here, Hitler!" Regen made a half-hearted kick toward his pet, and Hitler got the message. He vanished around the entrance to the command center.

"That pet of yours has been quite the talk of the camp since it killed that snake." Amalek looked back at the doorway and spotted a leathery head peering around the hatchway. "Would he sit on my lap?"

"Don't know. You could call him and see."

Amalek patted his lap and called to Hitler. "Come here,

Hitler. You can sit on my lap, if you like."

The skeen gave him a curious look then decided a strange lap was better than being excluded from the command center during the start of a mission. He walked cautiously toward the Zunid and sat for a moment looking up at him.

"It's okay, boy. Up here!" Amalek called, and Hitler jumped into his waiting lap.

"Oooof, he's not light, is he?"

"He's been eatin' pretty good lately. He'll slim down some afore we git back home."

Regen busied himself with the details of lift-off while Amalek followed his actions. Hitler loved to watch the changing displays on the instrument panel and would raise a claw in a vain attempt to grasp anything that remined him of food.

The ship lifted into the sky, and Amalek let out a wild call driving Hitler back out the doorway and causing Regen to jump with surprise.

"What the hell was that?" Regen asked.

"It's the war cry of the Zunid. I was so excited I couldn't hold back."

"Well, try t' keep it under control, will ya?"

Amalek scanned the displays. "You're using gravitational interaction drive now, aren't you?"

"Yup, it's th' only way t' get to th' spaceport to take on warp drive fuel. With your Space Force experience, I'da thought you'd knowed that."

"I do, it's just my excitement at being on a real space voyage at last."

The ship achieved orbit and phased toward the spaceport. Regen wasn't worried about customs on the way out of Terma. They didn't much care what left, but they taxed anything you brought in. He docked at the fuel station and took on enough warp fuel for the trip without any questions.

"You ready for warp speed?" Regen asked as he cleared the spaceport.

"This is the part I was really looking forward to. Let's go."

Regen set the controls and leaned back in the pilot's seat, tightening his harness as he did so.

The ship shuddered for a moment as the warp drive engaged then a full 12 g force pinned both men in their places. Amalek watched the viewing screen to see the spectacle of relativistic speed unfold. The pattern of white stars on the black velvet background of space vanished as the field created by the warp drive cleared even space itself from in front of the ship. Not even light could penetrate the absolute absence of any known entity. As the craft accelerated into the void, a new sensation of speed flooded over the men. Pinned to their chairs, the men could barely force their chests to move in order to suck in the life-giving oxygen of the cockpit. The noise of the warp drive drowned out even their thoughts, and they surrendered to the spell of the moment.

It only lasted a few seconds, though it seemed like hours to Amalek. The ship stopped accelerating and fell into a steady speed easing the pressure on their chests and allowing normal movements once more. Amalek changed the angle of the view screen to an aft view and marveled at the red shades patterning the display.

"God, it's beautiful!" was all he could manage.

"Ya git used to it," Regen assured him.

Hitler re-emerged from wherever he hid to survive the g forces and jumped into Regen's lap.

"Hitler, here, don't like that part of space travel much. He finds someplace he can curl up and ride it out. He's al'ays hungry after we start off, ain't ya boy?"

As if in answer, Hitler cooed imploringly and looked at his master with an expression of fondness, if one could say a skeen was fond of anything.

"I'm gonna git him one o' his rats t' eat. Be right back."

Amalek nodded his understanding as he scanned the controls and noted the changes brought on by warp speed. He barely noticed Regen's return to the flight deck.

"Ain't much t' see while we're in cruise at warp speed. Ya wanna take a nap, or sumthin?"

"No, I think I'll just stay here and pretend I'm flying this thing."

"Suit yourself, I'm goin' t' bed for a while." Regen stretched and yawned and headed for the cabin.

Amalek took an extended tour of the ship while Regen slept. It was a standard interplanetary system freighter in all respects but the stealth gear. It was an ideal ship for a smuggler, since they usually hauled small amounts of high value cargo. Both holds were full, and one held the live food for Hitler. He remembered he hadn't seen Hitler since they went into warp drive, and wondered how the skeen would react to him without Regen. He hadn't long to wait for an answer. The half rat-half lizard noticed him entering the food hold and quickly entered behind him. He rubbed against Amalek's legs like a cat wanting milk and cooed in a pleading manner.

"Well, looks like you're a friend of anybody who can open a cage." Amalek smiled down on the evil-looking thing and reached for a cage. His father's men managed to catch enough of the desert mice to fill Regen's cages. Amalek knew these rodents were more kangaroo than mouse, and he was curious about Hitler's ability to run them down. He lifted one of the cages and dumped the poor creature on the deck. It leaped away, clearing almost a meter with each leap. Hitler sped after it with more agility than Amalek expected and caught the animal before it could gain the cover of the weapons crates.

"You are a fast one, aren't you?" Amalek said, but Hitler was too busy consuming his treat to pay any attention to his benefactor.

Regen emerged from the cabin two hours later and found Amalek asleep in a command chair. He checked the instruments and found all in order before sitting down himself. Hitler immediately jumped into his lap and curled up in a ball.

"Ain't you hungry?" Regen asked, but Hitler only closed his eyes and went to sleep savoring the warmth of his master's body.

"Well, I aint' never seen you go this long without a treat, but you can take it easy for a while."

Regen took the chip Mulinor gave him and placed it in the communications unit. He played it back using the headphones so as not to arouse Amalek or Hitler. A middle-aged man in laser armor appeared on the screen and began to speak.

"I am Baddek, chief assistant for weapons to Princess Orianne. If you manage to make it through the defense system, you will need the navigation information on this chip to find your landing site. Use the coded message contained on the chip to contact me before you enter any orbit. I will prepare the landing site and send instructions to your ship for a direct reentry. I will also make sure there are no atmospheric interceptors in the area. At the next screen, connect this chip to your navigation system. When the handoff is made successfully, the options will be activated. Good luck."

The screen changed to a menu showing the options Baddek described, and Regen turned the unit off. Amalek stirred beside him.

"On, hi, Regen. Time to eat yet?"

"We just had lunch three hours back. You hungry already?"

Amalek stood up and stretched. "Not really, I guess I'm just bored. Maybe I'll get something to eat?"

"You kin gain ten pounds on a trip like this unless ya find sumthin' t' do. I use the exercise gear and watch movies a lot. We got a good selection o' movies – anything ya want. I used t' teach Hitler tricks, but I got tired o' that. 'Sides, he knows 'em all now anyway."

"What can *he* do?" Amalek gave the creature in Regen's lap a curious look.

"Oh, he kin sit up, beg, roll over, fetch, heel, and bite off fingers."

"Bite off fingers?"

"Yeah, that's a good way to take care o' wise guys in bars. I even taught him t' act like a god once."

"How good's his nose?"

"He's got a great nose. He can smell out a rat a kilometer away and blood at more n' that. He's like a shark when it comes t' blood."

Amalek rubbed his chin and thought for a moment.

"Maybe I could teach nim some things to pass the time?"

"You could try, but y' gotta have treats for 'im for rewards."

"We don't have that many desert rats aboard. Will he take anything else?"

"I use the fish pellets for the food synthesizer. He likes them 'bout as much as rats, and they ain't nearly as messy. I don't know how many we got left. Yer Daddy couldn't get me any t' replenish my stock."

"I'll check it out. By the way, I gave Hitler a rat while you were asleep."

"I thought it was funny he didn't want no food when I woke

up. Thanks."

Amalek went to the storage area for the food synthesizer and found the fish pellets. There were only two bags left in the box, but he calculated the number of pellets would be sufficient to get him through the voyage and help Hitler learn some new tricks. He took one bag back to the command deck.

Hitler was still asleep on Regen's lap while the Bremen was busy reading a book on one of the display screens.

"Do we have any explosives on the ship, Regen?" Amalek asked.

"Sure, we got any kind ya want – why?"

"I thought I'd teach Hitler to sniff out explosives. That could prove useful for this business and also for your smuggling operations later on."

"Sounds good t' me. Have at it."

Over the rest of the voyage, Amalek taught Hitler to find everykind of explosive they had on the ship. He even taught him a different pointing pose for each kind of explosive. Regen was amazed at the accomplishment.

"I knew he was smart, but I never gave him credit for that much brains. Pretty impressive."

"I've known dogs to take more time than Hitler required. He's a quick learner alright. The only problem is, I used up all the fish pellets training him."

"Don't worry 'bout that. We'll git more on Bardour if we can. If not, we'll just have t' do without fish on the way home. No big deal t' me."

"How close are we to Bardour now?" Amalek asked as he scanned the navigation display trying to make sense of the information.

"'Bout where I need t' send some kind o' signal for landin' coordinates. I got Mulinor's chip here, but I think I want t' double check it 'gainst what Orianne used when I dropped her off."

"Orianne? You mean *the* Princess Orianne? The one in command of the rebels?"

"That's th' one."

"You never told us you knew her."

"I didn't think you guys needed t' know. I dropped her off here afore I came t' Terma. I think I still got her stuff in the navigation memory."

Regen busied himself with the keyboard and the navigation display and soon found what he was looking for.

"Here 'tis – even still got the code software. I'll check it 'gainst the stuff on Mulinor's chip."

Regen called up the same information from the Mulinor chip and found there was a considerable difference in the code structure.

"Well, this new stuff sure ain't anything like Orianne's."

Amalek looked at the comparison. "I imagine they change their codes quite often. How old is the Orianne stuff?"

"Several months now, but she said it was a personal code 'tween her and one o' her most trusted buddies. I think I'll try her code first an' see what I git."

"Regen, the royal forces could be monitoring any of the old codes. You'll give yourself away."

"The way I see it, there's only two possibilities – they either can see me comin' in, or they can't. If they can see me, it's all over with from the start. If they can't, a communications transmission won't make no difference anyway."

"You'll give up any element of surprise. It may help if they can spot us, but it'd also be handy if they can't."

"I don't know why I don't trust Mulinor's contact, but I don't. It's just a strong feelin' in the back o' my skull. I know I kin trust Orianne. I'm gonna try her first."

"You're in command. I'll go along with whatever you want."

"Good man! Here goes."

Regen called up the Orianne code software and transmitted his message. Amalek sat poised on the edge of his command chair waiting for the console to come alive with various threats from the Bardour defense system, but the only response was the image of a lovely black-haird, blue-eyed woman with a puzzled expression.

"Who's using this code?" she demanded.

Regen turned on his camera and replied. "Just me darlin', Regen."

"Regen! What are you doing here?"

"Got a load o' goodies for ya. My guy named Mulinor set up the deal with your guy named Baddek, but I didn't trust the setup, so I called you t' verify it's all legit."

"It's all right. Baddek is a trusted member of my staff. You can follow his directions safely."

"Okay, I'll prob'ly be landin' in a few hours."

"We can't shut down the defense system for you this time. Our man in the defense center was arrested and shot."

"No problem, m'love. See ya in a while."

Regen signed off and placed Baddek's chip in the unit. He followed its instructions and was soon on his way to penetrating the Bardour system.

"I hope yer dohickey works," Regen said to Amalek.

"It's the best hope we got. I'll check it out." Amalek ran the system through its checklist and pronounced it ready for use.

"Here goes." Regen turned on the stealth device and watched for signs of their detection by the Bardourians.

CHAPTER 14

Amalek followed the ship's progress as the first warning lights came on signaling search radars and lasers were painting them. They tensed waiting for the missile warning tones, but none came.

"Let's hope they ain't got good passive systems." Regen voiced his concern, but there was no indication of any alert in the defense system.

"If he's taking us straight in, we'll make a helluva splash on re-entry," Amalek said.

"Yep, they'll see that allright, but there ain't nothing' we kin do about it. Brace yerself, here it comes."

The men buckled into their command chairs and watched as the space around them came back into view during the shift from warp speed to normal realms. They felt the shock of the ship entering the atmosphere. At that point Regen took over with manual controls following the guidance of his navigation display. The ship landed in a mountain valley, but just as it touched down, a jolt of energy shook the very ground they rested on.

"What was that?" Amalek almost shouted.

Regen only smiled and unbuckled his harness. "That, my friend, was a meteor strike. That's how they covered our re-entry signature. They set off some underground charges t' make it look like a meteor hit here."

"Won't that bring a bunch of scientists looking for it?"

"In the middle o' rebel country? You gotta be kiddin'."

The men checked the exterior cameras and saw a body of armed men approaching the ship.

"I hope those are the rebels," Amalek said.

Regen zoomed in on the group and recognized Baddek at once. "Yep, those are the ones we're lookin' for."

Regen left his seat as Hitler scurried around the doorway and skidded to a stop at his side. "Come on! We need t' see where they want this big hunk o' stuff."

He led Amalek to the entry port and lowered the ramp to the surface. They faced several laser rifles and men with stern faces. Baddek stepped forward.

"I assume you are the Regen Mulinor told me about?" he asked.

"Yup, nice touch settin' off them explosives underground."

Baddek stepped forward and offered his hand as the other men lowered their weapons. Regen took it in a firm grip and felt the vise-like pressure in return just as Hitler ran from behind his master and bolted for the forest.

Several rifles raised and were about to fire when Regen shouted. "Don't shoot, he's a pet."

Baddek raised a hand in the air, and the men dropped their bead on the skeen.

"We got rid of all our skeens years ago, but some of my men remember them. I'll get the word out not to shoot yours. Unless, that is, it's a female."

"Nope, he's male, and he only wants t' hunt any kind o' rat you got 'round these parts."

"He'll find plenty of good hunting in that." Baddek pointed to the thick undergrowth beneath the tall pine trees.

"Where do ya want me t' put my ship?" Regen asked.

"There's a hangar over there where we can hide you from

the satellites." Baddek pointed to a sheer cliff face, which opened as he spoke. "Better get you in there. The next bird's due over in ten minutes."

Once the ship was safely inside and the doors closed, Baddek joined Regen and Amalek on the command deck.

"Here's th' invoice o' what we brung ya." Regen handed him a data stick, and Baddek immediately plugged it into a device he pulled from a pocket in his armor.

"Hmmm. Not as much as I'd hoped for." Baddek's face took on a disappointed look.

"We had t' bribe a few more people than we figured on. We'll adjust th' price accordin'ly."

"I'll calculate a new figure." Baddek made some entries into his device and smiled. "I get 32 million. How about you?"

Regen worked a moment at his keypad then shrugged his shoulders. "I figur' it at 34, but I'll split the differ'nce with ya."

"33 million it is, then. You'll have to take a data card and transfer the funds once you're outside the Bardour defense system. They've got all financial channels blocked for us."

Baddek took a small plastic card from his belt and inserted it into his computer. After a few commands, he presented it to Regen. The Bremen verified the amount with his machine and nodded his approval.

"Good! My men will begin unloading at once. Come, I'll take you to Orianne. I know she wants to see you right away. By the way, what is this 'hashinah' on the cargo list?"

"Oh, I almost fergot 'bout that stuff. We used it t' fool the army back on Terma, but it's purdy good stuff."

"Is it a drug?"

"Yup, the Bedouins back on Terma smoke the stuff in water pipes. They claim it's better'n alcohol. You guys got any use fer it here?"

"Could be, what's the price?"

"I owe the chief back home 6 credits a kilo. You can have it fer that far as I'm concerned. I don't need t' make no profit on it."

"Done, I'll take the whole lot and pay you with my personal account."

"You got it," Regen said noticing the broad smile on Baddek's face as he anticipated a tidy profit from the hashinah.

"I'll take you to the Princess now," Baddek said indicating the way with a wave of his arm.

Baddek led Regen through a series of tunnels to a door guarded by two soldiers. He opened it and motioned for Regen to enter. Inside, Regen saw a busy command center with displays on each wall and men and women busy at computer consoles. Orianne stood with two men before a large map display. One of the men was pointing to red and blue marks on the map and talking heatedly. As they got closer, Regen overheard the discussion.

"Your Highness, our troops in this sector are being slaughtered by Royal armored columns. We need more anti-tank missiles immediately."

"And I got 'em," Regen said as he came up behind Orianne and placed his arms around her shoulders.

"Regen!" Orianne shouted as she turned and kissed him passionately.

The Generals were somewhat taken aback by the display of affection, but they waited patiently for the embrace to end.

Orianne pushed Regen back to arms length and her face sobered. "How many?"

"How many what?" Regen said as he regained his composure.

"Anti-tank missiles!"

Baddek consulted his palm computer and answered for Regen. "Two hundred, Highness."

"Great! Send a hundred to the Tullega front immediately." She turned to the General. "Will that help?"

"Yes, Highness. It's just what they need."

"Good! Then we are finished with this discussion." She dismissed the Generals with a wave of her hand and turned back to Regen. She took his arm and led him toward a door leaving Baddek and Amalek standing alone and perplexed.

"Regen, I'm so glad to see you. I was afraid you wouldn't get through after I talked to you. How did you do it?"

"I got hold of a new type o' cloakin' system, and it 'pears t' work real good. We didn't have no trouble at all, but . . ."

Orianne held a finger to her lips as she opened the door and pushed Regen inside. She closed the door behind her and locked it.

The room had no windows and very little furniture, outside of a large bed with silken sheets. She pushed him toward the bed.

"Make love now, talk later," she said as she began to undo her clothes.

Regen lay on the bed watching Orianne dress and marveled at his luck in finding not only a beautiful woman but also a princess.

"How do ya find time to run a revolution and make love at th' same time?" he asked.

"I make time for what I want to do. My people know to leave me alone when I enter this room and close the door. Usually, I'm asleep, but I think they all guessed what I was up to this time."

Regen shifted his feet to the floor and found his own clothes.

"How's th' revolution goin'?"

"We control over three fourths of the planet, but not the important three fourths. The crown still hangs on to the capitol and most of the industrial base. We need anti-tank and anti-aircraft missiles to make any assault on their main defenses. You've brought us enough to start with, but we'll need three or four times that to win."

Regen pulled on his trousers and launched a search for his tunic. "If you got th' money, I can git ya all ya want o' both."

"Money isn't really a problem. We've got plenty of financial support. You just get the stuff to me."

"With this new stealth device, looks like I can breeze through the defense system. It does take two weeks for the round trip, though."

"One more shipment and we'll be able to attack the defense system headquarters. If we can get that, they'll have to rely on the auxiliary command center on the moon. Your ship could take enough of my men up there to capture that facility, and you'd be free to come and go as you wish."

Regen finished dressing as Orianne was about ready to go out the door. He followed her into the busy command center where she was immediately accosted by a senior officer.

"Highness, we have bad news. The missiles did not work. They failed to track to their targets."

Orianne turned to Regen with a black expression. "What's this all about, Regen?"

"Hey, those missiles were supposedly checked out and workin'. Beats me."

Amalek joined the group. "Let's inspect the rest of them now. If there's something wrong, maybe we can repair them here. Can you give us a few hours, Highness?"

"I'll give you two hours to find out whats going on. I expect a full report then.   Until we settle this, I'm revoking the payment."

Regen expected to see steam rising from Orianne's head as she stalked off to attend to another subordinate's problem.

Amalek found the missiles in one of the many storage caves and uncrated one.

"Funny, this crate's been opened," he said.

"How can ya tell?" Regen asked.

Amalek pointed to a broken seal along one edge of the cover.   "The seal's broken.   All of them were sealed by the munitions ministry back on Terma when we got them. Someone's been at them since they were unloaded."

"Looks like Her Highness's got a saboteur 'round here.   Can you check 'em out?"

"I don't have a test set, but they've got some built-in test software."   Amalek turned on the unit and ran it through its paces.

"No problems here.   It checks out okay."

"They ain't been 'round here very long.   Whatever they did, it'd have t' be quick."

Amalek rubbed his chin and pondered the problem a moment before snapping his fingers.

"That's it.   It has to be."   He turned the missile over revealing one spot where a wire bundle was exposed.   He felt the wires carefully, then his eyes lit up with satisfaction.

"Here it is."   He pulled a small steel pin from one of the wires and held it up for Regen's perusal.

"That's it?" Regen said.

"I'll check some of these others to make sure, but this could do the job, and it could be done very quickly."

The next three missiles had the same problem, and the seals on all the cartons were broken.   Amalek grabbed one of the weapons technicians and instructed him on what to look for before he and Regen returned to the command center.

Orianne was with Baddek going over a tactical situation on a large wall map as Regen and Amalek approached.

"We got yer problem solved, Darlin'" Regen announced as Baddek and several of the other officers present recoiled at his choice of words in addressing their leader.

Orianne raised a hand to calm their concerns and turned to Regen.

"What did you find out?"

"You got a saboteur in yer midst. Them missiles had been tampered with."

Amalek stepped forward. "Highness, a pin like this one was shorting a wire critical to the target acquisition system. It wouldn't show up on the ususal checkouts. The person who did this must have a pretty thorough knowledge of the system." He presented the pin to Orianne.

The princess studied the pin for a moment then pushed a button on a console.

"Yes, Highness," a stern voice answered.

"Magan, someone sabotaged those missiles Regen brought in today. I want every man who even touched them interrogated. It was a pretty sophisticated job, so they had to know something about them. Call me directly if you find anything."

"Yes, Highness."

Baddek spoke. "Highness, those missiles are AZ-85s. They're very common around the galaxy. We must have a hundred men around this headquarters who are familiar with them."

"Then we'll interrogate every one of them. I want that spy found." She turned to Regen. "Take off as soon as you can, and bring me another load. You can save hundreds of lives with your shipments. I'll transfer your funds immediately. Is there anything you need?"

Amalek broke in. "If you have any fish pellets for our food synthesizer, we could use a case."

Orianne turned to Baddek. "Take care of it, Baddek. I want Regen on his way immediately."

"As soon as I can find the pellets, Highness." Baddek bowed and left the room.

Orianne moved to Regen and kissed him gently on one cheek. "I'm sorry I doubted you, but I'll make it up to you on your next trip," she whispered before pulling back to arm's length. "Come back as soon as you can, Regen." She offered her hand, and Regen kissed it tenderly.

"I'll hurry back for you, *Yer Highness.*" His voice had a mocking tone, but the nearby officers were already used to his brash manner.

At the hangar, they checked out Regen's ship. It was refueled and ready, and Baddek was just coming up carrying a case marked as fish pellets.

"You're lucky," he said. "This is our last one."

Amalek took the case as Baddek said his goodbyes.

"Is there any way outa this hangar 'sides the big doors?" Regen asked.

"Yes, there's a small door over there." Baddek pointed to a normal entrance to the right of the big doors. "Why?"

"I gotta git Hitler. He's still out in th' woods." Regen moved to the door and went outside. He blew Hitler's whistle and was relieved to see the skeen running out of the underbrush. It ran up to its master carrying a small snake in his mouth.

"Well, I 'preciates yer gift, but we gotta git goin'." He took the snake and threw it back into the bushes, much to Hitler's dismay.

Regen walked back toward his ship where Amalek was waiting on the ramp next to the box of fish pellets. As he got closer, Hitler bolted toward the box and assumed a rigid pose with one forepaw lifted in a pointing position.

"What th' hell is that all about?" Regen asked an astonished Amalek.

"If he's doing what I taught him, it means that box is full of Quantex," Amalek answered.

"What? Are you sure?"

"I'll tell you one thing. I'm not about to mess with it any more until the bomb squad boys say its okay." Amalek backed away from the box, but Hitler stayed focused.

"Can't ya call him off?" Regen asked.

"Sure, sure, down Hitler," Amalek commanded, and the skeen returned to his master's side.

Regen grabbed a nearby sergeant. "Call the bomb squad n tell 'em we got a suspicious package here."

The sergeant gave the Bremen a quizzical look, but he did as he was told.

A small truck arrived within five minutes, and two men approached Regen.

"I'm Sergeant Millis, what's this about a bomb?"

"Well, we think there may be some Quantex in that there box." Regen pointed to the fish pellet carton.

The noncom looked at the box and back to Regen. "What makes you think that?"

"Hitler, here, sniffed it out."

The man hadn't noticed the skeen before, but he recoiled from the pet out of instinct.

"Holy shit!"

"Don't git yer shorts in a knot. He's tame. Amalek, here, taught him how t' smell out 'splosives, and he pointed this box like a bird dog. I think y'd better check it out."

"Now, I've heard of dogs sniffing out explosives, but a skeen? Are you trying to tell me that thing can smell?"

"His nose is better'n any dog's, an' he kin take any dog you got with one claw tied 'hind his back. Now git busy checkin' out that box!" Regen's tone was forceful enough to make the Sergeant respond automatically. He lifted the box and placed it in the back of the truck.

"We'll know in a second of two about the Quantex," the Sergeant said. "This chamber sniffs that stuff out pretty quickly. Interesting that they put the stuff in with fish pellets."

"Why's that?" Amalek asked.

"The smell of the pellets throws off dogs. Whoever did this is a pretty smart cookie. If there really is Quantex in that box, your skeen's got one helluva nose."

Red lights began to blink furiously on the truck's console, and the Sergeant shook his head in disbelief before shutting it down.

"Find somethin'?" Regen asked with a satisfied smile on his face.

"Your skeen was right. There's enough Quantex in that box to blow this whole hangar to smithereens."

"It wasn't very heavy," Amalek said.

"That's the beauty of Quantex," the Sergeant replied. "It doesn't take much to do a whole lot of damage. I'll take care of this bomb and make my report to the command center. Just sign here."

He produced a device from his belt, and Regen used the stylus to sign.

"I'd better let the Princess know 'bout this," Regen said. He turned to Amalek. "While I'm gone, take Hitler 'round th' ship an' let him sniff anything they brought aboard here."

"Sure thing," Amalek responded.

"We'll wait around, just in case," the Sergeant added.

Regen made his way back to the command center, but the guards stopped him at the door.

"Only cleared people allowed in there, sir," one said.

"You tell th' Princess that Regen's out here. She'll wanna see me."

The guard spoke into an intercom box and seemed to be a bit startled by the response.

"Go on in, sir. The Princess will see you."

"I thought she would," Regen said as he pushed his way past the guards and into the room. Orianne was waiting for him.

"I thought you were on your way home. What's this all about?"

Regen took her by one arm and steered her toward the private room.

"I got somethin' we need t' talk about."

"Regen, I don't have time for that right now."

"This is real important. It'll only take a minute."

They entered the boudoir, and Regen closed the door. He glanced around the room.

"You sure this place ain't bugged?" he asked.

"They sweep it every day. What's so important you had to drag me in here?"

"I think yer man Baddek is a spy."

"You can't be serious. Baddek's been with me from the beginning. He gave up a title and a family fortune to be part of our rebellion. I'd trust him with my life."

"I'd think twice 'fore I actually did that. He just tried t' plant a bomb on my ship."

Orianne looked at Regen with unbelieving eyes. She moved to a communications console.

"This is Princess Orianne. Did the bomb squad find a bomb on Regen's ship?"

There was a slight delay before the voice on the other end responded.

"Yes, your Highness, they reported a sizeable quantity of Quantex hidden in a food pellet box. We're checking for clues now."

"Let me know personally when you find anything." She punched the device off.

"The stuff was hid in a box o' fish pellets Baddek brought to the ship. If you remember, he said he'd take care o' th' fish pellets personally."

"That doesn't prove anything. Several people in the command center heard you ask for the pellets. The explosives could have been planted by anybody before Baddek picked up the box."

"I ain't got time t' stick around for no big investigation. I recommend you check him out real good 'fore ya think about any big offensives. I'll leave the police work t' you. I gotta git goin'." Regen kissed her and left for his ship before any more bombs could materialize.

Amalek met him at the ship. "No more bombs. At least none that Hitler could find. We're loaded and ready to go."

"Let's git goin' 'fore they can plant any more."

The hangar doors opened, and Regen piloted his ship into the morning sky. They kept a close eye out for atmospheric interceptors, but none materialized.

"Guess they figur' Baddek's bomb'll do the job," Regen offered.

"Good thing. We don't have any defense against an

interceptor attack."

The ship made initial orbit safely and escaped the Bardour system in spite of the numerous radar hits recorded by the sensors. The stealth system was doing its job. Once they were safely on their way back to Terma, Regen broached what he thought might be a sensitive subject with Amalek.

"You suppose your Daddy'd let us use his helmet gizmo on our next trip to Bardour?"

"I don't see why not. He keeps a pretty close eye on it, but I'm sure he'd trust me with it."

"Do you know how t' use it?"

"Not as well as he does, but if you're thinking about using it on Baddek, I could tell you if he's a spy or not."

"Good, you talk to him once we git back. I don't think the Princess believed he was a bad guy, and she'll need positive proof t' get rid of him."

Regen pulled Baddek's card from his tunic and inserted it into the communicator slot.

"Better see if'n their credit's any good 'fore we goes much farther." He punched in several commands and watched as the display changed to reflect a new total in his account.

"Yup! He wasn't lyin'. The money's in my account now, and I'll split up with everybody when we get there. Your share's two and a half million, and your Daddy gits one and a quarter. Another one and a quarter for the Rugistani boys, and that leaves 20 million for me 'n Mulinor t' split. Not a bad haul fer one run."

Amalek smiled and relaxed in his command chair. "What do you figure, Regen—three more runs, maybe four?"

"Depends on what kind o' deal she gits from her other allies once the Bardour defense system's in her hands. She may not like our price after that."

"Can't we rely on your 'special' friendship with her?" Amalek's smile turned from greed to lechery, and he winked at Regen.

"Don't git yer hopes up on that account. Once she see's she can do without my help, she'll want some royal asshole 'stead o' me. I don't think I'd fit in with polite society on Bardour real well."

"She could make you a Duke, or something, couldn't she?"

"She won't do that. I'll be on my way after we finish this job."

"Back to the Velvet Saddle?"

"Don't know. I'm beginnin' t' get tired o' that too. I'd like t' quit runnin' 'round some day, but who knows when that'll be."

"You've got your pick of the whores plus Mariva back on Terma, and money's no problem for you now."

"I know, I oughtta be in hog heaven, but somehow I just cain't git used t' settlin' down. I al'ays loved th' hunt more'n th' kill, I guess. I was 'bout ready to pull out when Mulinor and this caper came up. Runnin' that Bardour system was th' most fun I've had in a long time."

"I guess you're doomed to die with your boots on."

"Looks that way, don't it? Hey, we'd better git our order in t' Mulinor so's he can have the stuff ready t' load when we git back. You got the card?"

Amalek produced a data card and inserted it in the communications console. He punched up Mulinor's contact information, and the familiar face soon appeared on the screen.

"Good to see you, Amalek. I assume you made the delivery."

"No problems at all except for a small bomb someone put aboard to blow us up on the way back. Thanks to Hitler, we were able to find it before we left."

"Hitler? You mean Regen's skeen?"

"Yeah, Favik, he smelled it out, thanks t' Amalek's trainin'," Regen said.

"Whatever it was, I'm glad were still in business. How much did you get for the load?"

"They beat me down t' 33 million, but that's still a tidy sum fer ever'body. You ready t' buy the next batch?"

"Just send me your list and transfer about ten million to my account for the buy."

"Here's the list," Amalek said as he transmitted the data on the card.

"Got it. What about the money?" Mulinor said.

"I'll do that soon as we're finished," Regen assured him.

"Okay, see you back here in a week." Mulinor signed off, and Regen handled the money transfer.

"Nothin' t' do now 'til we git back t' Terma." Regen reclined his command chair and closed his eyes for a nap, but Hitler jumped up on his stomach.

"Ooofff! Don't tell me yer hungry?" Regen protested, but the skeen only looked at him with pleading eyes and cooed softly.

"Let Amalek feed ya whilst I gits a nap. Git down!" Regen pushed the skeen off and looked at Amalek for his acquiescence.

"Okay, come on, Hitler," Amalek called as he led the skeen to the hold area containing the cages for his furry snacks.

Once inside the hold, Hitler went straight for the old fish pellet box, but it was empty. He stuck his head inside and rummaged around for a moment before looking back at Amalek with a puzzled expression.

"They're all gone, boy, and the ones Baddek brought had a bomb in with them. I thought you preferred your animals anyway."

Hitler gave the box a disappointed kick and moved to Amalek's side. Soon, a small creature was running for its life with Hitler in hot pursuit.

Amalek returned to the command center to find Regen sound asleep. He decided to nap himself.

Only an hour later, the alarm claxon awakened Regen and Amalek with its insistent and raucous blare.

"What th' hell?" Regen said as he scanned the displays for an indication of the problem.

"There it is," Amalek said pointing to the navigation console.

Regen turned to the display and moaned.

"Damn, seems like that bomb weren't th' only thing Baddek screwed around with. We're so lost it ain't funny."

Amalek punched in some commands and whistled sharply.

"You're not kidding. We're in a sector of the galaxy that isn't even on the charts, and we lost the last navigation signal a few minutes back. That's why you got the alarm. When this system goes one minute without a signal at warp speed, it shuts down and drops the bird to sub-light speed automatically."

"Well, th' system oughtta tell us how to git back t' civilization." Regen punched in commands and sat back in disgust. "That Baddek's a real smart cookie. He loaded up our memory banks with junk an' left just enough t' get us lost good an' proper. The computer don't have any idea where we came from or how to get back there. We're so far out in the boondocks there ain't even any familiar star patterns."

"There's got to be some intelligent life around here somewhere," Amalek said as he worked the console at surprising speed.

"Hey, you know this stuff pretty good for a mechanic,"

Regen complimented him.

"This particular model was one of my specialties." Amalek worked for several minutes before sighing in disgust. "Nothing, not even an old television station. This part of the galaxy is as barren as Caranis."

"Well, our only hope is t' find someplace that might have somebody with a good telescope. They might have some pictures that'll give us some stars we'd recognize. Check for human life planets."

Amalek turned to a different console and began a search for life supporting planets.

"Here's one. It's only a couple of AU from here, too."

Regen checked the fuel reserves. "We got 'nuf fuel t' git there and maybe still have 'nuf t' git home if we ain't too far out. Let's try it."

A few more commands put the ship on course for the planet representing their only hope of salvation.

In less than an hour, they were close enough for a scan of their destination.

"Hmmm, no radio or radar signals, and the infra red don't show no big cities. Looks like it's pretty primitive. Sensors do show human life all right, an' lots of it."

Regen projected an image of the planet on the main screen. It was the usual human inhabited world, large oceans and polar ice caps, but the land was composed of thousands of islands clustering within thirty degrees of the equator. Some of them were quite large, but most covered less than 5,000 square kilometers.

"Let's take a closer look at that one," Amalek pointed to a medium-sized island which showed up well in the infrared image.

Regen put the ship into a low orbit and caught a much more detailed image in the second pass.

"Yeah, that'un looks promisin'. Th' only thing is, how will those folks react to a spaceship?"

"Let's land here, away from the city." Amalek pointed to a clearing in the middle of what appeared to be jungle. "We can check them out and make contact on our terms if it looks like they're civilized enough to help us."

"Okay, sounds good t' me. Here we go."

CHAPTER 15

The ship came to rest in a clearing surrounded by lush green vegetation. As the boarding ramp touched the ground, Hitler streaked off after a small animal resembling a chipmunk. Regen and Amalek had barely reached the ground when a group of armed men appeared from the jungle. The pair halted at the bottom of the ramp, and Regen turned to Amalek.

"I think we'd better put our hands up and not make any sudden moves. These guys look like they mean business."

Amalek nodded his agreement, and the men assumed a surrender pose.

"Hey, take it easy. We don't mean nobody no harm." Regen smiled his warmest smile, but the grim-faced men dressed in green camouflage togas held their weapons at the ready and stared at him. They were normal-looking humans with bronzed skin and dark hair and eyes. Their weapons looked modern, which surprised Regen since the planet showed no sign of radio or radar signals and no indication of electrical power generation. He tried again.

"It's just us two an' Hitler, here." The skeen returned to his master's side with his kill, oblivious to any danger. "We're lost. Soon as we can find out where we are we'll be outa here. We come in peace."

Regen scolded himself for the last remark. He couldn't believe he could be so corny. A gray haired woman in a white toga trimmed in maroon emerged from the jungle and approached Regen. She was unarmed, but she walked with an erect posture and exuded authority. As she got closer, he could see the beginnings of age lines around her eyes and mouth, but she was still a very attractive woman.

"I see you speak Bremen. Can you understand me?" she said.

The accent was heavy, but Regen had no trouble understanding her words.

"How come you know Bremen?" Regen asked.

"We study the languages of the inner galaxy since we sometimes get stray travelers here. You may put your hands down now. They won't shoot unless I order them to. What brings you to Phoenicia?"

Regen was happy to lower his arms before they began to cramp. "Our navigation system went on the fritz, and it landed us in this part of the galaxy. I couldn't find any navigation signals, so I decided to land someplace to try an' get help."

"Did you repair your navigation system?"

"Nope, just re-booted it, but it's lost all its memory and can't do Warp speed til' it's fixed. I need somebody who knows sumthin' 'bout a NAV-438B and a course for civilization. Can you be of any help?"

"I think we can help you out. If you will come with us, we will see if our people in the capital can be of assistance. By the way, what kind of creature is that thing behind you?"

Regen turned to see Hitler tearing apart his victim. "Oh him? That's Hitler, he's my pet skeen."

"I've never seen anything like him. May I touch him?"

The woman reached for Hitler, but Regen grabbed her arm. "I wouldn't do that. He likes fingers real good."

The click of laser rifle actions caused Regen to look up into the barrels of several weapons.   He quickly released the woman's arm.   She waved a hand toward her men, and the rifles returned to the ready position.

"My name is Herion. I am the chief warden of this game preserve." She extended her right hand toward Regen. He took it in a gentler grip than normal out of respect for her age.

"Regen's my name, and I already told ya 'bout Hitler." He pointed to Amalek. "this here's Amalek. He's travlin' with me. By the way, can Hitler hunt 'round here?"

Herion surveyed the skeen as if trying to estimate how many animals the thing could kill in a day's time.

"We have a rodent we call a runiga that is particularly troublesome this time of year. I don't suppose your pet would cause too much damage for the short time you will be here, and it appears to like them." She pointed toward Hitler.

Regen turned to see Hitler swallowing the last of his kill before lapping up the blood on the ramp deck.

"Come this way, Regen, Amalek. We will go to my headquarters and have something to eat and drink while we wait on the Supreme Council's decision." Herion walked back toward the jungle, and the armed rangers fell in on either side of Regen and Amalek after searching them for weapons and finding none.

As they walked toward the jungle, Amalek spoke. "Do you trust this woman?"

"I think we're okay. Did you notice those rifles?"

"Yes, they're modern weapons, and if she knows Bremen, they're a lot more advanced than we figured."

"I don't know what's goin' on 'round here, but at least they ain't surprised t' see us, and I don't s'pose they's cannibals."

They walked for about a half hour along a narrow trail before coming to a group of huts in a large clearing. They were made of what looked like bamboo and had roofs thatched with palm leaves. The sides were open, and the floors were elevated about a meter above ground level. Herion led them to the large hut in the center of the complex.

As they walked up the steps to floor level, Regen was surprised by the scene before him. Men in various colored togas sat at low-level desks working with what could only be computers. Communication devices stuck in their right ear looked just like ancient cell phones. A young man in a beige toga greeted Herion. Regen could not understand their conversation, but Herion turned to them when it ended.

"This is Apalon, my secretary," Herion said. The boy bowed toward Regen then to Amalek, and the men returned the greeting in kind. "He tells me the Supreme Council wishes you to leave as soon as your navigation system is repaired. They're sending out a team of technicians from the capitol now. In the meantime, you are to stay with us. Apalon has arranged a luncheon and something to drink in my office. This way, please."

Herion showed Regen and Amalek to a small partitioned-off area at the rear of the hut where a meal was laid out on a table no more than three inches off the floor. Pits on either side of the low table were lined with cushions, and Regen and Amalek lowered themselves into one side while Herion did the same on the other side.

Apalon poured a yellowish liquid from a glass pitcher into three crystal goblets and placed one in front of each of the diners.

"This is Tannalah, a brandy made from one of the sweeter fruits native to this island. I hope you will enjoy it." Herion raised her glass and Regen and Amalek followed suit. They both took a sip.

"Mmmm, this is good stuff. I'll have t' take a few bottles o' this with me when I go," Regen said.

"I'll see that they are provided. Shall we eat?"

Regen was not too sure about the ingredients in some of the dishes, but each had a delicate flavor. As they ate, he questioned Herion.

"I see your people usin' computers and communicators, but my ship's sensors didn't find any evidence o' electrical generation on this planet. How are they powered?"

"By batteries made from a local mineral and seawater. They produce a great deal of energy in a small package, and they are cheap to produce. You may have noticed we do not use electric illumination." Herion waved her hand around the room to indicate the absence of lighting.

"No, I hadn't, but now that you point it out, it does seem strange not t' have any lights."

"We use candles or oil lamps for illumination at night. We have no need for much light after sunset, and we wish the rest of the universe to believe we are simple, primitive folk. There are no resources here of any importance to your people, so we hope they will leave us alone."

"I've known people who would come here for nothing more than the joy of raping your women and listening to you scream while they tortured you," Amalek offered.

"They would have a surprise in store for them indeed. We are a peaceful people, but we are not defenseless."

"If you're talkin' 'bout those laser rifles yer men had, you wouldn't be much of a contest for most bad guys I know," Regen said.

Herion laughed. "We employ the weapon appropriate to the occasion. We suspected you were a trader or smuggler of some kind from our analysis of your ship, so we calculated you had only laser rifles and pistols at best. You did not see the men I had hidden in the bush with more potent weapons."

"Hey, this green stuff's pretty tasty. What's in it?" Amalek asked.

"I'm glad you like it. It's made from the testicles of a local lizard."

Amalek choked a bit but continued to wolf down the dish.

"Why is it a people as advanced as you are live in these huts?"

"They serve the purpose, and they are cool during the day. The temperature here climbs to over 300 of your degrees at noon, and it doesn't drop much lower than 295 in the evening."

Regen was taken aback by the numbers until he realized Herion was using absolute temperatures on the Kelvin scale.

After another glass of the Tannalah, they left the table and walked around the complex. Men and women were busy at the normal duties associated with a nature preserve. Strange birds with exotic plumage filled bamboo cages while monkeys of various sorts cavorted in a huge enclosure. Herion showed Regen a large crocodilian usually found along the seacoast, but she told him it often swam up the rivers to seek its prey. She said they called it a zilla, and it reminded Regen of the coya on Gobra.

They strolled to the beach, and Herion cautioned Regen and Amalek not to walk close to the water's edge.

"In the evening, the zilla patrol the shallows waiting for something to venture close to the water."

"The water's beautiful. Do you ever get to swim in it?" Amalek asked.

"During the heat of the day the zilla move out to the deeper water, and we can swim then."

The sun hung on the horizon for a moment, and the group

watched as it sank below the water, pushed down under the weight of beautiful pink and purple clouds. They walked back to the compound as the light from a full moon filtered down through the leaves of the jungle canopy.

Now a large bonfire in a central fire pit made from native stone illuminated the complex. Candles and oil lamps began to flicker on in the huts.

When the central fire was down to glowing coals, the people gathered round it to roast an assortment of meats, fish and vegetables on steel skewers. As they waited for their kabobs to cook, they sang some of the most beautiful songs Regen ever heard.

Another woman joined the group and Herion introduced her to Amalek.

"This is Tira. She will be your companion tonight Amalek. She speaks no Bremen, but she has expressed a wish to sleep with you tonight. I'm sure you will be able to communicate as much as needed for that purpose." Herion smiled at Amalek whose jaw dropped to his waistline.

"That's very accommodating of you. Is this normal for your people?" Amalek asked.

"We have no problems with casual sex here. We see it as merely something people can do for entertainment. If she doesn't please you, you may send her away. She will not be offended."

Amalek looked at the woman. There was nothing displeasing about her. Her features were fine and delicate, and her jet black hair hung in a soft curl at her bronze shoulders. Tender brown eyes sparkled in the firelight, and her full lips almost begged to be kissed.

"No, no, she's beautiful. I'm quite honored," Amalek responded.

"Good, then it's settled," Herion said.

"This place is a paradise, Herion. If the rest o' the galaxy knew how you lived, they'd be here at Warp 10," Regen said as he tested the meat on his skewer.

"That's why our ancestors chose this planet. It's so far off the beaten track, nobody bothers to investigate us."

"They chose this place?" Regen looked at Herion with suspicion.

"We are not the native peoples of this planet. Fortunately, we found no native people when we came here over 400 of your years ago. Life here had not evolved to that point yet. In fact, there are still large reptiles on some of the islands, and huge animals and fish populate the deep oceans."

"Where did you come from?" Regen put down his skewer to concentrate on Herion's story.

"From a planet now consumed by a dying sun. Look just above that tree, there. Do you see the bright star among the cluster of four making a diamond?"

Regen studied the sky and found the target. "Yeah, the very bright one?"

"That's it. Your ancestors only knew it by a number. We called our planet Terra, but we named this planet Phoenicia to remind us of our old homeland on Terra."

"If you made the trip from that star to here over 400 years back, you gotta be pretty advanced people."

"Our technology then was even more advanced than yours today, and we have continued to do research. We do not wish to be surprised by any would-be invaders."

"But, I didn't detect any kind o' radiation as I came up to yer planet." Regen popped a chunk of meat into his mouth and gave an approving "hmmm."

"Our surveillance and communication systems are based

upon entirely different principles of physics, and the concepts are our most closely guarded secrets."

Regen noticed the men and women beginning to pair off and melt into the darkness. "Wow! Free love really is part o' yer philosophy."

"You have to understand our culture, Regen. There is no marriage here, and as I explained to Amalek, people are free to couple as they see fit."

"Well, I can see where men'd like that, but most women I know want somethin' more permanent."

"We are a matriarchal society. The women own everything and run everything. They prefer that status to being someone's personal slave."

"And the men go along with that?"

Herion laughed merrily. "What man wouldn't love to live free of responsibility and commitment? I deduce that's how you live right now. That aspect of our society always amazes you people from the inner galaxy. We developed this style of living long, long ago. You see, before DNA it was impossible to say who someone's father was, but there was no doubt as to the mother. We held on to that system because we found it to be very successful. Our legal system recognizes inheritance only through the female line. If a woman has no daughters, she must leave her wealth to the closest female relative. Men own nothing here but the clothes on their backs and what money they can save from their salaries. They are not permitted to own property or businesses."

"Well I'll be damned," was all Regen could say.

"You might well have been if the Supreme Council had deemed you a threat. They must have found evidence you are harmless." Apalon appeared with a silver pot and four mugs. He poured them each a mug of a hot black liquid Regen assumed was some kind of coffee.

"I don't have no invasion plans, and I ain't no spy. I make my livin' smugglin' stuff people really want and can't get any other way." He took a drink of the brew and almost choked on the bitter liquid. Apalon handed him a glass of water, and Regen consumed most of it in one gulp. "Damn! That's strong stuff."

"Sip it, the flavor is a bit dark, but the aftertaste is wonderful." Herion raised her mug and saluted Regen with it before taking a dainty sip.

Regen followed suit and found the bitter taste only lasted a moment before a soft, warm feeling enveloped his palate.

"Tell me, if women run everything here, are they doing any better job than men would?"

"Well, we have no war, and have had none since our race arrived here. The history books say that war was a constant condition on Terra. The original settlers were determined to avoid war if at all possible. One reason they chose this planet was the absence of any aboriginal population. They were resolved to wipe out any natives they found, but always hoped they would not have to resort to such a drastic measure. Phoenicia proved to be ideal even if it will not support a large population."

"How many o' you are there now?"

"The last census showed a bit less than two billion, but we're nearing the capacity of the available land. Our scientists are working to create artificial land by shifting the planet's tectonic plates, but it will be several generations before they can produce anything useable."

"What do you do in the meantime?"

"That's an aspect of our society I'm not allowed to discuss with strangers."

Regen noticed a more sober expression on the woman's face and decided that subject was best left alone.

"So women run everything and there's no wars. What about religion? That subject's al'ays good for a war ever' now an' then."

"We only have one religion here. No others are allowed. We worship Astarte, the mother creator of all things."

"Figur's you'd have a female god too."

"It's getting late, Regen. Since Amalek has been provided for, would you like to join me in my hut for the evening?"

Regen surveyed the woman carefully. Though her hair was solid gray, her face showed only minor wrinkling. He could tell nothing of her figure because of the voluminous folds of her toga, but she held a certain unexplainable attraction for him, and he felt himself becoming aroused.

"Sure, I'd love to," he heard himself saying.

"Very good," she said and turned to Amalek. "Tira will take you to her hut. I will call for you in the morning. Goodnight Amalek."

"Goodnight, Herion," Amalek said as Tira took his arm and led him away.

"My hut is this way." Herion led him to a hut near the edge of the clearing, and he followed her up the steps to a room lit by a single oil lamp. Silken cushions lay scattered about the floor and around a table similar to the one in her office. A few items of furniture made from a nearly black wood dotted the edges of the floor space. She moved to a pile of cushions and with one deft move dropped her toga to the floor.

She had the figure of a woman half her age, and her bosoms were firm and high. She noticed Regen's reaction.

"Are you surprised by my body, Regen?"

"Either you're prematurely gray or you people hold up to

time and gravity a lot better'n we do."

"Our average life span is over 120 of this planet's years. I'm 64 and still a very viable woman. Come join me."

Herion lay down on the cushions and beckoned to Regen. The Breman stepped out of his clothes and joined her for one of the most memorable evenings in his life.

The next morning, he awakened to find Herion gone and a tray of fruit on the low table. He found the bathroom and dressed without shaving, since he could not locate anything that resembled a razor. As he finished eating, Herion appeared.

"Good morning, Regen. I trust you slept well?"

"I sure did, and yer breakfast was damn good too." He moved to embrace Herion, but she turned away quickly.

"We don't have time for that this morning. Your navigation system is repaired and a course to your previous destination has been locked in. My people have restocked your food supply, and we've even filled the food cages for your pet lizard."

"He ain't no lizard, he's a skeen," Regen protested.

"I'm sorry, your skeen. We used some runiga we trapped for experimentation purposes. He seems to be very fond of them. We found about a dozen half eaten carcasses around your ship."

"Yeah, sometimes he only eats part o' 'em an' leaves the rest to ripen a bit. I hope your rats don't smell too bad."

"It's the best we could do. I'll escort you to the ship." Herion motioned toward a group of armed rangers waiting on the ground below with Amalek.

"What if I want t' stay here for a while? Amalek's good enough to pilot the ship back where we came from, and I'd sure be happy t' spend some more time with you."

"I don't think you'd like the conditions for staying here,

Regen. Let's get going." Herion started to descend the steps to the ground.

"Wait a minute! Tell me what the conditions are. Maybe they ain't so bad."

Herion came back to Regen and lowered her voice. "You'd have to have a vasectomy, and your spaceship would be destroyed. We're a pure race, Regen, and we can't allow our bloodlines to be corrupted by outworlders or take the chance on you leaving to tell the rest of the galaxy about us. Besides, the Council probably wouldn't allow it anyway."

"The vasectomy part ain't so bad. I don't plan on havin' any kids anyway this late in my life. Can't we ask the Council if it's okay?"

"No, they've ordered you off the planet, and I don't think they'd change their minds on my recommendation. We'd better go."

"I'd sure like t' come back here and see ya ag'in, Herion. I'll be sure t' save the coordinates o' this planet."

"Don't mistake last night for anything more than casual sex, Regen. That bitter tasting drink was an aphrodisiac. Remember, the women of this planet aren't interested in long-term relationships with men until well into their 90s. It just isn't profitable. Shall we go?"

The procession moved to the ship where Hitler was waiting in a strong steel cage. Regen moved to his pet at once to inspect him for any damage. The skeen appeared to be unharmed and fully fed. Herion explained.

"We had to trap him to make sure he was aboard when you left. You can release him once you're in space. I've also put several bottles of Tannalah aboard, but I thought we ought to share a parting toast." She waved her hand, and a man stepped forward with a tray holding a pitcher and three wine glasses.

He poured Tannalah into the glasses, and Regen and Amalek each took one as the tray was offered to them. Herion took the remaining glass and raised it toward Regen.

"To a safe and profitable voyage," she said.

"I'll drink t' that," Regen said as he downed the contents of the glass in one gulp.

"Goodbye, Regen. I'm sorry you can't stay longer. I really enjoyed your company." Herion kissed him gently on both cheeks and stepped back before Regen could return the parting kisses. She did the same with Amalek.

"Goodbye, Herion. I'll be back." Regen carried Hitler's cage to the flight deck and Amalek closed the entrance ramp. Neither of them heard Herion say, "I don't think so," before popping a small pill into her mouth.

The men took seats at the control console, and Regen checked the navigation system.

"Well, well, these guys, or I should say gals, got the nav system all locked up. We only got one course in th' system'n that's it. Oh well, I just hope it'll git us home. Strap in."

Regen started the launch sequence, and the ship leaped skyward.

Once in space, Regen released Hitler who jumped on the control console and looked at his master with pleading eyes, at least as pleading as a skeen could muster.

"Okay, I'll git ya a rat." He turned to Amalek. "Keep an eye on things whilst I feeds Hitler" Regen moved to the cargo hold and released one of the runiga for Hitler to pursue. He suddenly felt the urge to lie down and moved back to the control center to find Amalek snoring loudly. He checked the controls and navigation system before falling on his bunk sound asleep.

Regen awoke with a splitting headache. He took two pills from his medical store and proceeded to the flight deck. Amalek was awake and smiling broadly. "The navigation system's showing a lot of civilization now, and were getting signals from some familiar planets. We're right on course for Terma."

"Great!" Regen responded as he sat down to check the navigation system memory. He called up what should be the record of the course from Phoenicia and found nothing. It was as if they had never left the original course. There was no evidence of the planet in the sensor records either. No one would ever believe he'd been to the planet. He scratched his head for a moment then remembered the Tanallah.

"Where's that case o' wine they put aboard?" he asked Amalek.

"I put it over there," he pointed to a box in a corner of the cabin.

Regan opened the box and stood up stunned.

The bottles were labeled with the trademark of a winery from Bardour, and the box bore no markings at all. He would have sworn it was marked in what he assumed was the Phoenician language, but the lettering had vanished.

"They didn't put no Tanallah aboard. This stuff's reg'lar wine from Bardour."

"Hey, I saw the guy carry it to the ramp, and I brought it up here. I'll swear there was funny writing on the side and the bottles were labled in the same language."

Amalek moved to Regen's side and lifted one of the bottles from the box.

"Well I'll be damned! This isn't the same label at all." He held the bottle up to the light. "And this stuff's red. Tanallah was yellow."

"Well, they can't hide th' tast o' th' stuff." Regen opened one of the bottles and took a hearty swig. He spit out the mouthful in disgust.

"This stuff's really wine! That bitch tricked me. Now, how will I ever prove that damned place exists?"

At that moment, Hitler appeared carrying a bloody carcass in his mouth.

"Well, at least I got yer rats t' prove I was there."

Hitler looked at his master and gulped down the remainder of the runiga.

"Damn, boy. I can't let ya eat up all those things. I need 'em." Regen ran to the hold and opened the door. The chatter of animals greeted the appearance of Hitler's head around the sill. The cargo hold floor was covered with runiga scurrying to find shelter among the crates of food. Regen moved to the cages and found them all open and empty. Hitler busied himself seeking out another snack.

Regen noticed a small disc in one of the cages and pulled it from the plastic litter. It was a communication disc. He returned to the flight deck and inserted it into a player.

"What's that?" Amalek asked.

"A communication disc. It was hidden in one o' the rat cages. The rats are all loose and runnin' 'round the cargo hold like crazy. We'll never be able t' trap any of 'em 'fore Hitler eats 'em all. Let's see what this disc has t' say."

Herion's image and voice greeted him. "By the time you find this you'll know we erased all evidence of Phoenicia from your ship's data base. The runiga will have been released by now, and we trust that your pet will make short work of them. I really enjoyed our sex together, even if it was aphrodisiac induced, and I'd love to see you again, but unless the Council approves of your return, your ship will be destroyed once it's detected. I've petitioned them to allow you to immigrate under the normal conditions, but they move rather slowly on these matters. This disc will morph within thirty seconds of removing it from the player. The morphed form will bring you back to Phoenicia once you give it the command 'epistrepho'. I can't guarantee you will be welcome. You'll just have to chance it. Goodbye, Regen, and good luck."

Regen took the disc from the player and laid it on the console table. In a few seconds it began to change shape into a four centimeters tall silver statue of a woman in a toga. It was Herion. He kissed it and placed it on his navigation console for good luck.

Amalek sat in stunned silence for a moment. "Would you really like to go back there Regen?"

"Son, I've known a lot o' women in my time, but that gal is the best I've ever had. 'Sides, I like the way men are treated on Phoenicia. I got enough money t' live like a king anyplace, an' I don't see why that world would be any different from the rest. Money has a way o' talkin'."

"Well, I could never live where women were in charge. It goes against my upbringing. In our tribe, women are chattel. I'd never get used to being their property."

"Ever'body t' their own taste, I say," Regen said as he picked up the tiny statue and kissed it tenderly.

CHAPTER 16

Mulinor had the next batch of weapons ready when Regen and Amalek landed, but Regen had business with Jahallah while the cargo was being loaded.

"I need t' see Jahllah right away. You know where he is Favik?"

"He went back to his camp in Ausland, but he left Munjia in charge here."

"No good. I gotta see Jahallah in person." Regen turned to Amalek. "You know where yer Daddy's camp is?"

"I can take you there, but it's a good day's ride from here, and you can't get there with a truck or a plane," Amalek replied.

"Fine, git us some horses and whatever supplies we need, and we'll start as soon as you're ready."

Amalek checked the sun position before responding. "We don't want to leave until dark. I'm sure the army's still got the stronghold surrounded, and they've probably got drones watching every trail. Let's check with Munjia before we do anything. He'll probably have the latest information on which routes are safe. Besides, he's probably got some means of communicating with Father, and we need to see if he'll loan out the helmet before we go wandering off across the border."

Regen relaxed a bit and loosed Hitler's leash so the skeen could run. It immediately bolted for the brush area. "You're right. I'm just too itchy t' git that varmit Baddek what he deserves. Let's go see this Munjia guy."

Amalek led Regen to a tent where the Zunid captain was busy puffing on a water pipe and holding a heated discussion with two other Bedouins similarly occupied.

"Well shit!" Regen said. "Is he gonna be too high t' understand what we're talkin' about?"

Amalek laughed. "Don't worry about him. He's almost immune to hashinah. He just smokes it out of habit any more. They're arguing about the skills of some gals in the Stateen bordellos. Looks like they've been making trips into the Rugistani capital. I'll talk to him. He doesn't speak anything but Zunid, so you'll just have to wait until I can translate for you. Just don't get excited and do anything to offend him."

"How would I do that?"

"By not affording him the respect he deserves. These captains are very proud people. Just keep your mouth shut, and we'll be okay."

"Don't look like I got much choice. Go ahead an' find out what he knows."

Amalek greeted the captain in a very obsequious bow evoking a smile from the Zunid soldier and his companions. Munjia indicated he and Regen should take a seat on the carpets spread out around the water pipes. The conversation continued with Amalek being offered the water pipe in his turn. After he took several drags of the aromatic smoke, he passed the mouthpiece to Regen.

"Oh no, I don't do that stuff," Regen said as he held up one hand to ward off the pipe.

"Regen, don't be an idiot. It's an honor to be offered the pipe. Take it and give it at least two good drags. We'll never get anywhere if you don't."

Regen grudgingly took the wet mouthpiece and looked at it scornfully.

"And don't wipe it off either. That's considered to be very bad manners."

The Bremen took his first draw on the pipe and held the smoke in his mouth while pretending to inhale. He exhaled the blue smoke and smiled his best imitation of a satisfied smile.

"Don't fake it—inhale it. They can tell if you're faking. Try again!"

This time Regen inhaled the acrid smoke and fought to keep from choking on it. As he exhaled, he felt a bit lightheaded, but chalked it up to his inexperience. He tried to pass the pipe back to Amalek, but the Zunid indicated he should take another drag.

Once more he inhaled, and this time the feeling approached outright dizziness. It was all he could do to keep from falling over, but he held on in spite of the fact the tent was beginning to make lazy circles around the water pipe. He thought he saw Herion beckoning to him and Princess Orianne laying naked next to him. This time Amalek took the pipe and passed it on.

Regen had no idea how long they were with the Bedouins. He wasn't even aware of Amalek leading him to his bunk on the ship. He awoke to see Hitler studying him with a concerned expression and Amalek stirring up something in a mug. His head felt like Hitler had been inside it chasing rats.

"Damn! That hashinah's pretty potent stuff." He rose to a sitting position and waited for the cabin to quit turning.

"Well, glad to see you're back with the living. Here, drink this, it'll help." He offered the mug to Regen.

"What is it?"

"A private recipe for curing a hashinah hangover. Drink it down."

Regen took a tentative sip from the mug and cocked his head to one side. "Not bad, kinda sweet." He finished the mug and felt much better almost immediately.

"At least th' room's not spinnin' any more," he said.

"Good, because it's almost dark, and we need to be going. I talked with Father, and he'll consider letting us have the helmet as long as I'm the one who uses it. He doesn't want to take time to train you. Munjia told me which trails to use, but we'll still have to use thermal cloaks. The army will be scanning with infra-red after dark. We'll have to leave Hitler behind. His signature would be sure to give away our position."

Hitler looked at Amalek on hearing his name and seemed to smile. He obviously didn't understand he was not to accompany Regen.

"That's okay. I'll turn him out t' hunt 'fore we go, an' he'll never miss me."

"Just let me know when you feel like riding."

"Gimme a couple o' minutes t' get my gear together'n we can go."

Regen strapped on his favorite laser pistol and found two themal cloaks. He also added a heavy jacket as Amalek said it would be cold in the mountains.

Amalek met Regen at the corral and handed him a helmet.

"Put this on. We'll use it for commucications. Munjia says the army's dropped sensors on every trail into the mountains. We don't dare say anything out loud. I've even had the men cushion the horses' hooves. The army's shooting at anything that moves and finding out what it is later."

Regen donned the helmet. "This thing's a little confinin', ain't it?"

Amalek didn't respond, and Regen shouted louder. "I said, this here helmet's a bit on the claustrophobic side."

Again Amalek went about loading some supplies into his saddlebags. Regen pulled the helmet off. "I guess it works pretty good. I yelled at ya twice 'n ya didn't anwer."

"Don't put it on until we'er mounted and I have mine on. Don't forget, we have to get by the Rugistan border patrol also. They're pretty sparse around here, but you run into patrols every now and them. We don't want to pick a fight with them. If they've got us, just surrender. A few bribes'll square everything if they even bother to take us in. How much cash do you have?"

Regen checked his card. "'Bout a hundred thou'. That enough?"

"Plenty, don't offer them any more than a thousand. It'd be better if you had gold, but credits will do."

After sending Hitler out to hunt, the pair mounted their horses and headed for the border.

Amalek led the way, and Regen followed since the Bedouin knew the trail well. They hadn't been across the border more than a few kilometers when a sudden flash of light startled them.

"That was a laser gun!" Amalek shouted.

Another flash landed nearby as the sound of rocks splitting from the heat added to the confusion.

"Well, they either ain't aimin' at us or they're damn poor shots," Regen added.

"Hold your position. If they haven't hit us by now, they don't know we're here."

"Then what th' hell are they shootin' at?" Regen twisted in his saddle and scanned the darkness. The next laser flash illuminated two beady red eyes.

"Damn, it's Hitler. He picked up our scent and followed us." Regen dismounted and called to his pet.

"Commere fella!" He remembered the helmet and pulled it off as the next laser flash exploded only a few centimeters behind Hitler. Only the skeen's speed was saving his life.

"Commere, Hitler."

Hitler responded quickly to his master's voice and jumped into his arms.

"You just lost a few o' however many lives you got, boy." Regen pulled the thermal shield over his head then put his helmet back on. A laser flash struck the spot where Hitler had been, and Regen felt the heat even inside his thermal cloak.

"Get your horse covered, quick," Amalek shouted.

Regen sped to the horse and mounted awkwardly while holding a frightened Hitler. He threw the cloak over both ends of the horse as Amalek shouted, "Let's get out of here."

Both riders spurred their horses down the path as more laser flashes blasted the spot where Regen's horse had been.

"Good thing those guys're a little slow on pickin' up targets," Regen offered.

"They must be using the satellite for their infrared targeting. That adds about a half second to their reaction time, and the software they use builds in another half second. They must have a pretty slow guy on the joystick on top of that, judging from the time between shots."

Another laser blast hit far behind them, and Hitler hissed angrily at the sound before relaxing in Regen's arms.

"I gotta stop 'n git Hitler sitiated," Regen said.

"Okay, we can stop for a while, but don't uncover. Those bozos will be looking for more targets now that they've had some action."

Regen pondered the problem. "Damn, boy! You ain't made fer ridin'."

Working under the thermal shield made the problem even

more difficult. He tried laying the skeen across the horse's neck in front of the saddle, but the horse didn't like that arrangement and almost threw rider and pet in a frightened reaction to Hitler's claws scrabbling for a foothold.

"You'll just hafta ride in back, boy," Regen said as he draped his pet across the saddlebags and tied him in place with the cargo straps.

Once Hitler was taken care of, they made good time in spite of the darkness and raised Jahallah's perimeter guards shortly after midnight. Soon, they were escorted into the Zunid leader's cave.

"Phew," Regen whistled. "This place is more palace 'n cave."

"My Father loves luxury. Our people suffer a great deal to provide him with all the comforts of life, but we haven't had a revolt yet. One or two of his generals may covet his position, but they're content to wait for his death."

"Won't you inherit his place?"

"No, I've made it clear that I have no designs on the throne. I'm happy just to live on what wealth I gain from this venture and enjoy my harem."

"You got a harem? How many?"

"Only six now, but I plan to add several after we finish running weapons." Amalek smiled knowingly at Regen who only shook his head in envy.

"I don't know how ya keep six women happy at the same time. I have 'nuf trouble one at a time."

The guards on Jahallah's apartment recognized Amalek and saluted smartly before opening the door. The Zunid leader sat on a divan holding a conversation with a very lovely and scantily clad lady. He looked up as the door opened.

"Ah, my son and Regen. I take it your adventure to Bardour

was successful." He rose and embraced his boy then turned to Regen and offered his hand.

Regen took his hand and answered, "Yer account should be 'bout one and a half million bigger as of a few days ago."

"And my son's account is 3.3 million larger also. Welcome to my hideout, but why are you here instead of taking the next load to Bardour?"

"They got a problem there you can help 'em with, and I'm here t' see if you'd be willing to do it."

"If I can. Sit down." Jahallah dismissed the woman and clapped for a servant. When the man appeared he said, "Bring us something to drink and some refreshments for my son and his guest."

The servant bowed and left the room as Regen and Amalek took seats across from the divan.

"What is this problem you want my help with?"

"The Princess who's runnin' the revolt on Bardour's got a spy on her staff. He tried to sabotage the weapons we brought in, and he planted a bomb on my ship. I know who did it, but she don't believe me. I need your magic helmet t' make him tell the truth. Amalek says he knows how t' use it."

"Regen, you are asking me to send my most prized possession into a civil war. If I lost it, I could not replace it."

"Would five million make it any easier?" Regen asked.

"You could give me all the money you possess, and it wouldn't be enough. Those helmets are not for sale to persons like myself. You may remember, I only came by it through the capture of a psychiatrist after an airliner crashed near my desert camp. I doubt there will be another such fortunate occurance in the near future. I couldn't possibly let it out of my control."

"Father, I would be responsible for it and see that it is returned to you safely," Amalek said.

At that moment, Hitler jumped into Regen's lap.

"I guess you're hungry, big fella." Regen took a morsel of meat from the platter in front of him and held it up above the skeen.

"Do yer trick fer th' boys," Regen prompted, and the half dinosaur rolled over twice before standing on its hind legs, mouth open.

"Good boy!" Regen dropped the meat into the open maw, and Hitler swallowed it quickly before begging for another treat.

Jahallah's eyes brightened at the sight of the relationship between this miniature monster and its master. "Regen, there is a custom among my people that may enable you to use my helmet."

"What's that?" Regen asked as he held another piece of meat above the skeen's head.

"Whenever we wish to secure a treaty or an important contract, we always exchange hostages. The hostages are only returned alive if the agreement is fulfilled completely."

Hitler turned a somersault to the amazement of the men present then gulped down the food.

"What's that got t' do with us?"

"Leave your pet with me while you're gone. If you return my helmet safely, you may have him back. If you don't, he dies. It's a simple arrangement."

Regen looked at the Zunid chief then back to Hitler, who resumed his begging pose.

"How do I know you'd take good care o' 'im?"

"You have my word as a Zunid chief. Amalek will tell you it is a solid guarantee of my earnestness."

Regen threw another hors d'oeuvre without ordering a trick and stared at Jahallah.

"It's true, Regen. My Father would kill himself if he broke his word. A pledge is a very sacred thing among we Zunids," Amalek said.

"Okay, I'll go fer it. You can keep Hitler whilst we're gone, but if anything happens to 'im, you're a dead man, Jahallah."

The Bremen's eyes held a look that almost made Jahallah tremble. There was no doubt the man meant exactly what he said.

"We will make the blood pledge for this transaction." Jahallah clapped his hands, and a servant appeared, seemingly out of nowhere. He spoke to him in the Zunid language, and the lackey backed out of the room hastily. In a moment, he returned with two other servants carrying a tray loaded with golden objects and an older man in a long robe wearing a white turban. "Is this th' same thing I did t' seal th' weapons deal?" Regen asked Amalek. "What th' hell's goin' on?"

"This is the blood pledge ceremony. The old man is a priest, and he will perform the ceremony. I'll translate for you since he only speaks Zunid. Don't be concerned, it only takes a small cut."

"Cut? Cut what?" Regen protested.

"Your arm. You both bleed a little into the golden bowl and the priest says some mumbo-jumbo and that's about it."

"Pretty savage custom fer people as civilized as the Zunid, ain't it?"

"It goes back hundreds of years, and it's the only ritual recognized as absolutely binding."

Amalek led Regen to the priest, and his father joined them. The priest spoke something in a sing-song manner, and Regen looked to Amalek.

"Just boilerplate. The good part's coming up," Amalek said.

Jahallah spoke in the Zunid language, and Amalek

translated again.

"He's just told the priest about the deal. Time to offer your arm."

Regen held out his left arm.

"No, the other one," Amalek prompted.

The priest produced a gold-handled knife from his belt and spoke to Regen.

"What'd he say?"

"He's asking if you agree to the deal. Just say 'zalan', it means you do."

"Zalan!" Regen said.

The priest spoke again, and Jahallah offered his arm and responded, "Zalan!"

A quick movement of the knife opened wounds in both arms, and the blood ran into a golden bowl. Two servants bound the wounds with white cloth as the priest began a chant of some sort.

"We through yet?" Regen whispered to Amalek.

"Not yet. One more thing to do."

The priest took the bowl and swirled its contents around for a few seconds before offering it to Jahallah. The Zunid chief raised it to his lips and took a sip.

"Oh yeah, I coulda seen this commin'," Regen moaned.

"Only a sip is required. You don't have to drink the whole thing," Amalek responded.

Regen took the bowl and sipped the contents grudgingly. None of the men present was ready for Hitler's response to the smell of fresh blood. The skeen sat up before Regen in his usual begging position.

Regen pulled the bowl back from the priest and laid it on the floor in front of Hitler.

"Guess you kin drink too, boy. After all, you're the reason

for this whole shindig."

Jahallah laughed merrily, and Amalek smiled at the scene as the priest stood, mouth agape and eyes as big as saucers. He started to reach for the bowl, but Jahallah grabbed his hand and spoke in a comforting voice. The priest smiled also and nodded his head in approval.

After Hitler licked the bowl clean, the servants gathered the ritual paraphinalia and left with the priest.

"Well, Regen, our deal is sanctified by all that is holy to my people. I will have the helmet brought to you before you leave tonight."

"You'll also need a purdy strong cage fer Hitler too. He'll try t' follow me if'n he can."

"I'll see to it. In the meantime, get some rest, and I'll have my surgeon look at your cut later. If you need female companionship...?"

"Amalek's got his harem, but I could use a gal if you kin spare one."

"I keep a small stable of courtiers to entertain my guests. I'll send them around for your approval whenever you wish. Just give this to the servant at your door." Jahallah took a ring from one of his fingers and presented it to Regen. "Amalek will show you to your room now. I'll speak with you at dinner."

"Thanks fer ever'thing, Jahallah."

"Don't thank me until you are safely returned from your next trip."

Amalek bowed to his father, and Regen followed suit before the pair exited the room.

Amalek led him down a corridor to an ornate door guarded by a brawny servant holding a rather formidable sword. Amalek spoke to him in Zunid, and the servant bowed deeply to Regen.

"His name is Josesh. He only speaks Zunid, but there are buttons inside for whatever you need. Just press one. See you at supper."

Josesh opened the door for Regen, and Amalek walked off down the hallway.

The room was quite spacious, and light from recessed fixtures around the edge of the ceiling gave it a warm look. On the wall to his left, a digital window showed a seascape while a salt scented breeze wafted the curtains. The bed could have been used for a small soccer field, and a hot tub gurgled on his right. Regen decided to take advantage of it.

He hadn't been soaking long when Josesh led in a rather scholarly looking man with a small black case. Regen guessed he was the surgeon. The man tried Zunid then switched to Auslish when that failed.

"I am Doctor Amabad. His Highness sent me to look at your arm."

"Come ahead, Doc." Regen lifted the cut arm, and the doctor removed the bandage.

"Hmmm, not much damage. I'll just apply a mild dose of healing laser."

The medic opened his bag and produced a pen-like instrument. He pressed on the end of it, and watched as light reflected from a small mirror in the lid of his case. He twisted the barrel slightly and tested it again.

"That should be about right. Hold your arm still please."

Regen braced the arm against the edge of the hot tub and gritted his teeth. He'd done this before and was not looking forward to the sharp pain even if it only lasted a moment.

"That's done," the doctor pronounced. "You took it very well, I must say."

"Experience, Doc. Thanks a lot."

The doctor packed up his things and left, but he was replaced by four women in skimpy costumes. They swarmed around Regen, and one even shed her clothes and joined him in the tub.

"Any o' you ladies speak Auslish?"

"I speak Auslish as well as Rugistani and Bremen," a dark skinned beauty standing above him proclaimed. "These other women know other languages. What one would you like to use?"

"We kin start with Auslish. Who's the one in the pool?"

"Her name is Adullah, and she's a Zunid. She loves water."

"I kin see that," Regen said as the woman moved to massage his legs under the water.

"This one is Majuba," she pointed to the black woman. "She's from Nugambo, and her expertise is pressure therapy. If you have any joints or old wounds that bother you, she can make them better."

Majuba smiled broadly at Regen and knelt by the tub. She'd noticed his scars and began with the largest one across his left shoulder.

"Mmmm, that really feels good."

"The one on the bed is Carlina. She's an Auslander trained in the art of satisfying a man's sexual needs."

"An' you?"

"I'm Duma, your translator, but I am also skilled in many other areas. His Highness thought you might prefer Carlina, but you may have any of us, separately or together, we don't mind."

"Pretty broad minded o' you gals, but I only do one at a time, myself. I'll start with a better massage from the water baby there, then I'll let this black one go over my scars real good. I'll finish up with Carlina, if you won't be offended."

"Not at all. I'll stay around until you're ready for Carlina.

Since she's an Auslander, you won't need a translator for that segment of your entertainment. Dinner is in six hours. Take your time."

The women were everything he could expect, and he was soon sleeping very soundly after massage, therapy and a sexual experience like none he'd ever known before. The sound of a soft chime awakened him just as Josesh entered the room carrying a tray of fruit juice and snacks. Regen dressed and followed the huge man to the dinning hall. Jahallah and Amalek were there to greet him.

"Regen, I trust you are well rested and refreshed for your return journey," Jahallah greeted him.

Amalek was dressed for the trail, and a helmet-sized package rested near his place at the low table. "We're ready to go as soon as it's dark enough. We have fresh horses and new thermal cloaks."

"Right now I'm just hungry," Regen said as he inspected the dishes set before the guests. "Where's Hitler?"

Jahallah signaled a servant, and two men carried in a steel cage containing a contented-looking Hitler.

"You see, Regen. Your pet is being treated royally. You have nothing to fear as long as my helmet is returned safely to me. Now, have some dinner before you run the gauntlet of the Ausland army on your way back."

Amalek and Regen reached the ship near dawn the next morning. Molinar met them as they dismounted.

"The ship's loaded and ready to go. You can take off whenever you like. Here's the cargo list, and the price we paid for each item. I'm afraid the Rugistani left us less room to discount the stuff to your Princess this time. You're going to have to get at least 40 million for this lot to realize the same prophits as last time."

Regen perused the list and stuffed it inside his tunic. "That's okay.   Orianne says money's no problem."   He turned to Amalek. "You have any objection t' takin' off now?"

"No, none at all. I'd just as soon get going."

"Good. Favik, we may be longer getting' back this time. Orianne wants me to help with her revolution a bit 'fore we leave."

"Regen, don't get involved with that mess. Selling them weapons is one thing, helping fight the war is something entirely different," Mulinor scolded.

"Oh, it's just a little milk run t' ferry some folks t' one o' their moons. I wouldn't take it on if I was gonna git shot at. Just relax'n count yer money. See ya in two or three weeks."

The men boarded the ship and launched for Bardour.

CHAPTER 17

Regen called Baddek as they approached Bardour's defense system to get the landing coordinates.

"You can use the same ones you used last time," Baddek answered.

"Cain't do that. We had a nav system malfunction on the way home, and it erased the memory banks. You'll have t' send 'em again."

"Okay, but be careful. We've had a lot of air breathing interceptors around the last few days. You may have to make a run for it once you enter the atmosphere."

"The cloaking system's no good inside the atmosphere," Amalek advised.

"I think we kin outrun 'em," Regen said to both Amalek and Baddek.

"Very well, transmitting coordinates now."

A few hours later, the ship encountered no problems penetrating the defense system and was soon inside the atmosphere of Bardour. Amalek monitored the sensors for any interceptors and didn't have to wait long for action.

"Holy Zond, there's about six bogies coming up fast, Regen."

"From what angle?"

"Dead astern. They'll be in firing range in thirty seconds."

"Let's just hope the rebels has got some antiaircraft missiles. Otherwise, we're dead ducks." Regen tried to raise Baddek, but the frequency seemed to be jammed.

"Damn! Looks like no help from our buddy, but I didn't expect much. Those interceptors are prob'ly his work. Git strapped in."

The two men tightened their harnesses, and Regen began a series of violent maneuvers.

"They've launched missiles," Amalek shouted.

"Hold on." Regen threw the ship into a steep climb then a gut-wrenching left turn.

"They missed," Amalek shouted again, this time with some cheer in his voice.

"Those air breathers cain't do what we can. It'll take 'em a while t' re-acquire. I'll head for the hangar'n hope we kin git there 'fore they come back."

"Better make it quick. Here they come again."

Amalek snapped his fingers and turned to the cloaking device console.

"What good'll that do us?" Regen asked.

"It won't make us invisible, but it will send a powerful return signal back to any transmitter as close as those birds are. I think it'll jam their targeting radars."

"What if it don't?"

"Been good knowing you Regen. Oh oh, here they come."

Amalek pushed several buttons and watched the track of the missiles on the sensor display. To Regen's surprise, the three targets vanished completely.

"I think it worked. What th' hell happened?" Regen asked.

"The missiles thought they were here and exploded. Find the hangar. I'll keep them baffled."

Amalek thwarted another missile attack, but the interceptors closed on the spaceship for a gun attack.

"They're going to try guns now. Let's hope the rebel

defenses are watching this," Amalek said.

"Hangar's only a couple of kilometers away now, but I gotta slow down t' make it. Keep yer fingers crossed."

"Zunids don't believe in that stuff," Amalek said. "We do this." He rubbed his private parts then kissed his hand.

At that moment the interceptors turned off, and the track of three ground-based missiles appeared on the screens.

"Looks like th' rebels heard yer prayers," Regen said as he slowed for a landing in front of the cliff face that served as the hangar doors.

Inside the camouflaged hangar, Baddek was waiting at the bottom of the boarding ramp.

"Good to see you alive and well. I saw those interceptors jump you."

"I'm sure you know all about that," Regen said under his breath.

"Yeah, Amalek here did some fancy work with our cloakin' system t' spoil their attack."

"Mind if we unload you right away. We can use the missiles at the front right now."

"Go ahead, we'll negotiate th' price later. Is the Princess around?"

"She's in the control room. I'll tell her you're coming to see her." Baddek spoke into a communicator and handed it to Regen.

"Glad to have you back Regen. What do you need to talk to me about?" Princess Orianne's voice sounded more cheerful than the last time.

"I can't tell ya over th' phone. Kin we meet in yer private bedroom?"

"I'm kind of busy right now, Regen."

"Not fer that stuff. I'm bringin' in Amalek with me. He's got somethin' we want t' show ya. It may be th' answer t' one o' yer big problems."

"Ooooh, a secret weapon, eh?"

"Don't joke around. This is real important."

"All right, come on back, but keep it brief. I've got a staff meeting in an hour, and I need to get ready."

"This won't take that long. See ya in a few minutes." Regen handed the communicator back to Baddek. "She'll see us now. Back that way, ain't it?" He pointed toward a door in the far wall of the hangar.

"Yes, would you like me to lead the way?"

"Naw, we kin find it."

Amalek shouldered the box containing the helmet and followed Regen to the command center. This time the guards were prepared for his arrival and ushered him in at once. Orianne's greeting was much more subdued this time, but her smile was as warm as ever.

"What's so important you had to see me as soon as you landed?"

"We can't talk out here. You need t' hear this in private."

Orianne led Regen and Amalek into her private room and closed the door. Amalek placed the helmet box on the bed and removed the helmet. Regen picked it up and handed it to Orianne.

"This here's a special helmet that gits inside a man's head. You kin bring out his true thoughts on any subject. You remember I suspected Baddek o' bein' yer spy last time?"

"Yes, but I think you were jumping to conclusions. We investigated everything that happened and cleared Baddek on every count. The missiles were sabotaged by one of the armament technicians who supposedly checked them out before we sent them to the troops, and a cargo handler in the supply dump admitted to planting the bomb. Both of those men confesed and were executed. We don't need anything like this to solve our problems." She handed the helmet back to Regen.

"On our way back to Terma, our navigation system malfunctioned. I think Baddek was behind that too. The thing that should convince ya is th' fact we were jumped by interceptors th' minute we entered the atmosphere. Th' only guy who knew we were comin' was Baddek."

Orianne's face turned serious. "Interceptors normally don't come this far into rebel territory, and we haven't seen any for several days. They've been too busy supporting royal troops against our forces. I'll have the sensor guys check for transmissions in the last four hours."

She picked up a communicator and gave orders. "We'll know in a few minutes. If Baddek contacted the royal forces, he had to do it from here. He hasn't been outside the complex all day."

"You mentioned doin' a raid on th' defense system's moon base last time. If yer spy's still around, that could be a real disaster. It won't hurt t' make sure Baddek's not the culprit," Regen added.

The communicator buzzed, and Orianne listened for several seconds before closing off the conversation.

"There was a transmission out of here on a royal frequency just forty minutes ago. That was probably your spy. I'll get Baddek in here, and you can use that thing on him." Orianne pointed to the helmet.

"Better git a couple o' troops in here t' hold him down too," Regen offered.

"Good idea," Orianne said, and she left the room.

In a few seconds two burly troopers joined them, and

Amalek began to make preparations for the interrogation.

They didn't have to wait long before Orianne opened the door and pushed a surprised Baddek into the room.

"What's this all about?" Baddek protested.

"We're just gonna run a little test o' yer loyalty, Baddek," Regen said.

The two troopers pinned Baddek's arms to his side in spite of his struggle to free himself from their grip. Amalek came forward with a hypodermic and shot the sedative into Baddek's arm. The suspected spy grew limp in the troopers' grasp, and they placed him in one of the chairs, taking positions on either side in case he revived.

Amalek fitted the helmet and made several adjustments before turning to Orianne.

"You can't ask him any questions, but I can bring out his most recent thoughts for you to read on this screen. The words will be in Baddek's native language, but with Auslish script. Regen can pronounce them for you, and you should be able to understand their meaning. Are you ready?"

"Go ahead," Orianne said.

Words began to scroll across the small screen on the helmet's faceplate, and Regen read them off. They didn't seem to be making any sense to Orianne.

"Either you're not pronouncing them right or he's not speaking Bardour," Orianne said. "I haven't understood one word."

One of the troopers spoke. "Excuse me, Your Highness, but he's speaking an old dialect from a far northern province. I can translate for you if you like."

"Go ahead. Run it back again Amalek."

Once more the words scrolled, and Regen read them off.

The trooper translated. "Nothing worked. That Bremen is

back again. This time I'll make sure he's taken care of. I"ll call in some interceptors to deal with him. Baddek to Silver Four..."

"That's enough," Orianne commanded. "I'm convinced Regen. I'll have him shot immediately."

"Wait a minute, Princess," Regen cautioned. "He got a couple o' guys t' take the fall fer him on th' other stuff. He's prob'ly got some more buddies around here. We need t' get them too."

"I can regress him back as far as you like, but the memories grow fainter with age. How far should I go?" he asked Orianne.

"We got our last replacements a month ago. I don't think he had any help before that. Go back to that."

The words scrolled again producing several names. Orianne wrote them down and looked at her pad in disgust.

"These are all nobodys, but they're spread out in every corner of the command center. They must be his intelligence network—his flunkies and fall guys." She picked up her communicator and read the names off to her security chief, ordering their immediate arrest.

She turned to the troopers. "Take him out and shoot him. Then, search his quarters for anything he could use as a transmitter. Get security to help you. I want his communication device. We may be able to use it to our advantage."

The troopers left with a still groggy Baddek, and Orianne turned to Amalek.

"That is a remarkable device. Is it for sale?"

"No, Your Highness. I must return it to my father."

"'Sides that, Hitler gits popped if'n he don't git it back," Regen added.

"Ah, yes, your pet skeen. I wouldn't want anything to happen to him. After all, he's the thing that got me back to

Bardour." She turned to Amalek. "Leave it here in this room. I'll see you get it back safely before you leave."

"Yes Highness," Amalek said.

"You two can relax a bit and get something to eat if you like. I'll see that someone shows you to quarters. After dinner we'll meet with my staff to plan the raid on the moon base. Until then, I'm very busy with other aspects of our current offensive. Dinner is at 1900 hours sharp. I'll send someone for you." She moved to Regen and embraced him. "That's twice you've saved my bacon. I'll find some way to thank you properly later."

A trooper led Regen and Amalek to Spartan rooms and pointed out the mess hall on the way. Both men opted for sleep over food.

That evening they met with Orianne and two of her commanders. After introductions, one of the commanders called up a photo of a large complex situated on a barren landscape.

"This is the backup command center on the moon Gorin. As you can see it's defended by several missile installations and automated laser cannon pillboxes. It would be suicide to attack it from the moon's surface."

"I'll agree with that," Regen said. "But, how else would ya git in there?"

"Through this airlock." The colonel pointed to an airlock on top of the central building.

"Oh, I see, we just knock on th' door an' they open right up fer us," Regen mocked.

"Something like that. They get a supply ship once a week, and it docks at that airlock. The next one's due in two days, but instead of a royal freighter, they'll get your ship and instead of supplies, they'll get our troopers."

"I gotta see how you got this all figured out or start smokin' th' same stuff you are," Regen said.

"The ship scheduled for the next run is a ZHS-1160, just like yours. It alternates with a Mainstay 2200 that brings in any heavy stuff. You'll use your stealth gear to park in a 200 kilometer orbit just outside the atmosphere. The royal ship will take off and enter the same orbit but a few minutes behind you. You both go behind the planet blocking off the moonbase's view of their ship. Two ships go behind the planet, but only one comes out. That's you."

"What happens to th' real supply ship?"

"We destroy it on the side hidden from the moon. It will be over our territory, and no royal people around to observe the play. You go on to the moonbase and dock. We take over from there."

"Nice plan, but don't those guys have some security, like transponder codes and passwords an' th' like?"

"Yes, but we'll have all of that information before you leave. Any other questions?"

Regen leaned back in his chair and looked at Amalek. The man was deep in thought, but he felt Regen's stare. "Sounds good to me, Regen. I think it's worth the risk."

Orianne broke in. "Once you dock at the alternate command center, we will attack the main center here on Bardour. It should be no problem for our troops to secure it since we have it all but surrounded now."

"What about them royal cruisers in orbit around Bardour? The station's bound t' git off an SOS soon as they know we ain't the real thing."

"We'll be taking along some missiles to shoot them down if they head for the moon," the commander said.

"Won't you have the moon base's missiles?" Amalek asked.

"They're no good against royal cruisers. They won't home on anything with the current transponder code," Orianne said. "We'll have to bring our own."

"No laser cannon?" Amalek added.

"Same problem there," the commander said.

"Once we have the defense system, we can start bringing in weapons from our allies," Orianne said.

"I guess that'll mean th' end o' my gun runnin'," Regen said.

"We'll take all the weapons you can bring us as long as your price is competitive," Orianne said. A broad smile spread across her face. She felt sure Regen would not be able to match the figures she'd seen from other sources. He was too small a player.

"We ain't settled on th' price fer this batch yet, *Yer Highness*."

"My people make it 45 million. Is that satisfactory with you?"

It was Regen's turn to smile. Evidently, Orianne had no problem making his last delivery the most profitable.

"I'll take it." Regen turned to the commander. "Just let me know when we're ready t' go. Meantime, is there anything t' do 'round here fer entertainment?"

Two days later, Regen watched as rebel troopers crammed themselves into his cargo holds and any other available space on his ship. Amalek was forced to stay on Bardour so a combat soldier could occupy his position. The same commander who conducted the briefing supervised the operation. Regen just shook his head as several missile containers added to the payload.

"I don't know if'n I kin git this thing off th' ground with all that aboard."

The commander turned to him and smiled at the reaction. "Our computers calculated the maximum weight for your ship to make the moon, and you've still got 50 kilograms to spare."

"Well, Gen'ral, if'n th' computers are happy, what th' hell am I worried about?"

The officer laughed heartily at the sarcasm. "It's Colonel, Colonel Marden's the name, and we wouldn't overload you. This mission's too important. Besides, the supply ship would be near its maximum weight, and we want you to look like the real thing."

"Okay, but I just hope your computer knows what it's doin'."

The ship lifted off on time, much to Regen's amazement. He'd never operated anywhere near the maximum weight for his ship's class, and the sluggish response to controls was a new experience for him. Marden watched from the other command chair as the ship closed on the royal cargo vessel.

"They should be firing about now," Marden said. His voice held a twinge of uncertainty born of long experience with coordinated operations gone wrong.

"There it is." Regen pointed to a display panel showing a small blip approaching the large dot representing the cargo ship. The two dots merged, and then there were no targets to be seen.

"They got it!" Marden shouted. "Put me on the intercom."

Regen punched in the proper commands and nodded to Marden.

"This is Colonel Marden. The royal supply ship has been successfully destroyed. We're on our way to the moon now. I can't emphasize the importance of this mission strongly enough. The success of the entire revolution may well rest on how each of us performs his duty. With any luck, we'll have complete surprise on our side, but there'll still be a lot of heavy fighting to do before we secure the moon base for Princess Orianne. We'll never have another chance like this one. I expect each of you to fight to the death or the victory. That's all."

Regen looked at the colonel with a wary expression. "That's pretty grim talk, Colonel. I intend t' bring this ship back to Bardour in one piece even if'n I'm th' only one aboard."

"I understand, Regen. I'll let you know if you need to disengage. Your stealth capability should give you the protection you need to make it back safely regardless of what happens to us."

"Don't git me wrong, I wish you guys all th' success in th' world, but I gotta look out for number one."

The Colonel offered his hand, and Regen took it as the commander said, "You have my word. I'll give you all the warning I can if things start going badly."

Several hours later the first communication arrived from the moon base.

"Apple 46, this is Luna 1, please give recognition codes."

"That's the ones on this sheet." Marden handed Regen the list.

"Oh no, they'd spot my accent right away. You'd better do th' respondin'." He handed the list back. "That button there." Regen pointed to the correct control.

Marden read the list a moment before responding. "Luna 1, Apple 46. Go mix with raptor spaniel."

There was a moment of silence while the codes were processed. Then, the voice asked, "Is this Jessen?"

"No, he couldn't make it this trip. He's in the hospital with some kind of flu, or something. This is Sithers."

"You haven't made the run before, have you?"

"No, this is my first time. Any words of wisdom?"

"Just watch the nine o'clock latch on the airlock. It's been a little hard to engage lately. You just have to slam into it."

"Gotcha, see you in an hour or two."

The system went dead, and Regen scanned his sensors for any indication of hostile action from the moon base.

"I don't see no weapons activity, Marden. I think we fooled 'em."

"They'll be scanning us all the way in from here. I wouldn't be surprised if we get another call for ID codes."

"Well, you got th' list. Have at it."

Regen went into orbit around the moon Gorin before the next challenge came.

"Apple 46 this is Luna 1. Confirm identity please."

This time Regen's sensors showed several missiles locked in on the ship, and he pointed the signatures out to Marden.

"Let's hope these codes work," Marden said as he found the next set of words to use.

"If'n they don't, we're space dust judgin' from the number o' missiles they got aimed at us."

"Luna 1, Apple 46. Meadow, skyline, canyon, meander."

There was a long silence. Regen watched as the missile systems tracked his ship. He looked at Marden and noticed beads of sweat popping out on his forehead. They were dead ducks if the codes were wrong. He was even beginning to feel a little warm himself when the communicator panel came to life again.

"Sorry for the delay. Our display here went out for a few seconds. Glad you guys are bringing some replacement parts for it. You're cleared to dock."

"Phew!"   Marden exhaled sharply as he wiped the perspiration from his face. "I thought we were gonners for a while there."

"Better git yer men ready. We'll be dockin' in a half hour."

Marden left to inspect his troopers while Regen concentrated on guiding his ship into the docking port on the moon base. The computer did most of the work for him, but he always kept a hand on the manual override button in case of a malfunction. He remembered to hit the port latch hard, as the moon base had advised.

"We're here," Regen announced over the intercom, but the troopers were already entering the moon base.

He could only hear faint echoes of the fighting taking place inside the station, but his exterior cameras showed some of the rebel troopers in space suits setting up defensive missile systems. His communicator came to life.

"Regen, this is Captain Sonas. Do you read me?"

"I got ya. What's up?"

"I've got the defensive missiles set up, but we don't have any radar. You'll have to let me know if those Royal cruisers head this way."

"Don't worry. It'll take 'em at least one orbit t' head this way. How much range ya got on them things?"

"Up to 1,000 kilometers, in space, but I'd like to shoot at less than 500."

"Them cruisers kin shoot at 700. I sure hope their computers are lousy shots."

"At their speed they'll only have a little over thirty seconds before we down them. They can't get off many shots in that time."

"One's enough, but I'll keep an eye out fer ya."

Regen checked his sensors and saw the cruisers were still in orbit around Bardour. With any luck, they'd stay there until both defense command stations were secured, and the systems could be changed to allow the captured royal weapons into action against them.

Marden's voice interrupted his thoughts. "Regen, we're almost into the main command center. It's going very well, but they may have been able to get off a distress signal. Be on the lookout for those cruisers."

"Got ya. I got an eye on 'em."

The sounds of fighting began to fade, but the cruisers emerged from behind Bardour on a trajectory for the moon. Evidently, someone lived long enough to send out an alert.

"Here they come, fellas," Regen called to the Captain in charge of the missiles. "I'll let ya know when they're at 500 clicks."

"Bardour base to Regen." He recognized Orianne's voice and replied immediately.

"Hi, darlin'. You got things under control down there?"

"The defense system is in our hands now, but the cruisers are headed your way."

"I saw 'em. We got some o' yer guys out here with missiles, but they want t' wait 'til they're within 500 clicks. Can you shoot at 'em sooner?"

"It'll take my people several hours to repair the systems here and reprogram the computers to attack Royal targets. You're on your own until then."

"Let's hope yer guys are good shots, then. I ain't heard from Marden, so I don't know how it's goin' inside."

"This is Marden," a new voice joined the conversation. "The defenders here just surrendered, but we're in the same boat as the Princess. We may be a little quicker, but not much, and we'll need some data from the main base to finish the job."

"Then it's all up to our missiles," Orianne said. Her voice had an air of finality Regen was not happy to hear.

"We'll do our job, Your Highness." It was Captain Sonas.

Orianne broke in. "Marden, if the cruisers get through, destroy the station. Do you have any explosives?"

"No, but we can shoot up the place bad enough to do the same kind of damage. That is, if the cruisers don't do it for us."

"How 'bout I just take off and engage my stealth stuff?" Regen offered.

"We need your sensors, Regen," Marden called. "The moon base stuff was damaged in the fighting and isn't working yet."

"I'll second that," Sonas added.

"Okay, but if'n those cruisers start shootin', I'm gone."

"We've got eight missiles, Regen," Sonas said. "We'll fire two at 700 kilometers, but we have to save the other six for more certain range. Stay with us, and we'll give you all the protection we can."

"Yes, Regen, stay with them for my sake," Orianne added.

"I'll stay as long as I can fer you, darlin'." He blew a kiss into his microphone.

The sensors showed the first cruiser approaching the 700 kilometer range with the second about thirty seconds behind it.

"You got 700 clicks on my mark, Sonas. Five, four, three, two, one, mark!"

He watched as a missile arched toward the warship. An answering shot from the cruiser smashed into the moon base just to the right of Regen's ship, but the rebel missile exploded on target. When his sensors recovered from the blast, the first cruiser was still headed for moon orbit, but there was no more firing from it.

"I think you got the fire control system," Marden shouted.

"The sensors here show the cruiser not able to fire."

"I'll put two more into it at 300 kilometers and use two on the one behind it," Sonas said.

"300 clicks in seven seconds," Regen said as he began the countdown. "Six, five, four, three, two, one, fire!"

Two more balls of fire sped toward the crippled ship as the second cruiser opened up on the moon base. One shot rocked Regen's ship, and his panel went wild with yellow and red lights. He worked feverishly to control the damage while keeping track of the second warship. A bright flash of light temporarily knocked his sensors off line and marked the end of the first cruiser. When they recovered, the second ship was within range.

"You got th' second one at 450 now," Regen called to Sonas.

"Got him." Two missiles sped toward the cruiser as more shots rocked the moonbase knocking out the remaining missile positions.

"Sonas, you okay?" Regen called.

"They missed me, but they got the rest of my missiles. If these two don't do the trick, we're dead."

It seemed an eternity before the flash of light signaling the detonation of the missiles, but there were no more impacts on the station or Regen's ship. When the sensors cleared, the second cruiser was also gone.

"We got him!" Sonas shouted, and Regen could hear cheering from inside the moon base and over the communications system from Bardour.

"Great job, Captain Sonas!" Orianne called. "It'll take them two days to get another cruiser up. By that time, we'll have the defense system working for us. You can come back now, Regen. My people will stay up there to repair the moon base and man the station until we can send relief."

"I think my ship's okay fer that, but I'll have t' check it out 'fore I leave. It took a couple o' hits."

"Go on back to our headquarters. I'll meet you there in three days, and see that you're rewarded properly."

"I'll look forward t' that. See ya in three days."

CHAPTER 18

Making repairs to Regen's ship took most of the next day, and most of them were simply patches and wire-arounds with an eye toward getting it back to Bardour where proper fixes could be made. Amalek was waiting for Regen as the ship moved into the main hangar. He greeted his friend as Regen walked off the boarding ramp.

"Wow! They put a few holes in the old bird, didn't they?"

Regen embraced the Zunid and moved to inspect the damage in more detail than was possible on the airless moon base. He poked his fist into one rather ragged hole.

"This'n put the end t' our stealth stuff. I think it got the main control unit."

"That's too bad. We don't have any spares for the system, and I doubt they'll be able to reverse engineer it if it's been fried by a laser cannon."

"Well, as long it kin git us back t' Terma. I think my drug runnin' days are through. I'm tired o' puttin' my butt on the line fer money. 'Sides, I got plenty o' that now, an' where I'm plannin' on goin', I won't need it anyways."

"Are you going to return to Phoenicia?"

"Yup, there's not a night goes by I don't dream about that woman. I don't know what she done t' me, but I cain't git her outta my head."

"Most people would call that love, Regen." Amalek smiled broadly at his friend as he placed one arm around his shoulders.

"Hell, I bin in love a hunnert times, an' this ain't the same thing." He shrugged off Amalek's arm. "This is more like bein' comfortable than bein' in love. Ever' time I was in love, I was uncomfortable 'bout somethin', and I wasn't uncomfortable with Herion. I gotta go back an' find out if she'll have me."

"That's a pretty strong commitment for knowing the woman only one night, particularly since it includes conforming to all the crazy rules on that planet."

"I know, I know, but I just got a funny feelin' about her."

"Can a guy like you live on a planet run by women?"

"I'm ready t' swallow my pride an' just live comfortable-like. I don't know what they use fer money there, but gold al'ays talks. I'll take whatever this old ship'll hold." He reached up and patted the metal structure almost affectionately.

"As far as I'm concerned, we can leave whenever you want," Amalek said.

"I gotta wait fer *Her Highness* t' come back 'fore we leave. She might make me a better offer." Regen gave Amalek a sly wink. "Come on, let's see what kind o' booze they're servin' 'round here."

He took the Zunid by the arm and led him toward the bar.

Two days later, Regen and Orianne lay in bed together after a very wonderful evening of passion. Orianne rubbed one hand across the Bremen's chest and looked deeply into his sapphire eyes trying to discern his thoughts.

"You seemed far away tonight, Regen. What's troubling you?"

The Bremen pulled her head to his lips and kissed it gently. "Ya might say I was on another planet, but you certainly brought me back t' this un in a hurry."

"I'm glad I haven't lost my touch. You're the only man I"ve

made love to since I boarded your ship as a slave whore back on Gobra."

Regen smiled softly. "I know I'm good, but I didn't think I was that good."

"Don't flatter yourself. I just haven't had the time or the inclination, and anyone I went to bed with here would think they had an inside track to the position of royal consort."

"I kin understand that, but maybe I think I'm th' guy fer that job."

Orianne smiled warmly at her lover and slapped him playfully on the chest. "That wasn't the reward I had in mind for you, but if you'd like to stay here, I can make you a Duke or an Earl or something and give you the estate and income appropriate to the title. I have to marry some guy with bluer blood and have a couple of kids to inherit the throne, but that doesn't mean I can't visit my *loyal subjects* every now and then."

"Temptin', but I got other plans. 'Sides, I got all the money I need now, and soon as you pay for this last load o' weapons, I'll be set fer life without no fancy title."

"Are you going back to the Velvet Saddle?"

Regen snorted a quick laugh. "Well, it weren't a bad life, but th' place I'm talkin' 'bout's a lot farther off. I found it when yer man Baddek sabotaged my navigation system, and I got some questions that need answers I can only find there."

"Is she pretty?" Orianne pretended to pout.

"Well, I wouldn't call her pretty—more like comfortable."

"Comfortable!? I never would have guessed you'd go for *comfortable*."

"I've had wild, an' I've had exotic, an' I'm fed up with dangerous. I certainly don't want no homey type. I think comfortable's what I need from here on out."

"Well, I can't compete on that score. If you stay here, you wouldn't find comfortable with any of the women at court. I wish you all the comfort this woman can bring. You've been of great service to my cause."

Regen rose from the bed and began to dress. "I'm just a sucker fer a pretty figure, and you got one o' th' best, darlin'."

"I haven't told you what your reward is yet."

Regen turned to her with a surprised look on his face. "I figured this was it."

"No, no, as soon as we capture the capitol city, I want to present you with a brand new ship."

"That's mighty nice of ya, Princess, but I won't have no use for a ship where I'm goin'."

"What do you mean?"

"I mean, the people where I'm headed for'll destroy whatever ship I bring in. Might as well tear up th' one I got. That's why I weren't too picky 'bout how they fixed it up. All I need it for is transportation one way."

"My god, Regen! Are you telling me you plan to spend the rest of your life there?"

"Yup, if they'll have me. Don't matter though. It'll be th' rest o' my life one way or 'nother."

Orianne sat up in bed and cocked her head to one side. "Regen, what are you saying?"

"I might not be welcome back there. They don't like strangers, and they don't want people knowin' 'bout their little planet. If they decide you won't fit in, they ain't about t' let ya go on your way."

"Aren't you taking an awful chance for a woman who's only *comfortable*?"

"Yup, but if she ain't interested in me, I might as well be dead." Regen strapped on his laser pistol and walked over to the bed. He pulled Orianne to her feet and folded her in his arms.

"Yer still one o' th' best women I ever had, darlin'. If you wasn't a princess, I'd take you back t' Terma with me an' try t' fergit Herion, but you got a kingdom ta run, an' I don't fit in with royal society. See ya on down th' road." He kissed her tenderly, and she wrapped her arms around his neck as tears ran down her cheeks.

"You'll always have a place in my heart, Regen, and I wish I wasn't a princess, but my fate is here on Bardour. I wish you every happiness with her." She kissed him once again then released her hold.

Regen turned away quickly and strode out the door before Orianne could see the tears welling up in his eyes.

Regen walked past his ship, which more closely resembled a patchwork quilt with all the repairs. Amalek was waiting by the boarding ramp.

"We're all ready to go, Regen. It doesn't look pretty, but the ship's in good shape structurally, and all the systems are back on line except for the new stealth gear."

"Did ya git my old system workin'?"

"Yes, we could get parts for that, but there's no way to repair the Ausland experimental system."

"I got along fine with th' old stuff. Let's git goin'. I wanna git you home'n pick up Hitler so's I can be on my way back t' Phoenicia."

The pair seated themselves at the command console and received clearance from the Defense System, now in rebel hands. They moved to the launch pad past a half dozen freighters unloading weapons, supplies and allied troops.

"Looks like the weapons business here is over for guys like

us," Amalek said.

"Well, we made enough off'n it t' make us all rich men."

Amalek noticed the emotion in Regen's voice. "Pretty rough leaving the Princess, eh?"

"She's a great gal, but she's got a world t' run now. Ever'body says the war'll be over in a month or so, and she'll be crowned queen. She won't need me around then."

The flight back to Terma was uneventful. On the way, they radioed Mulinor about the new situation on Bardour.

"That's a shame. I was looking forward to another twenty million, or so, but I'm in good shape to retire now. The Rugistani boys'll be disappointed, but maybe they can get in on the deal directly now that the defense system's in the rebel's hands."

"We couldn't make no money now anyways. The big boys'd undercut us right an' left. 'Sides, this ship cain't carry 'nough t' compete on their level. The money should be in yer account b'now. Everything okay?"

"Yes, I'm happy and Jahallah's happy. You might want to land at his camp, though. He says he wants to talk to you right away. He wouldn't tell me why, but he was really worried about something. I'll break up operations here in Rugistan and see you back at the Velvet Saddle sometime."

"Okay, pleasure doin' business with ya Favik."

Regen turned to Amalek. "I wonder what yer daddy's upset about."

"I can't think of anything unless the Ausland army is getting serious."

"We'll find out soon enough. Plug in the coordinates fer yer daddy's place."

Jahallah was waiting for the pair as the boarding ramp hit the ground. The usual smirk of confidence was missing from his face, and he wrang his hands together in a nervous fashion Regen usually associated with drunks waiting for the judge to read their sentence. Amalek noticed the change immediately.

"Father, what's wrong?" He almost ran to embrace his parent. "Are you all right?"

"It's not me, my son, it's Hitler."

"Hitler?" Regen reacted with a mix of shock and anger. "What's wrong with Hitler?"

Jahallah lowered his head and held his hands together in a pleading position. "He's missing, Regen. Come inside, and I'll tell you all about it."

Jahallah led his son and Regen into the hideout/palace and to a small conference room.

"Sit down, would you like anything to eat or drink?"

"Not 'til I've heard 'bout Hitler," Regen said.

"It was two days ago. Your pet was not eating well, and my veterinarian thought he needed a change from the meat we were feeding him. He suggested we let him hunt. I was against it because I feared he would not return to his cage, but the vet assured me he would come back if we left some food and water in it. Well, he did not return. My men have been looking for him day and night ever since, but we've found nothing."

Regen leaned back in his chair, and the tension faded a bit from his face and body.

"Well, least ya didn't find no body. He's prob'ly still out huntin' somewhere. I'll try his whistle after I've had some lunch an' a drink."

"Regen, you don't understand. He was a hostage, and if we can't find him, I must pay the penalty."

Amalek's face now took on a concerned expression. "Father, it's only a skeen. You and Regen could surely come to some agreement on compensation if Hitler's lost."

"What's th' problem? Hitler's around, don't worry 'bout it," Regen said.

"What Father is talking about is our tribe's law concerning hostages. If a hostage cannot be returned after the conditions are met for that return, the one holding the hostage must kill himself or some member of his own family in compensation."

Regen's eyes widened, and his mouth dropped open a bit before he could compose himself.

"Now look here, Jahallah. Even if'n Hitler's layin' dead out there sommeres, he ain't worth no killin'. Sure, I'll miss th' little guy somethin' fierce, but he's just a pet. It ain't like he's my sister, or anything."

Jahallah shook his head sadly. "It's a matter of honor, Regen. You can't just forgive me and let it all pass. My word would no longer be good among our elders. I'd have to step down as leader of the Zunids."

"This is all nonsense anyways," Regen said. "I'll find Hitler right after lunch. Let's eat."

Lunch was a subdued feast even though it came with all the Gordian Bourbon Regen could drink. He was a bit on the tipsy side as he and Amalek mounted horses to scour the area for Hitler. When they were clear of the hideout, Regen blew several times on the whistle only dogs and Hitler could hear then waited for the sound of the skeen scurrying through the underbrush.

"I don't hear a thing, Regen."

"I don't neither. He must be a long ways off." The Bremen rubbed his chin and studied the mountains around him. "You suppose he went lookin' fer me?"

"If he did, he'd go back along the trail we used last time. We can't go there in the daylight because of the army. They're still looking for the stealth gear," Amalek said.

"Well, we kin give it to 'em now, cain't we?"

"I guess so, but it's pretty badly damaged."

"You could tell 'em it was tore up in th' crash, an' ya just found the wreckage, or somethin'."

Amalek pondered the situation a moment before replying. "It's worth a try. I'll contact them this afternoon and try to arrange a meeting. Meanwhile, I'll have some men strip the stuff out of your ship."

The men returned to the hideout, and Amalek made contact with the Ausland army contingent watching Zunid territory. They agreed to meet the next day/

That night after dinner, one of Jahallah's men entered the room with a message. He passed it to his chief on a silver tray then stood at attention awaiting furter orders. Jahallah opened the envelope and read.   As he read, his face brightened considerably, and a smile began to spread across his mouth.

"It's good news for you, Regen; but bad news for me. It's from Yussah, chief of the Rugistani Wamani. He has Hitler."

"I'm glad t' hear that. I'd hate fer you t' have t' blow your brains out over my skeen. Tell 'im I'll come git him soon as we kin git th' army off'n our backs."

"It's not that simple, Regen. He knows I was keeping him as a hostage, and he's taking advantage of my situation."

"I thought this here guy was a relative o' yers."

"He is, but he's also a Wamani, and that means he'll take advantage of any situation even if it's at his father-in-law's expense. He wants me to name his son as my heir, and I can't do that."

"There must be some other way outta this mess," Regen said.

"The only other honorable way out is to wage war on the Wamani."

"Whoa! Me an' Hitler ain't gonna be responsible for no war, and I sure don't wanna see Amalek disinherited. There's gotta be another way. Why don't I just offer him a few million fer Hitler?"

"That wouldn't be honorable. No money must change hands. There is no other way, and Yussah knows this. He must either give Hitler to me after I meet his terms, or I must take him back by force."

"You guys sure have a funny way o' dealin' with each other, but I gotta go along with whatever you want. I just hate t' see blood spilled over a skeen, even if he is my best friend."

"Perhaps there's another way?" Amalek chimed in.

"What is that?" Jahallah said.

"The only thing Yussah loves more than power is a beautiful woman. If we make it clear to him that war is the only alternative, he may relent and take the offer of a woman instead. I can't believe he really wants war."

"Oh, great. Now all we have t' do is find some good-lookin' female who wants t' be a whore for this Yussah guy. That should be easy," Regen said. His sarcastic tone made Amalek smile broadly.

"We could offer him a slave. He's always wanted a Cruzian woman. We could use your ship to fly to Cruzia and buy a whore," Amalek said.

"Yer fergettin', slavery's illegal on Terma," Regen responded.

"That's the good part, we offer the whore her freedom if she goes into Yussah's harem. He's happy, no money changes hands, and you get Hitler back."

"But, I'd have to buy the whore, and no money must change

hands," Jahallah said.

"Look, I'll buy the whore," Regen said

"I don't know," Amalek said. "If they're good-looking, they go pretty high on Cruzia"

"Well, I'm willin' t' have a go at it. Cruzia's only a few days away. What have we got t' lose?"

Jahallah raised a hand to halt the sudden rush to a decision. "Isn't there a Cruzian whore at The Velvet Saddle?"

"Yeah, Gaballa, but she's Mariva's whore, not mine."

"Considering the difference in circumstances, she might prefer life as one of Yussah's harem girls."

"Even if she'd jump at the chance, Mariva wouldn't be too happy 'bout it."

"As you said,Regen, slavery is illegal in Ausland. She's bound by law to treat her women as employees, and they are free to leave her at any time," Jahallah said.

"I hear what yer sayin', but Mariva's got some kind o' hold on all those girls, or they'd be off t' bigger n' better things by now. The Velvet Saddle ain't the poshest place in Ausland, ya know."

"As soon as we finish with the army, go back and sound both of them out. They may be willing to make a deal short of two million," Amalek said.

"I guess it won't hurt t' ask. Any more Gordian Bourbon around?" he said as he lifted his empty glass toward a servant.

CHAPTER 10

The Ausland army was glad to get their stealth gear back, even if it was a little worse for wear. Amalek explained it as damage from the crash, but the laser gun holes in some of the boxes made that hard to believe. They lifted their siege of the stronghold, and Jahallah returned to his camp in the desert near The Velvet Saddle. Regen left the next day for his apartment and discussions with Mariva and the Cruzian girl.

Regen entered his rooms and placed a call to Mariva, but he only got her voice mail. He left a message, then dialed room service for dinner. The liquor cabinet was out of Gordian Bourbon, and he had to make do with local stuff. Just as he was pouring water into his glass, the doorbell rang.

He opened the door to find Mariva pushing a cart holding his dinner and a fresh bottle of Gordian Bourbon.

"Welcome home, Regen," Mariva said as she pushed the cart into the room.

"Good t' be back, n' good t' see you too." Regen had almost forgotten how sensual this woman was, but one look at the trim figure and the promise in her deep black eyes reminded him. He took her in his arms and kissed her passionately.

"Your food'll get cold," Mariva whispered as she reluctantly broke off the kiss.

"We'll order more. I got an in with the owner o' this joint."

He picked her up and carried her into the bedroom.

Regen awoke first and moved to the abandoned cart to test the food. It was stone cold and ruined. He phoned in another order and helped himself to a bourbon and water. The clink of ice in the glass was enough to awaken Mariva, and she joined him wearing the top sheet like a toga.

"Pour me one of those, will ya?" she asked.

Regen made another drink and handed it to her.

"Where's Hitler?" she asked.

"That's what I need t' talk to ya 'bout. By th' way, I ordered us some dinner."

"What's wrong?" Mariva's tone turned somber, and her face took on a solemn expression. She didn't care much for skeens, but she knew Hitler was a special case.

"He ran off while I was gone, and some Wamani Bedouin chief over in Rugistan's holdin' him fer ransom."

"How much does he want? Can't you just pay him off?"

"I could if money was what he wanted, but he don't want money, he wants Jahallah t' name his son as heir t' the Zunid crown, and Jahallah ain't too keen on that. I offered t' pay off Yussah, but Jahallah says that ain't *honorable*, so we have t' make a deal t' git Hitler back with no money changin' hands 'tween him an' Yussah. We think we got a way t' git this done, but it involves your Cruzian whore."

"Gaballa?"

"Yeah, that's th' one. We think we can git this Yussah guy t' trade us Hitler fer her."

Mariva sat back in her chair and took a sip of her drink while she thought.

"Gaballa's the biggest attraction I've got. There's only about thirty Cruzian women on this planet, and twenty-some of them have husbands. There's only one other cathouse in Ausland with a Cruzian, and that's the Granada down in Union City. If I lost Gaballa, a lot of my clients would go down there, and my profits'd drop a good third. Besides, she still owes me 100,000 credits."

"If she's makin' ya all that money, how kin she owe ya so much?"

"I advanced her 250,000 to send back to her parents as an inducement to come in the first place. She's got four brothers and three sisters, and her old man's a cripple and can't work. She's their meal ticket and the source of college money for her siblings. She couldn't afford to give up whoring any more than I could afford to lose her services."

"What would it take t' git another Cruzian woman in here?"

"The gal down in Union City'd come here tomorrow, but she wants 250,000 up front and a bigger part of the take than Gaballa gets. I'd never make up the loss before she got too old to do the job."

"Let's see." Regen drummed his fingers on the end table and took a big sip of his bourbon. "A quarter million for her, say, another quarter million t' compensate you fer the lost income. Think a million'd be enough t' induce Gaballa t' live in luxury as whore t' that Bedouin?"

Mariva looked askance at Regen. "Wait a minute, all of this is pretty much speculation right now, and the biggest *if* is getting Gaballa to go for the deal. That doesn't even guarantee the sheik will bite. You've got a lot of ducks to get in a row here, Regen."

"*We've* got a lot of ducks to line up, darlin'. You're gonna help me do this ain't ya?" He leaned across the gap between them and kissed Mariva on the neck several times.

They were interrupted by the doorbell. "That's dinner, sweet lips. You can do more convincing later."

The next day, Regen and Mariva met with Gaballa in Mariva's office. Mariva opened the conversation. "Gaballa, you know Regen," she nodded toward the Bremen.

"Yes, lady, I know him very well." The soft, seductive tone caused Mariva to give Regen a stony glance.

"Good, he has a proposition for you, and I'd like for you to listen to it very carefully. I know all about it, and I'll tell you I'm fully in favor of it, if it meets with your approval. Go ahead Regen."

Gaballa turned to Regen with a quizzical look.

"I got two things t' offer ya. First, is enough money t' take care o' yer family in style." He looked at her for a sign of encouragement and noticed she was still interested. "Second, you'll get t' live a life o' luxury. How does that all sound?"

Gaballa sat back in her chair, and a wry smile spread across her face. "And just what do I have to do to how many to get all this?"

"All you gotta do is be part of the harem of a very rich shiek in Rugistan." Regen leaned forward trying to coax a positive answer out of the woman with body language.

Gaballa sighed in relief. "Is that all? I was afraid you were going to ask me to take on a Silurian Homopod, or something." She lapsed into thought for a moment before continuing, and Mariva and Regen sat in anxious silence. "I'd have to get a look at this shiek, and I'd have to know exactly how much money we're talking about before I say yes."

Regen relaxed visibly. At least she didn't reject the deal outright. "How much do ya need t' set yer family up right?"

Gaballa lapsed into thoughtfulness once more. "I'd say 400,000 up front, and another line of credit for 200,000 for the next four years. By then, my youngest sister will be out of college. If there's anything left in the line of credit after that time, it goes to my mother." She hesitated for a moment, and Regen was about to agree to the terms when she spoke again. "Also, you pay off my debt to Mariva."

"Done!" Regen almost shouted.

Gaballa gritted her teeth realizing she hadn't asked for enough, even though she'd doubled her bottom figure to allow some negotiating room.

Mariva entered the conversation. "I don't know what this shiek will give her in the way of money. She may need a bit more for her family, Regen." The pleading tone in Mariva's voice told Regen she was not satisfied with the deal being less than what they discussed for Gaballa.

Regen's expression turned sour. He thought Mariva was being very free with his money. "Tell you what I'll do, I'll throw in 300,000 in th' form o' an account in yer Mama's name. How's that?"

"Very generous, if this shiek isn't too bad to look at, I'll go for it, but doesn't this leave you on the short side, Mariva?"

"I'm being compensated for your loss, and I'll make an offer to Janea down in Union City to come take your place."

"Okay, when do I meet this shiek?"

"I gotta go back an' 'range ever'thin', but I'll be back in a week t' brief ya on th' whole deal. It'll prob'ly involve some play-actin' on your part, Gaballa, but I won't know how much 'til I talk with some other folks. Meantime, Mariva kin see if this Janea gal'll make a deal. I hope you kin help us out, 'cause it means a war if ya can't."

"War?" Gaballa said.

"Yeah, it's pretty complicated, but I'll explain it all to ya soon as I git ever'thing arranged." He turned to Mariva. "I'll leave in th' mornin' for Jahallah's camp, and I should be back within a week. We'll finalize ever'thing then. Thanks a lot, Gaballa." He kissed both women on the cheek and left the room.

After he left, Gaballa turned to Mariva. "What's going on here, anyway?"

"Like Regen said, it's pretty complicated, but the Zunids could be going to war with the Wamani in Rugistan if we can't get this problem settled. You're only one possible solution, and I don't want you to go along with him unless you really want to."

"He's offering big money. It'll be hard to turn down unless this sheik is a real loser."

"Honey, you'll just have to judge that for yourself, but I trust Regen to take care of you in this deal. Bremens've got a soft spot a mile wide when it comes to women. Want a drink?"

CHAPTER 20

Amalek met Regen as he rode into the Zunid camp. "Where's yer Daddy?" Regen asked.

"He's busy planning his campaign against the Wamani. He wants it to look real enough to Yussah. He also doesn't seem to think any Cruzian woman would go for Yussah, so he's certain there'll be war."

A servant took charge of Regen's horse, and Amalek led him into the chief's tent. "You can clean up and have something to drink before you brief us on your meeting with Mariva, if you like."

"No, I feel fine, but I will take a Gordian Bourbon and water."

"Coming right up." Amalek moved to a bar and mixed the drink plus one for himself. He handed the already sweating glass to Regen and sat down next to him. "Tell me what you found out."

"Gaballa'll go fer it, if this Yussah guy ain't too ugly. I got it all squared with Mariva too. Th' only problem now is how do we approach him?"

"Well, Yussah's not bad looking, but we gotta hope your gal is pretty enough to convince him to drop his demand for Father's throne."

"You ain't seen her, and you aint screwed her. Take it from me, any guy who don't think she's worth a kingdom is outta his gourd. Besides, I got a back-up plan in case he don't go for it."

"What's that?"   Amalek was suddenly much less skeptical about the prospects for success.   Regen was the type that always planned an emergency exit in any situation.

"It ain't that I don't trust ya, but I'd rather keep that my secret for right now.   Let's talk about how we tackle Yussah."

"Dad and I have talked this over a little, and we think it would be best if you went to see him as an informal peace envoy.   The Cruzian woman could be your companion, and you could judge his response to her as you tried to negotiate some kind of agreement.   Father would give you all the documentation you need to act on his behalf, and such an arrangement would also insure your safety in Yussah's camp."

Regen mulled the proposition over for a moment before answering.   "Yeah, I think that might be a good idea.   You git th' paperwork together, and soon as that's done, I'll go back t' git Gaballa an' a skimmer for th' trip into Rugistan.   With th' army happy, we don't have t' take th' back way in any more. I'll need the coordinates for the Wamani camp, too.   Meantime, I'll take some more bourbon."   He handed his empty glass to Amalek.

The papers were ready late the next day, and Regen left for The Velvet Saddle after getting the camp coordinates and a briefing on proper diplomatic etiquette from Jahallah.   He also advised the Bremen that any settlement other than trading the whore for Hitler was completely out of the question.

As soon as he reached the dude ranch, Regen briefed Mariva and Gaballa on the plan.   "Well, that's it ladies.   When can we leave?"

"I've talked to Janea, and she can be here by the end of the week," Mariva said.   "Gaballa's got customers booked through that time also.   Looks like first of next week, at the earliest."

"I'm ready to go any time," Gaballa said. "I'm anxious to get a look at this shiek, but I'll honor my commitment to Mariva."

"Good, first of next week it is," Regen agreed.

The next week Gaballa loaded her belongings into the skimmer and said a tearful goodbye to Mariva. Regen watched in bored resignation as the women did their thing, but they were soon on their way to Rugistan.

They passed the border checkpoints in a routine manner. Regen had no record on Terma, and Gaballa's papers were quite in order. The customs boys didn't find the 100 kilos of hashinah Regen sequestered in various nooks and crannies of the skimmer. He'd been careful to put the stuff in sealed bags to foil the sniff sensors, and visual discovery was impossible. As soon as they were safely inside Rugistan, Regen transferred the hashina to the luggage compartment of the skimmer.

The navigation system took them to the edge of the Wamani camp where Regen slowed down to accommodate the sentries sure to be posted far enough out for early warning purposes.

He'd guessed correctly. Two heavily armed Bedouins appeared from a group of rocks and signaled them to stop as they sighted the tents in the distance. Regen's practiced eye noted a heavy laser cannon hidden in some brush to the left of the rocks.

The guards noticed the Ausland markings on the skimmer and voiced their challenge in that language. "This is a private camp. Do you have business here?" the tall one asked in what Regen thought was a very polite manner.

"My name's Regen, an' I'm a special ambassador from Jahallah of the Ausland Zunids. Here's my papers." Regen shuffled through a briefcase and presented a folder bearing the royal seal of the Zunid king.

"Just a moment," the guard said as he opened the folder and read the papers carefully. The other one kept his rifle trained on Regen, just in case.

"Your papers seem to be in order, but who is the woman?" The guard handed the credentials back to Regen.

"She's my whore, an' she's got diplomatic immunity, too."

A smile spread across the faces of the guards as they stifled laughter. Women were chattel in this culture. "Just a moment, I'll let our sheik know you're coming."

The tall guard moved back behind the rocks for a few moments and reappeared with a piece of paper in his hand. "Here are the directions to Shiek Yussah's tent compound. He'll be waiting for you. Peace be upon you." The guard saluted and waved them on.

It was no problem finding Yussah's tent—the largest and most ornate in the camp. Gaballa was impressed.

"Wow! Some digs! I don't care if it is a tent, it's better than any place I've ever hung up my nighty in," she said.

"These guys make a fortune runnin' drugs, guns and whatever else is illegal anywhere. They're also some o' th' meanest critters there are. They'd cut you open just t' see what color yer guts are. Don't mess with 'em."

"I've heard the stories. Don't worry about me, it's you I'm afraid for. You have a tendency to say what's on your mind, and that may not be what these clowns want to hear."

"I'll be okay, you just remember what you're supposed t' do, an' ever'thing'll be fine."

"I understand. You can count on me."

An honor guard formed at the entrance to Yussah's tent as the skimmer came to a stop. A sharp command set the guard at stiff attention as a servant rolled out a red carpet toward the skimmer's door. "Looks like we rate first class treatment," Gaballa said.

"They do this fer people they're gonna behead too," Regen countered. "Let's go."

Gaballa stepped from the car followed by Regen. A rather short, middle-aged man stepped out of the tent entrance and walked toward the pair. He wasn't much more than 160 centimeters tall, but the wide shoulders and narrow waistline gave a hint of the athletic build under his loose-fitting top and pantaloons. Red felt boots ornately trimmed in gold and silver thread and studded with precious stones covered rather large feet, but his hands were delicate and almost feminine. His bronze complexion contrasted with the light beige clothes, while a red sash holding a bejeweled dagger circled his middle. He was handsome by any woman's standards with a chiseled face and dark black eyes. A neatly trimmed black beard outlined his jawline, and full red lips pouted sensuously. He radiated authority, but his smile seemed genuine enough. He moved to Regen extending his hand in greeting.

"Regen! It's so good to meet you. Welcome to my camp."

"Pleasure t' meet you too, yer highness." Regen took his hand and gave a perfunctory bow.

"And who's this lovely thing?" Yussah turned to Gaballa who knelt with her head lowered in the manner Regen briefed her about.

"This here's Gaballa, a Cruzian woman."

Yussah placed a hand under the woman's chin and lifted her face up to his. "A truly beautiful specimen. I must compliment on your taste in female flesh. Get up, Gaballa, and let me have a good look at you."

She stood, and Yussah found her to be at least seven centimeters taller than himself, but it didn't seem to dampen his ardor. "Yes, a truly beautiful specimen." He placed a hand on her shoulder and turned her around once. "But enough, come into my tent and refresh yourselves. I assume we have much to talk about, Regen."

"There's also 100 kilos o' hashinah in th' back o' th' skimmer as Jahallah's gift t' you."

"Fine, fine." He spoke to a servant in Wamani, and the drug was soon on its way to his private stores.

"Jahallah always sends the finest, but you've brought something even finer." He could not take his eyes off Gaballa.

"An' I'd like t' see Hitler, if ya don't mind."

"Later, later." He dismissed Regen's request with a wave of his hand as he extended his arm to Gaballa.

Yussah ushered them past the servants holding back the tent flaps and into a cool, well lit area carpeted with expensive rugs. Several divans surrounded the open space, and a low table laden with trays of food sat before one of them.

"Sit down and help yourselves to the food. What would you like to drink?"

"Ya got any Gordian Bourbon?"

"Alas, no. If I'd had more warning of your arrival, I would have stocked some. My spies tell me you're quite fond of it. What about you, lady?"

"If my lord pleases, I'd like some red wine."

Yussah nodded to a servant who poured the liquid into a crystal glass and presented it to Gaballa.

"I'll have some o' that, too, I guess," Regen said.

The servant poured two more glasses and passed one to Yussah and one to Regen. The trio sat on the divans with Yussah taking the one directly in front of the table while he indicated the one on his left for Regen and Gaballa. Regen took the divan indicated, but Gaballa sat down next to Yussah.

Yussah started a bit at the move, but a smile quickly spread across his face. He asked, "Why don't you sit next to your master?"

"Lord, Regen does not own me. Slavery is illegal in Ausland. I wanted to see if you smelled as good up close as you did from a distance."

"Well, do I?"

Gaballa sniffed the air and smiled coyly. "Yes, you do, Lord."

Yussah recoverd and took a sip of his wine before addressing Regen. "You asked about seeing Hitler. I assume that is the name of your pet skeen."

"Yeah, that's him. I wanna make sure he's bein' fed good and not mistreated in any way."

"I assure you he's quite safe and very well fed. He's even digested a few fingers from unwary servants."

"I'd like t' judge that fer m'self, if'n ya don't mind."

"Ah, but I do, Regen. You have a well deserved reputation for underhanded dealings, and I fear you may have some plot up your sleeve to rescue Jahallah from his dilemma."

"You know he's not goin' t' give in, don't ya?"

Yussah shrugged his shoulders and took another sip of his wine. "I was resolved to go to war before your skeen conveniently fell into my hands. I'm offering Jahallah a chance to save his honor while obtaining something I want, and all without bloodshed. It seems to me that I'm actually doing him a favor by making his death unnecessary."

Gaballa moved closer to Yussah and let her breast rub against his arm. "May I see the skeen, Lord? I've never seen one."

Yussah looked at her with a surprised expression. "I'd have thought you would have seen it around The Velvet Saddle."

Gaballa's face took on a pouting expression. "Lord, I spend most of my time in my room. When I'm not working, I'm sleeping."

Yussah broke into a merry laugh, slapped Gaballa on the backside playfully and spoke to Regen. "She's got a good sense of humor besides her beauty. You have quite a find there."

"I won her in a poker game, but strictly speakin', she's a free woman."

"But, you must have some hold over her."

"She owes me th' money I spent t' buy her freedom—th' money I should o' won in th' poker game. She's mine, in a way, 'til she pays that off, but we don't live together, or nothin'."

"I didn't think so. You're not the type to stick with one woman for very long." He turned back to Gaballa. "Yes, you may go see the skeen, if Regen approves." He glanced at the Bremen for support.

"Sure, sure, just let me know if'n he looks hungry, or anythin'."

Yussah clapped for a servant and spoke to him in Wamani. "Follow this man. He'll take you to the beast and bring you back when you're finished."

"Oh thank you, Lord." Gaballa jumped to her feet but leaned back and kissed the shiek on the forehead.

When she was gone, Yussah leaned closer to Regen. "Would you be willing to let me have a turn with your lady?"

"Well, I don't know. I was plannin' on havin' her myself while we was here."

"20,000 for one night. How's that?"

"A mighty fine offer, but what would I do for female companionship?"

"I'll call in my harem, and you may have your pick."

Regen smiled inwardly. Yussah was taking the bait, but he

decided to play him a little longer.

"That's neighborly o' ya, but Gaballa's got t' go for it. She only screws me an' the folks she wants to screw."

"I know she wants me. I can feel the magnetism, Regen. These Cruzian women radiate it, and I'm dying to experience their special skills at making love again. It's been over five years since my last one."

Regen swirled the wine in his glass and sat pensively for a moment.

"I kin sympathize with that. I gotta have her ever' now an' then myself. Tell ya what, let's see how the evenin' goes. If she's okay with it, I am. Meanwhile, we kin discuss how t' keep you two from killin' a bunch o' yer own folks in a silly war over a skeen."

Yussah waved a finger at Regen. "Ah, but it's not really about the skeen. It's about Jahallah saving his life and my son inheriting his kingdom. I can't really understand his opposition. The boy is his grandson, after all."

At that moment, a tearful Gaballa burst into the room. "Regen, see what your monster did to my beautiful necklace!" She held out a broken strand of beads to the Bremen.

"What happened?" Yussah asked.

Gaballa composed herself and turned to the shiek as Regen stared at the beads dropping to the floor from the shattered jewelry. "I was looking at the thing, Lord, when my necklace fell inside the cage. Before I could pull it back the beast bit off the pendant and swallowed it whole. It was a gift from a very good client, and I loved it very much."

She broke into fits of sobbing again, and Yussah took her gently into his arms. "There, there, my pet, you can tell my jeweler what it looked like, and he will make another just like it."

Regen laid the rest of the necklace on the table and picked up the loose beads from the floor. "Yeah, I'll pay fer it."

"Oh no, I insist on paying for it. The skeen is my prisoner, after all."

"Suit yerself. We'll just hafta stay here 'til it gits done, I guess."

"Please be my guest as long as you like. We should enjoy ourselves now. War may soon make all our lives unpleasant enough."

"I guess yer right 'bout that. I don't see Jahallah givin' in, an' I don't see you givin' me back my skeen."

"Then it's settled." Yussah summoned his jeweler who looked at the necklace and conversed a while with Gaballa before advising his master the item would be ready by the following afternoon.

"Well, now we can enjoy the evening. I've not planned anything special for you, but I'll have my chefs prepare an excellent meal and we can enjoy some music with dinner. Why don't you two settle into my guest tent and relax until then." Yussah summoned a servant and spoke to him in Wamani. "This man will show you the way."

The servant bowed low to Regen and led them out of Yussah's tent to a smaller tent nearby. Regen noticed the well armed guards on either side of the entrance and was glad he wasn't planning an escape. When they were inside, Regen made a quick check for sensors and found several well-placed units. Regen lifted a finger to his lips to indicate they should not talk.

A few moments later, two servants entered carrying their baggage. An inspection of the locks revealed the bags had been opened. Regen lifted an electric shaver from one of his bags and turned it on. "There, that'll keep their sensors busy fer a while."

"A razor?" Gaballa looked at the item in disbelief.

"That's what it looks like, but it's really a jammin' unit. That things transmittin' white noise on every frequency you kin imagine. We kin talk now. Good job gittin' Hitler t' eat th' pendant."

"It wasn't a difficult job. All I had to do was lean over the cage, and Hitler did the rest. You were right about the guards. They wouldn't come within two meters of that cage." Gaballa smiled recalling the wary look of Yussah's soldiers as they led her to Hitler.

"The dope'll take 'bout eight hours t' work. I need you in bed with Yussah by then. I hope he meets with yer approval."

"He's not bad looking at all, if you like short men. I prefer someone more your size." Gaballa moved to Regen and pressed her body against his.

"Now that you mention it, we'd better put on a good act for th' benefit o' his cameras." Regen wrapped her in his arms and let passion take it's course.

Two hours later, the intercom came to life. "Regen, dinner is in an hour. I hope you two are **refreshed**." The emphasis told Regen the cameras were working perfectly.

"We'll be there."

"Good, just walk outside and the servant will bring you to the banquet tent. See you in an hour."

Gaballa put on her most seductive outfit and modeled it for Regen. "What do you think?"

"I think Yussah'll go stark, ravin' mad when he sees that, 'specially after he's had a look at th' tapes from his cameras. You were better'n I ever seed ya afore."

When they were ready to go, Regen turned off his razor. "Better save th' battery. Might need it som'more."

The banquet tent was everything they expected. An open area ten meters on a side was surrounded by divans and low tables on intricately woven rugs. A small orchestra played what Regen guessed was native Wamani music on some curious-looking instruments. The sound was a mixture of wails and moans accompanied by a staccato drumbeat. None of Yussah's captains seemed to be paying any attention to it. They were too busy conversing with each other and fondling the silk-clad women at their sides. As Regen and Gaballa entered, the band broke into the Ausland national anthem, and the men rose to attention.

The last note of the strident anthem faded out, and Yussah raised his hands for quiet. He spoke briefly in Wamani then turned to Regen. "Come sit next to me, here." He indicated a divan next to his own.

The pair took their seats with Gaballa, again, next to Yussah. The woman on the chief's other side gave her a stony glance, and Regen guessed she must be his wife, and Jahallah's daughter. She spoke in perfect Auslander. "How is my father, Regen?"

"He was very well the last I seen 'im, yer highness. He's very worried 'bout a war 'tween his tribe an' yer husbands. I'm here t' try t' prevent that, if possible."

"I wish you every success. My husband can be a bit pig-headed in these matters." She gave Yussah a disapproving look, but he ignored her completely. His gaze was fixed on Gaballa.

The meal was excellent, though Regen was not sure about the ingredients of some dishes. Some excellent wines accompanied the food, and a fanfare from the band announced desert. Four servants carried in an ornately decorated cake on a gilded platform and sat it in front of Yussah. The shiek took a saber offered by another servant and struck through the several layers in a single stroke to the applause of his men. All eyes popped wide open as the cake parted along the saber cut and a sensuous woman emerged from under the frosting.

Whistles and shouts greeted the sultry brunette as she stepped gracefully from the confection and began to dance around the open area to the sound of a willowy tune. She was good, but Regen knew Gaballa was better. "Don't you know that tune, darlin'?" he said.

Gaballa took the hint and leaped to her feet. She shed the outer part of her gown revealing a black lace top of skimpy proportions and a black g-string arrangement with heavy fringe around the waistband. She pulled the tiara from her head, and her long, black hair fell in a cascade of ebony below her shoulders. The band stopped playing, and the men grew silent. The dancer glared at her with undisguised hatred. Yussah rose and spoke to the band. "Don't stop playing. Let's have a competition between our best and Regen's whore." He pulled a ring from his left hand and held it high. "This will be the winner's prize. Men, I give you Gaballa of Cruzia. Play on!"

The band resumed it's tune, and the Wamani dancer pranced to the center of the floor where she went into a series of provocative gyrations. Gaballa walked slowly to the edge of the area, cirlcling her opponent as she danced.

Gaballa was sex in motion. Her hips swiveled as if she had no pelvis, while her arms begged the men to embrace her. The steps coordinated perfectly with her body language, and her hair seemed to have some kind of control system of its own, assuming a perfect position to accent her face and bossoms. Soon, all eyes in the room were fixed upon her. The jeers and catcalls stopped, and the room grew eerily silent except for the band music.

The Wamani woman doubled her efforts, but it was obvious to everyone in the tent, man and woman alike, that she was a poor second. Yussah rose and clapped his hands together three times. The music stopped, and both dancers fell to the floor in obeisanse to the shiek. "Gentlemen, what is your decision? Is it Mooroa?" A smattering of applause greeted this question, and the Wamani dancer glared daggers at both Yussah and Gaballa. "Or is it Gaballa?" The air exploded with shouts of approval, and Yussah raised his arms again for silence. "You have won the prize, Gaballa. Come claim it."

The Cruzian rose and walked toward Yussan to the applause of the men while Mooroa sulked out of the tent. She knelt before him.

Yussah pressed the ring into her hand and lifted her to her feet. "The new queen of the dance!" he announced, and the men and women applauded wildly. He turned to Regen. "You must let me have this wonderful woman for one night. Name your price."

Regen's smile radiated intrigue as he answered. "Looks like she ain't opposed t' th' idée, and I don't mind doin' without her tonight." He rubbed his chin thoughtfully for a moment then looked at Yussah with a cunning grin. "My price is Hitler."

Yussah groaned and slumped into his divan. "You know I can't do that, why did you ask it?"

"Just doin' my job, that's all. I guess you kin have 'er since ya won't give Hitler back anyway."

Yussah's eyes lit up with joy, but the scowl on his wife's face told him the shiek would pay very dearly for his night of love. She rose from the divan and stalked from the room followed by two guards.

"I don't think yer woman's too pleased with yer choice," Regen said.

"She's a woman, Regen. In our culture, her feelings aren't important. She knows to keep her opinions to herself." He patted the divan where his wife had been. "Come sit with me Gaballa."

The woman moved to his side and gave Regen a surreptitious wink.

CHAPTER 21

A frantic servant burst into Regen's tent during the early hours of the morning jabbering in Wamani and gesturing toward the tent flap. The Bremen was barely able to don his pants and boots before the agitated servant practically dragged him into the night.

"Keep yer shirt on! I'm commin'." Regen protested, but the man only continued a string of Wamani and pointed toward a tent where light showed under the flap and other voices could be heard through the rough fabric.

As they entered the tent, a studious-looking man with a red beard greeted Regen in Auslandic. "I am Taman, the shiek's vetereinarian. This man called me when he found your skeen like this." He pointed to a steel cage where a limp Hitler lay on the floor, unmoving.

"Oh no! Hitler!" Regen ran to the cage, knelt down and opened the door. He pulled the skeen out on the rug covering the dirt floor and checked his pulse. Then, he bent his head close to the skeen's mouth and listened for any sounds of breathing while the other men in the room stood in silence. "He's dead," Regen pronounced. The big Bremen lowered his face into his hands and began to sob miserably.

"Sir, I assure you your pet has had only the best of care since his arrival in this camp. I can't understand what happened," the vet said.

Regen composed himself, and a servant handed him a cotton

towel to dry his tears. "What ya bin feedin' 'im?"

"I myself did considerable research in this area, and though it seems they thrive on anything, the literature indicated they preferred lean, raw, red meat. He's been given nothing but freshly butchered mutton and only the best water." The vet seemed to fear the Bremen would turn on him in revenge for his pet's death.

Regen moved to the cage and inspected the woodchip litter lining the bottom. He pulled a stool from the chips. "Somebody's bin feedin' 'im somethin' differ'nt. Look at this."

The vet leaned closer and saw the stool was stained a dark blue in contrast to the normal deep brown. Regen squeezed the stool between his fingers to show how fresh it was. "This here stool's prob'bly th' last one he did. See that blue color?"

"Yes, it reveals the presence of some chemical in the digestive tract, I would guess."

"Yer right, that's niobium trichloride, I'd bet my last credit on that."

The vet took the stool and passed it to a servant who looked to be his assistant. He spoke to the man in Wamani, and the assistant bowed and left the tent. "My man will verify your diagnosis in a few moments, but there is no possible way niobium trichloride could get into his food?"

"You bin fumigatin' fer rats lately? A lot o' people use that chemical for rats, but it's first use is t' git rid o' skeens. I seen it used on freighters a lot. It'll wipe out a skeen population in nuthin flat."

"We have no problem with rats here. There isn't a gram of niobium trichloride in the camp."

"Who might'a had some they used fer somethin' else?" Regen wiped his hands on the towel offered by a slave and stood up.

The vet thought for a moment. "No one. The only other use for niobium trichloride is coloring denemine gems to look like sapphires."

Regen snapped his fingers and his eyes brightened. "That's it! Hitler swallowed the pendant from Gaballa's necklace. She said it was a sapphire, but it was probably a denemine colored to look like one. At least it explains the bluish stool."

"Yes, it would do that, but I'd better perform a post-mortem exam just to be sure." The vet began to give orders in Wamani.

"Wait a minute! I don't want nobody cuttin' 'im up. I'm satisfied about how he died, an' you should be too."

Taman countermanded his previous orders and turned to Regen. "We will have him buried in the royal cemetery. What kind of memorial statue would you like? I'm sure Shiek Yussah will approve whatever you wish."

"I'd like t' burry 'im back home so's I kin visit his grave without crossin' no borders. Just put 'im in a refrigerated cooler so's he'll keep 'til I git back, if ya would."

Taman bowed to Regen and issued more orders. In a few moments two servants appeared carrying a rather large cooler. They sat it on the floor, and opened the lid. A cloud of vapor condensed over the opening, telling Regen the inside was the right temperature. Taman inspected the container and nodded to the servants. They gently placed Hitler inside and closed the lid.

A bustle of activity behind them caused the men to turn toward the tent opening. Yussah entered in a loose-fitting robe followed by Gaballa and two guards. The shiek's hair was in disarray, and Gaballa's makeup was smeared in several spots.

"What's going on here?" Yussah asked.

Taman bowed to his master and opened the cooler to show the dead skeen.

"My lord, there has been a terrible accident. The skeen is dead."

"Dead? How can he be dead?"

Regen stepped forward to shield the vet from Yussah's wrath. "Remember, Gaballa told us he snatched th' pendant off'n her necklace when she leaned too close to th' cage?"

"Yes, yes, but how could swallowing a small gemstone cause his death?"

"It was a denemine dyed to look like a sapphire, and the dye is a deadly poison to skeens."

"That gem was a true sapphire!" Gaballa blurted out. "The man who gave me the necklace assured me all the gems were genuine."

"And, who was this man?" Yussah asked.

"It was Gerbra, the Mollon. Everyone knows he's one of the richest men in the galaxy."

Yussah looked at Regen with a knowing expression, and the two men understood the situation immediately. Gerbra was well known as a con man who used what little wealth he possessed to convince suckers he was trustworthy enough to handle large sums of money for them. He was an expert at making small fortunes from large ones.

Yussah put an arm around Gaballa. "There, there, darling. My jeweler will replace your lost stone with one even finer, I guarantee it." He winked at Regen who covered a smile with one hand.

He placed his head close to Taman's and spoke in a low tone using the Wamani language. "Do you agree with Regen's diagnosis?"

Taman whispered back in Wamani, "Yes, lord. The skeen's stools bore a blue tint—a sure indication of niobium trichloride poisoning. I am satisfied."

"Very well, I don't want to upset this woman needlessly. Explain to her that you diagnosed a virus, or something. I'll take your word over Regens, and it will be over."

"Yes, lord."

Taman addressed Gaballa. "Madame, I do not agree with Regen. The gem was undoubtedly genuine. In my opinion, the skeen died of Durret's Virus. We've had some of our horses infected lately, and I fear one of the servants feeding the pet may have failed to clean his hands sufficiently before doing so."

"Who is he? I'll cut his guts out!" Regen shouted.

Yussah raised a hand to call for quiet. "Regen, I will get to the bottom of this, and the punishment for the guilty party will be the loss of his left hand." He turned back to Gaballa. "Go back to bed. I will return shortly. I need to speak with Regen a moment first." He kissed her tenderly on the forehead.

"I will be anxiously awaiting your return, lord," Gaballa said. She curtsied and left the tent.

"Well Regen, it looks like a cheap imitation gemstone has prevented a war. I'm sorry about your skeen, but you must agree that I had no part in his demise."

"Sure, sure, no hard feelins. It was a accident. I'll take off fer home after sunup, soon as Gaballa's ready t' go."

Yussah placed an arm around Regen's shoulders and led him out into the night. "That's something else we need to talk about. I've asked Gaballa to remain with me, and she has consented. I know she owes you money, and I'll be pleased to pay any sum you name, that is, any sum within reason, of course. What is your price?"

"Well, that Adran used her t' cover a 500,000 bet." He looked at the shiek to see the reaction to such an amount, but the man didn't blink an eye.

"Done! I'll transfer the funds to your account immediately."

He slapped Regen on the back. "You've made two men happy tonight, Regen. Jahallah doesn't have to go to war, and I have the woman of my dreams—quite an accomplishment for an amateur ambassador."

The next morning, Regen bid a tender goodbye to Gaballa and embraced Yussah in the Bedouin manner before boarding his skimmer. Hitler's cooler sat in the back seat with enough coolant to get him safely back to The Velvet Saddle. In a way, he was glad to see Gaballa in a decent situation, though he would certainly miss her services. He could only hope Janea was half as good.

At the border, customs was a bit skeptical of the dead skeen, but Regen assured them it was going to be a gift to the biology department at the university in the capitol city, and that calmed their fears. Soon, he pulled up in front of his apartment at The Velvet Saddle and hurried inside with Hitler's cooler. Mariva was waiting for him.

"How did it go? I don't see Gaballa, and I'm dying to know what happened. What's in the cooler?"

"Slow down, first things first." Regen opened a cabinet and pulled out a large, black bag. He rummaged around inside and took out a small brown case. He opened it to reveal a syringe and several vials of liquid. Carefully, he measured a small amount of the liquid into the syringe and expelled the air.

"What's that stuff?"

"It's fer Hitler." Regen opened the cooler, and Mariva recoiled in shock.

"Regen, Hitler's dead!"

"Not yet, but he will be if'n I don't git this serum in him real quick." He lifted the skeen from the box and placed him on the couch. Feeling for a vein, he held his finger over the correct spot and injected the serum. "Now all we kin do is wait t' see if he aint' been cold too long and if this stuff's still potent."

Mariva shook her head in dismay. "I don't understand any of this. You've got a lot of explaining to do, Regen."

Regen slumped into a chair to wait for Hitler's awakening and sighed heavily.

"I'm sorry I didn't fill you in on th' deal, but I only told Gaballa 'bout it on th' way over t' Rugistan. I was afraid somebody'd leak it out 'fore I could pull it off, an' the fewer people who knew, the better."

Mariva gave him a quizzical look but said nothing.

"Ya see, I needed a hedge in case Gaballa didn't go fer th' shiek. I found this-here necklace with a denamine stone colored t' look like a sapphire, an' I knew they'd done it with niobium trichloride, which is poisonous t' skeens. Now, I bin givin' Hitler small doses o' that stuff t' try an' build up some immunity to it, 'cause lots o' people use it as a way t' kill skeens an' he might run into it some places we go. I found out that a small dose put him inta like suspended animation, an' he'd stay that way fer hours 'less th' weather was real hot. Th' colder it was, th' longer he'd stay out. I figured he'd bite off anythin' that got within reach, so I had Gaballa wear that necklace when she went t' see 'im, an' I told her t' lean over th' cage an' let it dangle inside so's he could git it. She did a real good job, an' he was out 'bout eight hours later. They figured he was dead, an' I helped 'em confirm that. With Hitler dead, there was no way anybody could start a war. Jahallah's problem was solved, an' it didn't matter what Gaballa did. Turns out, she decided t' stay there anyway."

"Why didn't you just use the necklace yourself? It would have saved you a ton of money and me a damn good whore."

"I knowed Yussah wouldn't let me git near Hitler. He's a

pretty shrewd character, an' he was familiar with my reputation. Knowin' how those Bedouin folks feels 'bout women, I figured he'd never suspect Gaballa. 'Sides, th' necklace didn't look as good on me."

"Regen, you amaze me. I never gave you credit for that much intelligence."

"Thankfully, neither did Yussah. Hey! I think he's comin' 'round."

Hitler began to twitch a little, his eyes blinked several times, and he tried, unsuccessfully, to stand up. His legs gave out quickly, but his eyes opened wider and focused on Regen. Mariva later swore she saw real love in the animal's eyes as it lifted its head toward its master.

"That's a boy! Yer safe now. We're back home, fella." Regen reached forward and laid his hand on the skeen's head in what Mariva could only describe as tender affection. Hitler responded with a soft cooing noise she'd never heard before from the monster.

"I think he's going to make it." Mariva sounded almost relieved at Hitler's recovery, though she'd never had much love for the thing in the past.

This time, Hitler was successful in standing up. He wobbled for a moment then leaped into Regen's lap nuzzling his head against the Bremen's chest. "Looks like he's back t' normal. Guess the antidote was still good." He carried the skeen to the door and let it run off into the brush.

"Aren't you afraid he'll run into trouble in his weakened state?"

"Ain't nothin' 'round here kin give 'im any problems, and the fresh air'll do him good. He needs a good run afore we leave."

"Leave?" Mariva looked at Regen with disbelief. "I thought

this was your retirement home."

"It was, 'til I found Phoenicia." Regen stared out the doorway and watched Hitler chase a lizard across the sand.

"Phoenicia? I never heard of such a place. Where's that?" Her voice now held a note of anger mixed with jealousy.

"You ain't alone. It ain't on any charts, and I couldn't tell ya how t' git there if'n I wanted to. All I know is, I gotta go back." His gaze shifted to the sky.

"Is there a woman?" The tone was now pure jealousy.

"Yup, she ain't as pretty as you, and she ain't as rich, but fer th' first time in my life, I think I'm in love."

"Love? Did you say love? When did you start being interested in love?"

"I know it sounds crazy, but I can't git her off'n my mind. I dream about her, an' th' funny thing is I don't dream 'bout screwin' her like I do other women. I just see th' two o' us sittin' 'round and talkin'.'"

A sly smile spread across Mariva's face as she shook her head skeptically. "Regen, Regen, do you expect me to believe that?"

"Well, you kin believe whatever ya like. Tomorrow, I'm buyin' enough gold t' fill the hold o' my ship. Then, I'm takin' off fer Phoenicia."

"You said you couldn't tell me how to get there, what coordinates will you plug into the navigation system?"

"Oh, I got a way t' find th' place, but it's only good fer one trip, and that trip's one-way."

"Are you sure about this? It sounds so final, and I've never known you to take on any adventure unless you had a back way out."

"That tells ya how strong I feel 'bout this gal. I hate t' leave you behind, darlin', but I'm signin' over t' you all the credits I can't convert inta gold."

"Why gold?"

"I don't figure they got any contact with intergalactic bankin', but gold al'ays talks."

Mariva stood up and walked over to the big Bremen. She put her arms around him and lifted her face to his. "I guess I'd better take advantage of what may be your last night as a free man." She pressed her lips to his, and he responded with ardor.

CHAPTER 22

Regen calculated the weight he would have remaining after a full load of fuel and converted most of his credits into that weight in gold. Several armoured skimmers were needed to carry that amount to his ship near the Bedouin camp, and Jahallah provided armed escort to insure no other tribe would have a shot at the loot. His charge to Regen for the service was robbery enough in the Bremen's eyes. Jahallah did contribute a full load of rodents for Hitler's rations on the trip, and he treated his friend to a huge banquet the night before his departure.

As they watched a particularly boring dancing girl, Jahallah asked the question that had been bothering him ever since the Bremen's arrival in his camp. "Regen, Yussah informed me your skeen was dead. How is it that I saw him on your ship when you paid me with gold for my security service."

"That was his ghost. As far as anyone knows, he's dead, and I think it'd better stay that way. If'n Yussah knew I'd tricked him, he'd be in yer face tomorra with both barrels balzin'."

"How did you do it? Yussah is no fool."

"A little secret known only t' me an his new concubine, Gaballa. You'll have t' git 'im t' loan her to ya someday so's you kin get th' whole story."

A lecherous smile spread across Jahallah's face. "That sounds like a wonderful idea." As Amalik approached the pair, Jahallah's face turned sober. Regen rose to greet him.

"Regen! I'm glad I didn't miss you," Amalek shouted as he embraced his partner in adventure.

"I wouldn't leave without sayin' goodbye to ya. Sit down and have a drink."

"Don't mind if I do. Did Father tell you I'm to be married soon?"

"No, who's th' lucky lady?" Regen slapped his friend on the back just as a servant placed a drink in his hand, and the fruity concoction spilled over Amalek's expensive looking pants.

"Sorry 'bout that."

"Don't worry, with what my Father charged you for escorting the gold, we can afford to have them cleaned. You'll be surprised to learn that I'm engaged to Yasamina, Yussah's daughter."

"What? I didn't think he had any kids your age."

"He doesn't. Yasamina is only twelve, but it cements a bond between our tribes, and in our culture, I can have all the concubines I want, so her age doesn't matter. We only have to produce an heir, and that can wait until she's sixteen, at least."

The men fell into fits of laughter, and the dancing girl act left the floor to be replaced by a group of acrobats and jugglers. Regen's attention turned to Gordian Bourbon. It would probably be his last opportunity to imbibe since he doubted they'd heard of it on Phoenicia.

"Regen, tell me why you want to leave Terma for Phoenicia?" Jahallah asked. "Amalek told me the planet's run by *women*." The disgust in his voice was undisguised.

Regen poured another glass of bourbon and topped it off with only ice—no water. "Well, I think I found th' woman o' my dreams, Jahallah."

"You think? Hadn't you better be sure? My son says this is a one-way trip for you."

"I 'magine it will be, but I know that gal wanted me t' stay real bad, and I gotta believe I'll be happy with her."

"Well, in case you never have another good woman the rest of your life, I want you to meet Shaddar." Jahallah signaled a servant who vanished behind a drapery and emerged leading the most beautiful woman Regen had ever seen. She was tall and slim with bright red hair and flashing green eyes. Her whole body moved in sensual coordination as she walked toward him, and her filmy clothes swished about her perfect figure revealing long, slim legs and high breasts. She knelt before Jahallah and lowered her head in the Bedouin woman's fashion.

"Rise, my lovely. This is Regen, the man I told you about. I want you to make him very happy tonight. It may be the last happy night of his life."

She rose and turned to Regen. "My master bids me entertain you, sir. I can dance, play the lute, sing a little and perform some magic tricks. What do you desire?"

Regen's mouth watered as he surveyed the exquisite example of womanhood before him. "Tell ya what, darlin'. How 'bout you make my clothes disappear?" He rose from his couch and led her off to his tent.

The next morning, Regen slept in. There was no hurry taking off for Phoenicia, and he needed to fill his fuel hoppers at the space station anyway. He enjoyed one last fling with Shaddar before dressing and joining Jahallah and Amalek for breakfast. Jahallah greeted him warmly as he entered the royal tent.

"I trust you slept well, Regen." The wry smiles on the faces of both men said they knew there was little sleep involved in the previous night's activities.

"I really gotta thank ya fer that lady. She was first class. I can sleep on the ship." He sat down at the table, and a servant brought him a plate of breakfast. It was the usual Bedouin fare of lamb, vegetables and some kind of wheat paste, but it filled his stomach.

"I loaded two cases of Gordian Bourbon on your ship last night," Amalek said.

"Thanks, I just hope I don't need that much more fuel t' git t' Phoenicia, but if I do, I'll die happy."

The farewells at the ship were short and painful, but Regen was eager to be on his way. He lifted the ship into the orbit for the space station and phased into a docking orbit to refuel. At the station, customs and immigration were perfunctory. Terma officials didn't much care who was leaving the planet or what they were carrying, as long as no national treasures were involved. Regen had all the correct paperwork for the gold aboard, and all the inspectors gave Hitler a wide berth. He was on his way in only a few hours.

He took the small statue of Herion and placed it on the navigation console. "Here goes," he sighed as he spoke the command. "Epistrepho!"

The statue melted into a navigation disc, and he placed it in the console. Herion's picture appeared on the chart screen.

"I see you've elected to return to Phoenicia. I'm very glad you did. I don't know what kind of reception you will get, but by this time, I've done my best to insure you'll be welcome. If I've failed, you will at least know I felt very warmly for you. This disc will now take command of your ship. You will not be able to control it in any way until you land on Phoenicia, and then it must be destroyed whether you are welcome or not. You will land at the Ministry of Culture where you must stand trial as an alien. I wish you every success, and I look forward to seeing you again. I won't say goodbye, I'll only say adieu until I hold you in my arms again."

The image faded out, and the instruments went dark. He could feel the ship accelerating, and sat back in his command chair for a moment reflecting on his decision. The die was cast, and he would live or die depending upon Herion's eloquence in pleading his case. As he was thinking, Hitler leaped into his lap.

"Hey big guy, looks like we're headed for th' end o' th' line one way or t'other."

The skeen looked up at its master as if he understood the words. His face took on an almost sad expression, then he lowered his head to rest on the Bremen's chest. Regen stroked the leathery forehead gently.

"Well, it's bin a real good life even if'n this is th' end. Nothin' fer us t' do now but wait."

Ten days later, Phoenicia came up on the forward scanner screen. The deep blue planet seemed so inviting, but Regen tensed as the ship decelerated into a parking orbit 200 kilometers above the equator. Hitler joined him, sensing the change in motion.

"Here we are, fella. Won't be long now 'til we knows what these women'll do to us. I promise I won't let ya suffer, no matter what."

The communications screen came alive, and the image of a young woman in a royal blue toga appeared. "This is Phoenicia control. Please identify yourself."

To his surprise, the buttons on the communication system were not illuminated. He pressed "send". "This here's Regen. I come t' see Herion."

The woman turned her head slightly and nodded to

someone off camera before returning to Regen. "Identification confirmed. You ship will be guided to the Ministry of Culture landing site where our guards will meet you. Do not carry any weapons off the ship and make sure your pet is in a secure cage. You will be given further instructions after landing."

The screen went dark, and the ship began to enter the atmosphere of Phoenicia. Regen watched as a passenger while his craft was guided to a perfect landing on a high plateau at the North end of a large island. The vegetation was sparse, and there was no sign of life anywhere. The indicators showed contact with all landing struts, and he was about to cage Hitler when he felt the floor dropping from underneath his feet. A check of the view screen showed the ship descending into the heart of the plateau. After a few moments, the motion stopped, and he could see he was inside a large hangar.

"Please be sure your pet is caged. We will be coming aboard in two minutes." The words came from a group of armed men standing next to the boarding ramp door.

"Okay, fella, time t' cage ya up." He led Hitler to his cage and lured him inside with some fish pellets. He patted the animal through the bars. "You al'ays bin good luck fer me. I sure hope we're good luck fer each other now." He returned to the flight deck and waited for the guards to enter the ship.

The metallic noises of the boarding ramp were quickly followed by the sound of weapons being cocked and the tramp of boots on the metal deck. One of the guards appeared on the command deck, weapon poised and ready. "Mr. Regen, you will accompany me, please."

Two other guards entered, and one searched Regen. "I ain't got no weapons," he assured them. "What about Hitler?"

"Your pet is being well cared for. This way, please."

Regen was a bit consoled by the fact that the guards were at least being polite. He fell in behind the leader with the other two behind him. As they left the ship, he noticed two men carrying Hitler in his cage suspended from a stout pole between them. At least he was still alive.

The guards led him into a comfortable room with no windows and only one door. "Stay here please, and remove your clothes." The guards left him alone, and when he tried the door, he found it was locked securely.

"Well, I guess I'd better git with it." He stripped naked, and was surprised by a female voice coming from the ceiling.

"Please place your clothes in the hamper to your left."

He looked to his left and saw a box with the lid standing open. He deposited his clothes, and jumped back as the lid snapped closed. A grinding and sucking sound told him he'd never see that outfit again. He looked around the room. It was painted a stark white, and everything in the room was white— one bed, a comfortable chair, a nightstand, a small table and one straight-backed chair and a stainless steel toilet and sink in one corner. The floor was white ceramic tile, and everything was spotlessly clean. If this was a jail, it was the best one he'd ever been in. The voice spoke again.

"Please enter the medical testing booth." As it spoke, one section of the wall opened to reveal a small closet. He stepped inside and noticed marks on the floor where he should place his feet. They were pointing the other way, so he turned around just in time to see the panel close again and feel clamps bind his arms and legs and a wide strap close over his chest. He felt needle pricks in several spots and felt blood being drawn out of his veins. A helmet descended over his head, and he began to dream about his life. The images flashed by in rapid order and ended with him entering the medical booth. Next, he began to see mathematics problems, chemistry experiments, physics labs, atomic reactions, orbital mechanics problems, astrophysics equations, and other subjects he wasn't even aware of. The ordeal ended as it began. The clamps released and the panel opened. Once more the voice spoke.

"Please put on the robe you will find on your bed."

He walked to the bed and found a white bathrobe. Before he put it on, he checked his skin where he felt the needles and found no marks at all. The robe was very warm, and he found white slippers under the bed to warm his feet. The room temperature was warm enough, but the clothes felt good. He sat in the softer chair to wait for further instructions. So far, it had been painless, but what was next? A panel in the wall opened, and a tray slid out bearing a meal. The voice spoke. "Please help yourself to some food and drink. We are studying the results of your medical and intelligence tests now, and it may be a while before your next test. Thank you for your patience."

He moved to the tray and picked it up. The panel closed immediately. "Hmmm, don't look too bad. Can't tell what all this is, but if'n it's poison, they'll just keep feedin' it to me 'til I git so hungry I'll eat somethin'. Might as well go with a full stomach."

He sat the tray on the small table and dove into the meal. "Mighty tasty! Ain't much of it, but what there is is great. The drink was only water, but it was cool and refreshing. When he'd finished eating, he lay down on the bed for a nap.

"Please put on the clothes." The voice woke him from a fitfull sleep full of dreams about gruesome means of execution. On the wall between where the medical closet had been and where his food appeared, some clothes similar to what he had taken off appeared. There were no boots, only some soft, felt

slippers. He put the clothes on and found they fit perfectly.
Even the slippers were the correct size. There were no mirrors
in the room, and he had no idea what his hair looked like. He
ran his hands through it to groom himself as best he could. In a
moment, the door opened, and two guards appeared. The voice
spoke. "Follow these men, please."

The trio walked down a long hall to a door marked in a
strange language he guessed was Phoenician. One of the
guards placed a card in a lock slot, and the door slid open. The
other guard motioned for him to enter.

The room was a typical interrogation room. He'd certainly
seen his share of these in his life, and he figured the test results
hadn't been all he could hope for if this was the next step. The
small table and two chairs were the usual furniture, and what
was undoubtedly a one-way mirror hung on the left-hand wall.
Another door opposite the one he used opened, and a heavy-set
woman with short black hair and a pale complexion entered.
She was wearing a white toga with a navy blue stripe, and a
heavy gold medallion hung from a golden chain around her
neck. He guessed it to be a police badge. Things were
definitely not looking good.

She held a console of some sort and placed it on the table
between them. She sat in one chair and indicated Regen should
take the other. Two microphones popped out of the console,
and a small door opened to reveal a set of headphones. The
woman put on her set and nodded to Regen to do the same. He
donned the headset, and she began to speak.

"This is a translation and recording device, Regen. I do not
speak Bremen, and this is the only other alternative. I apologize
for this clumsy arrangement."

"No need, darlin'. I'm used to it. Tell me, how soon do I
find out what's gonna happen to me?"

"Very shortly, you will appear before the Governing Council, and they will make the final decision. You will have a counsel, and Lady Herion has agreed to appear as a witness on your behalf. The purpose of this interview is to answer some questions raised as a result of your medical and intelligence tests. You have the right to remain silent, but I should advise you that silence in these matters is never a good option." She looked at Regen with a somber expression, and that told him she was probably being honest. Besides, he was what he was, and there was no getting around that.

"I got nothin' t' hide. Fire away."

"Good. My first question concerns your bionic left leg. Tell me how that came about."

"Ten years back I did a stint in th' Bremen Space Force. I figured it was a good way t' git away from a gal who claimed I was th' father o' her baby."

The woman interrupted him. "And were you the father?"

"Could'a bin, but she was 'friendly' with 'bout six other guys I knew at th' same time, an' I wasn't goin' t' wait 'round fer th' DNA tests, just in case."

"I understand, go on."

"Well, I shipped out real quick, but it was right smack dab inta th' middle of a bunch o' dope smugglers. Ya see, our job was t' clean 'em out from their bases on our moon, Milia. One o' their laser cannons hit my battle station, an' I was wounded so bad they couldn't save th' leg. Th' Space Force gave me this'un." Regen tapped his left knee for emphasis.

The woman interrupted again. "It fits you remarkably well for being so old."

"Thanks, but this ain't th' same one they gave me. I had this'un done just a few months back."

"Thank you. I see you have quite an extensive criminal

record on several planets. Would you care to comment on that?" She sat back, obviously eager to hear what lies he could fabricate to soften this aspect of his resume.

"That all comes from th' same incident. I was in th' hospital ward when they brought in a couple o' those drug smugglers. Those guys had real fancy clothes an' acted like they owned th' place. They was offerin' mighty big bribes t' anyone who'd help 'em escape. I never figured there was that kind o' money in drugs. Course, I only seed it from th' street side. The pushers I knew never had th' kind o' money these guys was talkin' 'bout, and they was al'ays gittin' caught an' spendin' time in th' slammer. When they let me go back t' duty, I was sent t' help confiscate th' booty these guys'd accumulated. Let me tell ya, I was impressed. They lived like kings. We hauled million o' credits worth o' stuff outta their villas, an' I got t' thinkin', I'll never have two credits t' rub t'gether th' way I'm goin' now. I ain't got no education. I ain't got no family money. All I got t' look forward to is a lifetime o' workin' my ass off for peanuts. I decided then an' there t' git inta that business, an' as soon as my enlistment was up, I headed fer someplace where I could get inta th' drug business. I ain't proud o' what I done t' make my money, but th' gold on my ship should tell ya th' trade's been mighty good t' me."

The woman smiled, leaned closer to Regen and pushed a button on the portable console. "We're not recording now, so we can speak freely. The gold on your ship would make you the tenth richest person on this planet, man or woman, so I'll give you some friendly advice. Don't make a point of emphasizing how rich you are and how you're going to live high on your wealth. The members of the Council are only looking for an excuse to execute you so they can confiscate your gold. While you live, it's your gold, but a rich male alien is also a very dangerous thing in their eyes. You have to convince them you are no threat to their power structure, and given your record, that's going to be very difficult. I have to turn the recording device back on now or the gap will seem suspicious."

She reached for the button, but Regen signaled her to hold up a moment. "Why are ya tellin' me this now?"

"Herion is a good friend, and her happiness means a lot to me, that's all." She pushed the button again and faked surprise at the green light. "Oh my, for some reason we haven't been recording. I must have hit the stop button by mistake. We'll have to start over again. As I said, your mental scan shows no religious influence. Do you espouse any particular religion?"

"Like I told ya, no god ever did anythin' fer me, so I don't do nothin' fer them. I guess you'd say I was a agnostic, or somethin' like that." Regen cocked his head to one side and screwed up his mouth before adding, "Nope, that's not right. I do think there's a god som'eres, but I don't think he, or she, or it gives a damn 'bout any humanoid in th' universe."

She turned her attention to a small, hand-held device for a few moments before looking back at Regen. "I think that answers all of our questions for now. Your counselor will be appointed tomorrow, and she will interview you after that. Meanwhile, make yourself comfortable. Is there any particular food you would like?"

"I could sure use some Gordian Bourbon."

"I assume that's an alcoholic beverage, and I'm sorry, but you will be allowed no alcohol until after your hearing." She pushed a button on her console and a guard opened the door behind Regen. "The guard will return you to your quarters. Goodbye Regen."

The guard escorted him back to the stark white room. On the table beside the bed he found an electronic book. The control buttons were marked in the Phoenician script, but he guessed the green button was "on". The screen came alive with the title, "Phoenician for Bremens".

"Well, this is prob'ly a good sign. If'n they was goin' t' kill me, they wouldn't help me learn their language." He laughed a short, quick, snorting laugh. "That is 'less they 'spect me t' give the commands t' th' firin' squad." He sat down in the only comfortable chair and began to read.

He read for what seemed to be a long time before a chime sounded and another meal appeared from the wall. This one was as tasty as the last, but there was one item he didn't expect. He broke open his dinner roll to find a small bottle of Gordian Bourbon. Evidently Herion had some pull with his jailers. He poured the contents into his glass and was surprised to see the tiny bottle dissapear before his eyes. There would be no trace of the contraband to betray the donor.

As he ate, he wondered what time it was. There was no clock in the room, and they had confiscated his watch. He was beginning to get sleepy, but he figured it was just the bourbon and a good meal. He picked up his book again, but the lights in the room began to grow dim.

Must be bedtime by their reckonin'. He undressed and went to bed.

Breakfast appeared from the wall shortly after the lights in the room grew bright enough to wake him up. It even included a beverage that passed remarkably well for coffee. As he ate, he noticed a change in the area around the toilet. A shower now occupied what was once bare wall. *I think that's a hint I'm gittin' a little gamey.*

The hot water felt good on his back, and he let it run for a while before reaching for the soap. *Hmmm, nice masculine smell.*

I 'spected I'd have t' use some female beauty stuff. The shampoo was neutral scented. *Guess they's practical people an' ever'body uses th' same stuff.*

He'd just finished dressing when a guard appeared and motioned for him to follow. He led Regen to another room off the long corridor where a slim woman in a dark brown toga sat waiting. She was beautiful. Her brown hair was pulled back into a bun revealing fine features and a delicate jawline. She had sparkling brown eyes and full, red lips. She greeted him in Bremen.

"Sit down, Regen. I am your couselor, Jarva."

He took the only other chair in the room and responded, "Pleased t' meet ya, Jarva."

She nodded for the guard to leave and waited for the door to close before speaking again. "You need to understand how to proceed with the Ruling Council at your hearing tomorrow, and…"

Regen interrupted her. "Tomorrow! How can we put together a defense that quick?"

"This isn't a criminal trial, Regen. The Council has all the evidence they need to make a decision from the tests they ran yesterday. The only thing left is for you to appear and plead your own case. I'm here to help you understand what you need to say. You're very fortunate to have a witness in your behalf. The Lady Herion will speak for you."

He observed her as she spoke since something seemed strange about her face. It was her eyes, they didn't blink as often as they should, and a barely perceptible hesitation between her words gave her voice a mechanical quality. He tossed his head back and began to laugh.

"What is funny?" she asked.

"You, yer an android, ain't ya?"

"Yes, I am. How did you know?"

"I seed too many o' yer type in my lifetime. Is this all I git fer a defense lawyer?"

"I'm very good at what I do, and I am not biased in any way. The human females would be far too sympathetic to the Council's tendency to execute aliens, particularly rich males with a past like yours. I have defended many males in the past and achieved some degree of success in avoiding their deaths. You should be thankful the Lady Herion retained me."

Regen thought about the situation for a moment. He had to agree with the logic. In a world run by women, his resume would not win many sympathetic hearts. "Now that I think about it, you're prob'ly th' best choice. Tell me what I hafta do."

Jarva opened a folder and leaned forward with a serious expression. "You must convince the Council of three things. First, that you will not be a burden on our society. That will not be hard since you brought nearly a billion Drachmas in gold with you. Second, that you will not attempt to undermine our religion, and third, that you will not be a threat to our government. Your answer to the question about religion yesterday will help on that score, but your recent involvement with a rebellion on Bardour will be of considerable concern to the Council members. You will have to convince them you are no threat on both counts. Tell me how you would address those issues."

Regen sat back in his chair and pondered the question a moment before answering. "Well, I cain't give much more of a answer 'bout religion than I did yesterday. I ain't never been religious, and I don't much care how a man prays long as he don't try t' make me pray th' same way. I'll be glad t' take up your religion any time, long as it don't mean I gotta do somethin' weird. Far as th' rebellion on Bardour goes, I was just sellin' arms t' the rebels cause I was kinda fond o' th' princess leadin' 'em. It was a money makin' proposition fer me, that's all."

"But you helped with an attack on their moonbase."

"Man! You guys don't miss a thing, do ya? Yeah, it was a favor to th' princess cause my ship had some super-duper stealth gear capable o' foolin' their sensors. I got paid fer that too."

"And you'd have no problem living in a world run by women?"

"None at all, I never cared much who was runnin' things on th' planets I did business with. Ya might say I was a equal opportunity criminal."

"We should start your conversion to Astarte today. That would convince the Council you're serious about our religion. Would you mind that?"

"Nope, what do I have t' do?" He was secretly hoping the ritual might have something to do with temple virgins, but he was also afraid it might involve some kind of painful or embarassiug activity.

"I'll send in a priestess to give you the history of Astarte and instruct you in the rituals. You must authorize a gift of gold to the goddess so she can sacrifice a pig on your behalf at the temple. It isn't much, only two of the coins in your horde will suffice." She punched in some commands on her hand-held computer and turned the screen to Regen. "Just press your right thumb on the screen to authorize the deduction."

He didn't know if he could trust this android. He might be signing away his entire fortune, but he had little choice. He pressed his thumb on the screen.

"Good! I think you are ready to face the Council, but let me tell you something about the members and how the proceedings will be conducted.

The Council consists of seven women elected by the other women of our world. Council members serve for six years and may be re-elected once. Three new members are elected every three years, and the Council Chair is elected from the members going off their terms. The current Chair is Gilda. She will be the one in the center of the panel. She is very zenophobic and hates men. If she is the deciding vote, you are doomed, but I have every reason to believe she will not be the one who determines your fate. On your side will be Mallana, Gisselia and, possibly, Lunna. Selenia and Elektra will side with Gilda. The swing vote is Corrina. She will be the one you must play to. Lunna will like your answer to the religion question and the fact that you have started your conversion to Astarte. She already thinks you're very handsome, so smile at her with your best seductive manner. Corrina is a different matter."

Regen held up a hand to stop her. "Whoa, tell me what these women look like so's I'll know who to turn th' charm on fer."

"Sorry, I brought you some pictures to help with this." She opened her briefcase and handed Regen a blue folder. He opened it and whistled softly.

"Some o' these gals're real harpies, an' th' worst un is that Gilda you was talkin' 'bout." He fingered a picture of an older woman with sharp features. Her lips were thin and curved downward at the edges. She had steely gray hair, and age spots marred what was once a lovely face. The eyes drove daggers into your flesh even from the photo, and he knew they would be worse in person.

"Yes, she was a judge before being elected to the Council. The prisoners referred to her as 'Gilda the Garroter', because that was her sentence for people convicted of capital crimes."

"What a sweetie." He looked at the others and set aside the pictures of Lunna and Corrina. "This Corrina's a fine lookin' woman. What's th' deal with her?"

"Corrina is a lesbian. She doesn't care for the attentions of men, but she is very fair and logical. She thinks all men must have some redeeming value to be kept alive. Do you have any particular skill we could emphasize to her?"

Regen snorted a laugh before responding. "Me? I'm a good shot, an' I kin hold m'own in a bar brawl, but that's 'bout it."

"There must be something you're particularly good at?"

"What I'm really good at, this-here Corrina don't care for. Looks like I may be a cooked goose."

"Keep thinking about it. It doesn't have to be anything consequential. Even if it's just manual labor, she'll accept you. Think about it tonight, and we'll talk again in the morning. Your hearing isn't until after lunch. Is there anything else I can answer for you now?"

"I don't think so, darlin'. I'll try t' come up with somethin', but I don't know what it'll be."

Jarva stood to end the session, and buzzed for the guard. "I'll send for you before lunch tomorrow, and we'll go over everything once more. Until tomorrow." She extended her hand, and Regen took it in a gentle, but firm, grip. The guared appeared and escorted him back to his room.

CHAPTER 23

After lunch, Regen met with a priestess of Astarte in a small chapel dedicated to the goddess. She was not at all what he expected being rather on the plump side and not very attractive. She was young, he could tell that by her acne. She used the translator to tell him all about the Mother Goddess and what he must believe to be her true son. Regen took it all in and filed it in a remote corner of his brain except when she came to the part about completing his initiation into the cult by having sex with one of the priestesses. He hoped there were some with more visual appeal than the present example, or that would be the hardest part of the process. When she finished with him, he returned to his room and resumed his study of the Phoenician language.

It wasn't a difficult language to learn, but his mind kept wandering off the subject and landing in the hearing room. He picked up the folder containing the pictures of the Council members and studied the faces. None of them were what he would call attractive. Each had some characteristic he found objectionable. Gilda was too old, Mallana had a large nose and thick eyebrows, Gissellia's jawline was more like a man's than a woman's. Selenia was the best looking of the lot, but Jarva said she was with Gilda. Elektra projected the air of a woman very impressed with her own importance, and the grim line of her mouth said she was not impressed with anything but power, besides, her eyes were too wide apart. Jarva said Lunna thought him handsome, but Lunna was far from pretty. Her face was too wide, and her eyes too close together for his taste. He vowed to turn on the charm for her regardless of her looks. Corrina was a Lesbian, according to Jarva, and likely to be the swing vote.

Corrina would be looking for some logical reason to spare his life, and he could think of no reason that even convinced himself he should be spared. *What kin I offer this society? What kin I offer any society, fer that matter? I been a no-good all my life. I never did good in school, an' I weren't much of a soldier. What do I know—drugs, drug dealers, the worst dives an' th' best whore houses in any city in th' galaxy. I could git a PhD in rotten, but that ain't no good here. I can fly 'bout any spaceship ever built, but these folks ain't interested in leavin' their own planet. Looks like my goose is cooked 'less this-here gal takes pity on me, an' I don't see much pitty in those eyes.* He closed the folder and undressed for bed, but sleep eluded him. When he did doze off, all he could dream about were the various ways he could be executed, and Gilda the Garrotter kept popping in to solve that problem.

It seemed he'd only been asleep a few minutes when the guard awakened him. The room was brightly lit, and a tray of food awaited him in the usual place. The guard only nodded and stood by the door to the corridor until Regen finished breakfast, showered and dressed. Once he was presentable, the guard indicated he should follow him down the hallway. They entered the same room he and Jarva used the previous day. She was waiting for him.

"Did you come up with any reason you should be allowed to live?" she asked.

"Nope, it kept me awake most o' last night, but I couldn't think o' nothin'."

Jarva sighed and shook her head. "I didn't either, but I searched the data banks for jobs that are hard to fill on our planet, and I found these." She handed Regen a single sheet of paper.

He read the list with a look of disgust forming on his face. "Hog manure inspector? What th' hell do ya inspect it fer?"

"We use it as fertilizer, and we must be sure it contains no pathogens. An aromatic job, but it pays well," Jarva answered.

"I think I'd prefer this un here." He pointed to the next to last entry.

Jarva took the sheet and read the job title. "Ah, tunnel construction worker. A dangerous job, but no more so than running illegal drugs into hostile planets. We build a lot of tunnels on Phoenicia, as you will see if you are allowed to stay with us. Stand up, please."

Regen complied, and she rose also. She inspected his physique thoroughly before she nodded for him to sit. She took her chair and smiled a satisfied grin. "You have the build for that job. I think we should emphasize that today. Have you ever done any construction work?"

"A little bit in th' Space Force, but nothin' big."

Jarva waved a hand. "It doesn't matter. They're always looking for men to work the tunnels. I'm sure your willingness to take on that kind of job will be a point in your favor."

"I was hopin' t' have some kind o' job near Herion."

"That would be very hard to do. She's a wildlife expert and highly educated. Most of the people on her staff have advanced degrees."

"I see'd a lot o' flunkies around her place last time I was here. I could do any o' those kind o' jobs."

"There's a waiting list for any of her jobs. The island game preserves are very popular assignments. No, I think we'd best stick with the tunnel worker idea."

"You're th' expert. All I wanna do is make sure I git over th' first hurdle—stayin' alive.

"Now that we have that settled, I brought you your old clothes."   She pushed a button on the wall, and a guard appeared carrying a box. He set it on the table and left.

Regen dove into the box to find freshly cleaned clothes and highly polished boots. "Hey, they look great. I cain't wait t' get outta this stuff." He pulled at the fabric of his tunic.

"Let's go over the procedures and some stock answers for you. Then you can go change before the hearing."

Jarva covered the proper behavior before the Council and rehearsed Regen's testimony before calling for the guard. Regen returned to his room to change and to go over a few pages of his Phoenician language lesson. He was not quite finished when the guard opened his door, but didn't want to be late for his hearing.

This time, the guard took the first door off the hallway and entered a much more ornate corridor decorated with golden columns and murals depicting women doing heroic things or accepting the adoration of the populace. They stopped before a gilded double door, and the guard placed his palm on a pad at the left side of the entranceway. After a short pause, the doors swung open and Regen stepped into a large circular room with a domed ceiling. A raised gallery surrounded the central area, but the seats were mostly empty. Only a few women in pastel togas sat in a group above the row of tables he guessed to be for the use of the defense since Jarva was seated at one along with Herion. Opposite the tables, and along the other wall, a curved dais rose a meter above the floor. This was, undoubtedly, the place where the Council would sit. The room was paneled in a rich, dark wood with golden trim, and the floor looked to be marble with an intricate, veined pattern. He moved toward Jarva, and Herion rose to greet him. He embraced the woman he had come to Phoenicia for.

"It's good t' see ya again, Herion," he whispered as their cheeks touched.

"Welcome back, Regen. You don't know how I prayed you'd come back to me."

The sound of chimes caused Herion to break the embrace and face the dais. Regen followed suit, and the Council members filed in from a door on the left. He recognized all of them from their pictures, but Gilda seemed even more stern than the image the camera was able to capture. Corrina, however, seemed much more pleasant, and she even smiled at him as she took her seat at the far right end. Another woman appeared from a door on the right wearing a navy blue toga with the same badge he'd seen on his first interrogator. She strode to the center of the floor and spoke in Phoenician.

Jarva handed Regen an earpiece connected to a microphone. He put it on and heard the last part of the woman's speech.

"...to judge the suitability of one Regen from the planet Brem to join our society. The Ruling Council of Phoenicia is now in session." Another set of chimes sounded, and everyone took their seats.

The one he recognized as Mallana rose from her seat at the far right side of the dais and spoke. "Is the defense ready to proceed?"

Jarva rose and responded. "Yes, your grace. I am android Jarva for the defense."

"Welcome, Jarva, do you have any motions to present?"

"None, your grace."

"Then we will proceed with questions from the Council in order of seniority. Council Chair the worshipful Gilda will be first." Mallana sat down, and Gilda fixed Regen in an icy gaze.

"I have studied your mental scan and the reports from the medical analysis, Mr. Regen, and I must say, you are hardly a stellar example of your race. If this decision were mine alone, you would be resting on the bottom of the ocean along with your ship at this point." She stopped to let her words sink in.

Regen stifled his rage. He knew his ship would be destroyed, but he didn't need this bitch rubbing it in.

"I only have one question," she continued. "Why did you choose a life of crime?"

Regen rose and replied, "Well, yer worship, I tried some other things, but I found crime paid better'n they did." The gallery erupted with laughter, and Gilda gaveled for silence.

"Ya see, I don't have no edicashun, so there weren't too many good-payin' jobs open t' me. I looked at what a fellah could do t' make money on th' illegal side, an' I seen that dope dealin' paid th' best and there weren't too much violence associated with it, if ya did it th' right way. I never was a violent kinda guy." This last remark drew stifled snickers from three of the Council members, including Corrina. "Anyway, I threw in with one o' th' best dealers on Brem, an' he helped me 'til I could afford m'own ship. Th' rest was easy."

Gilda was not amused by his explanation, and her jaw set even more firmly. "I suppose they paid you well while you were incarcerated in the penal colony on Gaba 3?"

"Nope, I got nothin' fer that time, but they did git me a job on a space freighter, an' that's where I got Hitler."

"Hitler?" Gilda asked, and Gisselia, next to her, leaned over to show the Chairwoman a photo from the package of papers in front of her.

"Oh, your pet," Gilda said. "I must tell you that our zoologists find your creature to be quite interesting. They are not familiar with the species, and they are waiting to dissect it should you be condemned. I'd hate to dissapoint them."

"Hitler's a skeen, an' they're not that interestin' in th' rest o' th' galaxy. Most places, they're shot on sight, but I raised him from a egg, an' I'd hate t' see anything happen to 'im."

"That depends upon the decision of this Council. Tell me about the royal prison on Tabita."

"It weren't a very nice place."

Once more the gallery broke out in laughter which Gilda gaveled into silence.

"No, I don't suppose spending three years there is what anyone would call a vacation. Your witness Councilmember Lunna."

"Thank you, your worship. Mr. Regen, why did you decide to return to Phoenicia?"

"That's easy, I wanted t' see Herion, here." He nodded toward the woman.

"I assume you were aware of the possibility you would not be welcome here?"

"I was, but this lady's worth th' risk. 'Sides, I like th' idea of a planet run by women. I see'd a lot o' places where men've bin in charge fer thousands o' years, an' they ain't got it right yet. I'm willin' t' try one where the females run things."

"You understand we have no form of what other planets call marriage, don't you?"

"Yup, an' that's another good point 'bout your planet."

She looked directly at Herion as she said, "Yes, our men are free to consort with any woman, and any woman may try to lure any man into her bed. I have no more questions. Councilwoman Selenia?"

"I have no questions. Councilwoman Mallana?"

"Mr. Regen, I see by your mental scan that you intended to

retire on Terma. Could it be that you've seen the error of your ways?"

"Absolutely, yer grace. I finally got enough money t'gether t' live good th' rest o' my life, and I was content t' just enjoy things and take it easy. I knowed I couldn't do smugglin' forever. I was bound t' get caught an' do some serious time or git killed in th' process."

"Thank you. Your witness Councilwoman Elektra."

Elektra shuffled through her paperwork until she found the document she was searching for. "Mr. Regen, if you saw the error of your ways, why did you get involved with the rebellion on Bardour?"

"It was a chance t' make some money. Ya see, I was friends with Princess Orianne, th' rightful heir to th' throne. I got her back on her home planet after her family'd sold her inta slavery. She told me t' come back any time, an' I'd be welcome. I figured I'd be more welcome if'n I brought some guns along with me."

Again, some of the Council suppressed snickers, and the ladies in the gallery laughed outright. Gilda banged her gavel for order.

"I see. So you feel that violent overthrow of an established government is acceptable behavior."

"Normally, no, but it seemed t' me that Orianne'd been cheated outa her birthright by a low-down skunk who deserved all he got. 'Sides, I made several million on th' arms deals."

"But you took an active part in the rebellion, didn't you?"

"I helped a bit, but they'd o' won even if'n I didn't."

"No more questions. Councilwoman Gisselia?"

"No questions. Councilwoman Corrina?"

This was the one Regen was dreading. He didn't relish working in the tunnels, but it that's what it would take to gain his citizenship, he'd gladly do that in the hope of moving up to something better and a chance to be with Herion.

"Mr. Regen, I don't see any useful aptitude in your data. What would you do if we allowed you to live here?"

To Regen's surprise, Herion stood up. "I would like to answer that question, if I may, your grace?"

"Certainly, Lady Herion. Please go ahead." The defferential tone in Corrina's voice was hard to miss. Regen thought Herion must have a lot of respect from these women on some account.

"Mr. Regen's pet provides him with a very useful occupation."

Gilda broke in. "What could such a monster possibly contribute to our society? I understand it's already bitten off several fingers as thanks for trying to feed it."

"As your worship is aware, many of our islands are plagued by infestations of runiga. When Regen was here previously, his pet hunted freely on our preserve. It seemed to have a particular fondness for runiga, and it decimated the population of the pest in a little over one day. Since it only seems to obey Regen, I would propose to hire him as an exterminator. He could take his pet to any place experiencing problems with runiga and provide a very environmentally friendly solution. It would eliminate the need for poisoned bait or traps that may catch useful animals."

"I see," Corrina said as she tilted her head to one side. A wry smile crossed her face as she spoke, "That would be very convenient for you also, Herion, since you pleaded so eloquently for this hearing in the first place."

Herion lowered her eyes and smiled herself. "Your grace is very perceptive."

"I have no more questions, your worship." She nodded toward Gilda.

"Does the defense wish to call any witnesses?" Gilda asked.

Jarva looked at Herion who shook her head to indicate she'd said all she needed to say. She leaned her head close to Regen and whispered, "We don't need the tunnel worker ploy now. I think Herion made a good case for you with Corrina. Just tell them you're really pleased to be here and that you'll do your best to fit in with our society. Don't forget to say that you've started your conversion to Astarte." She rose and addressed Gilda. "Your worship, Mr. Regen would like to make a statement in his own behalf."

"Very well, go ahead Mr. Regen," Gilda said.

Regen rose and addressed Gilda. "Kalesapogevma, axiosebastos kyria."

A buzz of conversation swept the room, and even Gilda seemed to be impressed with Regen's use of Phoenician.

"I'm sorry, yer worship, but that's 'bout all I've had time t' learn. I promise t' do better in th' future. I really like yer language, an' I think I kin catch on to it in short order if you all let me stay."

The gallery erupted in applause, and Jarva couldn't conceal a smile.

"I know my life ain't been a great recommendation fer citizenship on any planet, but I really have given up on smugglin' drugs and runnin' guns. I brung 'nough gold t' keep me goin' fer life 'bout anywheres in th' galaxy, and I reckon it's still a lot o' money here, but I'm willin' t' work t' earn my keep. I also plan t' set up a fund fer supportin' some o' yer charities after I learn a little more 'bout yer society an' what it needs. I never had much education myself, so I think one thing I wanna do is fund some scholarships fer yer kids, 'ticularly them as can't afford no college on their own. I come back here t' be with this woman." He nodded toward Herion who took his hand in hers and stood up with him. "I only knowed her fer a little more'n a day, but I could never fergit 'er. Somehow I knowed this was where I belonged. I don't care who's in charge, an' I don't care what god ya worship. I once read a holy book that said somethin' like, 'your people will be my people, and your god my god.' That's th' way I feel, yer worship. My ship's gone now, an' there ain't no way I kin leave here, but I don't wanna leave long as Herion here wants me t' stay. You seen all th' stuff from yer tests, an' ya heard all my answers t' yer questions. I just want ya t' know that my feelin's fer her brought me back here. Even though I knew I might not be welcome, I couldn't think o' no other place I'd rather be, dead or alive. Ephkaristo!" Regen sat down to the applause of the gallery. Mallana, Gisselia and Lunna joined in, and even Corrina nodded her approval.

Gilda's face grew grim, and she banged her gavel for silence. "Thank you, Mr. Regen. The Council will now retire to consider its verdict."

Chimes sounded again, and the baillif called for all to rise. The Council filed out, and Jarva slapped Regen on the back after the door closed. "I think we did it, Regen. Good job!"

Regen turned to Herion who smiled warmly and pressed his hand more firmly. "Yes, I think we've done it," she said.

"Thanks to you, Lady," Jarva said. "That was a brillian idea about the exterminator business."

"Thank you, I just thought of it before I came into the councilchamber. I was ready to go along with the tunnel worker job because I knew I could use my influence to move him after a few months of good behavior, but this idea came to me out of the blue. I hope you agree, darling."

Regen enveloped her in his arms and kissed her gently. "I'd agree with anything that put me close t' you. Whada we do now?" Regen asked Jarva.

"We might as well wait here. It shouldn't take the Council long to decide. I figure we have four solid votes no matter how Gilda tries to slant things. Welcome to Phoenicia, Regen." She extended her hand, and Regen raised it to his lips to kiss.

"I never thought I'd ever like to take a android t' bed, but I'd make a exception fer you."

Herion laughed at the idea. "Regen, our female androids here have no sexual equipment."

Jarva smiled at the Bremen. "I'm flattered anyway, Regen. If I were human, I'd try my best to win you away from Lady Herion."

"That's another thing," Regen said. "I al'ays knew you was a lady, but I never knowed you was a 'Lady'."

"It's an honorary title because of my service as a judge and my twelve years on the Council. No money comes along with it."

"I got plenty fer both o' us." He turned to Jarva. "By th' way, I need t' take care o' yer fee, Jarva."

"The Lady Herion has already taken care of that," Jarva said.

"Then I owe you," Regen said to Herion.

"I'll take it out in trade," Herion said.

They sat for what seemed an eternity. Jarva slipped out once to return with some kind of fruit juice and something resembling cookies but tasting like fish to Regen. Jarva apologized for not being able to bring any alcohol into the Councilchamber. They were all relieved when the chimes sounded and the baillif appeared to summon everyone to rise.

The Councilmembers filed in, and Mallana shot a quick wink to Herion. Gilda looked more sour than ever, and Jarva nudged Regen and smiled at him in anticipation of a favorable verdict. When they were all seated, Gilda rose to speak. "Mr.

Regen, will you please rise."

Regen rose, but was suddenly not so sure the decision was in his favor. He'd been this route before in courts, and the outcome had always been grim.

"I regret to say that this Council has agreed to your immigration." The gallery came alive with conversation, which turned into applause. Gilda pounded her gavel for silence. "This decision is granted with provisions. First, you must make the appropriate sacrifice to Astarte and complete your religious training. Second, you must learn the Phoenician language within one year from this date. Third, you must establish a charitable foundation endowed with 25% of your gold to be administered by the Education Ministry. Award of scholarships will be with your personal approval, of course. Fourth, you must remain on the island of Kamara, Lady Herion's game preserve, for one year. You may not leave that island without the express permission of this Council. Fifth, you must undergo sterilization by vasectomy before you are released from custody. Sixth, you will pay an immigration fee equal to 15% of your gold. Are these terms acceptable?"

Regen was seething inside, but kept a cool exterior. All of this was a deliberate design by Gilda to cause him to rebel so she would have justification for executing him. He knew about the sterilization, but 40% of his fortune was a bit much. He composed his thoughts and realized it was this or death. "They are acceptable, your worship."

"Then this session of the Ruling Council is adjourned." Gilda banged her gavel, and the gallery cheered and applauded.

Herion embraced Regen and kissed him passionately. "It won't we long until we're together, Regen. I'll wait here in the city until you're released, and we'll go back to Kamara together."

Corrina joined them and offered her hand to Regen. "An eloquent defense by both you and Lady Herion. You almost make me want to woo you away from her, but Jarva has probably told you my tastes lie in another direction."

"Thanks fer yer vote. I'm real happy t' be back with this lady." Regen hugged Herion with his free arm as he shook Corrina's hand.

"I wish you every happiness." Corrina kissed Herion and left the room.

Mallana and Gisselia joined Herion who shrugged off Regen's arm and embraced both of her friends. "Thank you for your support. It must have been a difficult debate," Herion said.

"It was. We had to give in to Elektra's demands for the large immigration fee, but we carried the day five to two. Only Gilda and Selenia voted against Regen," Mallana said.

Both women congratulated Regen before the guard appeared to escort him back to his room to prepare for the surgical procedure mandated by the Council. A final kiss for Herion completed the temporary goodbye.

CHAPTER 24

The next morning, Hitler's cooing sound awakend Regen. He shook the cobwebs of sleep from his brain and sat up. A stout steel cage sat in the far corner of the room, with the skeen's front claws reaching through the bars toward his master.

"Hey, big fella!" Regen shouted. He leaped from his bed and opened the cage door. Hitler bounded into his arms and nuzzled his leathery head against Regen's chest. "I sure missed ya, boy. Looks like they treated ya pretty good, though." He inspected his pet from head to claw and noticed the stomach was as full as ever. The water bottle in the cage was full, and a container of dry food sat on top of the bars. Herion interrupted their lovefest. She entered through a new doorway in the wall opposite the one he'd used before.

"Good morning, Regen. Is it safe for me to come in?" She knew the skeen could be dangerous, but she was confident in Regen's ability to control the animal.

"Sure, sure, darlin'. I'll put 'im back in his cage." Regen stuffed a reluctant Hitler back into the cage and closed the door. He embraced Herion warmly. "You come t' git me?"

"Yes, get dressed, and we'll catch a tunnel train for Kamara. How do you feel?" She was familiar with the after-effects of the vasectomy procedure.

Regen shifted his hips a bit then answered, "Well, things are a bit tender in some spots, but it ain't as bad as I thought it'd be."

"I'll give you a few days to recover before we make love. Oh, there's your breakfast." A tray slid out of the usual slot in the wall, and Regen walked over to it. He drank the juice and placed the tray on the single table in the room.

"That's all I want. I don't go much fer th' green stuff, an' th' orange things've got a weird taste to 'em. Want it?"

Herion's nose wrinkled, and her mouth stretched into a grimace. "No thanks. I've had breakfast, and prison food never did appeal to me. The green stuff, as you call it, is minnea root. It has a lot of vitamins, but not much taste. It's redeeming quality for prison food is that it's cheap. The orange items are vegras—very high in protein and also very cheap. If you like, we can get some real food before we board the tunnel train."

"No thanks, I'd rather git t' yer island soon as possible so's I kin let Hitler out t' hunt. I figure he's been cooped up in a cage ever since I bin here. Make yerself comfy whilst I shower an' shave." He dropped his pajama pants and shed the top, leaving them lie where they fell.

Herion feigned embarrassment. "Regen, please, some modesty," she mocked.

"I figure it ain't nothin' you ain't seen afore. Be right back." He headed for the shower, and Herion picked up the pajamas and layed them neatly across the unmade bed.

"You'll have to learn to pick up your clothes," she shouted over the noise of the running water.

"Oh, I normally do, but seein' as how it's prison stuff, I figured they could take care o' it today." He broke into a baudy song as he scrubbed away, and Herion sat smiling as she waited.

Soon he was dressed and ready for a new life on a new planet. Herion complimented him on his outfit. "Nice clothes. Where did you get them?"

"They brought in my personal stuff from th' ship last night an' said I could have one outfit for th' trip t' yer island. They said they'd burn th' rest. Made me mad, too. Some o' that stuff cost me a lot o' money, but they said I'd have t' start wearin' them toga things."

"I'll teach you all about that once we're home. Ready to go?"

He looked down at Hitler's cage. "That thing looks mighty heavy. How we gonna git it on th' train?"

"No problem, it's a transporter cage." Herion pointed to a panel on the top of the cage. "You can set it to follow you under its own power. I'd do it for you, but I've been advised to keep my hands away from the cage."

"Just tell me how t' do it. Hitler won't bother me."

"Push the green button first." He did as she commanded and the cage lifted a few centimeters off the floor.

"You can raise and lower it with the arrow buttons on the left."

Regen tried them out and stopped the cage about thirty centimeters in the air. "Now what?"

"Now take the remote unit in the holder next to the pad, and push the green button on it. The cage will follow the remote unit, and you can guide it with the arrow keys on the remote."

He moved the cage around the room for a few minutes until he was satisfied he could control it well. Hitler was not too fond of the ride, but he settled to the floor of the cage and rested his chin on his front claws in resignation.

"Guess I'm ready t' go," he announced.

"This way to freedom." The door opened on a corridor leading to a foyer busy with toga-clad people. They drew some attention with Hitler, but managed to exit the building with only a few stops to answer questions about the animal.

Outside, Regen was surprised to find a sunny sky with some whispy white clouds. "I thought we was underground."

"We are, but people get depressed if they think they're in a cave all the time. We put up these artificial skies and a fake sun to give the impression of the surface. It even rains here every now and then."

They walked through a modern city with restaurants, shops, businesses, parks, and all the amenities anyone could hope for. The streets were broad, and silent electric vehicles carried people and cargo wherever needed. Herion hailed a taxi for the trip to the train station.

Regen settled into a comfortable seat after loading Hitler's cage on the top of the vehicle. Herion assured him it would be a safe ride for the skeen, but Hitler was not so sure. He hissed at each passing car, and his claws scraping on the cage floor could be heard clearly inside the cab.

"Ya know, I don't think I could git used t' livin' underground," Regen said.

"Most people don't live underground. They live topside and only work underground. We just don't want any casual observer to think we're an advanced society. In fact, we'd just as soon allow people to think there's nobody here at all."

"Well, that suits me fine long as we got each other." He took her hand in his and squeezed it gently.

The train station was much like any other he'd ever seen except the signs were all in Phoenician. He could make out a few words, but had to rely on Herion to get them on the correct train. Hitler had to ride as baggage, but Regen made sure he had plenty of water and food for the six-hour journey.

Most of the trip was underwater, and the tunnel in those areas had a clear roof allowing the passengers to observe the planet's marine life en-route. Whenever a particularly interesting fish or undersea structure appeared, a female voice came over the speakers explaining the sight. Herion translated for Regen.

Midway through the journey, an attendant served a delicious looking meal. Regen looked at his tray with curiosity, and Herion explained each dish in detail. Being used to unusual food, Regen tried everything. He pronounced several items excellent and only passed on one thing. Herion told him it was quite a delicacy and ate his portion as well as her own. The train arrived at Kamara on schedule after several stops along the way, and Regen reclaimed Hitler from the baggage car. A short elevator ride brought them to the surface just outside Herion's camp.

"I recognize this place," Regen said.

"I've had a shelter set up for you next to mine. Over this way." She pointed to her right, and Regen recognized her hut.

"Just a minute while I let Hitler out t' hunt." He opened the cage, and the skeen sniffed the ground for a long time before heading for the jungle. "Okay, lead th' way."

Regen's shelter was quite spacious and even featured a section designed for Hitler's comfort, including a cage for keeping the skeen under control when that was necessary.

"Nice digs," Regen complimented.

"I'm glad you like them. Shall we walk along the beach until dinnertime?"

"Sure, I'd like that, but we gotta keep it down t' a short walk count'a my recent surgery." He pointed to his groin.

Herion laughed and took his arm. "You make it easy on yourself."

They walked to the beach just in time to watch the sun set on the water. Regen found a rock large enough for both of them, and they sat down to watch the fantastic scene. The sun grew large as it fell into the pink clouds on the horizon, and the soft sound of the waves breaking on the pure white sand was almost a lullaby. As the stars began to make their appearance, Regen put his arm around Herion.

"Well, darlin', the sun's settin' on my past, but I know it'll rise tomorrow on a new future fer you an' me."

"For you and me and Hitler, don't forget him." Herion smiled up at the face she'd come to love in only a few short hours and surrendered to his kiss.

The End

Author M. L. Hollinger

received an Aeronautical Engineering degree from Purdue University in 1957 and went into the Air Force right after college. He worked on several space program projects including; Titan III Space Booster, Space Shuttle, Star Wars and several other special studies for the Air Force. He attended the Air Command and Staff College and the Air War College. He served in Viet Nam from 1971-1972. His decorations include The Bronze Star Medal, Meritorious Service Medal, Air Force Commendation Medal, The Vietnamese Honor Medal First Class, The Vietnamese Gallantry Cross and five unit excellence awards. He retired from the Air Force in 1980 with the rank of Lieutenant Colonel and came back to Indiana where he joined the Indiana Corporation for Science and Technology. He is now fully retired.

www.ingramcontent.com/pod-product-compliance
Lightning Source LLC
Chambersburg PA
CBHW020301120726
47904CB00001B/294